The
PEACH
Rebellion

ALSO BY WENDELIN VAN DRAANEN

Flipped

Swear to Howdy

Runaway

Confessions of a Serial Kisser

The Running Dream

The Secret Life of Lincoln Jones

Wild Bird

Hope in the Mail: Reflections on Writing and Life

Mr. Whiskers and the Shenanigan Sisters

THE SAMMY KEYES MYSTERIES

The PEACH *Rebellion*

WENDELIN VAN DRAANEN

EMBER

Text copyright © 2022 by Wendelin Van Draanen
Discussion guide copyright © 2023 by Wendelin Van Draanen
Cover art copyright © 2022 by Kimberly Glyder

All rights reserved. Published in the United States by Ember, an imprint of
Random House Children's Books, a division of Penguin Random House LLC, New York.
Originally published in hardcover in the United States by Alfred A. Knopf, an imprint of
Random House Children's Books, a division of Penguin Random House LLC, New York, in 2022.

Ember and the E colophon are registered trademarks of Penguin Random House LLC.

Visit us on the Web! GetUnderlined.com

Educators and librarians, for a variety of teaching tools,
visit us at RHTeachersLibrarians.com

Library of Congress Cataloging-in-Publication Data is available upon request.
ISBN 978-0-593-37856-4 (trade) — ISBN 978-0-593-37857-1 (lib. bdg.) —
ISBN 978-0-593-37858-8 (ebook)

ISBN 978-0-593-37859-5 (pbk.)

Printed in the United States of America
1st Printing
First Ember Edition 2023

Dedicated to
Compassion, Empathy, and Understanding . . .
and those who work to foster them

With special thanks to my sweet husband, Mark,
who tends to my heart when I shed tears over
my (imaginary) friends;
to my agent, Ginger, who brought sunshine into a
really difficult year;
and to my editor, Nancy, who held the ladder and
encouraged me to stretch for the high-hanging fruit.

1936

NORTHERN CALIFORNIA

PROLOGUE

Ginny Rose

It's August sixteenth.

My birthday.

I wake before sunup, excited. I'm not expectin' much in the way of gifts, but that's all right—it's still *my* day. And maybe there'll be cake.

A bird twitters a morning song, and I smile through the lifting darkness. But then I hear a high, sharp cry—like a squirrel, shot just off the mark.

I sit up.

There's no squirrel in our shanty.

It's Mama.

"Jeremiah," she cries. "The boys!"

Papa's quick to check on my little brothers, but everything goes still soon after.

"Mama?" I call, shootin' forward from the blanket bed she made for me when the boys turned sick.

"Stay where you are, Ginny Rose," Papa commands. His

voice is thick in a way I haven't heard before, and it sends me scuttlin' backward.

"They're gone, Mary," I hear him say to Mama a short while later.

At first the words confuse me. How can they be gone? They're right there! But Mama's wail swirls through the shanty and I understand.

"To Heaven?" I ask.

"Yes," Papa tells me.

My eyes sting. It's a sharp pain, sudden and fierce, and I'm grateful for the wash of tears that follows. For a few moments the room swims and sways and I can't hear anything but my own heart, poundin' in my ears.

Lucas.

Elijah.

Gone?

Lucas.

Elijah.

Gone.

Papa's voice cuts through. "No," he's tellin' Mama. "I'll take care of it."

Mama staggers up from the mattress on the shanty's dirt floor, but she stumbles backward and falls.

She tries again.

Falls again.

Papa puts a hand to her forehead and backs away quickly. "Mary," he says, like he's drivin' a stake into the earth. "Stay here."

"But, Jeremiah, I—"

"You're in no condition to go anywhere," he says, but more gently. "You'll need to say your goodbyes here."

"But . . . where will you take them?"

"I'll find a nice place," he assures her. Then he turns to me and says, "Load the water jug, the soap, and the shovel, and wait for me in Faithful. I'll be along shortly."

"But—" I say.

"Git!"

There's a heavy fog hangin' wet and cool over the camp, and the dirt shows signs of a drizzle. I don't mind the cool, because I know it'll give way soon enough to the sizzle of summer. But it does feel like the skies have been weepin'—like they knew about Lucas and Elijah while I lay dreamin' of cake.

I load the soap, water jug, and shovel in the bed of our jalopy, then go wait for Papa inside the cab. It's a long wait. One that gives me time to shed quiet tears for my brothers. One that gives me time to already miss my only friends.

When at last Papa comes out of the shanty, he's carryin' a tight blanketed bundle in his arms which I know holds the boys, wrapped together. I have a pang of jealousy as I step down from the cab. They'll always have each other, and who do I have now besides Mama and Papa?

I put on a brave face, and once Papa's placed the bundle in the bed of the truck, he uses the soap and a worn cloth to scrub my hands and arms, clear up to the elbows. He gives himself the same treatment, then wrings out the cloth, feels my forehead, and nods. "Let's go."

I climb back into the cab and watch as he cycles through the steps of startin' Faithful. It takes a few tries, but when she fires up, we putter through the labor camp slowly, then bump along across a field in silence.

At last Papa says, "Your brothers loved playin' around that

tree." He's got his eyes fixed on what Lucas called the Eagle Tree on account of the way it's shaped. And Papa's right—in the month we've lived at this camp, the boys were never so happy as when we'd picnic beneath its shady branches. "I'm thinkin' it would make a nice restin' place," Papa adds, more to himself than to me.

He parks Faithful near the tree, and once he's walked around a bit, he leads me down to the river. "I need rocks," he says. He picks one up and hands it to me. "This size is good."

The rock is smooth and shaped like a big egg. And, surprised by the weight, I nearly drop it on my bare feet. "I'll need dozens of them, Ginny Rose. Can you fetch them for me?"

I nod.

He kisses my forehead. "Good girl."

So while he digs, I carry rocks. Back and forth I go, back and forth. Down to the river, up to the tree. Down to the river, up to the tree. And when at last the hole's deep and wide enough and the stones are collected, Papa fetches the bundle out of the back of Faithful, steps into the hole, and lays it down. He looks around a little and frowns. "It should be deeper," he says, but climbs out and shakes his head. "It'll have to do."

I stand by, dumbly starin' into the hole.

Into the grave.

My eyes sting again.

"You don't have to watch, Ginny Rose," he says, but something inside me's refusin' to look away.

"They have each other," he says softly. "And their sock monkeys."

"Really?" I ask, and for some reason the sock monkeys bein' with them makes me feel better.

He nods. "And Mama's necklace, too, to protect them."

I know what necklace he's talkin' about. She's only got the one. But I don't know what Lucas and Elijah need protectin' from anymore, or what a little gold cross on a chain can do for them. I'm just glad they have their sock monkeys.

Since I don't move away, Papa says, "All right, then. Why don't we say a prayer together?"

I nod, and after a short quiet spell, he says, "Take Lucas and Elijah into your arms, O Lord. Release them to laughter and play in the company of their cousins Matthew and Jake, and bless them with the watchful care of family that's passed into your Kingdom before them. We thank you for the time we had with these boys, and we await a joyful reunion with them when it's our turn to be called home. We pray all of this in Jesus's name. Amen."

"Amen," I whisper.

And then Papa begins shovelin' in dirt.

I help by pushin' it in with my hands.

By layin' the river stones in tidy rows over the top.

By coverin' the stones with oak-leaf mulch.

Then, after we rinse off in the river and spend another quiet minute at the grave, Papa takes my hand in his and we walk back to Faithful. "Thank you for your help," he says gently.

I nod, and through the sadness and confusion in my heart, I feel a swell of pride at his look. Suddenly I *do* feel bigger.

So this is what it's like to be six years old.

1947

CENTRAL VALLEY,
CALIFORNIA

July

1

Peggy

REUNION

Each year, as the sweet smell of peaches filled the June air and ripened into summer, I found myself looking for Ginny Rose Gilley. For seven summers, I held on to a fading hope that she'd show up at our orchard, just like she had the summers I'd turned seven, eight, and nine.

The first summer she didn't come I was devastated.

Where was she? How was I going to survive harvest without her?

Growing peaches may sound romantic, but when your family owns twenty acres of them, reality is quick to replace fantasy, and when picking season is in full swing, farms all over need help with harvest, including ours. Especially ours. There's no shaking a peach tree to get the fruit down, or using a machine to harvest it. Peaches need hand picking, and every summer field workers swarm in to help.

The summer I turned ten, pickers came, but Ginny Rose and her father did not. That left me spending long, hot days sorting peaches in the field with strangers, and my family certainly didn't fill the void. Bobby, who was twelve and full of himself, and Doris, who was thirteen and full of spite, bossed me around, while Father ran the crew and Mother gave birth to twins.

"They're boys," I heard Father say when Willie and Wesley were born, his breath gusting out on a big sigh of relief, as though he could see himself resting at some future date.

Mother, on the other hand, seemed condemned to never rest again. Those babies cried. And fussed. And cried some more. "Boys," I heard her mutter, and in it was a whole wide world of weary.

My mother had been my only ally. Oh, my grandmother Nonnie, who lived with us, *used* to be, but the older she got—or maybe the older *I* got—the more she seemed to disapprove of me. And now they were both overoccupied with the twins and had little patience for my misery.

"They've surely moved on," Mother said that first summer, when I complained about missing Ginny Rose. "Maybe they've gone back to Oklahoma. You should hope for them that they've found something better than fieldwork," she said, changing Willie's diaper.

"But Ginny Rose is my *friend*," I whimpered. "My best friend!"

"You have plenty of friends, Peggy," Nonnie said, changing Wesley's.

"Not like her!" I wailed.

Nonnie raised an eyebrow in Mother's direction, indicating her disapproval at my tone. Nonnie is Father's mother, and that eyebrow of hers has done my mother in on more than one occasion.

"Well," Mother said to me, ignoring the eyebrow as she finished pinning the diaper tight, "friendship won't feed their family, and that's the same for us. Now go out there and do your part."

I did do my part. From dawn to dinner, I sorted peaches brought down by the field hands, hauled buckets of drinking water out to the orchard, and helped load wooden lug boxes of fruit high on a truck bound for the cannery. I did my part until peach fuzz coated my arms and face, until it permeated every pocket, every seam, every fiber of my being. I did my part until the trees were bare and the sickening rot of fruit on the ground buzzed with flies. I did my part until I never wanted to taste or touch or smell another peach for as long as I lived.

Anyone who's lived this life knows—farming's a roll of the dice, a prayer to the skies, and work. Endless, body-bruising work. And every nickel we earned seemed to be needed for repairs, supplies, and equipment.

But even farmwork can be fun when you've got a friend. Nonnie was right—I did have other friends—but Ginny Rose was special. Maybe that was because we did the same work—fieldwork. Words can't really explain what it's like, so mostly I didn't feel like talking about "my summer vacation" to other friends, or at school. Our family rarely went anywhere. And during harvest? We never took a day off, not even Sundays.

Summer meant working the farm.

Dawn to dark, we worked the farm.

So there was that, but there was also the way Ginny Rose could make me laugh. We'd giggle about everything, including Bobby, who was as bossy then as he is now, and Doris, who'd rather sting us with insults than work alongside us. Having Ginny Rose around made the days go by fast.

So even as I got older, even as I moved from working out back in the orchard to working out front at our fruit stand, I missed her. I missed *us*. But this summer after the month of June came and went, I finally stopped hoping she'd reappear. I'd be seventeen soon. It was time to let her go.

Besides, *so* many things had changed since those summers with her. The war had started and ended, rations were over, Franklin Delano Roosevelt—who'd been president for as far back as I could remember—had died, and Harry Truman was now in charge.

And the biggest change of all?

Everyone seemed more hopeful.

Also, if I'm being completely honest, instead of pinning my hopes on a friend who'd disappeared, I was putting them on Rodney St. Clair, a classmate who had already appeared at the fruit stand four times since school let out in June and had been especially friendly to me when I'd seen him at the Freedom Parade on the Fourth of July.

So that was where my mind was—firmly and fondly focused on sweet thoughts of Rodney St. Clair.

And then, suddenly, there she was.

"Ginny Rose?" I gasped. She was standing in front of the fruit stand, blue-eyed and freckled, her strawberry-blond hair braided in one long tail, just the way I remembered.

"Peggy!" she squealed. "That *is* you!"

We threw our arms right over the stand, right over the peaches, right over the years that had divided us, and wrapped each other tight.

I held on to her shoulders as we pulled apart. "Where have you *been*? Do you know how much I've missed you?"

"Aw!" she said, her eyes going glassy. "Honest?"

"What do you mean? Yes, of course! You were my best friend."

"Aw!" she said again, this time looking away as she blinked back tears.

"So what happened?" I pressed. "Where have you been?"

She shrugged noncommittally. "We moved around a lot. You know that."

"But . . . *where?* Mother said you might have gone back to Oklahoma."

Ginny Rose shook her head. "Papa lost everything there, so . . . no."

"But . . . are you still . . . are you still farmhands?"

"No. Papa found other work during the war, but he still hopped from job to job. We never really put down roots anywhere." She brightened. "But he's got a permanent job at the Ferrybank switching yard now."

"At the rail station?"

She nodded. "The job comes with housing and a little piece of land. We're plannin' to stay."

"That's wonderful!"

"All of us are tired of movin' around, and the Littles love that trains roll by."

"The Littles?"

"Oh!" she said, and her cheeks went rosy. "There's two more Gilley girls now. Katie Bee—she's six—and Bonnie Sue, who's seven. And of course there's Anna Mae, who's ten. So that makes four, and I'm mighty glad for all of 'em."

I couldn't help bouncing on my toes. "My mother had twins! They're boys and the same age as your Littles!" I laughed. "Maybe we'll get them to fall in love with each other someday!"

The idea of it really tickled me, but Ginny Rose barely smiled and seemed quick to change the subject. "What about Bobby and Doris?"

I grinned. "You mean Bossy and Dodo?"

That *did* get a reaction out of her—we both giggled like we were kids again. Then I said, "Bobby graduated high school and is practically running the farm now. And Doris eloped with a man right after the war. He was wearing a uniform then, but he's working the oil fields in Modesto now." I rearranged a few jars of preserves. "She had a baby."

"Doris is a *mama?*"

I nodded, then laughed. "It seems to have made her extra grouchy."

"It's a wonder that's even possible," she said with a grin. Then she waved a hand across the stand and said, "This is a smart idea."

"Father built it when I turned twelve," I said. But seeing it with new eyes now, I realized how weathered the raw sheet of plywood on four-by-four posts had become. "It's not much to look at, but it does the job."

"Well, it's in a great spot," Ginny Rose offered. "Folks can just pull right off the road, then get right back on it."

"You sound like my father!" I said with a laugh.

She laughed, too, then scuffed the dirt, her mood suddenly darker. "I wanted to write, Peggy, really I did. But . . ."

"So why didn't you? You have no idea how much I missed you!"

She was silent for a moment, then heaved a sigh. "Mama said there was more dividin' us than bindin' us. She said I should give up the notion of us bein' friends."

"What? Why?"

She kept studying the ground. "You know. 'Cause we were pickers?" She sneaked a peek at me. "Okies?"

"I never called you that!"

"But we were. We *are*." She gave another little shrug. "And Papa says to take it with pride when people say it. That it means we're *survivors*."

"So then . . . why . . . ?"

"Well, other folks don't see us as survivors. They still see us as trash."

Even though I could tell she was papering over painful memories, her voice held no sharp edges. It was the same as it had always been—cool and smooth and fast, like ice cream dripping quicker than you can lick it.

And hearing it now sent me back to the sleepover we'd had one August—a concession I'd begged from my mother for my ninth birthday. I hadn't understood Mother's objections, and eventually she'd lost the will to argue with me and had relented. It had been a magical time, with just the two of us playing crazy eights and old maid and whispering late into the night.

I was about to ask Ginny Rose where their house was when a car rolled up to the fruit stand. It was a sparkling new, deep red convertible with whitewall tires. And, as if tailor-made for each other, it was Rodney St. Clair sitting behind the wheel.

My heart went for a tumble.

"Hey, Peaches," he called, giving me a devilish grin as he stepped out.

I blushed.

So did Ginny Rose.

"You let him call you that?" she whispered.

"It's only the second time he's done it," I whispered back. "And what am I supposed to do about it?"

"Her name's Peggy," Ginny Rose asserted.

Rodney slipped his sunglasses down his nose as he approached. "And you are . . . ?"

I pulled Ginny Rose behind the fruit stand so she was standing beside me and said, "This is my friend Ginny Rose."

Rodney gave a little bow. "Pleased to make your acquaintance, Miss Rose."

"My last name's Gilley," she said. "I'm Ginny Rose Gilley." She tilted her head a little. "And you are . . . ?"

"This is Rodney St. Clair," I hurried to say, hoping to get things back on track. "His family owns Valley Motors, which is how he comes to be driving a brand-new . . ." I leaned around to admire his car and let him fill in the blank.

". . . Ford Super Deluxe." His gaze shifted to an old bicycle propped against a tree near the road. "I could set you up," he said with a grin in Ginny Rose's direction. "My dad offers great financing."

I stared at the old bicycle with its worn, oversized front basket, wondering for a moment where it had come from. But then it dawned on me—Ginny Rose hadn't just magically appeared. She'd ridden her bike.

"Not interested in financing," Ginny Rose said with a distinct huff.

"Well, cash is always welcome," Rodney said.

The air was feeling strangely charged, but not in the way I would have liked. "So!" I said to Rodney. "Are you here for peaches? Preserves? Pie?"

He flashed another grin. "Maybe all three?"

My brain had gone numb wondering what he was *actually* after when a black Dodge sedan skidded to a stop alongside the fruit stand. "Lisette!" I called out with a wave.

She emerged from the car, her skirt waist cinched impossibly tight, her smooth dark hair in a perfect victory roll. "Peggy!" she called as she hurried toward me, her saddle shoes flying. But when she realized that the boy with his back to her was Rodney St. Clair, her skirt came in for a landing and her voice took on an aloof tone. "Hello, Rodney," she said, turning her nose up slightly.

I'd kept my feelings about Rodney from Lisette because—not so very deep down—I knew they were foolish. I was a farm girl and he was . . . well, he was Rodney St. Clair.

I also hadn't told her because it felt disloyal to be head over heels for a boy she hated. She'd said time and again that he was annoyingly full of himself and not to be trusted. I'd never seen her give anyone the cold shoulder the way she turned it on Rodney.

But here he was, and here *she* was, which left me feeling stuck between love and loyalty. So when she turned her attention to Ginny Rose, I broke out of my paralyzed state and hurried to make introductions: "Lisette, I'd like you to meet my dear friend from childhood, Ginny Rose Gilley. Ginny Rose, please meet Lisette Bovee, my dear friend since ninth grade."

Nonnie likes to say that proper introductions put the hand that's attending to social encounters firmly on the tiller. And since I'd heard that expression my whole life, it was almost natural for me to put the notion to use. It seemed to be working, too, because as Ginny Rose and Lisette were saying their pleased-to-meet-yous, I could feel a calm settling over all of us.

That is, until my bossy brother came clip-clopping up on our white mare, Blossom, his cowboy hat wedged on tight.

"Bobby?" Ginny Rose gasped.

I did a double take, because instead of making a crack about him still riding a high horse or some such, she was looking at him like he was Clark Gable.

Unfortunately for her, Bobby only had eyes for Lisette— a relatively new development that made Lisette uneasy, to say the least.

Before he could dismount, I cut in with "Bobby, you remember Ginny Rose? She worked the orchard with us when we were kids?"

Bobby looked our way, but there was no light of recognition in his eyes, and before long he'd swung off Blossom and was talking to Lisette, stumbling through words, making no sense at all.

Desperate to wrestle free from the embarrassment we were all feeling, Lisette said, "So sorry, Bobby, but I have to dash." She locked eyes with me. "I've got things to tell you. Important things. Call me!"

Then, in a roaring cloud of dust, she was gone.

Bobby scared Rodney off, too, because the next thing I knew, he was back in his Super Deluxe, calling, "Great seeing you, Peaches!" which sent my heart into spasms and also made me want to hit my brother.

Bobby sighed, then swung up onto Blossom and headed off without a word or even a nod in our direction.

"Well," Ginny Rose said after the dust had settled, "I should be on my way, too."

"Wait! I need your phone number. And address! We should make plans."

She hesitated.

Looked away.

Scuffed the dirt.

"What's the matter?" I asked.

She shook her head and seemed ready to just leave, but then she snatched a pencil and a small paper bag from the stand and wrote down her information. "Here," she said, handing me the bag and pencil as if she'd done something monumental.

I looked it over. "Where's Carriage Lane?"

"Past the dairy, a little ways off River Road, just this side of the railroad crossing."

"Great! That's really not too far!" I pressed a bag of peaches on her. "Here. Unless you're tired of fuzzy-wuzzies?"

She laughed at the memory of us in young-girl hysterics, baby talking peaches as we sorted them. Then she smiled her sweet, sunny smile—the one I'd been missing for so long. "Never in a million years will I be tired of fuzzy-wuzzies," she said, and waved as she hurried back to her bike.

I let out a happy sigh as I watched her go.

Ginny Rose Gilley was back in town.

2

Ginny Rose

ANSWERS

Mama's rollin' out biscuit dough when I get home. The drop-leaf table she's workin' on takes up most of the small kitchen, but it'll soon be folded up and tucked away, leavin' room enough for all of us to gather for supper at the table that straddles the kitchen and the front room.

"Well?" Mama asks. "How was it?"

I know she's wonderin' about my applyin' for a job at the cannery, not my encounter with Peggy Simmons. "I start tomorrow," I tell her, pride slippin' out with the words.

"Oh my!" She turns her full attention to me and comes around to hold my cheeks, her firm hands powdered soft with flour. "That's wonderful!" she says with a brightness I haven't seen in ages.

"What's goin' on?" Anna Mae asks from the hallway. Like curious kittens, Bonnie Sue and Katie Bee appear beside her.

"Ginny Rose got a job at the cannery!" Mama exclaims. She

turns back to me, struggles a bit to contain it, then lets the question fly. "Does it really pay forty cents an hour?"

I nod, which sets her lookin' skyward. "Thank you, Harry Truman!"

Katie Bee, though, doesn't give a hoot about my new job or the hourly wage. Her eyes are locked on the sack in my hand. "What's in there?" she asks.

"Peaches," I say, gently pullin' out one, two, three gloriously ripe, perfectly shaped peaches.

"They gave you those?" Mama asks, her voice dancin' with delight. But then, slowly, a furrow forms between her eyebrows. "Those are too pretty to be canning peaches." She picks one up. "They're freestones, not clings."

So I confess. "Simmons Farm was on the way."

"And?" Mama asks, strugglin' to not say more.

"They have a roadside stand now," I reply. "Peggy was workin' it, so I stopped to say hello, and she gave me these."

"And?" Mama asks again, the furrow between her eyebrows now deep enough to plant.

"And Peggy was truly happy to see me."

"Was she now," Mama says, levelin' a stern look at me. "Well, don't say I didn't warn you." She turns her back on me. "And don't come cryin' to me when things turn sour."

"Mama, I don't understand," I blurt out. "You always said all farms could take a lesson from the Simmons family—that they were generous and kind. Why's it so hard to believe Peggy would want to be my friend?"

She turns slowly to face me. "I'm just tryin' to protect you, Ginny Rose."

"From what?"

She fists her floured hands and puts them on her hips. "Ginny Rose, face facts. Folks are keen on associatin' *up*, not down. You two are no longer children, and in any unbalanced friendship, the one at the bottom is sure to be dumped."

Mama's voice has been steadily risin', and Katie Bee retreats now, cowerin' with Bonnie Sue behind the cover of Anna Mae. I try to hold firm, but I know from years of accidentally pickin' at this wound that for all her thick skin, Mama's got a few sore spots that just won't heal. It makes me feel bad when I nettle this particular one, but I can't seem to help it. It's a sore spot with me now, too.

"I'm tired of bein' 'just an Okie'!" I blurt out. "I'm tired of apologizin' for it! I'm tired of survivin' the dust, only to be looked at like dirt."

"Well, I'm tired of it, too," Mama retorts. "But I'm more concerned with havin' enough food to feed all of us, and keepin' a roof over our heads." She wrenches the biscuit cutter into the dough. "And if that means doin' other folks' laundry and pinchin' pennies, well, I'm not too proud to do it."

"I'm not bein' prideful, Mama! Papa says we've got to stop lettin' the past cripple our future; that we need to pull ourselves up, dust ourselves off." I can feel Mama goin' dark, turnin' inside herself. And I know I should stop, but I've never challenged her this way and I need to finish with the point of it all. "Mama, right now it's *you* makin' me feel small, not Peggy. And I'm not gonna apologize for thinkin' I'm good enough to be friends with her."

The moment it's out, I can see I've pushed too far. And I could kick myself, too, because I know—this will grow inside

Mama like a dust storm, buildin' up and gainin' weight and power until it lands hard, smotherin' us in darkness.

But it's too late. My words are hangin' in the air and there's no takin' 'em back, and already I'm payin' the price. Gone is the feel of her pride on my cheeks, gone is the glow of her rare smile, her joy at my wages. The dust is still with us.

"Imagine," Mama says softly, "bringin' her here."

"What's wrong with here?" I cry, wonderin' what's come over me, wonderin' why I'm drivin' us both straight for the storm. But again, I can't seem to stop. "Here is so much better'n any place else we've been! We've got two bedrooms plus a back porch and enough land for chickens and a garden! We've got running water, cold *and* hot! An indoor latrine! Electricity! A *telephone*. Here is home, Mama. Or it will be once we settle in. And it's a *good* home."

Mama casts a long, level look my way. "We should probably make a cobbler from those peaches. So there's enough to go around."

I feel like screamin'. Her gratitude for the gift of peaches is to imply there's not enough? But then I catch a glimpse of my sisters cowerin' in the hallway, and from their faces I see that they're more shocked by my outbursts than they are by Mama's attitude, and *that's* what finally makes me bite my tongue.

Supper's a quiet affair. Papa eats his beans and greens and biscuits with gusto. He's worn out from his shift at the switching yard, content to simply bend over his plate and shovel. Mama eats, too, but slowly, silently, pausin' from time to time to fix me with a look that shifts between worry and regret. I see her fightin' against the dark cloud, but it's wrapped tight around her now.

All through supper, the girls give me cautious looks full of questions about things they don't remember, never knew, or can't understand. Later, I read to them from a worn storybook—one that was slipped to me by my teacher when we lived for a short time in Bakersfield. And after we're bunked down for the night—Anna Mae in the bed above me and Katie Bee snuggled close to Bonnie Sue in the moonlit bottom bunk on their side of our small room—the questions start.

Anna Mae hangs her head over and whispers, "What's a Hooverville?"

This sets off a spat between Bonnie Sue and Katie Bee. Bonnie Sue says, "It's where they make vacuum cleaners!" and Katie Bee demands, "How do *you* know?" and they're off like lightning bugs zappin' each other. . . .

"What else would it be?"

"Quit bein' such a smarty-pants."

"You quit!"

"But we don't have a vacuum cleaner!"

"So? Lots of folks do, and they're all Hoovers."

"How do you know?"

"How do you *not* know?"

"Shh!" I whisper, but Katie Bee's already scramblin' up to her top bunk with her rag doll, on the verge of tears.

Anna Mae's head is still hangin' above me, and one arm's joined in, doin' a lazy swing back and forth. "Didn't sound like a vacuum factory when Mama was cryin' about it to Papa tonight. Sounded like a bad place. A place she was afraid of."

"Were you eavesdroppin' again, Anna Mae?" I whisper, 'cause while all us girls were tasked with cleanin' up after supper, Anna Mae made herself scarce.

"Of course I was eavesdroppin'! How else am I gonna know what's goin' on? Nobody tells me a doggone thing!"

I consider doin' what I usually do when one of the girls asks me a question about the hard days they missed: find some fanciful way of shieldin' them from the truth. But tonight I don't feel like it. Tonight I decide they're old enough.

"So, Anna Mae," I say softly, "you're ten now, and I reckon you're old enough to understand." I cast a line across the room. "But I'm not sure about Bonnie Sue and Katie Bee."

Katie Bee bites first. "I am too old enough!" she says, swingin' back down to the bottom bunk. "I'm six!"

"And I'm seven!" Bonnie Sue says, stretchin' herself so she's sittin' taller than Katie Bee.

"Well, I *would* think you're too young," I whisper, reelin' them in, "but when I was six and seven, I *lived* in Hoovervilles, so I'm thinkin' you should be able to take hearin' about them."

Katie Bee's face scrunches tight. "You lived in vacuum cleaners?"

"You don't live in a vacuum cleaner," Bonnie Sue says with a scowl. "You live in the *factory*."

"Actually," I tell them, "Hoovervilles have nothing to do with vacuum cleaners."

"Ha!" Katie Bee crows. "You were wrong!"

"Girls!" we hear Mama shout. "Go to sleep!"

"Sorry, Mama," we all chime.

I drop my voice to barely a whisper, causin' the girls to lean in close. "Hoovervilles were places destitute people lived. They were also called shantytowns or Okievilles."

"What's *destitute*?" Katie Bee whispers.

"Poor as pig tracks," Anna Mae says darkly, and for maybe the first time ever, I see that she *is* growin' up.

Bonnie Sue whispers, "So we lived in Hoovervilles because we're Okies?"

"No!" I whisper back. "You two never did, and Anna Mae was too young to remember. And technically the three of you aren't even Okies. You were all born in California, not Oklahoma."

"I want to be an Okie," Katie Bee whimpers.

"Me too!" Bonnie Sue says.

Anna Mae's head swings back and forth. "You have no idea what you're sayin'."

I look up at Anna Mae, wonderin' if somewhere in her mind there's the memory of that time. But whether there is or not, I'm sure now that she's old enough to hear about it. So I take a steadying breath and let the truth out. "They were called Hoovervilles because Herbert Hoover was president during the Great Depression, and everyone blamed him because so many people couldn't find jobs, didn't have food, and had to live in houses that they made out of trash—wood scrap, sticks, cardboard, newspaper . . . anything they could find. The name stuck, and that's what lots of folks called the camps where we lived after we came over from Oklahoma."

"We lived in houses made of trash?" Anna Mae asks. "I *don't* remember that."

"Mostly it was before you were born," I whisper. "Each place was small. Smaller'n this room. And there was no water, no electricity, and no latrine or outhouse."

"No outhouse? Where'd you *go*?" Bonnie Sue whispers.

"In a bucket."

"Euuw!" Bonnie Sue and Katie Bee mew together.

"And we all slept on one thin mattress."

I can see Anna Mae calculatin' and not likin' the sum she's reached. "Mama, Papa, you, and . . ."

Her voice trails off, stoppin' short of the subject no one'll ever talk about.

"And the boys," I say softly. "Yes. And after they were gone, you."

"How'd they die?" Anna Mae asks.

"They got sick," I say, sidesteppin'. I didn't understand what dysentery was then, and I'm not keen on explainin' it now.

"Why didn't they get better?" Katie Bee asks.

"Papa couldn't get a doctor to come to the camp, and then it was too late."

The room falls quiet. Soon Anna Mae gets under her covers, sayin', "That's enough for tonight," and the Littles do the same.

I wonder if, once again, I've made a mistake; if I've gone too far. Maybe some stories are best left unspoken. Even for me, talkin' about those times feels like it's put a leak inside me. A leak I'm not sure how to plug.

A train rumbles by, long and slow, clackin' and screechin' along the tracks. After it's passed, and after its lonely whistle sounds in the distance, the soft purr of sleeping sisters soothes the air.

I stare at the bunk slats above me. What's the use in talkin' about that time when no amount of words can draw a true picture, and no picture can ever capture what it was like?

And even if they somehow could, Mama's right about one thing.

They'll never erase the heartache.

3

Peggy

BIG BAD NEWS

After dinner, I made a quick call to Lisette, who *did* have big news.

Her family was moving to Oakvale.

Oakvale was where we attended high school and was only five or six miles away, but it would mean a much longer bike ride to her house, and during summer harvest it was hard enough to spend time together as it was.

The sudden news hit me hard. "How . . . ? When did that . . . ? *Why?*" I sputtered into the phone.

She rushed to explain. "Valley Bank foreclosed on a house. There was an auction. Daddy won it. It all happened so fast!"

"The bank where your father works foreclosed on a house and *he* bought it?" My head was spinning. "Is that—"

"I know it feels like it happened overnight, but it didn't. Daddy said the owners stopped making payments more than a year ago. It's taken the bank forever to get them out."

There was a vague memory suddenly souring the pit of my

stomach. It had to do with something Ginny Rose had said when we'd worked the orchard. She'd told me that her family used to have a wheat farm in Oklahoma, one the bank had foreclosed on. I could still hear the sizzle in her words, though at the time I didn't really know what *foreclosure* meant. What I knew, though, was that she was spitting mad about it.

Despite the heat, I felt a shiver crawl through me.

Lisette was chattering on, but I was still stuck on the foreclosure. "But how could your father—"

She rolled my question flat with a rush of words. "It's going to take work to do repairs and get it the way Mom wants, but Daddy hopes we'll be moved in by summer's end. And since it's three blocks from the high school, it means that . . ."

Her voice trailed off as I caught up to what she was actually trying to tell me. "Oh," I said. "No more rides to school."

"I'm so sorry!"

I could tell that she really was, and I didn't want her to be. "You can't help it," I said, trying to sound cheerful. "But . . ." Something else wasn't adding up. "If the Oakvale house needs so much repair, why buy it? The house you live in now is so nice!"

I could feel her on the other end of the line, but she wasn't saying anything.

"Lisette?" I prompted.

At last her voice came, smooth tones over grit. "Well, you know."

"Know what?"

"That . . . well . . . look, Daddy just thinks that Oakvale is a more fitting place for a banker to live. He says that people need to have faith in their banker, and that if you're not successful enough to be living in Oakvale, maybe they shouldn't trust you with their money." Then she rushed to say, "It's different for you because you have land and that beautiful orchard. We don't. And Daddy's set on moving, so as much as I hate it, there's nothing I can do about it."

She didn't hate it, though. I knew her well enough to understand that. Ferrybank was where the farms and the dairy and the switching yard were. There were the sounds and smells of cows and pigs and tractors, and people *labored*. And one night last year when I was over at Lisette's house for dinner, her father had grumbled about how the outskirts of Ferrybank were turning into "Little Tijuana." He wasn't the only one complaining, and his weren't the harshest words, although the Mexicans rarely came into Ferrybank or Oakvale unless they were on a job. And the truth is, I just didn't get it. Why complain about hardworking people? I think I have more in common with the field hands than I do with Mr. Bovee.

So people in Ferrybank turned up their noses at people from Mexico, and people in Oakvale turned up their noses at people from Ferrybank. But people from Modesto turned up their noses at people from Oakvale, and city dwellers in San Francisco did the same toward people from Modesto. So where did it end? And what did it matter?

Mother appeared in the kitchen and gave me the time's-up signal—two taps on her wristwatch. During the war, when the phone company had asked families to not use their phones in the evening so lines would be open for people in the military to call home, Mother had restricted our talk time to one minute. But now that the war was over, she still gave the signal when I was on the phone for more than a minute, claiming she didn't like me "wasting my life talking nonsense."

Tonight, though, she had a reason for the double tap. Bobby was waiting for me to help set the lug boxes. "Time's up," I told Lisette.

Lisette no longer had such restrictions and so was easily annoyed by mine. "Already?" Then she hurried to add, "I know you've got to work the stand tomorrow, and I've got a shift at Woolworth's, but . . . but there's more to talk about and—"

"Like what?"

"Nothing I can say while your mother's tapping her watch. Maybe we can get malts at Dolly's after work and do a toast?"

Lisette was always wanting to make a toast to something. It had started when the war was ending. "To Hitler's demise!" she'd cried, clinking milkshakes with me at Dolly's. But since then she'd taken to toasting everything from cars to cardigans. Mostly it was just Lisette enjoying life, but now I was going to have to toast to her new house—something I really didn't feel like doing. Still, I put a smile on and said, "Sure. Sounds like fun."

"Great! I'll pick you up at . . . how about five?"

To my annoyance, Mother gave the signal again, so I simply said, "Okay. I'll look for you then."

"You'll come out?" she asked, which was code for her not wanting to run into Bobby.

"Of course," I said. Then, trying to sound more cheerful than I felt, I added, "I know you're going to love it in Oakvale."

"Nothing will change," she rushed to say. "I promise you— nothing will change!"

I hung up and went out to find Bobby and set the lug boxes. Aside from dawn, this was my favorite time in the orchard— a time when the sun cast the trees in a soft glow and gave the day over to the Delta breeze, which swept in cool, damp air from the rivers and ocean. It was a time when the trees, the land, the house, and everyone on the farm breathed a big sigh of relief.

The empty lug boxes were already loaded on the flatbed trailer. The sturdy wooden crates saw their fair share of action during harvest. Filled at the orchard and emptied at the cannery in a seemingly endless cycle, they were thumped and bumped, filled and spilled, and served as the final reset at the end of each day.

As usual, Bobby had scouted the orchard with Father before dinner to determine which trees would be harvested the next day, so he knew exactly where the crates needed to go. And, as usual, he hopped on the tractor first, leaving me to ride the trailer and distribute the boxes.

Setting lug boxes is not a hard job or a precise one. You dump them off the side of the trailer as the tractor rig moves forward, and however they land in the dirt alongside the trees is just fine.

It's easy to get lost in your own thoughts while setting lug boxes, because talking's not practical over the noise of the tractor—something that had never been a problem when working with Bobby because he rarely said much, at least not to me.

So I was already lost in thought, conjuring sweet images of Rodney St. Clair, when Bobby's voice invaded.

"What did you say?" I called forward as I shoved two boxes off the left side.

"Is she going out with Hot Rod?"

It took a moment for me to catch on that Bobby was thinking of Rodney, too. "Lisette?" I asked. "With Rodney St. Clair?"

"Yeah. It seemed there was something doin' between them."

"No!" I called with a laugh. "She hates him!"

"So why, then? Where am I going wrong?"

I could hardly believe what I was hearing. For one thing, he was *asking* me something instead of telling me what to do. For another, he was asking me about a *girl*.

I couldn't help but have a pang of sympathy for him. If it had come to him talking to *me* about it, he must be in a world of hurt.

But . . . what to say? I was about as fond of him as Lisette was.

I attempted diplomacy. "You . . . you come across pretty stern."

"Stern?" He looked shocked. Like he couldn't imagine anyone describing him this way.

I tossed out a group of boxes, then tossed him some truth. "Yes! You seem very stern. All the time. To everyone."

We lurched to a halt, and he craned around the tractor seat to look at me. "Did *she* say that?"

I almost blurted out, *No. She said you give her the willies. Is that better?* but I bit it back and lied. "Yes."

Even with the kindness of the lie, he seemed crushed.

"Look," I said. "I know you don't know what to say to her, but lurking in the next room, or watching us from behind the house, or shadowing her around the grocery store . . . it makes her feel uncomfortable. It would make anyone uncomfortable!"

"I don't mean to do those things! I just don't know how to approach her. I tried going right up to her, but that was a bust, too."

"You're talking about today? When you rode up on Blossom?"

He nodded.

I now realized that what had felt like an intrusion at the fruit stand had actually been an act of bravery. "What were you trying to say to her today?"

"I was trying to ask her out."

A dozen incredulous comments sprang to mind, but again I held my tongue.

I scrambled forward on the trailer so I wouldn't have to shout. "Bobby, look, I can see you have feelings for her, but I'm not sure Lisette is right for you."

"I'm not a kid, Peggy," he snarled.

"You haven't been a kid since you were about ten," I said. "Which is the problem. You act angry and burdened. Like life is nothing but hard work."

"It *is* nothing but hard work! In case you haven't noticed, that's all I do!"

"It's all I do, too, but I don't take it out on the rest of the world!"

"It's different for you."

"What are you talking about? I work dawn to dark, just like you!"

"It's not the same!"

"How? How is it not the same? You're the foreman. It's not like you're out here climbing ladders and picking fruit."

He turned his back on me. "Someday you'll be gone, just like Doris."

I stared at the back of him, stunned. The very last thing I wanted for my life was to end up like Doris. Why was he saying this?

He ground the tractor into gear. "At the end of the day," he called back, "you can walk away. You don't have the weight of the *farm* on you. I do." Then he let out the clutch, and the tractor lurched forward, sending me tumbling backward into the boxes.

4

Ginny Rose

PATCHES

The sun risin' before five o'clock makes it easy to wake on time for my first day at the cannery. I slip from bed, mindful to not wake my sisters as I tuck the bedsheets into place and gather my work dress from the small wicker chair where I'd laid it out. It's clean and ironed, starched stiff from a fit of nerves last night.

I've had odd jobs before. Some were paid in food—biscuits and beans, maybe an apple—but for us, that could make the difference between starvin' and just bein' hungry. And sometimes I got nickel jobs. Especially before the war, those nickels felt like gold.

But mostly my jobs had paid nothing at all. During the war, I was Mama's helper, doin' other folks' laundry and darning. Before that, I was Papa's helper. Free extra hands that knew how to work—even if those hands were small—could help Papa land a job that he'd likely be passed over for alone. We'd be in a line of hungry pickers beggin' for work, and Papa would holler, "I got an extra set of hands," up to the foreman. "They're free and fast and won't complain!" Folks around us would grouse, but Papa didn't care and neither did I. Our stomachs were in charge, not our pride. First Mama and the boys and then Mama and baby Anna Mae were countin' on us bringin' home something to eat, and I was more'n glad to be Papa's ticket to the front of the line.

But now here I am, startin' my very own job.

And gettin' paid forty cents an hour!

By the end of my eight-hour shift, I'll have earned three dollars and twenty cents!

At the end of the week, I'll be bringin' home sixteen dollars.

Sixteen dollars!

That'll be enough to feed the whole family for two weeks, maybe three if we stay heavy on potatoes and light on meat. By the end of summer, we'll have a nice cushion—maybe enough to splurge on new clothes for school!

I finish dressin' with a song in my heart, then find Mama fixin' breakfast in the kitchen.

"Good mornin'," she says, and yesterday's cloud seems to have lifted. She's bustlin' around the stove, cookin' flapjacks, eggs, and beans, but instead of askin' me to give her a hand, she nods at the table. "Sit."

It fills me with unexpected pride to take a seat beside Papa. And that feeling swells when Mama slips a plate identical to his in front of me. On a regular day I'd be havin' porridge with a splash of milk along with my sisters. Today I'm lookin' at more food than I can possibly eat.

"You'll need your strength, Ginny Rose," Mama says. "Eat every bite."

I do, and before long Papa's chuggin' off to work in Faithful and I'm gettin' a sack lunch from Mama and a nervous kiss on the cheek besides. "I'll have supper waitin'," she says. It's the very last thing on my mind at the moment, but after years of livin' so close to the bone, keepin' us fed is always on hers.

The air's already warm as I push off on my bicycle and pedal down the dirt lane to River Road. I turn right toward Oakvale and ride by the dairy and the hog farm, pedalin' quick to get past the smell. A long white bus full of Mexican field workers roars by and turns north onto Santa Fe Road. I have a pang of sympathy for those men, knowin' the hard, hot day they're in for, which is followed by a wash of gratitude for the change in my own family's fortunes.

As the smell of manure gives way to the sweet scent of orange blossoms, my mind wanders back to that hopeful day so many years ago when we caught our first true whiff of California. Papa had pulled Faithful to the side of the road to breathe in the wonder of an orange grove, and we reveled in the miracle of three fresh oranges, just sittin' there on the soft dirt shoulder of the road. After weeks of mishaps crossin' what seemed to be an endless desert out of Oklahoma, the five of us ate those three oranges under the clear blue California sky like songbirds splashin' in a springtime puddle. The boys and I had never even tasted an orange, or breathed air so sweet, so to us it was a miracle beyond compare. And Mama and Papa were all smiles and murmurs about havin' reached the promised land.

That day was a drop of joy in what became a sea of misery, and as I pedal by the acres of farms burstin' with fruit and nuts, I wonder how anyone in California ever went hungry. How is it possible that people starved to death?

I come upon Simmons Farm and picture Peggy out in the orchard, probably doin' tally work instead of sortin'. I coast for a few yards, takin' in the sight of their farmhouse with its yellow and white rosebushes in full bloom along the wraparound porch, moss baskets of cheerful petunias danglin' from the shaded eaves.

I'd slept over in that house once. It felt like being a princess in a castle.

A princess with a bath and fresh pajamas.

A princess with a full supper, and frosted cake besides.

It was a truly magical night.

Then I'd awakened, worked the orchard, and returned to our one-room shack made of trash, where Mama, thin as a rail, was fixin' biscuits and beans while Anna Mae squalled at her hip.

I shake off the thought of the shanty and again count my blessings about where we are now. But the memory of that one night—and how I dreamed about it for years—makes me see Mama's concern.

Peggy and I are not on equal footing.

Not by any stretch.

I push on. It's hard to get past the picture of us as children. It's hard not to go back to that simpler view. One where we couldn't see the things stoppin' us from bein' friends, and instead just saw each other.

I ride along River Road, pedalin' past River Park on one side, the cemetery and Valley Church with its tall white steeple and marquee announcin' nine a.m. Sunday service on the other. And then, next door to the church, tucked back from the road, buttoned up and silent like an usher waitin' patiently at the exit, sits Merrihew's Funeral Home.

In another mile or so, I come upon the WELCOME TO OAKVALE sign, and then, just past it, West Side Grocers and the yellow

Signal gas station, where a short line of cars waits their turn at the pump.

A milk delivery truck passes me by. So do dozens of cars. With the war's gas and rubber rationing over, new cars seem to be everywhere now. We could sure use one, seein' how Faithful's nearly twenty years old and showin' every mile, but we're still a long way from bein' able to afford one—a thought I'm havin' just as I breeze past Valley Motors and its full lot of cars sparklin' with chrome.

Farther into town I pass by Dolly's Diner, Valley Bank, the library, and the post office, which are all across the road from Oakvale High School, where I'll go come September. It's always hard startin' a new school—something I've got more experience with than I care to recall. And it *has* been a struggle keepin' up, but I work hard at it, which most teachers have been more'n kind in helpin' me with. So, puttin' the Okie slurs and jokes aside, I *like* school. Especially the books. Not just havin' a whole library to pick through, but the subject books, too—especially history books. They're always chock-full of such fascinating things.

I pedal on, and a little ways past the high school, I take a quick right turn through a yellow light at Depot Street, only to have to wait for a long, slow freight train to lumber by before bumpin' over a wide stretch of railroad tracks. In another minute, I turn onto cannery property and park my bike.

The sudden hammerin' in my chest has nothing to do with the long bike ride. It's my first day at a real job and I'm nervous . . . and so excited!

I make my way over to the warehouse, where I've been told to report for orientation and training. A man at the entrance finds my name on a list and directs me to a woman named Miss

Robinson. I'm the first new hire to arrive, but soon we're joined by three others—all women older'n me. There's no introductions, just nerves. And at last Miss Robinson issues us aprons and leads us over to the punch clock.

"This will track your time and attendance," she explains, handin' each of us a thick tan card. "Anytime you are not working the line, you must punch out, then punch in again when you resume work." There's hundreds of cards in metal slots on the wall, but the one I'm holdin' has GILLEY, GINNY ROSE typed on top.

It makes me feel . . . official.

I have a real job!

Miss Robinson has each of us push our cards into a slot at the top of a sturdy metal box with a clockface that's mounted to a wall near the time cards. When it's my turn, I press my card in, and with a solid *thunk-clunk,* the machine stamps the date and time on it.

"At the end of shift, workers will file out along this corridor," Miss Robinson explains. "You must learn to become quick at selecting, stamping, and returning your card to the wall or you'll be very unpopular!" She says this with a warm smile, but I make a point of rememberin' where I place my card among the others.

The noise level goes up as we follow Miss Robinson through a large open doorway into the main room of the cannery. Women stand facin' each other across long, wide conveyor belts, their arms movin' quickly as they work. They stand on metal grates—grates that keep them off the cement floor, which looks soiled and sticky with peach goo.

A little farther down the warehouse, cans bump and clatter

as they move up and snake along overhead, travelin' on narrow metal conveyors.

"We start new hires at the beginning of the line," Miss Robinson calls to us over the noise. "Your job is to pull sticks, stems, leaves—anything that's not peaches—from the harvest as it rolls along and drop it in the pail on the floor at your station. Down the line they'll sort the peaches, so don't pull any fruit regardless of condition. Beyond that, they'll clean and process them for canning." Then, after she's called out some quick instructions about breaks and the whereabouts of the toilet, she has us put on our aprons and join the line, standin' alongside workers whose shift is about done.

Men at the front of each line empty lug boxes of peaches onto the two long conveyor belts that stretch nearly the length of the warehouse. The fruit goes by quickly, and though the job's simple, I'm surprised by the number of things that need to be plucked out. Besides sticks and stems and leaves, there's bits of trash, clumps of mud, cigarette butts, pits, and rocks and feathers.

I've just gotten a feel for how fast I need to work when the shift whistle blows. It's shrill and long and loud, and without so much as a nod in my direction, the woman I'm workin' beside steps off the metal grate we're standin' on, undoes her apron, and hurries away.

The excitement I'd felt comin' in fades fast. By lunchtime, my legs ache, my hands are thick with sticky goo, and my arms are covered in peach fuzz. By the end of my shift, I can barely find the energy to smile at the woman who's startin' swing shift. Even with two short breaks and thirty minutes for lunch, a full day of standin' on a hard grate watchin' peaches roll by has made me dizzy, more'n a little nauseous, and sore all over.

My hand shakes as I slip my time card into the slot. *Thunk-clunk*. There's no joy in my first day done, just weary relief.

Outside, the sun burns my eyes, and my ears still hum from the noise inside. I see two women rinsin' off their hands and arms with water from a hose, so I do the same, then take a long drink before handin' the hose to another worker. I stagger toward my bike, exhausted and dazed. *Tomorrow will be better,* I tell myself, breathin' in fresh air, tryin' to steady my legs.

But I don't know how I can do that again tomorrow.

Think about the money, I tell myself.

But at the moment I'm havin' trouble carin' about three dollars and twenty cents.

I get on my bike and push off, strainin' to figure out what three dollars and twenty cents really means. *That's . . . a pound of bacon, a dozen eggs . . . five pounds of sugar, a gallon of milk . . . a pound of cheese . . . and a few loaves of bread,* I tell myself.

And this helps.

A lot.

The day's still hot, but the breeze that comes from ridin' my bike cools the sweat that's soaked my body since the warehouse began swelterin' around noon. The stretch of road near the river is a welcome relief, and my mind begins rallyin', figurin' out how to paint a different picture of my day when Mama asks me about it. I can do this. I *must* do this. Mama was so happy. It serves no purpose for her to know.

I pedal harder, but the bike resists, and when I look back, I see that my tire's gone flat. I let out a wail and nearly break down cryin'. I'm well past the gas station where I could probably patch the tire, but still miles from home. And by the time I walk home, Mama'll be sick with worry.

Then a hopeful thought bubbles up:

Peggy Simmons.

Her farm's only a bit farther down the road, and I could ask to call home. And surely they'll have a tire repair kit.

But . . .

I look down at my dress, my legs, my hands and arms.

I'm a mess.

No, I decide, I'd rather be late than have anyone in Peggy's family see me this way.

So I push the bike along, and I pick up the pace when I reach Simmons Farm, hopin' to pass by without bein' seen. But then I spot Peggy's friend Lisette sittin' in her car near the fruit stand.

I stop, not sure what to do. Maybe I should hide behind a tree until she drives away?

And then Peggy appears, hurryin' across the road to join her.

It's too late to hide, so I hold real still and pray that Peggy won't notice me. But just as she reaches Lisette's car, she does a double take. "Ginny Rose?" she calls. When I don't answer, she moves toward me. "Are you all right?"

I'm so exhausted and embarrassed that my chin starts quiverin', but I force back the rising tide of tears. "I . . . I've got a flat," I manage to say.

She studies my back tire, and suddenly Lisette's out of her car and comin' toward us.

Peggy takes me in—my appearance, my situation—then glances at Lisette, who's castin' a worried look at the farmhouse. "Do you need a ride?" Peggy asks.

I'm quick to give her a firm "No." Maybe it's her friend's

stylish clothes, or maybe it's the clear difference between Peggy and me just now—her lookin' fresh and pretty in a lovely dress and lacy ankle socks, and me lookin' slopped 'n' dropped.

"My," Lisette says, her eyebrows liftin' at the sight of me. But then she asks, "Do you need a ride?"

I'm more'n a little surprised by her offer. And I'm just re-calculatin' my impression of her when she says, "We're actually in a bit of a hurry," and then goes kickerjawin' on about a house in Oakvale that they need to get to. None of it makes sense to me—and I'm too embarrassed to give a hoot—but with her next few sentences I know that Lisette Bovee and I will never be friends.

The house is a foreclosure.

Her father's the banker.

He's movin' her family into the house.

Peggy tries to quiet Lisette, but the girl just won't shut up.

"Go. Please," I interrupt, pushin' the bike forward. "Thank you kindly for your offer, but I'll be fine."

"Ginny Rose!" Peggy calls after me. "We can fix it right here. We've got a kit."

I can hear Lisette whisperin'. She's like a teakettle fixin' to boil, and I don't need to make out the words to understand their meaning. But if life has taught me anything, it's that just when you're sure a situation can't get worse, it up and does. Because right then, Bobby appears.

Peggy hollers, "Bobby! Could you do us all a huge favor and patch Ginny Rose's tire? She lives miles from here and needs to get home."

Peggy hurries to catch me and says, "I'm so sorry! I don't

want to leave you, but I'm guessing you'd rather get the tire fixed than have Lisette give you a ride, is that right?"

It is, so I nod and look away.

"I promise I'll make this up to you!" she says.

"No need," I tell her. "Just go."

Bobby doesn't have much to say as he leads me past a line of forlorn palm trees to their shed. And the truth is, I don't have much to say to him, either. Maybe seein' him yesterday did something strange to my heart, but it's clear as day he's smitten with Lisette, and there's no competin' with that. Even if I didn't look such a fright, I will never look like her.

He pushes open the heavy wooden door, rollin' it to the side, then flicks on a light—a single bulb danglin' from a rafter. The shed's large—probably big enough for two tractors—but it feels small because it's crammed full of equipment parts and things that seem to have rusted or crumbled in place.

I step inside, pushin' the bike along. There's a wide workbench against one wall and another down the middle. Both are piled with tools and parts and tubs of junk. Propped here and there are shovels, rakes, trimmers, and orchard ladders in need of repair, and against the far wall is a rack of irrigation pipe, with scraps of plywood and two-by-fours beneath it.

As I follow Bobby deeper into the shed, we pass by an old hand plow that sends me straight back to Oklahoma, back to watchin' Papa work soil that was beyond givin' back any wheat, back to dust risin' and hope fallin'.

The memory darkens my mood further. I believed Papa when he promised me rain would come. I resented Mama for sayin' it would not; for whisperin' through the dark that his long, hard day had been a fool's errand, throwin' away more good seed after bad.

But she was right.

Rain didn't come.

And then, at last, with nothing but dust left in our pockets, he agreed to go to California.

"Back here," Bobby says, because I've stopped dead in my tracks.

So I move forward and watch as he gathers a patch kit, a foot pump, and a screwdriver. But when he goes to pry off the tire, I stop him. "I can do it," I tell him, takin' the screwdriver from him.

He studies me without smilin'. "I'll get a pail of water."

While he's gone, I pry back the tire and pull the inner tube from inside it. The tube's got odd-sized patches all over, some almost touchin', and when I pump in some air, I find the leak without needin' to dunk it in water.

It's a whistler.

Bobby returns with the pail. "Scissors?" I ask, ignorin' his water and usin' some spit to zero in on the puncture.

He fetches a pair and watches as I mark the leak, wipe the spot dry, trim a patch, smear on glue, and seal the hole. "You've done this before, I see," he says, his eyes on the tube's many patches.

"I have," I say curtly. And as I reseat the tire and pump it full of air, I start thinkin' about how a tire is like life itself. When it springs a leak, you can moan about the flat, or you can patch it, pump it full of air again, then get back on and ride.

'Course people don't usually see the patches of your inner tube, which is how a tire and life are different. On a bike, you can buy a new tire and tube and change them both. But in life, you can change the tire—what folks see on the outside—but the tube? No matter how much money you earn, no matter how others see you, you only get the one, and you carry it inside you wherever you go, patches and all.

I hand Bobby the tools, the kit, and the pump, and say, "Thank you kindly."

I say it like a stranger. The stranger that I am to him. Because despite the fact that he's seen my patches, he can't begin to imagine what they mean.

I push out to the road without lookin' back.

Then I get back on and ride.

5

Peggy

QUANDARY

I felt awful leaving Ginny Rose, but I didn't know what else to do.

"Poor thing," Lisette said, glancing in her rearview mirror as we drove away.

I was twisted around in my seat watching my brother lead Ginny Rose across the street. "Maybe I should go back."

"She'll be fine," Lisette said, her eyes now focused on the road ahead. "Bobby knows how to fix a flat."

I watched them disappear from view, then faced forward. We were both quiet for a time, but I could feel Lisette losing the battle to keep something to herself.

Finally, she just came out with it. "But putting aside whatever happened . . . a flour-sack dress? Who wears those anymore? The war's been over for two years!"

"Lots of people do," I said. It sounded defensive, and I knew it. Making clothes from big cotton flour sacks was something almost everyone in Ferrybank had done during the war. Like planting victory gardens, and giving metal and rubber to the scrap drive, and living off rations, making do with less was part of serving on the home front. And since cloth was one of the things rationed, flour mills began printing pretty patterns on their large cotton bags so people could turn them into garments, or dish towels, or stuffed bunny dolls. The sacks even came with ideas for how to use them.

And life may have been different for Lisette, but the only way *I'd* ever lived was by making the most of what little was around. Older people talked about times "before the Depression" and "before the war," but since I'd never known anything *but* those times, it had always sounded like a fantasy world to me.

Things *did* feel different now. Other people seemed looser with their earnings, freer with their smiles, and they were dressing with flair and *color*. But at our house, the routines and attitudes hadn't changed. Mother and Father and Nonnie were always concerned about the gamble of peach farming and countered any lighthearted outlook with dire predictions. "Things can turn on a dime" was the refrain inside our walls. The result was that our family didn't toss out anything, and that included worn flour-sack dresses.

The only reason I no longer had to wear those dresses was that Lisette had taken to giving me her hand-me-downs. They were mostly outfits she'd tired of, or ones she'd deconstructed and sewn into her own creations, which eventually found their way to me. They did have flair, if not particularly refined seams, and anything beat the coarse scratch of flour sack.

I was lost in these thoughts when I realized that Lisette was dividing her attention between me and the road ahead. "Tell me you don't still have yours," she said with alarm.

I shrugged and looked away.

"Peggy, *why?* They're dowdy and stiff and scratchy and . . . Whatever are you thinking, holding on to them? I know things were tight . . . they were tight for everybody! But that's in the past! Life is *good* now."

My mind was spinning—not just about my flour-sack dresses but about the worn, dirty one Ginny Rose had been wearing and the proud, desperate state she'd been in. By the grace of Lisette giving me her castoffs, I now had a decent wardrobe. But it was a generosity Lisette could afford because her parents were well-to-do. Which was also something that allowed them to buy a house in Oakvale. A house that another family had been forced to leave. So obviously life wasn't good for everyone.

"What *are* you thinking?" Lisette asked.

"Maybe I'll give them to Ginny Rose," I murmured.

"Yes! Yes, that's the perfect thing to do." She nodded and gripped the wheel tighter. "Poor thing, right?" A heartbeat passed, and then, "Did you know she'd be by?"

I shook my head.

"I wonder where she was coming from. She looked exhausted, didn't she? Like she'd walked from Oklahoma just today!"

"Lisette, don't."

"Don't what? What did I do?" Again a beat passed, and then, "And why did she get so hostile? I offer to give her a ride and suddenly she's going off in a snit?"

"Let's change the subject, shall we?"

"So you *do* know why?"

I sighed. "Lisette, she's had a really rough life, all right? And part of that had to do with banks and foreclosures."

Lisette's mouth formed a tiny red O. "I sure didn't mean to upset her," she said. "I guess I shouldn't have tried to explain.

I was just wanting to leave before Bobby showed up. Which he did!"

"I know. And *I* understand all that, but Ginny Rose didn't. Through her eyes, it's a different situation. She heard *bank* and *foreclosure* and that was a bad combination."

"I didn't know," she said with a sigh. "And now I feel bad. Remember how Miss Anderson read *The Grapes of Wrath* to us last year? So I get it. But *I* didn't do anything to her . . . or to anyone!" And after a quiet moment at a stop sign, she asked, "So can we change the subject?"

I laughed. "What a good idea!"

We were in Oakvale now, and a short while after we passed by the high school, she turned onto Bardo Street. "It's right up here," she said. "See why the location's so great? You can walk to anywhere!"

"Except my house," I said, trying to make it sound like a joke.

"But you can come over every day after school," she said. "It'll be great, I promise!" She pointed ahead, toward a two-story blue-and-white clapboard house. "There it is! I can't wait to see inside."

"You haven't yet?" I asked with surprise.

"No! It hasn't been vacant until today." She gave me a smile, her eyes twinkling. "And I wanted my best friend in the whole wide world to be with me when I did."

My heart swelled. "Aw! Thank you."

But as we approached the house, the twinkle disappeared and she gasped, "Oh no!"

A man standing in the front yard beside a sprawling pile of things—furniture, kitchen equipment, clothes, a radio console— was yelling at a sheriff's deputy who stood guarding the front door while workers emptied the house. His eyes had heavy bags, and his clothes and fedora were dirty and rumpled. Seeing him sent me straight back to my days working with pickers in the orchard; to the memory of men appearing at the door, begging for food.

"How can you do this to me, Mac?" the man in the yard was yelling at the deputy. "You served in the war, just like me! You know the struggle I've had. And you've got a family, just like me! How can you do this?"

The deputy was stoic, looking in a different direction, trying to ignore the yelling.

"Mac, answer me! How can you do this?"

The deputy faced him. "There's a court order that's doin' it, Carl, not me," he shouted back. "And I'm sorry it's come to this, but it's my job to enforce the order. Don't make me feel worse than I already do!"

"I should be worried about *your* feelings right now?" Carl yelled. "You and that yellow-bellied Bovee? He couldn't find the courage to put on a uniform but isn't afraid to force a family from their house?"

Lisette gasped again and sped away, and neither of us made a peep as she drove to Dolly's. Even after she'd parked in the lot, we stayed in the car, silent. Clearly, neither of us felt like going inside to toast the new house.

At last she whispered, "That was Carl Sunderwood. He's in Daddy's bowling league."

I tried to hold my tongue, but in the end it wrestled free. "How could you live in that house knowing—"

"Stop it, Peggy! Just stop! Do you think *I* have a choice in this?" She turned to face me. "Daddy's not a mean or heartless man. And he's not a coward. That's just not fair! Maybe he didn't enlist, but he was exempt from the draft, just like your dad!" She looked down and shook her head. "And everyone knows that if someone's not paying their mortgage, the bank has to take the house back!" She gave me a pained look. "I didn't know it was Mr. Sunderwood, though. . . ." She faced forward again and seemed to double down. "But Daddy said Valley Bank gave him every chance in the world to make it right, and he didn't."

I *did* understand the financial angle of it, though it was still hard to swallow. But it was the rest of the situation that really bothered me. "But why did your father—"

"Buy it. Right. I know," she snapped. She turned to me again, this time with pleading eyes. "It looks really, really bad, doesn't it?"

I shrugged. She knew it did. There was no reason for me to say it.

Just then there was a *tap-tap-tap* on Lisette's half-open window, echoed by a *tap-tap-tap* on mine.

We both jumped.

On the other side of her glass was Rodney St. Clair. Outside mine was Rodney's best friend, Jimmy Dickens, wearing his usual cowboy hat and cockeyed grin.

We cranked down our windows farther and Jimmy tipped his hat. "Hi-de-ho, Miss Simmons," he said to me, then looked across at Lisette. "Miss Bovee."

Rodney was grinning, too, his gaze focused on me. "You girls going inside, or staying out here?"

"Or . . . ," Jimmy said as he eyed the back seat, "*we* could come inside." He looked across us to Rodney. "Plenty of room for the four of us, wouldn't you say?"

"Plenty," Rodney said with an approving nod, then gave me a sly grin. "Whaddya say, Peaches?"

I, of course, blushed, and my tongue became instantly paralyzed.

But Lisette had no problem taking action. She cranked the motor to life as she shot a withering look at Rodney. "You will mind your manners around us, Rodney St. Clair!" Then she called across me, "That applies to you, too, Jimmy!"

"Hey!" Rodney called as Lisette threw the gearshift into reverse. "It's just a nickname! She sells peaches!"

But Lisette was already tearing out of the parking lot.

I knew Lisette disliked Rodney because of the way he flirted, but in the three full years she and I had been friends, I had never, *ever* seen her behave this way. And I'm afraid I was gaping, because when she glanced over at me, her face screwed down tight and she said, *"Peaches?* And did you see the way he was looking at you?"

I had. It had sent quivers running through me. The sort I'd only ever felt around Rodney St. Clair.

"Well?" she demanded.

"Watch out!" I cried, because we were drifting into the oncoming lane.

She clamped down on the steering wheel and kept her eyes focused straight ahead.

Once again, I was at a loss of what to say. Mostly, I was confused. I'd seen boys say really cheeky things to *her* and she'd never reacted this way. She'd either shut them down or flirt right back. Lisette was a honey that sent boys buzzing. I was more her honeycomb—a practical, steady harbor where she knew she could go to rest and collect herself. Being Lisette's friend came with a need to be comfortable in that role, and I was.

I'd never even questioned it.

Until now.

Now I sat beside her, staring straight ahead, trying to work out whether her overreaction was because of what had happened at the house or because she really was this offended by Rodney's behavior. And *was* Rodney's nickname for me something to be offended by? Or was it just an innocent name because of my family's farm? There were lots of peach expressions, and all of them meant something good. *Isn't that peachy? Sweet as a peach. That's a peach of an idea.* And I'd heard my own mother use the expression *peaches and cream* about the flawless complexion of a girl we saw at church one Sunday.

So maybe Rodney just thought it was cute. The more I mulled it over, the harder it was to believe that he was being anything more than playful.

But Lisette was clearly in a mood, and the last thing I wanted was to start an argument. Instead, when she pulled to a stop off the side of the road in front of my house, I said, "Thank you for coming to my defense."

Even at a standstill, she kept gripping the wheel. "You are not equipped to deal with the likes of Rodney St. Clair."

I could feel my face flush hot. It suddenly seemed like it was my sister, Doris, not my best friend, making me feel like a foolish little girl.

"And I'm sorry about that horrible scene at the house," she said. She gave the door handle beside me a pointed look. "I need to go."

This, too, had never happened before. Not unless Bobby was approaching. But he was nowhere to be seen, and there was no doubt what her look meant.

I should leave.

Now.

I hurried out, then leaned in through the open window. "Did I do something—?"

She shook her head emphatically. "I will call you tomorrow."

And in a cloud of dust, she was gone.

6

Ginny Rose

WEATHERIN' A STORM

After fixin' the flat, I roll up to our house wantin' nothing more'n to collapse into bed. From my heart to my toes, everything aches.

The girls are waitin', sittin' on the short run of worn wooden steps that leads to our front door. Faithful's parked alongside the house, so Papa's home, and the smell of supper floatin' through the open doorway causes my stomach to let loose a mighty growl.

Quick as crickets, Bonnie Sue and Katie Bee spring up and fly inside, chirpin', "She's here! She's here!"

Anna Mae's slower to rise, and her look is appraising, leanin' toward suspicious. Before she can speak, Mama appears in the doorway. She, too, takes in the sight of me.

I remind myself to perk up. To not let on how hard my shift at the cannery has been, or how the stop at Peggy's has done me in. "Sorry I'm late!" I call out with as much cheer as I can muster. I lean the bike against the house. "Flat tire."

Anna Mae's still studyin' me. She's a magnifier, burnin'

through my mask. Soon Mama's voice is the only part of her lingerin' in the doorway. "Supper's waitin'."

As I mount the steps, Anna Mae speaks at last, her voice a forceful whisper. "You're a mess," she states. "And you've been cryin'."

I look at her in horror.

"Your face is streaked."

I rush back down the steps to the spigot, scrub my face with water, then use the inside of my dress hem to dry it.

"Better?" I whisper when I'm back at the steps.

Anna Mae nods, but there's a winning-hand look in her eyes now. "All it's gonna cost you is the truth."

"All *what's* gonna cost me?"

"Me not tellin'," she says like she's holdin' aces.

"Nobody's gonna give a hoot if I did a little cryin'. So what? Who cares?"

"Well, it seems *you* do. And besides, you never cry."

"Cryin's no big deal, Anna Mae. You can attest to that."

She takes the hit without flinchin'. "So you won't mind me mentionin' it at supper, then?"

"Anna Mae! Why are you blackmailin' me?"

She moves in close, her whispered voice comin' fast and furious. "I want the truth about Mama. About why she went from hummin' to frettin' to fumin' in the time it takes to set a table. I want to know why you bein' a little late is the end of the world, and how she can be this mad at you when, from the looks of things, you had a hard day."

"She's *mad* at me? Not just worried?"

"Mm-hmmm," she says, stretchin' it way out.

I blink at her, wonderin' when my first baby sister had become this sassy big girl. And at all of ten years old? What had this vagabond life and Mama's dark moods been doin' to *her*?

So I say, "I reckon the only one who can answer that is Mama."

"Well, she's not tellin' and I'm not about to get my head bit off again askin' . . . which is why I'm blackmailin' you."

"Well, I don't know, and surely she's not mad anymore."

Mama's voice snaps through the air like a whip. "Girls!"

Anna Mae raises an eyebrow. "Surely you're wrong."

Inside, we find everyone else seated around the table, the serving dishes clustered in the middle. I take in the sight of potatoes, baked beans, creamed corn, and pork chops—a true feast.

Or, I'm realizin', a celebration. One to honor my new job.

Only nobody's smilin'.

Mama sits under her dark cloud, a fork clenched in one hand, a knife in the other, though food has yet to touch her plate.

Anna Mae scurries to her seat beside Bonnie Sue, and with a gentle smile and encouraging nod, Papa eases me forward to my chair across from Mama.

"We took a minute to wash up," I explain.

Papa says a few words of thanks as we all clasp our hands and bow our heads. Everyone's eyes are dutifully closed, but Anna Mae and I are side-eyein' Mama, who's still holdin' tight to her fork and knife.

Dishes get started around the moment Papa proclaims, "Amen." The Littles go heavy on corn, Anna Mae on potatoes, Papa on meat. Mama doesn't take much of anything, and as everyone else eats, my appetite fades fast.

She *is* mad.

But why?

After a long, prickly spell of us all eatin' in silence, Papa casts a cautious glance Mama's way, then turns his attention to me. "So. How was your first day, Ginny Rose?"

Papa's not one to begin a conversation. He more seems to endure them. So him settin' this ball in motion is unexpected, and also a little alarmin'.

"Everyone was very nice," I say in the optimistic tone I'd rehearsed. "Friendly and helpful."

"And the work?" Papa asks.

"Simple enough," I answer, then give him a knowing look. "I've had worse."

It's another line I worked up on the ride home, but now that it's crossed my lips, I can taste the lie in it. The truth is, for all the pickin' we've done, for all the farms we've worked, for all the hot summer days we've spent fryin' in the California sun, I hadn't felt so suffocated since we left Oklahoma. In the fields we may have been hungry and tired and sunburned raw, but Papa always pointed out that at least we had fresh air to breathe. And, everything else aside, wasn't that what we'd left Oklahoma for? Dust pneumonia had taken my cousins and more'n a few of our friends and neighbors. At least *that* wouldn't get us here.

But today was a different kind of suffocation. It wasn't dust billowin' miles high, expandin' like a wall across the plains. The cannery was a closed-in, swelterin' kind of suffocation, but it *had* sent my mind back to bein' desperate for air.

Mama breaks me from my reflection. "You'll be needin' a clean dress tomorrow," she says, givin' me a hard look.

"Yes, Mama," I reply. I hear my voice quiver. Why's she mad at me?

"The gas station didn't have a phone?" she asks next.

Before I can make sense of the question, I ask, "What gas station?"

"The only one between here and the cannery," she says, holdin' my gaze. "Where else would you have fixed a flat?"

"I . . . I . . . The Simmons had a repair kit."

"The Simmons," she snorts.

I've landed here enough times to know—this is the calm before the storm. My mind reels with ways to stop what's comin', to block it. But I know, too, that no matter what I try, it's comin'. Like the dust, blinding and unstoppable, it's comin'.

"Mary . . . ," Papa says, placin' a hand on her arm.

"No!" she says, shakin' him off.

"Mary, please. It was kind of them to help her fix the bike."

But Mama's eyes have gone dark. "They had a kit, but not a phone?" she asks. "Or did they not want you in their house?"

The storm's upon us now, but still, I try. "It wasn't like that! It was Peggy's brother who helped me. And afterward I hurried straight home!"

The lie in my words tastes bitter this time, and sticky. Though what choice do I have but to lie? What would she say if I told her the truth? That I was blinded by tears and stopped to let them out—to let all of it out? That I needed time to find the strength to face what waits for me tomorrow? And the next day? And the next? That I'm feelin' close to broken and am tryin' with all I've got to hide it?

Mama studies me, makin' the air feel thick and charged— like movin' a muscle will send sparks flyin'. At last she says, "So it was *you* who didn't think to call?"

"Mama! I was . . . I just wanted to come home!"

"Mary," Papa says, "can't you see she's exhausted? Leave her be."

I hate that he's read me despite my efforts, but I slip him a grateful look nonetheless.

Still Mama doesn't stop. Her nostrils flare, and with each word her voice gathers strength as she says, "She. Didn't. Even. Think. To. Call!"

"Mary!"

But Mama bears down on me without so much as a glance in his direction. "Do you know where I pictured you? Do you know all the ways you died in my mind? Hit at the crossing! Run off the side of the road! Dead in a ditch!"

"MARY!" Papa bellows, jumpin' to his feet, commandin' her to silence in a way I've never seen him do before.

And she does fall silent.

For a moment.

Then the winds of pain inside her rise up, and the whole table trembles as darkness moves in. She faces him, lashin' out with a forceful blast. "I've lost two children already! I cannot go through that again! I would be no good to this world if I lost another—you understand me?"

Papa tries to calm things. "*We* lost 'em, Mary," he says gently. "*We* did."

"But *I'm* the only one still mournin'!" she shouts, pushin' away from him and standin' up.

"That's not true! They were my *boys*, Mary. My *boys*."

"And *I* gave them life!"

Suddenly the winds shift and Mama's collapsin' in her chair, breakin' down in tears.

Tears.

High-pitched, moon-howlin' tears.

The Littles look at me and so does Anna Mae, all of them ghost-faced. I'm torn between wantin' to scoop them out of the house and hunkerin' down, when it dawns on me that this might be the storm we've been prayin' for.

Maybe the rain's come at last.

I pull the Littles in close, and Anna Mae scoots in on her own. And through Mama's sobs and gasps, we hear her say, "But I wasn't strong enough to keep them alive, was I?"

Papa's at her side again, his voice low and soothing now. "There was nothing you could have done, Mary. You nearabout died yourself."

She sits, defeated, bent over and sobbin'. "We left them, Jeremiah. In a ditch grave. One I've never even seen."

Papa looks up sharply and sees the girls holdin' on to me, wide-eyed and horrified. "Git," he commands me. "Take them outside. Now!"

I begin to do as he's commanded but stop short. "The girls are always askin' questions about the boys, Papa. I reckon it would help if we could just clear the air about all of it."

"No," Papa says sternly. "What's done's done. There's no way to undo it, and there's no sense pickin' at the scabs of the past."

"Papa," I say in the calmest voice I can find, "it doesn't take a doctor to see that Mama's got an infection under her scab. Tellin' her everything's all right is not makin' it go away."

My heart's gone wild inside my chest and I feel light-headed. I've never challenged him before. Ever.

Behind me, I hear Anna Mae whisper, "*Now* she's dead," to the Littles.

But Katie Bee's hand is suddenly inside mine, and then, on the same side, so is Bonnie Sue's.

"We want to know what happened to our brothers," Katie Bee chirps.

"We know they got sick and you couldn't get a doctor," Bonnie Sue says, like she's answerin' a teacher's question.

And from behind me Anna Mae mutters, "And now we know you buried 'em in a ditch."

Fortunately, Papa doesn't hear Anna Mae. And to my surprise, he doesn't bark us away with commands. He stares at us. Each of us. Takin' us in one by one, seemin' to toggle between confusion and conviction.

But most surprising of all?

A small smile has crept up Mama's lips.

I blink at her, wonderin' if this time she's slipped right over the edge.

But . . . hers doesn't look like the smile of a madwoman.

It looks like the smile of a mother.

The one I had a long, long time ago.

She puts her arms out for the Littles to fill and they do so, though their eyes seek mine for reassurance.

"Well," Papa says, findin' his voice. "You know what happened, then. And what matters now is the boys are with the Lord in Heaven."

Mama releases the girls, gives them each a sweet kiss, then turns to Papa. "I have very little faith left in the Lord, Jeremiah."

He seems as shocked by these words as he was by her tearful outburst, but she pays him no mind. She stands and looks us girls over. "So who's helpin' with dishes?"

We each utter a meek "I will," but Mama comes over to me, holds me at arm's length, and says, "You've done enough work for one day, Ginny Rose."

Then she pulls me in and hugs me like she might never let me go.

7

Peggy

PEACH PIE TANGLE

Lisette did *not* call me the next day, but I barely noticed. The twins were sick, which meant that Nonnie and I did many of Mother's chores on top of our own so she could take care of them. From the sound of things, Nonnie and I got the better end of the deal.

With all the baking, cooking, canning, and cleaning being done, it was sweltering in the house by noon, even with fans in the doorways. Mother finally shooed me out to work the stand around three, and it was sweet relief to escape the house, despite the fact that the thermometer nailed to a front porch post was pushing a hundred degrees in the shade.

But there was no rest for me. Two cars were parked near the stand, although since our hours varied widely, theirs was a wait of optimism. "I'll be right there!" I called across the road.

I rolled the wide, double-level handcart Father had built up to the porch steps, where Nonnie helped me load it with peaches, pies, jams, preserves, an assortment of paper sacks, and the cash box. Then I pulled it over to the stand.

Some of our regular customers have seen me there since I was twelve. They greet me like family, and I do likewise in return. At the beginning of each season, the comments about how much I've grown have slowly been replaced by compliments about what a pretty young lady I've become, which is always the blush side of nice.

But apparently I wasn't looking too pretty or ladylike at the moment. Mrs. Gustoff's comment was the most direct. "It *is* a hot one, dear, I'll give you that. But, my Lord!" She looked me over as she paid for a pie and half a dozen peaches. "Your daddy should fashion a canopy to protect that beautiful skin of yours."

"That would be nice," I replied, because at the moment I *was* sizzling.

"Insist," Mrs. Gustoff said, heading off. "You need to watch yourself before it's too late. At least wear a sun hat."

I worked through the next string of customers with as much pleasantry as I could muster, telling myself that Mrs. Gustoff had always been one to slip bitters into the sweet tea of her comments. But several other people made remarks, too. Mrs. Prager said, "You look positively wilted!" and Mrs. Quimbly said, "Dear . . . your hair!" in a voice of complete despair.

"My . . . hair?" I asked, resisting the urge to touch it because my hands had just become sticky with pie sugars.

"Yes, dear. A brush is most definitely in order."

I wiped my hands and tried to tie my hair back—what if Rodney came by? But thoughts of Rodney put me back inside

Lisette's car in my mind and how she'd made me feel like a naïve little bumpkin.

Well, I *wasn't* a naïve little bumpkin and I *did* like Rodney, and wasn't that my choice, not hers? And why hadn't she called?

As the afternoon wore on, my thoughts began to froth. I knew Lisette showing up at the stand with an explanation would calm me within minutes, but I'd be embarrassed for *her* to appear now, too. Because, as always, she would be completely put together, lipstick on, not a hair out of place.

And yet, by the time I was ready to close down the stand, I was even more frothed because she *hadn't* appeared, and doubly terrified that Rodney might. But it wasn't either of them who came by as I was rolling the nearly empty handcart back toward the house. It was Ginny Rose.

She was riding fast, her face locked forward, seemingly intent on barreling by. "Ginny Rose!" I called out.

She kept on, full steam ahead.

"Ginny Rose!" I called again.

She eased into a coast and glanced my way but didn't put on her brakes.

"Ginny Rose!" I called. "Stop!"

She didn't stop, but she didn't pedal, either. So I dropped the cart handle and chased after her. "Ginny Rose!" Was she mad at me for yesterday? For leaving her to fix a flat with my brother instead of helping her myself? For being friends with a banker's daughter?

She glanced over at me chasing her and finally stopped.

"Don't be mad at me, please," I panted as I caught up to her.

Her stony look dissolved almost immediately. "How can I be

mad at you," she said, trying to stifle a laugh, "when you look worse'n I do?"

I checked us both over and laughed along with her. "You're nowhere near the disaster I am, apparently," I said. "The twins are sick, so I've been doing double duty and haven't had a moment to breathe. Customers have been dropping hints all afternoon about how bad I look."

She leaned over and pulled something out of my hair. "You do look like you tangled with a peach pie and lost."

I sighed. "That pretty much sums things up."

She peeled out another chunk of who knows what and flicked it to the ground. "Tell your mama you've earned a bath." She smiled at me. "You still have that big white tub? The one with iron claw feet?" Before I could tell her we did, she said, "I loved that tub," like it was something out of a fairy tale instead of just an old farmhouse bathtub.

"We do, but . . ." I couldn't help asking, "Where *are* you coming from?" because, once again, her dress was in real need of washing. It was wet at the armpits and the bodice, and dirty along the sides and at the hem . . . like she'd been sweating all day while wearing an apron.

Just like me.

Her eyes flicked away from mine. Then she seemed to find her resolve, straightening up as she said, "I've got a job at the cannery. It pays forty cents an hour."

My jaw dropped. "Forty cents an hour! That's wonderful."

She gave me a wry smile. "It's nothing like workin' your own orchard, but it'll help put food on our table." She started pushing off. "I do need to get home. I was late for supper yesterday, which was not good. And I got wash to do before work tomorrow, so—"

"Wait!" I called, suddenly remembering. "Don't go! I'll be right back!"

I raced away from her protests, flew into the house and up the stairs to my bedroom, folded my flour-sack dresses and placed them inside a bag as quickly and neatly as I could, then raced back across the road.

"These are for you. If you want them," I panted.

She shook her head and said, "I can't take it," without even looking inside.

"Sure you can," I insisted, shoving the bag into her arms. "It's just hand-me"—I realized how what I was about to say would sound and made a quick switch—"hand-me-overs. It's what friends do. So if you don't want them or don't need them or don't *like* them, just pass them along. Do whatever you want with them."

Her curiosity got the better of her. She peeked inside the bag, understood what was there, then seemed to analyze the simple cotton summer dress I was wearing. All the while, she stayed completely silent, which sent me into a tailspin of doubt. Had I just insulted her? If *I* would never wear them again—not because they didn't fit, but because they were out of style and just scratchy—had I just given her my garbage?

Finally, she said, "We're not leaners."

"But . . . do you want them? Can you use them?"

"I'm on a rotation of two dresses, so I *could* sure use them," she admitted. "But Mama will be . . ." She heaved a sigh. "We're not leaners."

"Don't be silly. You're my friend. Take them and save yourself from doing laundry tonight." I pulled the bag from her grasp and placed it in her basket. "I've got to get inside," I said, "and if I remember right, you were in a hurry."

She quit protesting and said, "I'll get you back!" the same way she'd done when we'd worked together in the orchard as kids.

"Not if I can help it!" I called as I hurried to the handcart, and we both laughed with the memory of the fun we'd had those summers.

After dinner, after the lug boxes were set and the dishes were done, after the Delta breeze had cooled the house to almost bearable and the twins were settled into bed with Vicks ointment smeared on their chests, I was helping Mother and Nonnie with a final scrub of the kitchen when the phone rang.

Mother leaned the handle of her mop against the wall and gave me a reproachful look as she moved to snatch up the phone, because who would be calling this late besides Lisette?

But it wasn't Lisette.

It was my sister.

I knew it was Doris by the way Mother crumpled onto the little stool that finds its way from one purpose to the next in the kitchen. And although she didn't say my sister's name, the way she twisted the phone cord and the set of her mouth said it loud and clear. Mother did her best to bite her tongue and accept Doris's decision to run off with a man who'd yet to have dinner at our house, but her disapproval always seeped out in her voice, in her words, even in her breathing.

Nonnie, sensing the troubled nature of the call, took the broom and went out to sweep the back porch, but I'd learned from Mother not to be so polite. I hung on every word as I wiped down the counters, trying to piece together the conversation.

When Mother was finally off the line, I wrung out the rag I'd been using, draped it over the faucet, and asked, "Is Doris okay?"

Mother looked up but didn't get up. Whatever it was had clearly been one straw too many.

I moved closer. "Mother?"

"She's expecting again." There was no joy in her words. No attempt to put a little lift in her voice.

"But . . . that's good news, isn't it?"

She stood. "Another grandbaby who'll never play in the orchard?" It was exhaustion that allowed the words to slip out, and she moved quickly to cover them up. "She's got morning sickness all day long, and Tommy's up half the night squalling. She's asked me to come tomorrow, but I don't know how I can. Not with the boys sick."

"I'll go," I volunteered. The words were out before I could think better of them, perhaps because a trip to Modesto—even if it landed me at Doris's—would be easier than another like today.

Mother looked at me now. Really took me in. "Would you?" she asked.

"I could go in the morning and be back by three or four to work the stand."

She let out a heavy sigh. "Thank you."

And since I was finally done with my chores and it felt like this might be my only chance, I asked, "Is it all right if I call Lisette?"

"It's much too late to call!"

"Anytime before nine is okay with the Bovees."

Mother frowned and grumbled, "Banker's hours," but with it came a curt nod of permission.

So I dialed the Bovees', asked for Lisette, and was told by her mother that she was "having a bubble bath."

I felt a strange sort of heat rise up inside me but tamped it down. "Is she working at Woolworth's tomorrow?"

"Yes, she is."

"Could you tell her I'll be visiting my sister in Modesto tomorrow and hope to have time to stop by Woolworth's while I'm there?"

"I most certainly will."

"Thank you, Mrs. Bovee," I said as pleasantly as I could, then went upstairs to take a long-overdue bath of my own.

8

Ginny Rose

SURPRISES

Not wantin' a repeat of yesterday, I pedal hard to make up the time I've spent with Peggy. I'm both grateful for the dresses she's given me and terrified of them. The thought of havin' to scrub, dry, and iron my two dirty dresses before bed feels like a mountain too high to climb after my cannery shift, so Peggy's gift is a godsend. But it *is* a gift, one I can't repay—something that's bound to bring in Mama's dark clouds.

The girls are on the steps again as I roll in, but this time Mama's put them to real work—the Littles are shuckin' peas on the bottom step, and Anna Mae's darnin' a sock on the landing.

"She's here!" Bonnie Sue and Katie Bee cry, jumpin' up and nearly upendin' the bowl of peas.

Anna Mae stays put as the Littles race inside to sound the alarm. Her eyes are fixed on the sack in my basket. "What's that?" she asks.

"Something that'll save me hours of scrubbin' and ironin' before bed tonight."

Anna Mae anchors the darning needle in the sock and stands. "New clothes?"

"Hand-me-overs from a friend," I say, repeatin' Peggy's description as I park the bike.

"Anything that'll fit me?" Her eyes are hopeful, childlike.

I give her a gentle smile. "Not yet, but someday."

Inside, Mama's busy fillin' serving dishes but still takes notice of my bag. "What do you have there?"

Papa's told me over and over that there's no path less painful than the one that leads directly to the truth, so I dig deep for courage and come out with it. "Hand-me-overs from Peggy Simmons." Then I explain how grateful I am to have received them.

Papa's waitin' on supper at the table, and he turns a keen eye from me to Mama as the room goes quiet. I signal the girls, and we all help Mama get the serving dishes placed, but we're each holdin' our breath the whole time.

We keep right on holdin', too, as Papa says grace and Mama starts the dishes around. "So how are you repayin' this kindness?" Mama asks at last.

"I need to give that some thought," I say.

"Yes, you do," she says firmly. But to everyone's surprise and relief, that seems to be the end of it.

During supper, I notice Papa's eyes on me. They flick away when mine meet his, but then I feel them on me again shortly after, and can't help wonderin' what he's thinkin'.

He's sure as shootin' thinkin' *something*.

After supper, he invites Mama to walk with him. It's plain to see she doesn't want to, but since this is his way of sayin' he'd like to discuss something out of earshot of the rest of us, she obliges.

No one needs to tell us to clean up. We fall into the task like marching ants, the Littles deliverin' dishes to the sink while Anna Mae collects cuttings and scraps for the chickens and I wipe down the table's oilcloth and ready the sinks and drainboard. Soon, we've all lined up in position, Anna Mae rinsin' and the Littles dryin' the dishes I wash. We conserve water, even though it runs hot and plentiful from the faucet—a luxury I still can't quite believe is ours.

With only half the dishes washed, Anna Mae suddenly abandons her post and hazards a peek out the back door. We watch her look one way, then the other. Then she ventures outside.

"Uh-oh," Bonnie Sue whispers.

"If she gets us in trouble, I'm tellin'," Katie Bee says with a pout.

"Tellin' what?" I ask.

But then Anna Mae's back, wide-eyed and rosy-cheeked. "Show us!" she whispers to me. "I checked around the whole house—they're gone."

"Show us!" Katie Bee squeals with little hops up and down.

All eyes are on me, and I realize it's the dresses they're wantin' to see.

And, I'm realizin', so do I.

I dry my hands quick, open the bag, and pull out the dresses. One has a pattern of bluebells, the other, kittens with umbrellas.

I can't help smilin', and the girls all squeal with delight because . . . well . . . is there anything cuter than kittens with umbrellas?

"I can't *wait* 'til this fits me," Bonnie Sue says, holdin' the skirt wide as she pictures herself big enough to wear it.

"Me too," Katie Bee says with a sigh.

"Quick!" Anna Mae whispers, because there's no mistakin' the sound of voices outside.

We hurry to tuck the dresses away and are back at our posts in a flash, but our guilt is broadcast by our silence and our hands workin' a little too fast.

Mama and Papa don't seem to notice. Instead, Mama goes straight to the bag and pulls the dresses from it. She inspects them, turnin' them back and forth before hangin' them over the back of a chair. She, too, is silent, and my side glances to figure out just what sort of trouble I might be in end up tellin' me that something strange is goin' on between Mama and Papa. Out of the corner of my eye, I watch them have an unspoken conversation. Nods and head shakes and little hand waves, frowns and furrowed brows.

Anna Mae and I take up signals of our own, mostly me tryin' to still her jabbing elbow and questioning looks.

Then, at last, Mama says, "Ginny Rose, when you're done there, please meet us outside."

"Yes, Mama," I say, like it's an everyday occurrence rather than something that's never happened before, and my eyes roam wide and worried over to Anna Mae's.

"Doesn't *sound* like trouble," she whispers when Mama's gone.

"So why's it feel like it?" I whisper back.

Outside, I find Papa on the porch, readin' the Bible. It's nice on the porch, the sun's rays filtered through a row of trees while a gentle breeze shoos the day's heat toward tomorrow.

Mama's in the garden goin' after weeds, and when she joins us, Papa begins by sayin', "Ginny Rose, you'll be turnin' seventeen next month."

I look back and forth between him and Mama. I know Mama's keenly aware of my birthday and the heartbreaking anniversary it marks, but Papa lives from one sunrise to the next, so why's he summoned me outside to tell me my age?

"You'll be eligible for marriage soon," Mama says bluntly.

I gape at her, dumbstruck.

"Mary," Papa says gently, "let me." He puts the Bible aside and faces me. "Your mama and I had a few years of true joy before hard times hit us. There were socials, church functions, dances . . . especially dances. Your mama and I met at one, did you know that? We were both fifteen, and she was quite a dancer."

I try to hide my surprise, but . . . *Mama*? Quite a *dancer*?

I *am* stupefied.

And that wistful tone in his voice . . . is the man sittin' there lookin' every bit like my papa really my papa? And the woman— the one with the wash of pink heatin' her cheeks—is that really Mama?

Feelin' a little light-headed, I shake my head in reply.

"Well, it's true. You, though," Papa continues, "have had none of that. You were born durin' the Great Depression, spent your childhood fightin' dust or pickin' crops, and have braved hardships no child should ever know. You've lived your teen years under the shadow and sacrifices of war, and now you work long, hard hours at the cannery—something I know more'n a little about from what folks at the switching yard tell me."

My chin takes up a quiver, but I fight hard against it. Despite my efforts, though, I'm in danger of losin' the battle, because at no time in my life have I heard words like these come from Papa—or Mama either, for that matter.

"And in all these years," Papa says gently, "your mama and I have never once heard you complain. Not from hunger, not from weariness, not from fear."

Tears seep free, and I wipe them aside with the back of my hand.

"School's startin' soon," Mama says out of the blue.

Papa gives her another gentle look and picks up the talk. "Your mama and I are grateful for the wages you're earnin', but we think it's time for you to have money of your own."

Of all the directions things might have gone, this is a swerve I had not seen comin'. "What are you sayin'?" I ask, my voice choked and hoarse.

"You need proper clothes for school," Mama says, shakin' her head at the sight of my shoes. Then she adds, "And you need a little spendin' money for social gatherings."

My jaw goes for a dangle, and then Papa cuts in. "What we're thinkin', Ginny Rose, is that you give half of what you earn to the family while you're still livin' with us, and keep the rest for things you need to enter into a life apart from us."

Inside me, there's a strange mix of excitement and fear. Like a bird must feel, peekin' out from the nest for the first time. And it's true—I know how to clean. I know how to cook. I know how to build things and fix things and stretch a dime clear to Texas.

But . . . life apart from my family?

My mind's never even *touched* those thoughts.

"Are . . . are you sure?" I ask.

"We are," Papa's quick to say, castin' a firm look at Mama. Then he picks up his Bible, signalin' the end of the conversation, which sends Mama back to the garden and me back inside.

Anna Mae has, of course, eavesdropped the whole thing, but when she corners me later, what she says takes me by surprise.

"You cannot run off and leave me here alone with her, you hear me?" She wraps me in a hug that nearly cuts me in two. "I don't know how to fix her the way you do!"

"Fix her?" I whisper back. "I'm the one who's always breakin' her!"

She pulls back, wipes away a spray of tears, and is suddenly Anna Mae again. "Ew," she says, wrinklin' her nose. "Go wash. You stink."

I laugh because, hard as it is to hear, she sure does know how to take a path directly to the truth.

So I fetch a bar of soap, a worn washcloth, and a hand towel, and I fill the latrine's sink with water. Then I give myself a thorough scrubbing, grateful for the day's surprises and the miracle of warmth flowin' through the pipes.

9

Peggy

THE ROAD TO MODESTO

The morning was half gone by the time I arrived at Doris's doorstep. The box of fresh cobbler, preserves, and peppermint tea Mother had sent along was manageable when Father dropped me off at the bus stop, and for the thirty-minute ride into Modesto it sat comfortably on my lap. But it seemed to increase in both weight and size with each step of the six-block walk to Doris's apartment, threatening to slip free more than once. With aching arms, I was grateful to finally arrive.

And then the door opened.

My sister looked dowdy and *old* in a worn cotton nightdress, her hair unkempt, her feet bare. Yet her face pinched at the sight of *me*, making me feel like a worm in her apple. "Mother couldn't be bothered?" she snarled.

My cheeks were already warm from the walk, but now they burned. "The twins are sick. Mother told you that." I shoved the box into her arms. "I can turn around and go home, if that's what you want."

She softened, the weight of her obvious exhaustion taking over. "No. No, I'm sorry. Come in."

I'd been to the apartment only a couple of times since my mother had patched things up with Doris. It was baby Tommy who'd finally made Mother shelve her hurt feelings, but that shelf was at chest height, easily reached.

Father, on the other hand, had washed his hands of the whole business. "She made her bed—let her lie in it" was all he ever said about Doris, and he only said *that* when he wanted to put an end to Mother's attempt to discuss her. He had never once been to Doris's apartment. He had never even met Tom, Doris's husband. "I know all I need to about the man," he would say flatly, and from her little snorts and eye rolls it was clear that Nonnie agreed. So Doris, in turn, had stopped coming home.

I wished I could say I missed her.

The apartment was small—one bedroom with a tiny front room and a cramped kitchen—but stepping into it now, I was struck by a smothering confinement. Had the ceiling always been so low? The interior so dark? It was already very warm inside, but there was no fan in the window to circulate the air, which smelled like dirty diapers.

And what a mess! There were dishes everywhere, toys strewn about, washed diapers on a drying rack and draped over the sides of a playpen. And the *noise*. Tommy was banging a large spoon against an overturned pan on the kitchen floor.

"Stop that!" Doris barked at him, and he did for all of two seconds before starting up again.

Doris put Mother's care package on the kitchen counter and grabbed Tommy roughly by the arm, yanking him to his feet. "I said stop that!"

The banging did stop . . . but then the screaming began. He just *wailed*, spoon still in hand, his diaper dangling heavily. And then, his face blotchy red, his nose and eyes streaming, he whacked the spoon against Doris's leg.

She whacked him back, on his bottom, and *hard*, only it never made it through. "Oh!" she wailed, her hand now smeared a goopy brown. And since it looked like she was about to explode—either into a geyser of tears or a rage—I eased Tommy's hand free from hers and said, "You clean up. I'll change him." I looked around. "Where . . . ?"

"I use the bathroom counter," she said, then burst into tears.

"It'll be okay, Doris," I said, snatching a dry diaper from the rack and pulling Tommy along, but rather than having a soothing effect, my words made her cry even harder.

I'd had plenty of experience changing the twins, so the state of Tommy's diaper and the fountain he produced when I washed him down with warm water were nothing new to me. He laughed when the stream erupted, and since I was ready for it with an edge of the old diaper, I laughed right back.

"Mama," he said to me as I pinned on the clean diaper. "Mama."

"Mama's in the kitchen," I cooed at him. "You want to see Mama? Why don't we get you dressed first?"

But when I asked Doris about clothes, she said, "Just leave him. It's been way too hot for clothes."

"Don't you want me to take him out to the park?" I tried not to look around at the mess surrounding us as I said, "So you can . . . catch up on some things?" I hastened to add, "Or rest?"

I didn't have to ask her twice. Tommy was dressed and we were out the door in record time. And after an hour and a half of swinging and chasing pigeons and riding with him down the slide, I took Tommy home to find the apartment in the same state I'd left it, and Doris sound asleep on her bed.

I closed the bedroom door quietly, got Tommy some juice and cereal, made myself a quick bologna sandwich, then set about doing dishes and straightening the apartment. I tried to keep Tommy quiet, which was impossible, but somehow Doris slept through it.

It was nearly two o'clock when Doris woke up. But rather than appearing a little rested, she looked like she'd been dragged through a knothole. She took in Tommy, sleeping in the playpen, and seemed to recognize the dent I'd made in cleaning the apartment. She looked at me, her eyebrows quivering, her chin joining in, then withered into a kitchen chair and began sobbing.

My hopes for stopping in to see Lisette at Woolworth's were fading fast, but I pushed those thoughts aside and put a kettle of water on to boil. "Mother sent along some peppermint tea. She says it'll help with your morning sickness."

"She told you, then?" Doris asked miserably.

I nodded. "You'll feel better in a few weeks. It'll be fine."

She looked at me wordlessly. *Stared* at me. And finally she said, "It will not be fine. It will never be fine again."

This was *the* most personal, confessional thing my sister had ever said to me. I sat down across from her and hesitantly asked, "Are you and Tom . . . are you having problems?"

She gave a derisive snort. "We're the same as always."

"What does *that* mean?"

She sat up a little straighter and said, "So Mother didn't also tell you why I left?"

"Why you . . . ?" I could see in her eyes that I was missing something, but I didn't know what.

She leaned forward, her face hardening. "Why I *eloped* . . . ?"

I had no idea what she was getting at, so I simply said what I believed. "Because you fell madly in love with Tom and were sick of living at home?"

She hacked out a laugh, one full of bitterness. "Tom happened because I was *angry*."

I bit my tongue. She'd always been some shade of angry.

In response to my silence, she asked, "So . . . do you want to know why?"

I *didn't* want to know. But since it would be rude to say that, and since the kettle was coming to a boil, I said, "If you're sure you want to tell me," and got busy making a pot of tea.

"Well, you're almost seventeen, so you better start facing facts."

I turned to look at her. "What does this have to do with *me*?"

"You know we're just free labor to them, right?"

I gave her a hard squint. "What *are* you talking about?"

"They're leaving it all to Bobby. The orchard. The land. The house. Everything."

As I set two cups and the steaming teapot on the table, my legs turned to jelly and I landed in the chair across from her again.

"Ha!" she said, taking in my shocked expression. "I knew they wouldn't tell you!"

"But . . ." I had never given this—any of this—any thought. It was our *family* farm. It belonged to *us*. We had all worked it dawn to dark. Why would one of us inherit more than the others? "Who says?" I finally managed to ask. "How do you know?"

"You don't question enough, Peggy. You just work. You accept. You *trust*." She rolled her eyes as she reached for the teapot. "And with your looks, it'll be no problem."

"What are you *talking* about?"

"Daughters marry a man who can provide. Sons inherit. That's what Father told me. And no amount of my arguing that we had all worked equally hard in the orchard, no amount of my *reasoning* with him to look at it differently, made any difference. Bobby gets the farm." She crossed her arms and leaned back. "That's how *he* got it, you know."

"Who?"

"Father!"

"But—"

"His sisters knew the deal. Why do you think they left? Why do you think they never visit?"

"They don't visit because they live clear across the country!"

She snorted. "Look, Peggy, when Poppie died, he left everything to Father with the understanding that he'd take care of Nonnie. It's the same for Bobby."

"But . . . what about the twins? They're boys."

"They're way younger. Bobby gets to decide."

"You're *serious*?"

"Those are Father's exact words. And knowing Bobby, he'll cut them out as quick as he'd turn his back on the two of us." She poured me some tea. "So I got mad. I went out. Tom told me I was beautiful, I quit resisting, and now I've got *him*," she said, nodding over at the playpen, "and live *here*."

Pages of a calendar fluttered by in my mind. "So Tommy wasn't . . . early?"

Doris snorted.

I didn't stay long after that. And on my walk back to the bus stop, I felt more than just weighed down by what I'd learned.

I felt *betrayed*.

I had never even *thought* about what would happen when my parents passed on. It seemed like something way in the future. I *hoped* it was something way in the future. But when it happened . . . why should Bobby inherit everything?

Just because he was a son?

The *eldest* son?

Granted, the twins had yet to spend a day working the orchard, but they would.

Of course they would.

We were a *family* farm. We all worked together. Everyone played a part.

And all parts were hard.

But now I felt a surge of panic. I *was* turning seventeen in a few weeks. And I *was* going into my last year of high school. So . . . *then* what? It felt like the momentum of farming and school had never stopped long enough for me to give it any thought. But walking along, I realized that I *didn't* want to live at home after high school. I didn't want to sweat out summers in the kitchen. I didn't want to work the farm.

So . . . what *did* I want?

And why hadn't I ever thought about what *I* wanted instead of what the family needed?

I knew I'd be late getting back to Ferrybank, but at that moment I didn't care. I needed to talk with Lisette, even if she hadn't called me like she'd promised. And since Woolworth's was only a few bus stops from Doris's apartment, I got off there instead of going straight back home.

When I walked through Woolworth's double glass doors, I had a new appreciation for why Lisette enjoyed working there. It was bright and cool inside, and the luncheonette counter across the store made the whole place smell wonderful. I'd been inside lots of times, but walking through it now with what Doris had said weighing on me, I started seeing it in a new way. Everything was clean and modern. The women around me were wearing stylish dresses with matching hats and handbags, and the men wore polished shoes and sharply knotted ties.

This felt like . . . the future.

And it made me and everything about my life feel like the past.

Why *did* I work so hard at the farm? My allowance didn't cover a fraction of the places Lisette wanted to go, or allow me to buy new clothes or even a lipstick every now and again. Maybe if I worked the cosmetics counter here instead of the fruit stand at home, I'd be able to fuss over my hair and makeup like Lisette did. Maybe Rodney would stop calling me Peaches and start calling me Beautiful.

I worked my way across the store and arrived at the cosmetics counter ready to spill my thoughts—well, except for the ones about Rodney—but neither girl working there was Lisette. "She left an hour ago," one of the girls said. "Crippling headache," the other one added as her wrist floated dramatically to her forehead, and they both laughed.

I was more than a little disappointed. I'd been counting on talking to Lisette. I needed her to help me sort through my feelings and figure out what to say to my parents, what to *do*.

As I strode back across the store, I felt completely untethered, my thoughts flying away in all directions. And then from over by the luncheonette counter came a whistle, followed by "Hey, Peaches!"

My entire body flushed hot. And although the embarrassment of any boy whistling across a busy store and calling out "Peaches!" should have sent me marching by without so much as a glance in his direction, it did not.

Because this wasn't just any boy.

This was Rodney St. Clair.

His hair was groomed back except for a breakaway curl in front and crowned with sunglasses. And with his Haggar slacks, pinstripe shirt, cap toe shoes, and disarming grin, he looked every bit the movie star.

He waved me over and gave a good-natured shrug, acknowledging that his behavior had been out of line while silently asking me to forgive him.

Which, of course, I did.

"What brings you out to the big city?" he joked when I joined him at the counter.

It flashed through my mind that his reason for being at Woolworth's might be the same as mine, but I knew that couldn't be. Lisette hadn't been here for at least an hour, and she never would have invited him. So I shoved that thought aside and said, "My sister lives nearby. I've been helping her today." I perched on the empty stool beside him, grateful I'd taken the time to freshen up before leaving Doris's. "What about you?"

"Errands for my dad," he said with a little wobble of his head. "Don't tell him I've blown his profits on a milkshake, okay?"

I raised an eyebrow playfully and said, "I won't if you'll share." It just tumbled from my lips, shocking my own ears.

He seemed surprised, too. "Deal!" he said with a grin, then

reached over the counter, plucked a straw from a glass jar, and popped it into his milkshake so that it was facing me. His eyebrow arched as if daring me to take a sip, so I did. And while I did, he leaned forward and sipped from his own straw, holding my eyes with his.

I could barely breathe, let alone swallow. Rodney St. Clair's face, his *lips*, were only inches from mine. I could feel my heart spilling helplessly open.

Then he broke away and the moment was gone, and I could feel myself blush. Had I just made a gooey-eyed fool of myself?

"Oh!" I said, feigning surprise as I checked my watch. "I've got to hurry or I'll miss the bus. I need to get home to work the stand."

He sprang up, saying, "Wait, wait!" then slurped down the milkshake fast enough to make his brain freeze. "Ooooh," he said, gripping the side of his head, pulling faces, laughing. When it had passed, he said, "I've got to get back, too. Let me give you a ride!" And before I could even imagine a reason to protest, he was leading me outside.

The car Rodney was driving was different from the last one I'd seen him in. But then he was always in a different car. And he *did* make an effective ambassador for his dad's dealership. Who wouldn't want to be like Rodney St. Clair, all style and charisma in a brand-new Ford?

"Not a convertible today," he said regretfully as he started the motor.

It was another sizzling day, so a convertible would have been nice, but we could have been in a dump truck for all I cared. "I know how to operate a window crank," I said, doing just that.

He followed suit, then turned on the radio.

Lisette's car had a radio, but it was older and hard to tune. This one was clear and bright, and as we started toward Ferrybank, Perry Como came over the airwaves singing "Chi-Baba, Chi-Baba."

"You like this song?" he asked, and—although everyone else seemed to—I told him truthfully that I didn't care for it. He seemed relieved, switching stations as he said, "I'm with you, but they play it all the time."

"Now *this* one . . . ," I said with a laugh as the Andrews Sisters challenging Bing Crosby and Dick Haymes in their new hit "Anything You Can Do" came through the speakers, "*this* one I like!"

He laughed, too, and picked up the men's lines, singing, "Anything you can do, I can do better."

"I can do anything better than you," I sang back with the Andrews Sisters.

"No you can't."

"Yes I can!"

"No you can't!"

"Yes I can!"

"No you can't."

"Yes I can, yes I can!"

By the time the song was done, we were nearly halfway home and laughing really hard. And as another song played and I'd finally settled down, I tried to remember the last time I had laughed like that.

When had I ever felt this carefree?

Rodney St. Clair was . . . *magic.*

"That was fun," he said, giving me a happy grin.

We drove along, not saying anything more while Dinah Shore sang, and then, just a little ways from home, "All of Me" came on and Rodney pulled off the side of the road, parking in the shade of a grove of red oaks.

I looked at him questioningly.

He turned off the motor but not the radio, tossed his sunglasses onto the dash, and slid my way.

My breath caught.

My heart popped!

He smiled sweetly as he stroked my hair, his fingers caressing a strand that fell along my face. He was looking at my mouth now, softly singing along with Frankie Laine, "Why not take all of me? Can't you see I'm no good without you?"

I knew the next line. Everyone knew the next line.

Take my lips, I want to lose them. . . .

And with those words from the radio, his mouth met mine.

His lips were warm and soft, and I was suddenly floating outside myself, dissolving into him. He kissed me and kissed me, and oh, the sweet things he whispered in my ear as he kissed me there. How much he'd wanted to be with me. How different I was from other girls. That I could trust him. That he would never, ever do anything to hurt me.

But suddenly my buttons were coming open. And his hands were . . . everywhere. And I could hear Lisette warning me, *You are not equipped to deal with the likes of Rodney St. Clair.*

And then thoughts of Doris and how she'd let one night change her whole life came crashing into my mind. "Stop," I said, hoarsely at first, then with conviction and a firm grip around his wrists. "Stop!"

"Sorry," he said, pulling back, panting. "You're just so . . . beautiful."

I was too confused, too *embarrassed,* to know what to do.

"Peggy?" he asked, using my real name for the first time.

Which for some reason made everything worse.

And so, not knowing what to say, not knowing what to *do,* I scrambled out of the car, ditched him through the trees, and *ran.*

10

Ginny Rose

BABYLAND

On Thursday I wear the bluebells dress to work. It's a little large, but not by much, and with its sweetheart collar, short puff sleeves, and accent pockets, it's fancier than anything I've ever owned.

Thanks to Peggy once again, I feel almost like a princess.

And then I'm on the line, pullin' twigs and trash and stones from among a never-ending river of peaches while cans move and clank on the overhead conveyors. The temperature inside the warehouse rises like the sun, and my scalp soon tingles with sweat. As morning wears on, it trickles down my neck, my back, my chest, behind my knees. My princess sleeves are sticky now, ruined from the inside out. I go through the motions, tune out the noise, the smell of machine oil and moldering fruit, the peach fuzz collectin' on my arms, and think of the money. My half of the money. What in the world will I do with it?

Shoes, I decide at last. I will start with shoes. My very own brand-new shoes. What *will* that feel like? To put my feet inside shoes not already formed to someone else's feet? Not already stained by someone else's life?

The thought—just the *thought*—makes me dance inside, but my daydreams disappear when the woman beside me collapses. She goes down in a swaying slant, nearly knockin' me over on her way. I manage to break her fall a little, grabbin' hold of her apron as she buckles.

Once she's landed, I check her breathing and feel her heartbeat. She seems to have simply fainted, and who can blame her in this sweltering heat?

I know her name's Mrs. Smith. We were introduced when she joined the line yesterday. I tried to help her the best I could, because she was weepy and seemed preoccupied, but when I asked her what the matter was, she shook her head, lettin' me know she didn't want to talk about it.

She sure isn't sayin' a thing now, and above us, peaches keep movin' by while women on both sides of the line keep workin'. "Can someone get help?" I shout over the noise. "She's fainted!"

I shake Mrs. Smith gently, callin' her name. I tap her cheek with my hand, but she's out for the world. "Help!" I holler. I want to get her off the floor, away from the pails of trash, and out of the sticky slop of fumbled fruit.

At last the woman workin' to my right gives up her post and hurries off. "I'll get Miss Robinson," she calls to me.

When Miss Robinson appears a short while later, she dabs water on Mrs. Smith's forehead and cheeks. "Oh, Betty," she says with real care in her voice.

"Is she . . . a friend?" I ask, because from their similar ages and the way Miss Robinson's lookin' at her, that's what it feels like.

Miss Robinson nods. "A colleague."

Considerin' our workplace, this sounds a little highfalutin to me. But there's no time to question it, because right then Mrs. Smith's eyes flutter open.

She looks around like a scared doe, and when it dawns on her what's happened, she bursts into tears.

"Oh, Betty," Miss Robinson says again as we help her up. "Let's get you home."

"I'm so sorry, Kay," Mrs. Smith whimpers through her tears, and Miss Robinson guides her away.

During lunch break, a small cluster of line workers comes up to me. And after they've pumped every detail from me, they go into a whispered buzz about a stillborn baby.

"It was a boy, then?" one of them asks.

The second one nods and says, "Six months of bed rest, and that's the outcome. She's devastated."

"They placed him in Babyland," the third woman says. "I don't think I would have done that."

Babyland? I wonder. *What on earth?*

"But you can see why she did!" the first one says.

"So she can be tortured for the rest of her life?" the third one retorts. "They didn't even give the child a name!"

"Still. It's a beautiful corner of the cemetery, and he'll be with other—"

"Please, can we not?" the second woman says. And then, with a disapproving shake of her head, she whispers, "I don't understand why she's even here. We're back at work in seven weeks. She should be recuperating."

"They have bills," the first woman says, lowerin' her voice. "They've had no income since April." And then, as if she just can't hold it in a moment longer, she whispers, "Andy was let go!"

"He *was?*" the other two women gasp.

"He was having an affair. With his boss's wife!"

The second woman's face clouds over. "While his own was bedridden with his child?"

"The monster!" the third woman snarls.

Then one of them nudges the woman beside her, and like dominos fallin', all eyes land on me. "Excuse us, dear," the woman who let loose about the affair says to me, "but this is a private matter?"

I'm no stranger to invitations to leave. Most have shown less tact than this one, so I simply pick up my things and go, even though *they're* the ones who came over to *me*. Then, before I've had the chance to finish my lunch, our break's over and everyone's hurryin' back to their post.

The gossipers vanish somewhere down the line.

The space where Mrs. Smith was workin' is filled by someone else.

Peaches roll by.

The rhythm of work takes hold and my mind wanders off again.

Only this time, it doesn't spend time thinkin' about shoes.

I've got more important things to consider.

At shift's end, I'm as tired as ever but also determined not to be. I've decided to make a stop on the way home, one Mama . . . and, especially, Papa . . . can't know about.

I bump over the train tracks, then pedal hard through Oakvale. The air's like a hot breath down my neck and against my cheeks, but the town goes by in a blur because I'm thinkin'. Thinkin' hard.

I coast along past the church, feelin' a twinge of guilt,

wonderin' if it'll matter to anyone—or to God—that the Gilley girls quit prayin' long ago.

The church is behind me now, but its property stretches on. First there's the picnic area with long rows of tables and firepits for roastin' meats. Then there's the cemetery, deep and wide, shielded from the road by a tidy hedgerow.

The roadside gates are open, so I stop and enter the cemetery, pushin' my bike along. Inside is quieter than out on the street, and cooler, too, thanks to well-watered grass and the plentiful shade of large jacaranda trees.

I lean my bike against a tree and walk along a dirt path that leads away from the road. This is my first visit to a real cemetery, but after the heat and the noise of the cannery, the cool stillness here's invitin' in ways I hadn't expected.

So I keep walkin'. And I marvel at the tombstones. They seem like sentries, guardin' each grave, the words etched upon them proud badges recallin' lives now passed.

They are beautiful.

Worthy.

And they're a world apart from the lonely graves I'd seen in Oklahoma and on the long trek west—simple crosses staked into parched earth.

I walk along, passin' by graves of soldiers lost to the war, their plots decorated with crisp flags and fresh flowers. I have a pang of guilt thinkin' on how the war gave Papa jobs with better wages, improvin' our lives while these soldiers were off losin' theirs. I think about the boys laid to rest here and picture their families, left to carry on. And I wonder at the ties that bind us to those who've passed and the ache to not let go.

How long can the spirit of the dead cling to the souls of the living?

Or is it the other way around?

A short while later, I come upon a simple wooden sign posted beside a small bridge. The bridge arches over a pond and leads to an area canopied by jacarandas.

My breath catches as I read the sign.

BABYLAND.

I step onto the bridge and move forward. There's lilies in the pond, and a statue straight ahead—an angel with a sleeping child in her arms. I wander between the grave sites and am drawn to one with fresh earth showin' through a heavy blanket of flowers speckled with baby toys—rattles and wooden blocks, stuffed bears and little airplanes. I read the grave marker:

BABY SMITH.

I find myself tearin' up for the woman who fainted beside me, and soon tears begin to form for Mama. And when I can no longer hold them back, they spill for my brothers, and for that awful day when Papa and I buried the boys.

"You must be one of Betty Smith's students," a voice says.

I wipe my face quick and turn to find a middle-aged woman. She's wearin' a gray skirt, white blouse, and black shoes, and she has a basket of white carnations looped over one arm. "I didn't mean to startle you," she says. Then she starts replacin' withered flowers at each grave site with fresh ones. "I just think it's nice that so many of her students have come to pay their respects."

I blink as bits of the lunchtime conversation begin to make sense.

Mrs. Smith. Miss Robinson. The gossipers.

They're teachers workin' the cannery on their summer vacation.

"I'm Mrs. Poole," the woman says, breakin' the silence. She casts a look at me over her shoulder. "The reverend's wife?"

I shake myself clear of cannery gossip and revelations and find my voice. "Pleased to meet you, ma'am. I'm Ginny Rose Gilley."

"Well, Ginny Rose Gilley," she says, switchin' another carnation, "it's very kind of you to come pay your respects."

I feel guilty. Like I need to confess. Or, at least, explain. But I've lost track of time and I'm worried about how long this has already waylaid me. I need to get home!

Still, it's out before I can stop it.

My question.

"How . . . how much does a grave site here cost?"

She straightens from her stoop and turns to face me. And she must see all the emotion churnin' inside me, because she sits down on a bench and pats the space beside her. "Why don't you tell me what this is about?"

"I don't have time," I blurt out. But then I find myself sittin'. And soon my chin's quiverin' and I'm tellin' her about the boys, about . . . everything! All my efforts to be strong blown to bits in mere minutes.

"Oh, you poor dear," she says.

I fling away tears and stand, strugglin' to collect myself. I don't want her sympathy. Gilleys are *not* leaners. Not in any regard. And I'm torn! Do I really think this is a good idea? Good enough to fight for it? Because it will be a fight. Mama's pleaded with Papa to give the boys a proper place to rest, but Papa wants them to rest in peace where they are. And in the end, Papa holds all the cards.

Doesn't matter about the way Mama treats me.

Doesn't matter that I've got a strong bond with Papa from all the things we've been through.

Him holdin' all the cards seems wrong to me.

So I sit.

And I ask again what I need to know.

Because for the first time since I helped bury my brothers, I have a glimmer of hope.

One tellin' me that maybe things can change.

And that maybe *I'm* the one to make them change.

11

Peggy

BATTLE LINES

After I bolted from Rodney's car, I charged blindly through the oak grove. But after a few minutes, I slowed. Why was I running like a scared rabbit? Rodney had stopped when I'd asked him to. . . . Why hadn't I just set boundaries after that? Yes, he'd been way out of line, but why was I acting like such a *child*?

I walked the rest of the way home, wishing I could go back in time. I was embarrassed and affronted, but mostly I was confused. After all, I'd encouraged Rodney's attention—had I given him the wrong signals?

And did he know . . . could he tell . . . that he'd given me my first kiss?

It wasn't easy to avoid Mother's questions about Doris when I got home. Not that I didn't want to answer them, but aside from all my confusion over Rodney, I was even more muddled about my family and what it meant to be part of it. I didn't trust myself to start talking about my trip to Modesto. I needed time to cool off.

Cool off and *think*.

So I escaped to the stand, promising Mother I'd fill her in at dinner. And although I did have time between customers to think, all thinking did was confuse me even more about Rodney, and rile me up about my family. If what Doris had told me was true, why was I roasting out here in the sun? Why wasn't I working a job with a future, or one that actually *paid*? Why wasn't I working somewhere cool and clean and *stylish* like Woolworth's?

And Rodney. What was *he* thinking right now? Maybe Lisette was right. Maybe I *wasn't* equipped to deal with the likes of Rodney St. Clair. But a wild part of my heart couldn't stop thinking about him—the touch of his lips against mine, the caress of his words in my ear.

Would he stop by and see me?

Suggest we start over?

Make plans for a real date?

And then it was dinnertime, and I still hadn't figured out what I was going to say to my parents. At our home, dinner was a time of weary relief, a heaved sigh after another day done . . . or nearly so. It was the one time we all sat together as a family, and it was usually a time of gratitude and news sharing. During the war, that news had focused on battles against Axis forces. Some nights we didn't say a word to each other and instead clung to every bit of news crackling through the radio. I'd been grateful each and every day that Father didn't have to go, and Mother had held her breath and prayed the war would be over before Bobby could be drafted. All anyone in town had talked about was the war, and there seemed to be no avoiding the dreaded *Did you hear about So-and-So's boy?*

But since the war had ended, the radio had been put aside

and talk around the dinner table had become increasingly about the orchard and farming. Father and Bobby would talk about new equipment they'd heard of, new methods for planting, pruning, irrigating, and spraying for pests. They'd talk about water tables, the ditch flow, the benefits of grafting new varieties, avoiding brown rot, disking weeds . . . it went on and on and on. It almost made me miss the war.

Aside from farm talk or community news, Father wouldn't tolerate topics that interfered with him "eating in peace." He enforced a strict rule against sibling spats or scuffles at the table. Even the twins had learned to mostly control their squirming during meals.

Tonight, the twins were still sick and resting in bed, so dinner should have been relaxed. But Mother was keyed up and kept glancing at Father, who was silent tonight and, like Bobby, going after his fried chicken, gravied potatoes, and peas like he was racing a clock.

Nonnie sensed that something was off, because her eyes switched keenly from Mother to Father to me as we ate.

I pretended not to notice Nonnie or Mother and just waited, biding my time, steeling my nerves. A plan had now formed in my mind, and it relied on Mother's need to mend fences with Doris. The only way that would happen was if she could get Father on board, and the only time she seemed to be able to discuss touchy subjects was with the civility of dinnertime etiquette backing her up.

The timing, I knew, was crucial. Put things into motion too soon, and dinner would be ruined. Too late, and Father would escape with the excuse that there was still work to be done in the orchard.

So the subject of Doris sat like an invisible stick of dynamite on the table, and as I ate and watched the others through my lashes, I prayed hard for Mother to strike the match.

When Father had almost finished his meal, she finally did. "So," she said, trying to make it sound casual, "how was your visit with Doris today, Peggy?"

I gave a noncommittal nod and said, "Interesting."

"Interesting?" she asked, lighting the fuse. "How so?"

I knew I didn't have long, so before the subject could be snuffed by Father, I helped it ignite. "Interesting because I learned that Bobby is going to inherit everything from you, and that a fight over *that* is the reason she got herself into trouble and had to marry Tom."

Nonnie's eyes went wide.

Bobby's jaw dropped.

Mother went pale.

And then Father exploded. "Oh, so it's our fault now?"

"So it's true?" I asked, somehow managing to lock eyes with him and hold them steady. "Bobby gets everything while Doris and I—who have worked every bit as hard as he has—get nothing?"

"Peggy . . . ," Mother said, trying to calm things.

"No!" I snapped. "If this farm isn't truly a *family* farm, if it's a farm that goes entirely to *him*," I said, pointing at Bobby, "why am I sweating from morning to night here? Why wouldn't I get a job like Lisette's? One in a clean, cool building? One that *pays*?"

"Peggy . . ."

I turned sharply to face my mother. "The war is over, Mother! I can't count on buying my way into the movies or the roller rink with *peaches* anymore. The allowance you give us"—I turn to glare at Bobby—"or at least the one *I* get, won't afford me anything."

"You do not—"

"Ginny Rose Gilley—you remember her?" I said, plowing ahead. "She gets forty cents an *hour* at the cannery. For all the work I do around here, I get fifty cents a *week*. Which was fine when I thought we were a *family* business. But now that I know—"

"ENOUGH!" my father bellowed. "If you want to go the way of Doris, that's your choice."

"*What?*" I cried.

But before I could say anything more, Bobby's voice cut through the sound of Father scraping back from the table. "Peggy's right," he said firmly, then stood, too.

Silence fell again. And as my father and brother faced each other, I noticed with some shock that Bobby had grown taller than my father. Taller, and larger. He looked *stronger*.

For the first time ever, I realized that my brother was . . . a man.

And he had just *agreed* with me?

"We all work hard here," Bobby was saying. "I didn't like knowing it when Doris told me, and I like it even less now. I can't blame them for being mad, and the truth is, I don't want the burden of this place."

"The burden of it?" my father shouted. "The *burden* of it?"

"That's how it feels to me," Bobby said, looking down. "I know it's your life's work"—he glanced at Nonnie—"and I know it was Poppie's, but I . . . I've got no life away from it, and nothing built up that feels like my own." He tossed me a grateful look.

"Peg's right about the allowance, too. I'm a grown man, with nothing in my pockets but peach fuzz."

Father's mouth gaped. Mother looked from Father to Bobby, back and forth, as a fevered hush engulfed the room.

And then Father stormed out.

"Robert!" Mother called, then chased after him.

Nonnie rose and began collecting dinner plates. "Peggy, dear," she said softly, "you're not going to get the sun to start rising in the west, so make your plans accordingly." She stacked another plate. "And, Bobby, for the love of peaches, don't look a gift horse in the mouth. Plenty of folks would—and have—killed to be in your shoes." Then she picked up the stack of plates and left the room.

Bobby stood silent, his chin set against all that was churning inside him, and I sat stock-still, doing the same. Could my parents' thinking really be so . . . archaic? Hadn't they noticed that views on women had changed? Could they have missed all the ads showing women who'd stepped into "man-sized jobs"? Lisette and I had marveled at these women welding, or building planes, or holding wrenches. . . . They were images that put women on an equal footing with men.

But . . . now that the war was over, things did seem to be drifting back. Today's ads for women were all about homemaking or fashion or pleasing your man.

So . . . was it all just a glitch? *Was* expecting a new way of thinking and believing women could be on an equal footing like hoping the sun would rise in the west?

Bobby shook me from my trance. "Well, I suppose we should set the lug boxes."

"Wait," I said, because the strength inside me had vanished, and with jelly legs and a gut to match, I sure wasn't ready to work the orchard. He did wait, and when he turned to face me, I said, "That was really brave."

"Me?" He slipped into the chair beside me. "You've never challenged them, and then *that*?"

"And you have?" I asked. When he looked away, I put my hand on his arm and said, "Thank you." Suddenly tears were stinging my eyes. "I wasn't expecting . . ."

"Well, it's wrong," he said angrily. "It's just wrong. And as much as Doris and I fought when she was living here, she was right to be mad." He looked straight at me now and his words began speeding up, rushing out. "The more time I spend here, the older I get, the more trapped I feel. At least you have friends. At least you get out. Since I graduated, I've got . . ." He looked down again and sighed. "I've got nothing."

I battled back the thought for a solid minute, but in the end I lost. "Bobby," I said gently, "I can help you with that, but you're going to have to agree to a few things."

"Like . . . ?"

"First and foremost, you have to trust me."

"I can do that."

The ease with which he said it . . . the conviction in his voice . . . suddenly years of distance between us were gone. I squeezed his arm. "And you have to *take* my advice, not argue with me or think you know better."

He nodded. A little ruefully, but he nodded.

"And"—I let go of his arm and leaned back a little—"I know this is going to be hard, but if you don't agree to it, you'll be sitting in this same seat of sorrow a year from now." I locked eyes with him. "You have *got* to—"

"Give up on Lisette," he said, cutting me off. "I know."

I laughed a little. "Bobby Simmons, you are full of surprises tonight."

He gave me a pathetic look, then turned away. "I didn't say I know *how*."

As gently as I could, I said, "Stop looking at her, stop dreaming about her, and stop thinking she's the only girl for you."

"But—"

"Because, Bobby? She's not. She's a terrible match for you. She will never look at you the way you look at her, and you should have someone who does."

"But . . . how's that ever gonna happen?"

I gave him a small smile, and in a rash rush of wanting him to feel better, I whispered, "It already has."

"What? What are you talking about?"

"Well," I said, taking in a deep breath, "if you weren't so blinded by Lisette, you'd have noticed the way Ginny Rose Gilley looks at you."

He stared at me blankly, then pulled a face. "That Okie girl?"

Angry blood rushed to my cheeks. I shot back out of my chair. "You did not just say that."

"Say what?"

"Oh!" I said, furious now. Ginny Rose had told me during our one sleepover how much the name hurt. How the *No Okies* signs and the jeers and the way people snarled *Okie* made her feel like crawling into a hole; made her feel like she *belonged* in one; made her think that waiting out a choking dust storm had been easier than waiting for people to see the good in her and her family.

I'd shared that with everyone at dinner the day after our sleepover, and maybe that was years ago, but I hadn't heard Mother or Father use the word since. And now this from Bobby?

"What?" Bobby demanded. "What is wrong with you?"

"Me? What's wrong with *me*? Ginny Rose Gilley is a sweet, courageous, hardworking girl. She was also my *best friend*. Don't you *dare* call her that. Don't you *dare*."

"But . . . she's from Oklahoma!"

"You know darned well that's not what people mean when they say it!"

"Besides," he said, his brow furrowing as regular Bobby returned, "you're wrong. She barely spoke to me when we patched her tire. She seemed mad the whole time."

I replayed that evening in my head. The desperate way Ginny Rose had looked, the way she'd tried to act so strong despite the state she'd been in. "Well," I said evenly, "maybe if you'd bothered talking to her instead of thinking about Lisette, you'd understand why."

"I talked to her!"

I spun on my heel and beelined outside to where the tractor was waiting. I hadn't taken the wheel in ages, but it was about time he took a turn at setting the boxes. I clambered up and cranked the motor before Bobby could stop me.

"You don't even know what section to set," he called.

"So tell me!" I shouted.

He gave in and then tried talking to me as we did the rows. But it was all justifications and excuses, so I just kept driving, facing forward, not saying one word back.

When we were finally done and I'd cut the motor, he seemed all worn out from calling his excuses out to deaf ears. He climbed off the trailer, heaved a sigh, and said, "I just don't get why saying *Okie* about someone from Oklahoma is so bad."

"It's not the word," I said, finally acknowledging him. "It's all the meaning that comes with it. It's the way it makes her *feel*."

"Well, maybe she just shouldn't feel that way."

I gave him a hard look. "Or maybe you just shouldn't say it."

"Why are you picking a fight over nothing, Peg?" Then slyly he added, "It doesn't seem too bright"—he caught my eye—"considering."

I read his meaning loud and clear: *Considering he was getting everything and had actually stood up for me but could change his mind if he wanted to.*

"You know what?" I said, leaping off the tractor. "If you still think it's okay to call her an Okie, you can have it. You can have all of it. Live your miserable, lonely life here forever." I drilled him with a look. "Just don't think for one minute you're better or smarter or more worthy than Ginny Rose Gilley *or* me. Because you're not."

And for the second time that evening I stormed off, leaving him to catch up.

If he could.

12

Ginny Rose

ALL WRUNG OUT

I leave the cemetery and pedal on down the road with a sense of purpose in my heart. It's mixed with fear and no real plan, but that doesn't matter now. I agree with Mama—my brothers deserve better'n a ditch grave.

The trouble is Papa. He will never agree to move them. I heard him tell Mama during a fight last year that it had been too long. He also said he wouldn't be able to find them back, but that was a lie. It wouldn't be easy, but I reckon *I* could find them. But since it's his wages that would pay for any change, when he says no to something, it's no.

Though in a twist of irony set in motion by Papa himself, I'll soon have money of my own. And since Mrs. Poole took pity on me and said she'd reserve a nice plot for the boys that I could pay off over time, I don't have to ask Papa to give the boys a proper grave and Mama a place she can go to release her grief. It'll take a while to own it, but then I'll have a place to move them.

The question is, *should* I? I understand Mama's agony over

leavin' the boys behind, and in a ditch grave, no less. But the thought of *un*buryin' them seems . . . grisly. Especially since they were simply swaddled together in a blanket when Papa placed them in the ground.

Thinkin' about that day gets my eyes burnin' again.

Thinkin' of undoin' it gives me shivers.

After all these years, what'll be left of them?

So if I know Papa's against it, and talkin' it over with Mama will cause nothing but trouble, where does that leave me? And even if I do manage to pay for a site on my own, how in the world would I manage to move them?

I pedal harder, and though there's a breeze from ridin' fast, the sun's still a fireball, and heat blasts up from the pavement. I long for a dip in the river. If only I had the time.

As I near Simmons Farm, my thoughts turn to needin' something truthful to say about why I'm late. Something that has nothing to do with Babyland. If Peggy's still workin' the stand, maybe I can stop and ask her about ways to repay her kindness. Havin' an idea to share with Mama—or just that I've stopped to discuss it—will help explain away my tardiness.

But Peggy's busy with customers, lookin' as singed as I feel. As I coast past the fruit stand unnoticed, I wonder why there's no canopy over the stand. Why is she bakin' out there in the sun when a simple roof would protect her?

It isn't until I'm almost home that it strikes me that *that* could be my kindness. *I* could build the canopy.

Mama seems unsure about the idea when I break the silence during supper to suggest it, but Papa nods and says, "That sounds like a fine idea." Then he asks, "They have tools? And supplies?"

"Lots of 'em," I assure him, rememberin' all the scrap lumber and equipment I saw in the shed when I patched my tire. And then from my mouth springs "I'd like to do it this weekend, if that's all right."

Though Mama's the one insistin' on my repayin' Peggy's kindness, I can see from the set of her face and the way she's pokin' at her potatoes that she's on the verge of sayin' no. But Papa says, "That'd be fine," leavin' no room for Mama's protests.

Anna Mae breaks the tense silence. "Can I help her?" she asks, her pleading eyes turned on Papa.

"No," Mama says, beatin' Papa to it this time. "There's plenty to do around here, and you're not beholden to the Simmons, so—"

"But—"

"No," Mama says, slammin' the door.

Anna Mae knows better than to push against it, but she sits in silent fury for the rest of supper. Afterward, while we're doin' dishes, I whisper, "I'm sorry she won't let you go," though I can't even *think* about havin' her along, seein' how I haven't asked Peggy about it yet!

Anna Mae turns to me suddenly and pleads, "Don't wear the kittens dress tomorrow."

"What?"

She wrinkles her nose at my armpits as she rinses a plate. "You'll ruin it."

I give her a dismayed look. "I can't help it!"

"I know. And Mama says my time's comin' soon enough. So I'm not bein' mean, just *please* don't ruin the kittens dress. I'll help you wash the others."

"But—"

"It's still hot outside," she says in a rush. "They'll be dry by morning." I see her cast a look at the Littles before addin', "Besides, none of us has three dresses, let alone four!"

The Littles, who've been quiet as mice as they've dried dishes, stick their noses in now. "That's right," Bonnie Sue squeaks. "You should give the dress to Anna Mae."

"You should!" Katie Bee says with gusto.

Anna Mae works to conceal it, but she's hidin' a canary in her mouth. I look at the three of them, my eyebrows stretched high. "You're gangin' up on me?"

Katie Bee hurries to explain. "Anna Mae says we can have pockets!"

"Katie Bee!" Anna Mae cries.

"You promised them *pockets*?" I ask Anna Mae. "What does that mean?"

Anna Mae stands stock-still beside me, wide-eyed and mute.

So Bonnie Sue says, "When she gets the dress and cuts it smaller . . ."

". . . because it's *way* too big on her," Katie Bee chirps.

". . . she'll make pockets for us!" Bonnie Sue says, her eyes sparklin'.

"You weren't supposed to tell!" Anna Mae cries. "You *promised*." Then she abandons her post at the sink and bolts outside.

"Oops," Bonnie Sue whispers.

Katie Bee looks stricken. "Does this mean we don't get pockets?"

I take a deep breath and begin a count to ten. "She should never have promised you pockets," I tell them when I reach three. "It's not her dress to cut up."

But tired as I am, after we tidy the kitchen, I *do* set up the washboard and tub outside and scrub my dirty dresses. Not because I'm givin' away the kittens dress, but because Anna Mae's right—wearin' it to the cannery will ruin it, and now that I have other plans for my wages, I want to save the dress for . . . I have no idea. Maybe the first day of school in September?

It's after dark when I finish scrubbin' the other dresses. The Littles are already in bed, and if Mama had her way, Anna Mae would be, too, but she's somehow snuck outside to keep her word. "I'm sorry," she whispers as she helps me twist a dress into a long, hard rope, wringin' all the water we can from it. "I know I did wrong."

It's not like Anna Mae to say she's sorry, and it softens me up right away. "It's okay," I whisper back. "Kittens-with-umbrellas would turn anyone into a criminal."

She laughs. "Not a *criminal*."

"Pardon me?" I toss her a playful glare as I give the dress a hard flap to shake out some wrinkles. "Weren't scissors part of the scheme?"

She laughs again and helps me pin the dress to the line. And we've just started twistin' the second dress when out of the blue she whispers, "Can you keep a secret?"

I almost make a joke about *her* bein' the untrustworthy one. But I can see she's serious, so instead I whisper back, "You know I can."

"Cross your heart."

So I do.

"Hope to die?"

Again, I'm sorely tempted to make a joke—something about death by scissors. But her look's one teeterin' between life and death, so I simply nod.

"There's a boy," she says, her eyes dartin' toward the house.

"He lives up the road. His ma sends him out a couple times a week for sundries. He used to just walk by, ignorin' every little thing, includin' me, but a couple days ago I hollered at him that his shoe was untied, and yesterday he kissed me."

"What?" Did she just go from hollerin' about an untied shoe to kissin' in a single sentence? In a couple of *days?* I sputter a little, then manage to ask, "Where?"

"On the lips, silly."

"No! I mean how on earth . . . ? Where was Mama?"

She twists her end of the dress so tight it coils back around itself. "In her own little world, like usual. She doesn't know where I am half the time." She watches me flap out the second dress, then whispers, "Since you started workin', she spends hours shut in her room cryin'."

I pin the dress to the line. "But . . . why?"

"The boys, I suppose. She had another fight with Papa about them."

"About where they're buried?"

She nods. "Guess she'd rather cry over them than mother us." She hurries to add, "Not that I'm complainin'. I couldn't meet with Liam if she was payin' attention."

We're wringin' out the last dress now. "How old's Liam?" I ask, slippin' in the name she used. I try to hide how stupefied I am by her casual manner, her steely nerves, and the disturbing news that, though she's seven years younger than I am, she's beat me to a first kiss.

"Same as me," she answers. "Only I reckon he's richer. He's always clean."

She looks away, and suddenly it all makes sense. Kittens-with-umbrellas is more'n just cute.

It's clean.

Practically new.

I don't breathe a word of what I'm thinkin'. I thank her for her help, promise again that her secret's safe, and shoo her off to bed. But as I'm dumpin' out the tub and tidyin' up, there's no doubt left in my mind.

Kittens-with-umbrellas will be meetin' its fate with scissors long before September.

13

Peggy

THE PITS

Plop, plop, plop.

Plop, plop, plop, plop.

Plop, plop, plop, plop, plop, plop, plop! The building rhythm of peaches being harvested drifted through my open window, breaking the stillness of dawn. In my mind, I could see the workers standing on orchard ladders, buckets strapped across their chests, their nimble fingers plucking fruit from the branches.

Plop, plop, plop.

The reveille of peaches was calling me to work.

I pulled the covers over my head, trying to block out the sound. When I was a kid, I was thrilled to race outdoors to help, hoping Ginny Rose would be part of the day's crew. But that was ages ago. A whole wartime ago. So much had changed. There were no children working the orchard now. No families. With so many men going off to war, and so many war-related jobs springing up on the home front, many of the people who used to work farms had found better jobs, and now most of the Valley's field hands were braceros—men from Mexico who mostly spoke only Spanish and lived in barracks built by the government. Father appreciated the way the hands arrived early and worked hard, and he'd picked up a lot of Spanish in the last few years.

I burrowed under the covers, hiding from the day, wanting desperately to go back to sleep. But soon memories of yesterday stirred inside me: my visit with Doris, the clash at dinner, my argument with Bobby—they darkened the day as the sun rose to lighten it.

Thoughts of Rodney might have swept everything else aside if things with him had stopped with that magical first kiss. But they hadn't, and although my heart raced at the thought of him, it was a confused beat, part anxious, part offended, but also full of longing.

Lisette, too, pushed her way into my mind. I was dying to talk to her and at the same time afraid to tell her the truth. Hadn't she warned me? Wouldn't she just call me naïve? But Rodney irritated her, so how could she possibly understand the way my heart leaped every time he looked at me?

The orchard was fully awake now. Voices called, the tractor growled, a spigot squeaked, and underneath it all, the rhythm of harvesting peaches continued. There was no sleeping through the energy, no denying my duty.

Nonnie was in the front room busy with sewing repairs, and I found Mother alone in the kitchen, blanching a box of yesterday's peaches. Steam rose from the large kettle, the moisture curling stray hairs that had escaped the knot of her high bun. A cool morning breeze running between the screened front and side doors helped, but it was already hot in the kitchen. Hot and humid.

Mother's back was to me as I stood in the doorway between the kitchen and dining room, watching her scoop the peaches from the kettle into the cooling bath to prepare them for peeling. In the slant of morning light, her head looked electrified, her movements robotic.

"Well, don't just stand there," she said without turning around. "Get in here and help."

I hurried to put on an apron, then fell into line, rubbing the cooling peaches with my palms and fingers. The skins came off easily and I collected them in a bowl to add to the spoiled-fruit pails outside—slop that Father would trade at the hog farm for bacon.

Soon we had a large container of peaches ready for pitting. Through it all, Mother didn't say a word, and neither did I.

Finally, she retrieved two paring knives, handed one to me, and said, "What you and Doris have to understand is that this is the way things are. Men pass their property to their sons, who carry on their name." She ran the tip of her knife around the seam of a peach, twisted the halves apart, flicked the pit into an old lard pail, and placed the peach halves in the large bowls between us. "If a man left his life's work to his daughters, it would become their *husbands'* property, and control over it would be lost." She picked up another peach and gave me a pointed look. "You must see why they don't want that! Daughters marry—and we hope wisely. They become part of another man's family and take on the benefits of that."

I sliced angrily around a peach, twisted it open, and shot the pit into the lard pail, *ping!* "So I'm just supposed to cook and clean and marry well? You act like we're living in the Middle Ages!"

"No, but it's a system that works," Mother said. She whipped the tip of her knife around another peach. "Do you really think the likes of *Tom* deserves any part of our farm?"

"Do you really think there'd *be* a Tom if things weren't set up the way they are?"

My words cracked the air like a snapped towel, and they found their mark. I could see the sting of them on Mother's face. But after pitting a few more peaches, she sighed and said, "I believe there would. Doris came into this world angry, and she'll go out the same way." She gave me a pleading look, one I'd never seen on her before. "But you don't have to take her path, Peggy. Think about what you want. Don't just react."

I was about to tell her that what I wanted was to be treated as an equal to Bobby in family matters, but the temptation to do so was interrupted by a voice floating through the screen door. "Hello?" it called. "Is Peggy here?"

I recognized the voice immediately. "Ginny Rose!" I called back, my mood suddenly lifted. "I'll be right there!"

Mother gave me a curious look—one that was tinged with disapproval—and I gave her a defiant one back as I rinsed my hands. What on earth could she have against Ginny Rose?

I hurried over and pushed the screen door open. "Hi! Come in!"

Ginny Rose shook her head. "I'm on my way to work, but I wanted to ask you . . ."

She suddenly seemed uncertain, so I prompted, "Yes?"

"Well, I know you gave me those dresses with no strings attached, but I'd like to return the kindness by—"

"Oh, Ginny Rose, no. You don't owe me a thing. I was happy to give them to you!"

"I know, but I've thought of something I'd *like* to do in return."

I waited, because I could see she was set on offering, even though she knew I was determined to turn her down.

"When I fixed my flat the other day," she said, "I noticed lots of scrap wood in the shed."

"And . . . ?"

"And I'd like to build a cover for your fruit stand. To shield you from the sun? I see you out there and . . . well, you should have a shelter."

My eyes were suddenly stinging. How could anyone *not* love Ginny Rose?

I shook my head. "Really, you don't—"

"I know how to swing a hammer," she rushed to say. "I've helped put up lots of shelters." She caught herself, pulled back from explaining. But I knew what shelters she was talking about. We'd often driven by the shantytowns where pickers lived before the war started. They were trash and scrap wood pieced together, whole little cities built from garbage that Father had called Hoovervilles and Mother had called "plumb sad."

Ginny Rose shook me from my memories. "Please?" she said. "Just let me, okay?" And then, as though she was remembering, too, she added, "I promise it'll look good."

Something about this—her on my porch, the thought of how she used to live, her offering to build me a sun shelter in exchange for two old dresses—clamped my throat down tight.

"Please?" she asked again. "I'd like to."

And since I couldn't seem to speak, I simply nodded.

She bounded off the porch and was on her bicycle in a jiffy.

"Wonderful!" she called with a happy wave. "I'll be by after work!" Then she pedaled away.

"Who was that?" Nonnie asked from the front room as I closed the door.

"Ginny Rose Gilley," I replied. "A dear friend."

"I should say," Nonnie said, then turned back to her work.

When I'd returned to the kitchen, Mother asked, "What did *she* want?"

There was a bit of a sneer in her voice that annoyed me. "She wants to build me a shade cover for the fruit stand," I said, gouging the pit from a peach half. "*She,* at least, has noticed how I stand out there frying in the sun."

"You could just wear a sun hat," Mother said defensively. "And why on earth would she want to—"

"Because she's *nice,*" I snapped. "And she thinks she should repay me for giving her two old flour-sack dresses even though they're completely out of style and nobody wears them anymore."

Mother's knife hovered over a peach. She looked at the clothes she was wearing. Flour-sack apron over flower-sack dress.

I sliced a peach in half, twisted it, flicked the pit, *ping!* "Fashion on the ration is *done,* Mother. People are dressing with *style.*" Slice, twist, *ping!* "And since, according to you, I need to *marry* my way into a good situation, I'd better start investing in my appearance. And to pay for that, I'll need more than what you give me for allowance." Slice, twist, *ping!* I turned to face her. "So why *wouldn't* I get a job working at Woolworth's or the cannery instead of sweating here all day for nothing?"

"For *nothing?* We pay for all your needs! We put a roof over your head and food on the table!"

"So do the Bovees and the Gilleys and all the other parents I know." I picked up another peach. "And if that's the reason you gave Doris"—slice, twist, *ping!*—"no wonder she ran away!"

The words hung like daggers in the humid air of our kitchen. Mother's eyes were wide and horrified, and I could see her wondering where her helpful, compliant daughter had gone. Part of me was shocked at the change in me, too, but it was too late to back down. There was no closing my mind to what I'd learned. Something had to give, and for the first time in my life, I was determined it wouldn't be me.

"Things can change on a dime, Peggy!"

I held her gaze. "Yes. I know. You say that a lot."

"We've barely come out of a world war, and that was on the heels of the Great Depression!"

"I'm aware, Mother."

"Well, before that was World War I! So you cannot fault your father and me for being careful with money!"

"It's not that so much as it is the unfairness of Bobby getting everything. In your heart of hearts, do you really think that's okay?" I held her gaze, and after another long moment, she blinked.

"I should never have had you go see Doris!" she cried, ripping off her apron. "Never!"

She stormed out of the kitchen and I soldiered on, pitting peaches as I stewed in the heat of our conversation. I expected her to return, but as the minutes ticked by without her, I became overwhelmed by a need to call Lisette. Why she hadn't gotten in touch with me suddenly didn't matter. I needed to talk to my best friend!

I cleaned my hands quickly, picked up the handset, and dialed, looking over my shoulder for Mother the whole time.

The rotary seemed to tick extra loudly as I dialed, first the quick rasp forward, then its measured return. My heart pounded as the last digit—a zero—finally finished. Why was I so nervous? Why couldn't I just call a friend like everyone else I knew? Why was my life so . . . restricted?

The connection hadn't even registered a single ring when someone snatched it up. "Hello?" the voice whispered.

"Lisette?" I whispered back.

"Peggy?" She sounded wide-awake, something I wasn't expecting at this early hour. The Bovees are, after all, a banking family.

I wanted to ask, *Why haven't you called me!* but there was no time for that, so I got straight to the point. "When can I meet you? I have so much to tell you!"

"Me too!" she whispered. "But I have to work today."

"Are you feeling okay? I heard you had a headache yesterday."

"What?" There was a pause, and then, "Who told you that?"

"Didn't your mother tell you I was going to stop by Woolworth's?"

"When did you talk to my mother?"

We were getting way off track. "Never mind!" I whispered, worried that *my* mother would return any minute. "Can you meet me tonight?"

"Come to the roller rink."

"The *roller* rink? We can't talk there!"

"But that's where I'll be, starting at seven."

"Do you have a date?"

"Long story. I'll explain tonight."

"Who is it?"

"I'll explain tonight!"

This made me unbearably curious, but the complete impracticality of meeting her at the roller rink rushed in. Roller World was on the far side of Oakvale. If she was on a real date—not just meeting a boy there—she wouldn't be able to give me a ride. And the last thing on earth I wanted was to ask Mother or Bobby if they would drop me off. Plus, even if I rode my bike, if Lisette was on a date, where would that leave me? Standing off to the side, waiting for her to break away for a minute or two? I didn't want that!

There was also the price of admission to consider. Why waste money on skating when what I wanted was simply to talk?

But instead of conveying any of this to Lisette, I stammered, "But I don't have any . . . All I have is . . ."

"Don't worry. Gordy loves your peaches. And you. He'll be glad to take them."

Two weeks ago, I wouldn't have thought twice about what she'd just said. But since Rodney St. Clair had entered the picture, I really didn't want to hear that the old man who ran the roller rink box office loved my peaches. Or me. "Fine," I said, not feeling at all fine about it.

"Seven?" she asked.

"If I'm meeting you there, I probably can't make it until seven-thirty."

I was fishing for her to offer me a ride, but she didn't bite. "Seven-thirty it is," she whispered. "See you there!" And with a click she was gone, leaving me wondering who in the world her date was, and why in the world she wouldn't just tell me.

14

Ginny Rose

AN INVITATION

It's only my fourth day at the cannery, and already I've advanced two stations. Mrs. Smith isn't the only one who's fainted, and fainting's not the only reason for quittin'. This morning the woman across from me fell to pieces when the stick she plucked out of peaches rollin' by turned out to be a snake. It was just a small garter snake, but it sent her screamin' from the building.

But now with the snake taken away and forgotten, my mind turns inward again as I work, findin' refuge in thoughts of buildin' a shade cover for Peggy. I do love makin' things. It can be with a hammer and nails or a needle and thread—doesn't matter. What matters is it bein' around long enough afterward to remind me I've done something helpful. Cookin' may be important, but I don't get the joy from it I do from makin' something that lasts. Give me a chicken coop to build, or steps to fix, or a quilt to sew out of scraps, and I'll be keen to work on it. Ask me to sweep or scrub and I'll do it—and do it right—but my heart and mind will be elsewhere. Ask me to *dust* and I might just refuse.

Pluckin' trash and twigs and rocks from between peaches leaves me with nothing afterward. Peaches keep comin', keep rollin' on by. So as my hands work, my mind goes off tryin' to re-call what supplies I saw in the Simmons' shed and how I should go about buildin' the sunshade for Peggy. I have an idea, but I'm not sure if there's enough plywood for the roof . . . or if there's maybe something else I could use.

While I'm thinkin', my mind drifts back to an afternoon of scavengin' a trash heap with Papa for things to fix up our shelter. We'd been in California more'n a year and were on a long stretch of lean days when we had little to eat about half the nights, and nothing to eat the rest. Mama sent me along to help Papa while she tended to the boys, who were whiny and feelin' hot to the touch.

I picture Papa wanderin' farther and farther from me while I did my best to stack cardboard and pieces of corrugated tin and pluck rusty nails from sandy dirt. I was barefoot and my stack was bulky, slippin' from my arms. I heard Papa cry, "Eu-reka!" and spotted him in the distance, silhouetted by the harsh angle of the late-afternoon sun. I couldn't see his face, but I knew he was smilin'. "No more cold nights!" he called, and as he picked his way around trash to reach me, I saw that he'd found a stovepipe—one he'd push through the roof so our trash-burning potbellied stove could sit all the way inside with us.

But even after Papa put up the stovepipe, even after a gift of potato peelings from a new neighbor—scraps that Mama stretched into a delicious soup with the help of an onion and spices—Mama fretted about the boys.

After dark, when we were all restin' on the mattress in a corner of our shelter, Mama's voice was soft as she asked, "Ginny Rose, are you awake?"

I used to answer truthfully, but one night when I was driftin' off and slow to answer, I learned that this is the time to discover truths rather than speak them. So I played possum and waited, and when she was sure I was asleep, she whispered across the mattress to Papa, "They're listless."

I wasn't sure what *listless* meant, but I could hear the worry in her voice.

"They're hungry," he whispered back. "Tomorrow I'll find work and food. We'll be all right."

But two weeks later, Papa and I buried the boys, and Mama looked likely to go next. First from illness, then from heartbreak.

The memory has wormed its way in, causin' my heart to race and my eyes to burn as I pluck through the peaches goin' by. And I wonder—how in the world will I be able to move my brothers if just the *thought* of that day guts me this way?

The woman beside me touches my arm. "Are you all right?" she calls over the noise. "Do you feel faint?"

I *am* breathless and light-headed, but I shake her off. "I'll be fine," I call back with more backbone than I feel. Then I force the memories into a dark corner of my mind. I can't change the past, but if there's any hope of ever puttin' it to rest, I cannot lose this job.

When she's sure I won't faint, the woman hollers up the line, "I'm going to demand they get us more fans. This is unbearable!"

She gets a chorus of encouragement from other women on the line, but three hours later she hasn't returned, and the only thing blowin' is the shift whistle.

Instead of dashin' out as I've done the days before, I take a moment at the sink in the women's toilet to freshen up. The room's badly soiled, and the trash bin's overflowin', but the tap runs cold and fast. I splash water on my face and throat and use it to tame and rebraid my hair. Then I do my best to wipe the stickiness and sweat off me with a wet paper towel. When I've done all I can, I try on a smile in the mirror and hurry outside to my bicycle.

Peggy's busy with a customer at the stand when I roll up, but she interrupts the sale with a friendly smile and wave in my direction. "I'll go over to the shed with you," she calls. "Give me just a minute."

But then another customer pulls up. And another. So at last I tell her, "I'll just go myself, if that's all right with you."

"Sure!" she says. "I'll come when I can."

"I'll be fine," I tell her, then ride over to the farmhouse and around back to the shed.

The shed door's closed, so I lean my bicycle against the wall and roll the door open enough to slip through. I flick up the light switch, but even with the bulb on, it takes a little time for my eyes to adjust after bein' in bright daylight.

Once I can see better, I make my way over to the back wall and start sortin' through the wood. I find several tall fence posts, some two-by-fours, and plenty of plywood scrap. I pull out the pieces I think I'll need, then begin rootin' around for tools. And I've just found a hammer when a voice barks, "Freeze!"

My heart scampers like a rabbit, but the rest of me holds stock-still. There's a figure silhouetted in the doorway—a man wearin' a cowboy hat, his head cocked sideways as he peers down the sights of a rifle that's aimed right at me.

I've faced the business end of a gun before, but it was always with Papa by my side, and always with the same cold words comin' from behind the sights: *Your kind's not welcome here.*

But now the gun's not on me because I'm an Okie.

It's on me because someone thinks I'm a thief.

"Put your hands up," says the voice.

I don't dare do anything other than what he's commandin', so the hammer's still in my hand when I raise them high.

"Put that down!" he barks.

I ease the hammer onto the workbench, and I *want* to say something, but my heart's beatin' so hard it's closed off my throat, and I'm also afraid to. Words have only ever been met with threats when Papa's tried usin' them to lower a gun.

The rifle barrel flicks up. "Now raise your hands! High! Where I can see them!"

My hands go up, and at last my voice quivers its way out of me. "Bobby? Is that you? It's me, Ginny Rose. Peggy said I could."

His head rises off the sights as he squints to get a better look at me, but the rifle stays up. "She's got no business saying you can take a thing!"

"I'm not *takin'* anything," I tell him. "I'm gonna build her a sunshade."

"You're gonna what?"

"Build her a—"

But suddenly Peggy's there, screamin', "Bobby Simmons! Are you out of your mind?" She dives in, pushes the muzzle aside, then sticks a finger in his face. "What's the *matter* with you?"

"I didn't know!" he cries. "How was I supposed to know it was her?"

"Her bike's right outside!" Peggy shouts.

"Well, I didn't see it! I thought someone was in here swiping tools!"

"Apologize!" Peggy demands. But he just stomps off grumblin', so she rushes toward me, sayin', "I'm so sorry!"

I tell her it's all right, and after we spend a few minutes calmin' nerves, I show her what I've gathered and explain how I'm plannin' to put it all together. "Does that sound all right to you?" I ask.

She's quiet for a long minute, then says, "It does, but it also sounds like a lot of work."

"No more work than stitchin' two dresses," I tell her with a smile. "This'll be easier'n that."

She gives me a look I can't quite figure, though there's a tinge of pity to it that I do not like.

"I'll tell you what," she says. "*If* you let me help you, then okay. Because, really, it's too much, and a lot of it's going to take two people." She studies the pile of parts. "Maybe we should take everything across the street and build it in place? That way I can help you between customers." She gives me a sunny smile. "It'll be fun."

I'm surprised by the rush of relief inside me. I *could* do it alone, but she's right—it wouldn't be easy. "That does sound fun," I say, and since she's walkin' toward the door, I follow. "What time can I start tomorrow?"

"Come anytime," she says, steppin' outside. "Although I'll be in the kitchen until around eleven, so maybe after that?"

"If I want to get started before then," I say as we push the door closed together, "nobody's gonna shoot me, right?" I'm grinnin', so she'll know I'm kiddin', but there's also truth behind my words, and she knows it.

"I am so sorry," she says with a cringe. Then she kids me back, sayin', "I'll be sure to tell the whole family not to shoot you!"

I laugh as I fetch my bicycle, and when I'm set to push off, I call out, "I'll see you tomorrow!"

But after only a few pumps of the pedals, there she is, runnin' alongside me. "What are you doing tonight?" she asks.

I backpedal to brake, then hop down, straddlin' the bike. "What?"

"What are you doing tonight?" she asks again, and before I can answer, she says, "Do you want to go to the roller rink with me? It's a Friday-night thing in Oakvale. Everyone goes."

My heart leaps, then falls. I'm tickled by the invitation, but . . . I've got no skates or money to rent them, let alone money to get inside.

As if readin' my mind, Peggy says, "You can use Doris's skates. And I think I can get us both in with peaches."

"With peaches?"

"Gordy—he's the old man who runs the box office—he lets me pay with peaches. Usually. If I'm discreet." She gives a little shrug. "Let's hope, anyway. Otherwise I don't have the money, either."

"But—"

"Oh, just come. Please?"

"But . . . I've never been. I don't know how!"

"I'll teach you! It'll be fun, I promise!" She bites her lower lip, then blurts, "But we'll have to ride our bikes. Is that okay?"

"Sure, but—"

"Great! So . . . why don't you just stay? Have dinner with us and we'll go after."

"I . . . I can't," I say, lookin' down at my dress. "I need to go home and clean up and . . . and get permission and . . ." I'm feelin' more'n a little flustered, but giddy, too.

Am I really goin' skating?

"But . . . you'll go?" Peggy asks. "Promise?"

"If it's okay with—" And then I remember Mama and Papa's talk, and I say, "Yes. Yes, I'll go." It comes out like a gavel comin' down. Like it's decided and official and not to be questioned.

"Can you be back here at seven?"

Seven will be hard. Mighty hard. But I tell her I'll see her then, and as I push off for home, I promise myself that, even if it means missin' supper, even if Mama's changed her mind about me doin' social things, even if her dark cloud zaps lightning all around me, this is the first true social invitation I've had, ever, so come hell or high water—or dust ten stories tall—I'm goin'.

15

Peggy

TRUTHS AVOIDED

Dinner was a quick, silent affair. The twins were well enough to be back at the table, but even they were subdued, sensing the tension that had not dissipated since the night before. Father shovcled in his food, eyes down. Bobby did the same. Mother's eyes flicked about as she picked at her meatloaf, and Nonnie's one eyebrow was permanently raised as she surveyed us all.

"May I be excused?" I asked when I'd finished my plate, but I was already standing before I got permission. "I'm meeting friends at Roller World tonight, and I need to get cleaned up."

Bobby's eyes lifted. "Who's all going?"

I cleared my plate, saying, "Nobody who's aimed a gun at my friend with no apology, that's for sure."

Father was suddenly interested. "What was that?"

"Ask Bobby," I said, and made a speedy exit.

I'd spent the day stewing about my family and the Dark Ages logic Mother had used to justify the *in*justice of it. But as miffed as I was over all of that, as the day wore on, I'd found myself thinking more and more about Lisette. What in the world was going on with her? Why all the mystery? I had a bad feeling about it, but I couldn't put my finger on why. Even a bath didn't calm me.

Compounding the anxiety over meeting Lisette at the roller rink was wondering if Rodney would be there. It was true that high schoolers congregated at the rink on Friday nights, and ordinarily I'd be thrilled at the thought of seeing him there. But now? He hadn't called since he'd kissed me, hadn't stopped by the stand . . . there hadn't been a peep from him. So . . . what was he thinking? Had I ruined everything by bolting from his car?

So I was relieved that Ginny Rose would be going with me. If Lisette was on a date, she wouldn't be spending much time with me, and I sure didn't want to make a fool of myself looking around for Rodney or standing by like a lonely wallflower.

I put on a rose-colored skirt that flowed easily from side to side and spun out wide in a twirl. It had been part of a full outfit Lisette had made, but I liked pairing the skirt with a white cotton blouse. I ribboned my hair into a ponytail, put on a light coat of soft pink lipstick, and dabbed a little on my cheeks. Then I collected my skates and Doris's, too, and ran downstairs.

Mother was waiting.

I tried to dodge her, but she moved to block me, sizing up the skates. "Are those Doris's?"

"Ginny Rose is borrowing them," I explained, fighting to stay calm.

"Does Doris know that?"

And that was all it took for me to lose the battle. "Does Doris *live* here?" I snapped. I moved past her into the kitchen and got busy packing peaches, angrily filling two large lunch sacks.

She stood by, watching. "You're taking *all* of those?"

"Prices at the rink have gone up," I said as I folded down the tops of the sacks. "It's thirty-five cents to get in now." I glared at her. "Nearly a week's allowance."

I moved to pass by her, but again she blocked my path. "That's quite enough lip from you, young lady!" she said in a fierce whisper. She wagged a finger in my face. "I have a good mind to ground you for this attitude!"

I had never been grounded in my life. She'd never even used that term before. And now all her threatening did was make me madder.

I gave her a hard look and asked, "How well did restricting Doris work?"

"You are not Doris!"

"But I understand her much better now!"

She blinked at me. "Don't," she said, her voice choked. "Don't do this to me!"

"I'm not doing anything to you! All I'm doing is dealing with the facts," I said. "And the *fact* is nobody's offered to raise our allowance. The *fact* is I'm still trying to buy my way into places with peaches. The *fact* is nobody's even *discussing* how things might change." I dropped my voice, letting the words come out strong and steady. "Ignoring this is *not* going to make it go away."

We were interrupted by a knock at the door. I moved to answer it, but Mother held me by the arm. "Lisette can wait a minute. We need to finish this."

"It's not Lisette," I said, breaking away and heading toward the door. "It's Ginny Rose." And then, because I could feel what was coming next, I said, "We're taking bikes, and yes, that means I'll be riding home after dark."

"But—"

I spun around to face her. "Mother, you need to stand up for me. And Bobby! He's lonely and miserable, and I wouldn't be surprised if *he* ran off someday!"

"What? He would never! Where would he go?"

"Anywhere but here!" I snapped. And then I let fly something I knew I probably shouldn't. "You were worried that the war would drag on so long that he'd be old enough to get drafted, but he was dying to enlist—did you know that?"

From the look on her face, she did not.

I barreled on. "This place is killing him, Mother! He works all day and then holes up in his room reading *Popular Science* or old comics. The highlight of his life is listening to *The Shadow*. He has no friends, and no hope of finding them."

"But . . . that's not true!"

I held her eyes with mine. "Name one friend of Bobby's. Go on, name one."

She stared back, then blinked and looked away.

"Exactly. And today he aimed his Winchester at the only girl who's ever had stars in her eyes for him." I went to the door. "Things need to change, Mother."

I escaped through the front door, relieved by the cooler air, the open space, and the sight of Ginny Rose.

"Hi!" she said, her face glowing.

I tried to shake off what had just happened inside and gave her a bright smile in return. "You look so cute in that dress!" I said, because although it was a little large on her, she really did.

"Kittens-with-umbrellas would look cute on anyone," she said with a laugh. "Though my sisters are mighty upset with me for wearin' it tonight. Especially Anna Mae."

Her saddle shoes were the same pair she'd been wearing earlier, but the toes were now chalky white from a new coat of polish, which seemed to spotlight instead of hide how worn they were and that the toes were pushed free from the soles.

I felt a pang of worry for her. People would definitely notice. But offering her a pair of mine to borrow would be insulting, and besides, once she'd switched into skates, no one would see.

I pulled my eyes away. "But she's only ten, right?" I placed both pairs of skates in her bike basket and both sacks of peaches in mine. "The dress would be way too big for her, wouldn't it?"

"Scissors were part of the scheme," she said as we got on our bikes.

I laughed. "Oho!"

Ginny Rose laughed, too. "She's bold and sassy and I love her so much," she said as we pushed off. "I don't know where she gets her nerve. One day she's tellin' a boy from up the road that his shoe's untied, the next day she's kissin' him on the lips!"

"Uh-oh!"

She glanced my way. "She beat me to a first kiss, can you believe it?"

"Does your mother know?"

"I'm sworn to secrecy," she said as we rolled along. "Which I guess I've just betrayed, but . . . I reckon it's only Mama she cares about not knowin', because Mama . . ." She caught herself and began picking her words carefully. "Mama doesn't need more to fret over."

I rode along, wondering what she was sheltering behind the words she chose, when she asked, "Have you had your first?"

"My first?"

"Kiss!"

My cheeks were suddenly burning.

"Oh my!" Ginny Rose squealed. "You have! Tell me!"

My face went up another few degrees. Where to begin?

"I'm sorry!" she said in response to my silence. "You don't have to if you don't want to. I didn't mean to pry."

But I *did* want to tell her. I'd been dying to confess it all to Lisette, but suddenly Ginny Rose seemed a much safer choice. A *better* choice. So as we rode along, it all spilled out. About going to visit Doris, about walking into Woolworth's to see Lisette and walking out with Rodney St. Clair, about the fun ride home and singing "Anything You Can Do" together, then about our first kiss and the feeling of being lifted into the clouds.

And then I told her about the fall back to earth and how things had spun so madly out of control.

"So I ran," I said. "Just jumped from the car and *ran*."

"Oh!" she gasped. "Oh my!" And if she hadn't been gripping so tightly to the handlebars, I'm sure she would have been holding her cheeks in shock. "So . . . what are you . . . has he . . . are you . . . ?" Her voice just trailed off.

"I have no idea!" I wailed. "I don't know what to think. I'm so . . . embarrassed. Especially since he hasn't called or come by the stand."

We were in Oakvale now, waiting for the stoplight at Depot Street to turn green. And after staring straight ahead for a minute, Ginny Rose turned to face me and said, "*He's* the one who should be embarrassed! And if he doesn't call you or apologize, well, that tells you all you need to know."

She said it with finality, but there was also sympathy in her voice. And it was the sympathy that made me hear the truth of her words—a truth I'd been avoiding because . . . oh, Rodney St. Clair!

The light turned green, so we pushed off and turned left through the intersection.

And we were just gathering speed when I said, "He'll probably be there tonight. He and his friend Jimmy Dickens usually show up. At least for a little while."

Ginny Rose slowed to a coast. "So . . . maybe I should turn around?"

"What? No!"

"But . . . I don't know anybody, and if you have hopes of fixin' things with Rodney, I . . . I don't want to be in the way."

"You won't be, I promise! I'm so glad you're with me!"

I could see her weighing things in her mind, and when she started pedaling again, I thought things were okay. But then she asked, "Will Lisette be there?"

The question threw me. How did we get from Rodney to Lisette? Regardless, the look on her face told me that I wouldn't get away with fudging the truth. "Sure," I said. "She's—"

But before I could explain that Lisette had a date, Ginny Rose said, "Well, please don't stick me with her."

"Stick you with her?"

"When you're with Rodney."

I rode a little closer to her. "I know you didn't hit it off with Lisette, and I know the two of you are different, but I would really like my two best friends to get to know each other."

She shook her head and huffed like I was out of my mind for wanting this. And since the whole situation felt very delicate and I didn't want her to think the only reason I'd asked her along was because Lisette was unavailable, I decided against telling her that Lisette was coming with a date.

Not long after, we were at the roller rink, parking our bikes, taking the skates and the two sacks of peaches up to the box office. "Hi, Gordy," I said, slipping him the sacks when it was our turn at the window.

His eyes widened at the sight of them, then took in Ginny Rose standing beside me.

"I see," he said.

"Please?" I begged. "I packed extras."

"You know I'll let you in," he said. "Just don't tell nobody—that's our deal." He eyed Ginny Rose again. "And two's the limit, you hear me? Much as I enjoy these peaches, this is a little outta control."

He hid the sacks away, then gave us a toothy grin as he passed us tickets. "Have fun, girls."

"Thanks, Gordy," I said, smiling back.

And just like that, we were in.

16

Ginny Rose

ROLLER RINK

I don't have time to sit down with the family for supper on Friday, and Mama's none too happy about that or the flurry of all I do to get ready to go skating. But Papa gives her stern looks and little signals that somehow keep her tongue still.

He hushes Anna Mae, too, when she sees I'm goin' out wearin' kittens-with-umbrellas. "It's her dress," he says. "Let her be."

She pouts, but there's nothing I can do about that now.

And then, as I'm scamperin' to leave, Papa shocks me by sayin', "Since skatin' will be over after dark and you'll be workin' at the Simmons' early, if Peggy invites you to stay the night, that would be all right."

Mama starts about my havin' chores to do at home, but Papa hushes her again with a single look. Then he turns back to me and says, "Just make sure you call here if that's the case."

"I will," I tell him, and give him a look reflectin' the wide-sky gratitude I feel.

When I arrive at Peggy's front door, I'm breathless and a little giddy. But it seems to take ages for someone to answer, and during that time my mood falters. I *am* five minutes late. Did she leave without me?

I sense something to my right, and when I look, Bobby ducks out of view behind the house. I picture him rushin' off to fetch his gun and my mood stumbles. It's plain as day I'm just an Okie to him, one he's itchin' to run off the property.

And then Peggy whooshes out of the house lookin' pretty as a picture, and my spirits lift. Soon we're off, pedalin' down the road, and I can't help smilin' at the skates she's placed in my basket—white lace-up ankle boots with wheels, just like I've seen in magazines—a pair for each of us!

We ride along the road side by side, and soon we're talkin' the way we did all those years ago. It's like time's been standin' still, just waitin' for this moment to take up tickin' again.

But during the conversation I begin to fret. She tried to hide it, but I saw Peggy eyein' my shoes. I polished them the best I could, but the fact is you can't paint over poor. My family still gets sneered at and shunned, or just looked at with suspicion—like we're sure to give folks lice or some disease if we get too close, or steal their wares if they're not watchful. I also can't seem to help slippin' up and "talking funny," and as kind as Peggy is, she may not know what she's gotten herself into by askin' me along.

The urge to go home grows stronger with each turn of my pedals. But Peggy seems to sense my mood and works at pullin' me along with assurances. My years in California have taught me how to build shelters, includin' a sturdy one around my heart. It's not easy to move the hinges on the door to that one, but for Peggy I'm willin' to try.

When we get to the skating rink ticket booth, we park our bikes, stand in line, and pay our way inside with peaches. The area around the box office is buzzin' with excitement. There's small groups of teens huddled together, the girls laughin' and whisperin' with each other, the boys lookin' at the girls and doin' the same. My heart scampers in my chest. I'm excited, but also a little terrified!

Peggy gives me a reassuring smile. "You'll be fine!" she whispers, then takes my hand and leads me inside.

Sounds swirl all around us. There's organ music playin' over loudspeakers, people talkin' and laughin', and the low rolling roar of skaters in the rink. I hear the roar before I see it, but once we pass by the skate rental counter, the rink comes into view on the other side of a wide carpeted area that has rows of long wooden benches.

"They're goin' so fast!" I gasp.

Peggy pulls me along and points out a big lit-up board on the wall. "That's why." The board's divided into about a dozen sections, each with a large word or two—words like ALL SKATE, COUPLES, REVERSE, SPECIAL, and CLEAR FLOOR—in bold black letters. All are dimmed except for MEN ONLY, which is lit up. Peggy grins at me. "They like to show off."

We pass by a snack bar with Coca-Cola signs on either side of a large soda fountain. Three men work the counter, sellin' fountain drinks and snacks, includin' hot dogs, which are doin' a lazy turn on a roaster. My almost-empty stomach twists and flips at the smell of them.

A railing divides the refreshment center from the carpeted area, and the whole space is crowded with people our age standin' at the counter or near the railing. One of them's Lisette, and who could miss her? Her hair's in a beautiful shoulder-length bob, with curls so smooth they're reflectin' light. And with her flowing red skirt and frilly white blouse, she looks like the star of a roller rink movie.

Peggy sees her, too, and when they wave at each other, my insides start to shrivel up.

I don't belong here.

As Lisette comes toward us from her place at the counter, I get a fearsome urge to bolt for the door. The boy she's with seems surprised by her quick departure, but he's midbite into a hot dog and stays put at the counter.

"Your date is *Jimmy?*" Peggy whispers to her when they're face to face at the railing.

Lisette looks tall and slender on her skates, and a fresh scent has sailed in with her. Her eyes drift to me, and she smiles as she says, "Hello," but it's an uneasy greeting, made more tense by the way she side-eyes me from head to toe . . . and lingers on my toes.

When she turns back to Peggy, she whispers, "He's serving a purpose."

It's not meant for me to hear, so I turn my eyes away, but my ears stay tuned. "What do you mean?" Peggy says, and I can feel the wheels churnin' in her mind.

"There's so much I need to tell you!" Lisette whispers with a quick look over her shoulder.

"So why haven't you?" Peggy asks, her voice tinged with irritation. My stomach takes a different sort of twist as I wonder if Peggy's invited me as a backup plan—her way of not havin' to be here alone.

"Well, I can't explain it now," Lisette huffs, and I catch the annoyed look she shoots my way.

My cheeks go hot. "I can leave," I say, givin' away that I've heard every word.

And I do start for the exit, but Peggy grabs me by the arm and pulls me back. "Don't be silly," she says. "I'm sorry. Let's go skate."

Lisette's already gone back to her Jimmy and whatever purpose he's servin', and Peggy keeps her eyes straight ahead as she leads us past the refreshment counter to a door marked LADIES.

Through the door is a small locker room with toilet stalls and sinks on one side, wooden benches between rows of small metal lockers on the other. Peggy sits on a bench and begins rippin' loose the laces of her shoe.

I sit beside her. "What's goin' on?" I ask. "Looks like you knew Lisette would be here with a date, so . . . what's got you so upset?" I pause. "Now, if that boy was Rodney . . ."

"Shh!" she says, checkin' around for who might have heard.

Then in a fierce whisper she says, "Did you see her? New hair, new outfit, new makeup . . ."

"She smelled pretty nice, too," I say with a shrug.

"Yes!" she fires back, sparks flashin' in her eyes. "Whatever that is, it's new, too!"

"But isn't that just part of bein' a banker's daughter?" I try to make it sound light, to keep the bitterness out of my voice. It's there, though. Even if she can't hear it, I surely can taste it.

"I thought she was sick!" she says. "Or that something traumatic had happened! Or that she'd been fighting with her parents about moving to Oakvale! Or . . . or . . . something!" She yanks on a skate boot, her heel thumpin' hard inside it. "But no. She's been off putting together a whole new look!" She pulls the laces snug and double knots a bow, then starts on her second boot. "And Jimmy? *Jimmy?*"

I get busy unlacin' my shoes. "What's wrong with Jimmy?" I ask, because he seemed handsome enough, that's for sure.

"He rides rodeo! All he talks about is horses and riding, and how he's going to win the Clover Roundup next year. Lisette makes fun of him for it!"

I take off my shoes and reach for Doris's skates. "But rodeo stars are—"

"He's not a star," she says, sizzlin' and poppin' like water-splashed bacon. "And even if he becomes one, Lisette's not interested in boys with horse poop on their boots." She double knots the second skate, mutterin', "Of all the boys she could have, why's she toying with him?"

Suddenly she goes still as a statue, and the color drains from her face. Then she turns to me and whispers, "No!"

"What's wrong?" I ask.

"Jimmy is Rodney's best friend."

My mind leaps from thoughts of the four of them double-dating to what "serving a purpose" might mean. I drop my voice way down. "But . . . you've told her *you* like Rodney, haven't you?"

She looks like a cornered rabbit. "No!"

"But . . . why not?"

"I couldn't even admit it to myself! And when I finally did, I was *going* to tell her, only she always acted like he disgusted her and I was worried she'd be disgusted with *me* if she knew. And then we were parked at Dolly's Diner and he started flirting with me in front of her and . . . and . . . well, she seemed to get mad and told me I wasn't equipped to deal with him!" She gives me a sorrowful look. "I haven't really spoken to her since."

I strap up a boot, ponderin' all of it. At last I say, "Do you think she *does* like him and is usin' his best friend to make him jealous?"

She looks at me with tears swimmin' in her eyes. "That's the only thing that makes sense." She covers her face with her hands. "I can't believe this is happening."

My boots feel big and clunky, and with Peggy so down, I'm not lookin' forward to skating anymore. So I say, "Do you want to just go home?"

"No!" She swipes away her tears and stands. "Absolutely not." She gives me a hand up. "I'm sorry I dumped all of that on you." She rallies, smilin' as she eyes my feet. "How do those feel?"

I take a few baby steps forward. "Mighty strange."

"Wait," she says. "Let me give you some pointers." So right there in the ladies' room she shows me how I should keep my knees bent a little to help me not fall, how to do a plow stop by pointin' my toes inward, and how to push off. I practice a little, keepin' one hand on the lockers and walls for support. "So," she says after I've stumbled around a bit, "are you ready to go out and give it a try?"

"Sure," I say with a nervous laugh.

She tucks away our shoes in a locker; then we clomp through the door, across the carpet, past a guardrail, down one step, and onto the hardwood track. The lighted sign says ALL SKATE, and the track is whirrin' with skaters.

At first all I do is hug the wall, feelin' like a wobbly baby foal. Peggy takes my hand and coaxes me along, remindin' me again and again to keep my knees bent. I feel silly and clumsy, and my legs keep tryin' to walk like I'm on land instead of wheels. But before too long I start to glide in little spurts. Peggy cheers me on, sayin', "That's it! That's it!" until at last I can roll along without touchin' the wall.

Peggy guides me forward by the hand. Her smile's like sunshine, and I feel such a swell of affection for her. She was in tears not long ago, but she's put her troubles aside and turned her full attention to teachin' me how to skate. I almost can't believe it, but Peggy Simmons *is* my friend.

And with that thought, I lose my concentration and slip, landin' fanny down, legs spread forward on the track.

My cheeks are blazin', but Peggy swoops around to face me toe to toe and pulls me back to my feet. "That was your first, but it won't be your last," she says. "Everyone falls."

As I work at gettin' better on the skates—which includes practicin' comin' to a stop without crashin'—I do see a few other people tumble—boys and girls—and it takes some of the embarrassment out of it when I fall again.

But after our second full turn around the rink, I start glidin' along, start pushin' forward, start feelin' wind on my cheeks and the thrill of speed buildin' beneath me. I know I'm smilin' like a little kid, but I can't help it.

This is *fun.*

"See?" Peggy says, coastin' along beside me. "It's like riding a bicycle. Once you get your balance and a little momentum, it's easy."

We finish another lap without me fallin', and then over the loudspeaker a man's voice says, "All right, all right, all right! It's time to let couples rule the floor. Everyone else, this is your chance to quench your thirst at the refreshment center. Couples only now. Show us what you've got!"

The lighted sign changes from ALL SKATE to COUPLES, and we file out of the rink and up the steps to the carpeted area where other skaters either sit on benches or clomp over to get a soda.

I follow Peggy, but she seems unsure about where to go. She's lookin' around . . . but tryin' not to look like she's lookin' around.

"Is Rodney here?" I whisper, doin' the same thing she is.

"I don't see him," she whispers back, and after we've taken turns at the water fountain, she leads me to an open space on a bench where we sit facin' the rink.

I'm happy to watch the couples skate. The music's soothing now, and most of the couples glide along side by side, in step with each other. A few couples get a little fancier, facin' each other with one partner skatin' backward, then switchin' positions. "Can you skate backward?" I ask Peggy.

"A little," she says with a smile. "But I'm not great at it." Her face falls, and I follow her gaze to Lisette, who's just stepped into the rink with Jimmy. "Nothing like her," she says.

I watch Lisette and can hardly believe my eyes. Not only can she skate backward, she can skate backward with one leg high in the air behind her. She can skate backward and switch to forward without a hitch. She can skate backward and twirl forward. She's a beautiful, graceful dancer on her skates.

Jimmy, on the other hand, can't seem to do any of those things, so he just faces forward while she grandstands, swishin' and twirlin' and glidin' all around him.

"She's something," I concede.

"Yes," Peggy sighs, "she is."

Out of the corner of my eye I spot Rodney. He's barbered up and dressed sharp, standin' with his back against a wall. My heart falls for Peggy, because though he's got a clear sightline of her, he's not lookin' our way.

His eyes are fixed on the rink.

Fixed on Lisette.

17

Peggy

OFF TRACK

By the time we entered the skating rink, I had confessed everything about Rodney to Ginny Rose. Everything! It felt a little rash, but I was desperate and there was no doubt in my mind that I could trust her. And she turned out to be such a good listener! Which, now that I was comparing, was more than I could say about Lisette. Conversations with Lisette often ended up being about her, even when they hadn't started out that way.

Ginny Rose also showed herself to be observant, which included her thoughts on why Lisette was at the rink with Jimmy. Was it really to make Rodney jealous?

To make *my* Rodney jealous?

I hated the idea, but the more I thought about it, the more sense it made. Ignoring someone you liked was the oldest trick in the book. How could I have been so naïve?

So *blind*?

If it was true, it was an impossible situation. Lisette was my best friend, and despite everything, I had to admit it—I was helplessly in love with Rodney St. Clair.

But I'd never told Lisette that!

So . . . what was I going to do?

I tried to shove the worry from my mind and focus on Ginny Rose. What an awful friend I'd be if I spent the whole night worrying about Lisette and Rodney.

Ginny Rose was a quick study on roller skates, taking only a couple of tumbles before she really began to move around the rink. It was fun teaching her, and a relief to have my mind occupied with her learning to skate. But after they announced couples only and we were seated on a bench overlooking the rink, my thoughts turned back to my dilemma.

If Lisette was really after Rodney, I didn't stand a chance.

After a while, I noticed Ginny Rose staring across the room, and when I followed her gaze, it landed on Rodney.

I swooned at the sight of him. He looked so dapper! But as hard as I willed him to turn my way, he never looked over. He only had eyes for Lisette.

Ginny Rose's voice came low and firm. "Do not look at him, do not go to him, do not talk to him."

I understood what she was saying and knew she was right. My heart was breaking over it, but I nodded and turned my eyes back to the rink.

Back to Lisette.

Back to a different sort of pain.

Or maybe it was the same pain, only piercing my heart from behind instead of straight on. Which was not an entirely fair thought, but still, I couldn't help having it.

When the song ended and ALL SKATE lit up, I began rising

from the bench, but Ginny Rose held my arm. "We can leave, if you want," she said.

"No," I replied with more conviction than I felt.

Our skates clacked as we walked along the carpet toward the step down. Lisette and Jimmy were still whizzing around the oval, and Rodney was still watching them.

"Do not look at him," Ginny Rose warned.

"I can't help it!" I whimpered.

She pulled me along firmly. "Yes, you can."

Ginny Rose seemed to have a new determination about her as we began rolling along. At first I thought it was her resolve not to tumble. But after a couple of laps I realized she was determined to not let my *heart* tumble. Each time my gaze wandered around for Rodney, she would stop me. "Don't look," she'd command, and then she'd spy and report, saying things like "He's behind us, back by the curve," or "He's jokin' around with Mister Servin'-a-Purpose like he hasn't a care in the world," or "He's skatin' with two other girls."

With every spin around the rink, I was on pins and needles, wondering when he would catch up to me and say something.

Not looking was so hard!

Then, after three songs and countless times around the track, it dawned on me that he might not come say hello to me at *all;* that he must be avoiding me. He hadn't skated beside me, or even acknowledged me once, and he'd had plenty of chances!

My spirits sank even further. What more evidence did I need? I had to face the harsh truth: my romance with Rodney St. Clair had ended the moment I'd bolted from his car.

But . . . how could he shatter my heart this way?

The music changed again and TRIO lit up, with the voice on the loudspeaker announcing, "Trio now, in a line! Trio *only* now, and *only* in a line!"

"What's that mean?" Ginny Rose asked.

"Groups of three, holding on to each other like this," I said, sliding in behind her and placing my hands on her waist.

"Do we have to leave the floor?" she called over her shoulder.

"Usually a third latches on," I said to the back of her head.

The words were barely out of my mouth when hands clasped my waist. They were small, their grip light. I glanced back.

Lisette.

"Why are you mad at me?" she asked over the music and the whirring of skates. I glanced back again to say . . . *something*, but she went on before I found the words. "Do you like Jimmy—is that it?" Again, there was no time to reply before she said, "How was I supposed to know that? And I *don't* like him, so it's not a problem! You can have him!"

Something about that really irritated me. Something beyond her using poor Jimmy. And that irritation helped me find some words. "I know you're just using Jimmy to make Rodney jealous," I snapped at her as we rounded the top curve. I chanced another look back and caught the shock in her eyes.

Good.

But after I faced forward again, she leaned closer and hissed, "Well, it's *working*."

I felt slapped by the sting of her words. And the way she'd said them . . . it was as though she was miffed at *me*.

"So have Jimmy," she said. "He's all yours." Then she peeled away, skating past us, her ruby-red skirt flying.

Ginny Rose slowed and looked over her shoulder at me, but in an instant her eyes grew wide and she quickly faced forward, pushing off hard.

Before I could look behind me, another pair of hands gripped my waist. These were firm and warm and came with a voice that purred in my ear. "Hello, Peaches."

The sound shivered down my spine and immediately infected my heart. I knew I should swat him back, but . . .

How could I want to hit him . . . and also *kiss* him?

I was desperate to hear him say I'd been on his mind, to tell me he was sorry. Instead, what he said was: "Don't believe everything she tells you," and before I could react, he let go of my waist and peeled away toward the step up to exit the rink.

"What happened?" Ginny Rose asked, because I'd let go of her, and although I was just coasting along, I was having trouble catching my breath. She grabbed me by the elbow as though *I* might fall. "Are you okay?"

The song had changed, ALL SKATE was now lit again, and the rink was flooding with people who'd been waiting for TRIO to end. We were trapped center track with skaters buzzing by, bumping and dodging us as I drifted along in a trance I couldn't seem to shake.

That was all Rodney had to say to me?

After everything he'd whispered in my ear before?

Then Lisette was upon us. "What did he say?" she asked.

I felt like I might faint and must have looked it, but Lisette wasn't seeing *me* at all. She was all about *her*.

How had this happened to our friendship?

"What did he say?" she demanded.

I felt a rush of color come to my cheeks, and then . . . anger. At him *and* at her.

I forced myself to look directly at her. "He said, 'Hello, Peaches,'" I replied, mimicking the same sultry voice Rodney had used.

"He said it like *that*?" she gasped. "Why do you let him call you that?"

In that moment, I realized that she *wasn't* scandalized by the nickname.

She was jealous of it.

I held Lisette's gaze for a moment, then gave Ginny Rose a nod toward the exit step. And as we drifted in that direction, I said to Lisette, "He also said not to believe everything you tell me, which isn't hard, considering you haven't told me anything at all."

Jimmy was beside us now. "Hi-de-ho, ladies, what's going on?" he asked as we all came to a stop at the wall near the step up. It was obvious that Lisette had ditched him to ask me about Rodney, and although I could see he was hurt, he was bravely trying not to let it show.

Lisette brushed him off and kept her gaze on me. "Why are you being like this?"

"I'm sorry," I said icily. "I misspoke. You *did* tell me *one* thing." I gave Jimmy a meaningful look. "But nothing you'd want me to repeat, I'm sure."

Lisette's jaw went slack. Ginny Rose's eyes went wide. And I felt really . . . strange. First my parents, now Lisette?

When had I ever spoken to her this way? I always just went along, and now I was speaking in barely veiled threats?

"Look," I said, calming myself. "A lot has happened that you don't know about, and—"

"Yes! It has! And I was going to tell you all about it tonight, but—" She shot a resentful look at Ginny Rose.

"I don't believe this," I said.

"Don't believe what?" she demanded. And when I went up the step without replying, she came after me. "Where are you going?"

I turned to face her. "Home." Then I added, "I have a pretty good picture of what's been going on with you. If you want to spend a minute hearing about what's been going on with *me*, ask. You know where I live." I shot a look at Jimmy. "I promise, it has nothing to do with *him*."

She didn't chase after me as I marched into the ladies' room with Ginny Rose scurrying behind. She didn't show up as we were changing back into our street shoes. She didn't try to stop me as we walked right past her and Jimmy on the way outside. And, I realized, this was it. The end of us. She wouldn't call me, or come over, or chase me. She would put her nose in the air and blame me for . . . for everything!

I stopped short of the exit. Because as upset as I was right then, I didn't want to lose our friendship.

I didn't want to let a *boy* come between us.

Even if that boy was Rodney St. Clair.

So I told Ginny Rose I'd be right back, marched over to Lisette, and said, "For the record, you might not want to believe everything *he* tells you, either. Especially when he's whispering sweet nothings in your ear!"

Jimmy looked at me, confused. "What did I do?"

I gave him a sad shake of the head. "Not you, Jimmy."

"What are you saying?" Lisette demanded.

But I couldn't say any more. Not with Jimmy standing right there and Ginny Rose waiting for me. "Ask Rodney," I told her. Then I hurried toward the exit, hoping I'd said enough to make her think.

18

Ginny Rose

A DARK SECRET

Learnin' to skate is so much fun . . . until Lisette sweeps in and things turn ugly.

I do not like that girl.

Not one whit.

So it's a relief when Peggy and I are out of the building and back on our bikes, with the night air coolin' everything down.

"I'm sorry," Peggy says as we pass by the Oakvale sign on the way home. It's the first thing either of us has said since ridin' away from the rink.

"Don't be!" I hurry to say. "I had a great time! And you were so nice to take me and teach me. I just feel awful about the . . . the Rodney predicament."

She snorts. "That's exactly what it is. A predicament."

We're ridin' beside each other, our headlamps bobbin' through the darkness. "Do you know what you're gonna do?" I ask at last.

She sighs and shakes her head. *"Bobby* saw it—why didn't I?"

"Saw what?"

"He asked if there was something doing between Lisette and Rodney, and I laughed at him." She shakes her head. "And believing Rodney might actually like me? He was probably just using me the way Lisette's using Jimmy." Her voice about breaks as she says, "I was such a fool."

"*He's* the fool, not you," I scold. "That boy's just a smooth talker gettin' by on dash. And Lisette's—" I catch myself, but not in time.

"She's what?" Peggy demands.

I shake my head.

Shrug.

Bite my tongue.

"Just say it," she says.

"She's . . . she's a mite self-centered is all."

Peggy laughs. It's a merry laugh, too, which I don't get. Does she agree? Does she not mind? Then, after a little more ridin' along, she says, "I guess it's hard to see things when you're standing too close."

All the way to Peggy's we talk about what happened at the rink. And when we reach the farmhouse, I pull to a stop and hand over the skates. "I'm sorry about Rodney and Lisette," I tell her. "But I did have a nice time learnin' to skate. Thank you for invitin' me."

She checks her watch. "Do you have time to come in for dessert? It's barely nine." Then she lures me, sayin', "Peach pie and ice cream?"

"You sure?"

"Of course I'm sure! We have to be quiet, though. My parents go to bed early."

So we park the bikes and tiptoe in through a side door. We're careful to keep the hinges from squeakin' and the floor from creakin', only to find her folks and Bobby all sittin' around the kitchen table, fully awake, lookin' mighty serious.

"Oh!" Peggy says.

"Come in," Mrs. Simmons says. "We were just talking about the need to replace a big section of old trees, and how much that's going to cost."

Her words seem like daggers flung at Peggy, though I don't understand why.

Peggy stiffens, but then she puts on the armor of a smile and says, "Well . . . Mother, Father . . . you remember Ginny Rose Gilley, don't you?" She casts a sharp look at her brother. "And, of course, Bobby does."

They murmur hellos, but they're more interested in studyin' the table than they are in lookin' at me, and it's plain to see I'm intrudin'.

But Peggy flies into action, retrievin' pie, dishes, ice cream, and forks, chatterin' about how I took to skatin' like a fish to water. When she sees I'm still standin' on the outskirts of the kitchen, she waves me in, sayin', "Sit!"

There's two chairs available. One across from Bobby, one beside him. Across is farther from him, so that's what I choose.

He glances at me through lashes that look like fine bristles of gold. "Sorry," he murmurs. Then, as if there might be some question as to *why* he's sorry, he adds, "About earlier."

I mean to tell him it's all right. And maybe it's because I know he's crazy about Lisette and I'm mad at him for it, but what pops from my mouth instead is "No need to say it if you don't mean it."

He looks straight at me now. "But I do mean it!"

"Then don't act like a whipped puppy about it. *Say* it like you mean it."

I go prickly all over.

Did I just say that?

In front of his *folks?*

He stares back. And I can see him thinkin', *Did you just say that? In front of my folks?*

But over on my left there's a chuckle. It's a man's chuckle, deep and . . . rusty. Like it hasn't been worked in ages. I sneak a peek at Mr. Simmons and see Mrs. Simmons nudge him to quit laughin'.

Peggy serves up pie and ice cream, shovin' plates in front of everyone, tryin' to smooth things over. And while Mrs. Simmons protests that they've already had dessert, it doesn't stop Mr. Simmons from diggin' right in.

And since I've had little to eat since lunch, there's nothing refined about the way I start in on my own serving. Only after three bites do I manage to pause long enough to say, "Mrs. Simmons, this is *heavenly.*"

"Heavenly?" she asks, her voice crackin' a little.

"Mm-hmm." But after two more bites, I stop eatin' because it occurs to me that I might never again have the opportunity to say something I've wanted to say for years. "You were always so kind when we worked the orchard," I say, lookin' at Mrs. Simmons. "You brought us biscuits and beans and fresh water. Some days it was the only food we had." I turn to Mr. Simmons. "And you didn't run us off when we slept at the back of the property. The other farmers"—I look away—"they weren't that way."

Silence settles over us. And once again, I feel like I've made a mistake.

Like I don't belong.

And then Mr. Simmons says, "*Who* are you?" His gaze is now squarely on me, his eyes sharp slits.

"Ginny Rose Gilley, sir," I choke out, because for as much of an impression as he made on me, I can see I made none on him. "I spent summers workin' your orchard when I was younger."

"She's Peggy's little harvest friend from her peach-sorting days," Mrs. Simmons whispers. "Her father was a picker."

"Okies?" Mr. Simmons whispers back, though it's plenty loud enough for the rest of us to hear.

"Father!" Peggy cries.

"What?" he asks.

"*See?*" Bobby says, givin' Peggy a glare.

How thankin' someone for their past kindness could turn ugly so quick is beyond me, but I try to put the whole thing to rest. "If by Okies you mean survivors, then yes, sir, we are."

He studies me and I hold his gaze, reachin' deep for the strength not to flinch.

I refuse to let *Okie* hurt me anymore.

It's become a steel rod holdin' up my spine.

"So you've settled here, now?" Mr. Simmons asks.

"Yes, sir," I reply. "We've taken to callin' Ferrybank home. Papa's workin' a job he likes at the switching yard, and we've got a little place near there." Then my mouth keeps yammerin'. Maybe because I want him to know Okie means a whole lot more'n poor trash, scrapin' by. "He had eighty acres of his own land back in Oklahoma. I reckon he'd trade his soul to farm again, but he tries to stay grateful for what he has now and not think so much on what he's lost."

Mr. Simmons rubs his stubbled jaw. "He farmed winter wheat?" he asks at last.

"Yes, sir," I answer. It's a safe guess, seein' how that's what most farmers there grew, but I'm still a little surprised he knew that.

His attention turns back to his pie, which he finishes with a clean sweep. Then he scoots back from the table and gives me a curt nod. "Well, you're welcome here anytime, Ginny Rose. Good night."

Silence grips the table for a moment, but then Mrs. Simmons is up, too, sayin' good night, and Bobby's mutterin' something about needin' to get an early start in the morning, leavin' Peggy and me suddenly alone.

Peggy stares after them but says nothing, and soon an uneasiness settles around us.

"I should get home, too," I say, all the strength I had moments before knocked flat by a worry that Peggy will never again invite me into her home.

"What? No!" Peggy says, snappin' out of her thoughts. "Why don't you stay over?" And in a flurry she assures me that everything I need I can borrow from her and that it would not just be sensible, but also fun.

So I call home.

And then we scurry upstairs.

Peggy's bedroom is the same one I slept in all those years ago. And though it seems smaller, it's just as magical—cozy and tidy and clean, with the same starflower quilt on the bed and floppy dolls on the dormer window seat, their cloth faces smilin' like they haven't a care in the world.

I smile back at them and feel barely nine again, joyful and excited and not at all sleepy. I think back on that night when we were kids and about how I never told Peggy that my birthday was the day before hers, or how I pretended her beautiful fluffy white cake with scrumptious buttercream frosting was also *my* birthday cake. It was hard not to say anything as she blew out the candles, but Mrs. Simmons was keepin' a watchful eye on my every move, and I didn't want to do or say anything to break the magic of bein' there.

Peggy *did* give me something that night, though—a playing-card souvenir. She spread the deck we'd been playin' with faceup in front of me. "Pick a card, any card," she said. The pack was already missin' a few cards on account of Bobby havin' swiped them to clip to the spokes of his bike, and for some reason she wanted me to have one to keep in my pocket. "To remind you of tonight," she said. "Here—take the queen of hearts."

"I don't want her," I said, siftin' through the cards.

"How about the jack?"

"Don't want him, either." Then I found the one I'd been lookin' for. "Can I have this one?"

"The *two* of hearts? Why the two?"

I just smiled at her, and she understood right away. "Aw!" she said. "Yes, take it."

Now all these years later, we fall right back into the enchantment of that night. We don't play cards, but we whisper through the soft moonlight for hours. First, we talk more about our night skating, but after we've run the subject of Rodney deep into the ground, Peggy switches to memories of us sortin' peaches as kids, which leads me to tellin' her what it's like workin' at the cannery, sortin' peaches now.

"People *faint?*" she asks.

So I tell her about poor Mrs. Smith, and to my dismay I hear myself repeatin' the gossip about her bein' bedridden, only to lose her child, and about her husband's unfaithfulness.

"That's awful!" Peggy says. She sits up suddenly, struck by a thought. "What did this Mrs. Smith look like?"

So I describe her, and I add, "I'm pretty sure she's a teacher. There's a group of them workin' there."

Peggy hops out of bed, sayin', "I'll be right back," and returns a short while later with an Oakvale High School yearbook. "It's Doris's senior book," she says, flippin' through it. Then she stops and points to a small photograph on a teachers' page. "Is that her?"

"Yep," I answer, then point to another picture. "She works there, too . . . and her!" Then I see Miss Robinson. "And she's the line supervisor."

Peggy seems shocked. And after givin' me a quick summary of each of them—what subjects they teach and how strict or nice they are—she sits back against the headboard and sighs. "Mrs. Smith is the nicest teacher at school. She was out most of last year, so I haven't really thought about her lately, but now . . . I'm so sad she lost her baby."

"A lot of people are. The grave site's covered in flowers and toys." Peggy gives me a curious look, so I'm quick to add, "Her baby's buried in an area called Babyland at the cemetery next to Valley Church. It's a real peaceful spot."

"Does your family go to Valley Church?" she asks. "We do,

but we haven't been since harvest started." Then she confesses, "And our attendance was getting spotty before that!"

I don't want to lie to her, so I say, "No . . . I . . . we . . ."

She sees how painfully stuck I am and says, "Don't be afraid to tell me."

So it's my turn to confess. And though my intention is to hold back, one thing leads to another, and soon out tumbles the whole story of how my brothers died, how Papa and I buried them swaddled with their sock monkeys, and the way their death is like fine black dust lingerin' in every crevice of our lives.

I take a minute to catch my breath and wipe my eyes dry, then begin again, tellin' her about my talk with Mrs. Poole at the cemetery, about usin' my wages to secure a Babyland grave site, and about why I can't breathe a word of it to Mama or Papa. And then, at last, I confess: "I'm plannin' to move them."

"Move your brothers?" she asks. "But . . . how? If your parents can't know?"

I study her a moment, weighin' the sanity of the plan and the sanity of tellin' her.

And then I let it out.

"I'll do it myself."

She waits, her eyes earnest.

And I can tell she's still not gettin' what I'm sayin', so I spell it out.

"With a shovel."

Even to my own ears it sounds horrible. Horrible and gruesome. And even in the shadows, I can see Peggy turn white as a ghost. "How on earth are you going to manage *that*?" she breathes.

"I don't know yet. But my folks *can't* find out!"

"I would never say a word to them," she promises.

We both go quiet, and then silence spins a cocoon around us. Soon our heads are restin' on pillows, and it doesn't take long for the full weight of the day to settle into my bones.

I am so, *so* tired.

But just as I'm driftin' off, surrenderin' my cares for the night, Peggy's voice slips into my ear like a dream.

"I'll help you," she whispers. "We'll do it together."

19

Peggy

SHADE

After everything Ginny Rose told me, I had a hard time falling asleep. I knew about the Dust Bowl, of course, and about the people from that area coming to California to start again. And Miss Anderson *had* read *The Grapes of Wrath* to us last year. There was a rumor that she'd gotten into trouble for it, too, but she'd never explained why.

So I'd honestly believed that I understood how hard and awful that time had been for migrant families, but hearing Ginny Rose tell of it—knowing the horrible things she'd endured—I felt bad for not understanding in my *heart* before. When we were kids, I'd worked with her in the orchard like we were the same. Like her life was the same as mine. Like her tummy was as full as mine. She'd never once let on about how dire things were, or that living like that had killed her brothers. Blinded by the joy of having a friend to work with, I hadn't noticed a bit of her pain.

And now that she'd shared it . . . now that I knew how the past was still haunting her family . . . how could I not try to help?

But . . . had I really offered to help her move—*to dig up*—her brothers? The more I thought about it, the more insane it seemed!

It was after midnight when we stopped talking, and although Ginny Rose fell asleep right away, it took me a long time to drift off. And when I awoke the next morning, it was with a start. A bad dream, I thought. But when I looked around, it was instantly forgotten.

Ginny Rose was gone.

My alarm clock said it was 4:35. I put it to my ear and listened. It was still ticking.

Her clothes and shoes were right where she'd put them, so I figured she'd gone to the bathroom. But when she didn't return, I checked down the hallway and found the bathroom door open and the light off. There was no sign of Ginny Rose.

I went back to my room and heard a rustling sound coming from outside. It was getting light out, and when I looked through my open window, there was Ginny Rose, wrestling an orchard ladder into the branches of a peach tree.

She was barefoot, wearing the pajamas I'd lent her, and she had a picking bucket strapped across her. I almost called out to her, but I held back and just watched as she gave the ladder a shake to test it, then went up, up, up, plucking fruit at each rung and placing it carefully in the bucket. There was no thump. No plop. Just gentle . . . reverence.

When was the last time I'd treated a peach that way?

Maybe never.

Near the top of the ladder, she held a peach to her face and took a long moment to inhale its fragrance, then took a bite. She laughed aloud as she flung juice off her hand, then bit again like it was the most scrumptious thing she'd ever tasted.

Suddenly Bobby was at the foot of the ladder, fully dressed in his jeans, boots, and hat. "What are you doing?" he demanded.

She gazed down at him. "Looks like I'm stealin' your fruit, Bobby Simmons. Best run fetch your gun."

He sputtered, then marched off; and I stifled a laugh. Poor Bobby. Sweet on Lisette and sassed to confusion by Ginny Rose, he was clearly baffled by both.

"Pssst!" I hissed through the window when he was gone, and in the still morning air it carried to her.

"Oh, hi!" she whispered from the ladder, and waved. "I'll be right up!"

"Meet me in the kitchen! If we get the peaches prepped early, I'll have time to help you with the shade before the stand opens."

"Okay!"

We had the day's baking peaches blanched, pitted, and sliced, and breakfast started, before Mother came into the kitchen. She just stood by, sizing up Ginny Rose squeezing orange juice and me turning flapjacks.

Then Nonnie appeared. She took in Ginny Rose and me, still barefoot and in our pajamas, and she stayed silent, as usual, but cocked a meaningful eyebrow at me.

"Oh!" I rushed to make formal introductions between Nonnie and Ginny Rose, and after their pleased-to-meet-yous, Nonnie moved forward to inspect the prepared peaches. "What time did you girls get up?"

I laughed. "Well, *Ginny Rose* was up gathering peaches from the orchard at dawn."

Nonnie looked her over. "Were you now."

Ginny Rose didn't seem to mind her tone. "I was happy as a bee in clover," she gushed. "The air was cool and clear and smelled so sweet . . . and all those peaches!" She sighed. "Millions of them."

"Yes," Mother said wryly, "at least it feels that way."

"It's not just the peaches," Ginny Rose hurried to add. "I see plenty of peaches at the cannery. It's the *orchard.* Bein' out there so early . . . it was still, but so *alive.*" She twisted down another orange half, squeezing the juice through the metal press. "And I couldn't help considerin' the *wonder* of it all. I mean, a tree startin' from a seed smaller'n a thumb and growin' into something taller 'n' wider'n a haystack? Bloomin' year after year and somehow combinin' things as different as earth and air and sun and water, and turnin' them into a bounty of sweet-tasting fruit?" Her eyes were shining like she was bearing witness in church. "It's nothin' short of a miracle when you stop'n think about it."

Mother stared at her.

Nonnie stared, too, and now *both* of her eyebrows were raised.

Then Mother said, "Well, that's very poetic of you, Ginny Rose," and got busy setting the table.

After breakfast, I lent Ginny Rose a shirt and some dungarees and managed to escape outside with her by promising Mother I'd be back in a jiffy. I didn't intend for it to be a lie, but while we were weeding through scrap lumber in the shed, I was delayed by a thought. "What's your plan?" I asked. And when she began explaining how she planned to build the sunshade, I stopped her. "For transporting your brothers, I mean."

"Oh," she said, and grew quiet.

"Because I'm thinking the blanket you said they're wrapped

in will be disintegrated. And who knows what state *they're* in. So we're going to need something to put them in." I took a deep breath. "Have you figured that piece out? And is there a car? Do you drive?"

Her face twitched around, and soon her eyes were brimming with tears. I thought I had upset her, but then she threw her arms around me and said, "You weren't foolin'? You'll help me?"

I laughed. "Well, it does seem more than a little crazy, but I can't let you do it alone."

She pulled back. "I don't know how I'll bring them to the cemetery. They're buried in Garysville and—"

"Garysville? Isn't that way up north?"

"It would take three, maybe four hours to drive there from here," she said with a little shrug, like it was no big deal. "We have a truck, but . . . I'll have to come up with an excuse for usin' it. And there's no guarantee I'll be able to find them . . . or that they're still there."

I could see her mind running to horrible places, so I tried to bring her back to the here and now. "But if you do find them, you'll need to be ready." I turned back to the scrap wood. "So . . . what if we build a box for them out of this?"

"A . . . a coffin?" she asked, her eyes wide.

"Yes."

"But . . . there isn't enough wood here to build one *and* the sunshade."

"Say!" I said, suddenly struck with an idea. "Come with me!"

Ginny Rose followed me outside and over to a place near the property line, where Bobby and I had stacked palm fronds that had blown down from the trees. "Instead of covering the roof frame with wood, why don't we lash some of these on top? It would look like an island paradise stand, which would be very inviting, and it would leave us wood for . . . the other thing."

"That's a wonderful idea!" she said. "But . . . are you sure? About helpin' me with the boys, I mean?"

"After what you told me last night? Yes. I'm sure. I don't think many people would understand, so I agree that we should keep it quiet. And I *do* think things are made all the more complicated by keeping it secret from your parents, but if that's how it has to be, we need a plan. A real plan. One that's secret from my parents, too, because"—I shook my head—"they would forbid me to help you."

"I don't want to get you in trouble," she said.

I could see that Ginny Rose was wavering, and that she was a little scared we might actually do this. So at that moment I might have been able to turn her away from the idea altogether, but I'd spent the night thinking about her family. My heart had ached from the pain in Ginny Rose's voice as she'd talked about her brothers and her need to find some way to put the past to rest.

So instead of trying to turn her away from the idea, I tried to sound decisive as I said, "I won't get in trouble for building a box. Let's plan on that."

Ginny Rose nodded. "But first, the shade."

And since she thought it would be handier to do some of the cutting and framing work near all the tools instead of by the fruit stand, we set up sawhorses outside the shed. Then we dragged some palm fronds from the property line to a spigot by the shed, because they were filthy and full of spiders. And I'd just gotten a hose and a broom to clean them when Mother's voice came cutting through the air. "Peggy! I need your help in here!"

"Darn," I said, and promised Ginny Rose I'd be back to help move things across the road when my duties inside were done.

My mind was so full of other things that I had no problem ignoring Mother's agitation as we worked together in the kitchen. She had the radio on low, and it ran through tunes by Guy Lombardo, Benny Goodman, Glenn Miller, and Count Basie. But even "the sweetest music this side of heaven" couldn't seem to create a truce between us. I rolled the pie crusts, filled and topped the tins, and rotated the baking as she worked at restocking our supply of jam. Through the heat and steam, the only sound from either of us was Mother's heavy sighs. And there were a lot of them.

At last she turned off the radio and said, "I'm sorry about my reluctance toward Ginny Rose earlier. She seems like a fine girl." She sighed again. "And I'm working on your father regarding that other matter. But it's going to take some time."

Her comment about Ginny Rose was a shock. Of course it was true, but apologies in our house went one way, and her saying she was sorry was, I could see, a difficult swim upstream. "Thank you," I said. "For saying that about Ginny Rose." Then I added, "And for talking to Father." I began pulling the last batch of pies from the oven. "But meantime, am I still bribing my way into places with peaches?"

"Meantime, you have to have a little patience."

It was my turn to sigh. I was pretty sure this meant Father would put her off for eternity. Which also meant that I was the one who needed to make a change.

But what?

Unexpectedly, a change of sorts started with a stranger

passing through as I was setting up the stand. He was driving a gleaming Cadillac convertible with spotless whitewall tires and was dressed in a sharp suit. "Hey, sweetheart. How much for a pie?" he asked, pulling up next to me. The woman beside him had a beautiful silk scarf wrapped around her hair, stylish sunglasses perched on her powdered nose, and perfectly painted cherry-red lips and fingernails.

I was suddenly self-conscious of my steam-frizzed hair, my farm-girl hands, and my sweaty face. Something snapped in me, and out of my unpainted lips came "Pies are two dollars each."

It was twice the usual price.

And then those lips of mine added, "Fresh-baked this morning with peaches from our family orchard."

He reached for his wallet and said, "I'll take two."

When he was gone, I put two dollars in the till and two in my pocket. In one transaction I'd made as much money as I did in a *month* from allowance. My head felt light, swimming with excitement. Talk about pennies from heaven!

It did feel strange, though. Because in all the years I'd worked the stand, I had never even *thought* about doing something like this. Not just because Mother kept a tally of everything that rolled out of the kitchen and reconciled those tallies with the money I delivered at the end of the day, but because I just wouldn't.

I'd be stealing from my *family*.

But now that view had been shaken. Wasn't I putting in my labor, spending my *life* working for something that I wasn't a partner in after all?

So I felt justified in pocketing the two dollars. And I didn't stop there. I started a tally sheet of my own to keep track of the extra quarter or two I charged likely prospects who weren't regulars. Doubling the price had been brash, and I certainly didn't want to drive customers away, so I adopted a slow-and-careful approach to price hiking. If Mother couldn't convince Father to cut me in or increase my allowance, I'd do this until I figured out a better way.

The stand was busier than usual, even for a Saturday. So I didn't have a chance to check on Ginny Rose or find out why she hadn't brought the parts over to assemble the way we'd planned. There wasn't even time for a lunch break. Thank goodness for Nonnie, who came out with a sandwich and said she'd given one to Ginny Rose, too.

I could hear hammering from time to time in the distance, but I didn't actually set eyes on Ginny Rose until almost five o'clock, and then I couldn't *believe* my eyes. She and Bobby were waddling toward the stand, each holding two posts of the finished sunshade, and it was *beautiful*. The wood was painted white, with wide front and side boards boasting *Fresh Peaches! Homemade Pies & Jams!* done in deep blue-and-orange lettering, and there were smiling yellow suns bursting from the corners. All that cheeriness with the palm-frond roof *did* make it look like it belonged on a paradise island.

"Oh, *wow*," I cried, and positively danced around as they settled it into place. "Look at that! Just look at it!" Then we all stood back and admired it together.

"You won't be able to bake enough pies to keep up," Bobby said, tipping back his cowboy hat with a grin. "And you'll move more peaches, too."

He was beaming, proud as a peacock. And I was just piecing together that he'd done more than simply help Ginny Rose carry the shade across the street when Lisette rolled up in her car.

The world seemed to freeze in place. Lisette held still behind the wheel and stared at us, Bobby's mind was clearly stunned beyond function, Ginny Rose's face had switched from joyful to placid—a calm surface with unknowable forces churning beneath—and I stood trapped in between.

Lisette stepped out of the car and, like a switch had been flipped, everyone began moving.

"I've got to get back," Bobby said, giving Lisette a wide berth in one direction.

"And I've got to get home!" Ginny Rose said, doing the same in another.

"Wait!" I called, but neither turned around.

"Well," Lisette said, admiring the shade. "This is a big improvement." She was carrying a cardboard box, the top flaps woven closed.

"What have you got there?" I asked, because the box was hard to ignore.

"A peace offering," she said, passing it to me.

I opened the flaps and knew immediately what was inside—hand-me-downs.

"I'm really sorry about Jimmy," she said as I looked through the box. "I know your pride wouldn't let you admit it last night, but if you are sweet on him, he's all yours! And I'm really, really sorry."

I kept my eyes on what was in the box, trying hard not to lash out at her. I'd been perfectly clear last night that Jimmy had nothing to do with what was going on with me. And yet, here she was, acting like she knew better. For the first time in all the years I'd received them, I didn't want her clothes. Or, more precisely, I didn't want what they represented.

These were her discards.

Jimmy Dickens was her discard.

Was that all she thought I was good for?

But at the bottom of the box was a pair of shoes that I really *did* want.

Not for me.

For Ginny Rose.

So instead I said, "Thank you for these." Then I closed the flaps and said, "But you're wrong about Jimmy. I've never had feelings for him." I leveled a look at her. "There *is* something you should know, though."

And then I just let loose. I told her how I'd fallen for Rodney. How the mere sight of him made me swoon. How I'd longed for him, dreamed of him, could lose whole hours to thoughts of him, but had never told her because I thought she would disapprove. I laid myself bare, and the whole time Lisette looked at me—not with shock or sorrow or even regret—she looked at me with *pity*, her head shaking ever so slightly.

I didn't need a translator to read her thoughts. They were coming through, loud and clear:

How could I think that Rodney St. Clair would ever have feelings for *me?*

Naïve, simple, farm-girl *me?*

But all her look did was convince me to tell her the rest— about running into Rodney at Woolworth's, about our ride back to Ferrybank, about singing along to the radio together, and about what had happened after he'd parked the car. And as my story unfolded, the look of pity vanished along with the color in her cheeks.

"No!" she gasped at last.

"Yes," I replied.

And then all the color rushed back to her face, and she cried, "You're lying!"

Her words hit me like a hard, painful slap. "What?"

"You're lying!" she cried again, moving quickly to her car.

It took a stunned moment before I ran after her. "Lisette! Stop!"

But she didn't stop, or even look back. She just got in her car, slammed the door, and raced away.

20

Ginny Rose

MAYBE SOMEDAY

The dry trill of a Brewer's sparrow wakes me near dawn. I slip over to Peggy's window and breathe in the cool, damp morning. The trill stops, leaving the air still—like the orchard's holdin' its breath, too, waitin' for the warm glow of sunrise.

I spot a ladder lyin' beside a tree a few rows back. During the summers Papa and I worked for Peggy's family, I always wanted to climb an orchard ladder but wasn't allowed, and I stayed dutifully on the ground. But now I'm swept up by the same urge, and with nobody to stop me, I tiptoe downstairs, sneak outside, scurry into the orchard, and climb up the ladder. The air's sweet, and the miracle of the gifts nestled in the green arms around me fills me with a profound sense of awe.

Later, when Peggy and I are workin' in the kitchen, I get a little carried away as I try to explain myself to her mother and grandmother. They tolerate my gush of words but eye me like my collecting basket might be holdin' an egg or two that's cracked, which I *do* understand.

It's hard explainin' a miracle.

But their reaction keeps me from complimentin' them on the kitchen, which is its own sort of miracle. It's large, with a wood-block worktable in the center for preparin' food, deep double sinks under a window that overlooks the orchard, two large ovens with gas stovetops, and the biggest electric icebox I've ever seen. When Peggy asks me to fetch a pitcher of buttermilk from it for fixin' pancakes, I can't believe how much is stored inside.

But the miracle of the kitchen's more'n the size of things and the appliances. Like the orchard, it's how it *feels* bein' there. All around me are pots and pans, canisters of sugars and spices, and every kind of utensil you can think of. And with the room's blue-and-yellow paint trim and sunflower-patterned curtains, just standin' in this kitchen makes me want to trill like a sparrow.

Our own kitchen is tiny, rough-sawn, and old, with shelves built into unfinished walls. Even our kitchen in Oklahoma couldn't compare to this one. It was neat, with an ample work counter and a cast-iron stove, but we had no running water and no icebox. Milk and butter and such were kept in the pump shed, set in the cool stream of water the windmill pulled up from deep inside the earth. It kept things fresh enough, but gettin' from the house to the shed and back to fetch supplies often meant gettin' grit in your eyes and teeth, and dust in every pore. Winds may have turned the mill and pumped the water, but they also stirred the earth.

Still, I tell myself, livin' doesn't have to be *this* good to be good. Our kitchen now feels like luxury compared to cookin' on a potbellied stove fueled by trash and cow chips, but seein' this one gets me thinkin' that it wouldn't hurt to sew a pretty curtain for our kitchen window and bring some cheer into the place.

At breakfast, I meet Peggy's little brothers for the first time, and my heart leaps, then breaks. They're darling, so full of laughter and mischief, and they make me think of my own brothers and what they might've grown to be. I force back tears and finish breakfast quick, fightin' to keep dark thoughts at bay.

I have work to do.

Upstairs, Peggy lends me clean clothes and suggests we wash up before gettin' to work, which, after the steamy time in the kitchen, is a most welcome idea. But as we're sharin' the bathroom, Peggy holds out a small jar and asks, "Do you want to try some?"

"What is it?" I ask.

"It's called Mum," she says. "It helps stop odor." She swipes some from the jar with two fingertips, raises an arm, and smears it along the armpit.

An armpit that's shaved clean.

"I . . . I . . . ," I stammer. I understand now that Anna Mae isn't the only one to notice my problem, and it fills me with shame. "I've never shaved."

"Do you want to?" Peggy asks. And before I can blink twice, she's teachin' me how to wield a razor, first under my arms, then along my legs. It takes some time, and the Mum stings a little when I apply it, but I'm grateful beyond my embarrassment to have a friend help me out this way.

"Keep it," she says about the jar of Mum. "I have another one."

Afterward, as we head downstairs to begin work on the shade, I feel grounded again, and happy. But when we get to the back door, we run smack-dab into Bobby, who's on his way inside.

"Oh!" I say, takin' a little leap aside.

He keeps his head down as he walks past us with a grunt,

and I watch him go, wonderin' if he was ever full of laughter and mischief like his little brothers.

Which sends me straight back to thinkin' about mine.

On our way across the property, Peggy breaks the silence. "I'm sorry about Bobby. I don't know why he's such an oaf."

"I reckon he's mostly just shy," I say with a shrug.

Peggy gives a little snort. "That's very charitable of you, Ginny Rose."

Later that morning, Peggy's gone and I'm outside the shed nailin' two-by-fours together, ponderin' the buildin' of a box— a coffin—for my brothers, when Bobby comes up from behind. "Can I brace that for you?" he asks.

I jolt upright and the pieces fall apart. "Don't sneak up on folks!" I snap at him.

For a blink or two, he looks hurt but then clouds over. "I wasn't sneaking!" Regret grips me as he storms off, only before I can say I'm sorry, he turns back and says, "I just have trouble knowing if I'm wanted someplace or not!"

So now I feel awful. I recall seein' the way Lisette's treated him, and sure don't want to be put in that camp. So I call, "I'm sorry!" And when he stops and turns, I add, "And yes, I could use a hand. Kind of you to offer."

He hems and haws a bit and grumbles at the ground, but he does come back, and he helps me fasten two legs to a crosspiece— the side edge of the roof. Then he disappears into the shed, returns with a box of metal angle braces, and says, "These'll help secure those joints." And then he's off, without a nod or a smile or even a tip of his cowboy hat.

The angle braces do wonders to keep the joints tight, and I've got both the left and right sides of the shade framed when Bobby returns. "Good job," he says after inspectin' my handiwork. He says it with a frown, like he wasn't expectin' it to be, which rankles me. Who's he to tell me "Good job"? How many shacks has *he* had to build? And if he's so good at it, why's he never built a shade for his sister?

My mind turns back to workin' their orchard when I was young, and how Bobby, even back then, had approached things with a frown. And while my life then was worse than his by any measure, I'd *loved* workin' here.

Mainly because I'd loved bein' with Peggy.

Which makes me wonder if Bobby's ever had a true friend—someone who'd take time to teach him things the way Peggy has done for me; someone to help him find joy in even the hard things.

I have a pang of sympathy for him. And since I'm pretty sure his "Good job" was meant as a compliment, and since I'm figurin' out quick that he may be even less comfortable with himself than he is with other people, I smooth my ruffled feathers and say, "Thank you," then set about layin' out the roof frame.

He pitches in without my askin', and we work in silence awhile. It feels unnatural at first, but then I start to appreciate how skilled he is, how intent on the job, and how quickly the roof frame comes together with his help.

"Gotta get back," he says, leavin' me to tackle the metal bracing. But a short while later he returns—this time in a manner that doesn't spook me. "You thirsty?" he asks.

I've just taken a nice, long drink from the hose, so instead of an answer, what comes tumblin' from my mouth is "Do you happen to have a spare peach? I'd love one if you do."

He breaks out laughin'. It's a horsey hee-haw laugh—like he's laughed so little in his life, he hasn't quite figured out how. But when he sees me lookin' at him, he stops and says, "Whoa. You serious?"

I give him an even look. "Yes, Bobby Simmons, I am."

"Lord," he says, tippin' back his hat. He heads off without another word, and when he returns, it's with two ripe, perfectly blushed freestones.

I bite right into one and can't help but slurp at the juice and grin. There's nothing on earth more glorious than a tree-ripened peach.

I hand the other back for him to eat, but he shakes it off. Then out of the blue he asks, "Did Peg and Lisette have a falling-out?"

I'm struck dumb, peach juice oozin' between my fingers and down my wrist. When I recover, I ask, "What gave you that idea?"

He shrugs like it's no big deal. "Lisette usually drives her to the rink. Peg says she was there but . . . then she got all testy."

"Maybe she didn't want you nosin' in her business?"

"She wasn't testy at *me* for once—she was mad at Lisette." He takes a deep breath, holds it, then sets it free on a gush of words. "So what happened?"

I size him up as I rinse my hands. "You sure you want to know?"

"Yes!"

I take a long, slow count to ten. "Well, then," I say, but I make him wait while I turn off the spigot. And wait some more as I fetch my hammer.

Then I get back to work, swingin' nails into place as I talk. "Lisette thought she'd use Jimmy Dickens"—*whack*—"to make Rodney St. Clair"—*whack*—"jealous." *Whack, whack.* "Your sister"—*whack*—"doesn't see that"—*whack*—"as honorable be-havior." *Whack, whack, whack!*

"Are you . . . are you sure?"

I stand upright and look him straight on. "Yes, I'm sure."

"Maybe—"

"No maybe. She admitted it herself!" I get back to hammerin'. "So tell me this:"—*whack*—"*Why* do you like that girl?"

"Peggy *told* you?" he says, like he's accusin' her of high treason.

My head snaps up. "No one had to *tell* me. It's all over your face every time she's around."

He sputters like porridge on the boil, then rushes off without a word.

I get back to whackin' nails, which is far more satisfyin' than dealin' with some fool boy.

Peggy's grandmother brings me a sandwich around noon. She doesn't say much more'n "Thought you might like a bite to eat," but the sandwich says plenty—roasted chicken that's still a little warm, layered on with tomatoes and creamy mayonnaise, all of it burstin' out the sides of fresh-baked bread. I gobble up every last crumb.

By midafternoon, Bobby hasn't shown his face again, and though Peggy hasn't been by, either, I've made good strides on my own. The three parts—two sides and the roof—are now cross-braced and coated with some leftover paint I found in the shed, and palm fronds are lashed to the roof frame with scraps of wire. And I've just reached the point where I need help attachin' the roof to the sides when Bobby comes shufflin' along with a tall glass of lemonade in his hand.

I give him an even look, not sure if he's plannin' to offer me the lemonade or drink it himself.

He steps closer. "Because I'm an idiot," he says, holdin' out the glass.

It's taken hours, but I realize he's come around to answer my question. "Well, I'm not gonna argue with *that*," I say, acceptin' the glass from him.

He heaves a sigh and shakes his head and gives the earth a hangdog look. "Don't tell her, all right?"

"Lisette?" I snort. "No danger there." I take a long, grateful drink of the lemonade. "But my tellin' her wouldn't exactly be breakin' the news."

His hands go skyward. "How's it everyone knows?"

"I already explained that," I say.

"Swear anyway, okay?" he asks, and the poor boy looks ready to cry.

I frown. "Look, the only thing I've got in common with Lisette Bovee is your sister, which, as anyone can see, holds true for you, too."

"But—"

"So swearin' me to secrecy's not necessary, but you do have my word." I finish the lemonade and set the glass down. "Now, if you can put thoughts of that wreckin' ball aside for a few minutes, I could use a hand puttin' these parts together."

With his help, it doesn't take long. And as we're nailin' some wood braces at the top corners to stop the shade from rackin', Bobby asks, "How'd you learn to do all this?"

I give him a keen look, thinkin' that *he's* the one whose basket might be holdin' an egg or two that's cracked. Either that, or he's just plumb ignorant. "How d'you think?" I snap, drivin' in a nail with a single dead-aim swing.

His eyes pop at the swing, but then he turns away quick. "Sorry," he says, and I can tell he's pieced it together.

After we're done hammerin' and tackin' and fluffin' palm

fronds, he fetches a second brush from the shed and helps me finish paintin'. The coats dry quick in the afternoon sun, so I'm able to add lettering and festive touches to the sides. Bobby sticks with the job until it's done, and when we stand back to look at the shade, Bobby grins like a fool. "Well, will you look at that!"

I can't help grinnin', too. It surely does look good!

Bobby helps me put all the tools away and clean the paint-brushes, and soon we're walkin' the shade across the property to the fruit stand. It's heavy and hard to handle, but I'm determined not to let that show. Besides, I'm too excited to see Peggy's re-action to let the strain of it slow me down.

Peggy *is* thrilled. She dances around as we put it in place and is more excited than I've ever seen her. And Bobby's *still* grinnin'—something that I'm realizin' looks mighty fine on him.

So I watch, full of joy and pride and . . . belonging. And then who comes rollin' up to ruin everything?

Lisette Bovee, of course.

She steps from her car like she's on a movie set, her hair stylish, her hands gloved, her lips a silky red. All at once, I'm aware of my own appearance—dungarees, frizzy braid, hands and arms blotched with paint . . .

And then she takes a good long look at my shoes.

Bobby turns to jelly at the sight of her, and I've already shriv-eled up inside. So, like summer lightning, I excuse myself and hurry away.

Maybe someday I'll be strong enough not to feel like this.

Today is not that day.

21

Peggy

BIGGER THINGS

Father was very talkative at dinner, and all of it centered on what a fine job Ginny Rose had done building the shade. Bobby elbowed in a few times, pointing out that he'd helped, but his words were just spectators to Father's main show, and soon he bowed out and went back to his meal, though I noticed he was poking at his mashed potatoes more than he was eating them.

And then Father asked, "What was her motivation for building that thing?" and to my absolute horror, Mother replied, "The girl seems fond of climbing ladders."

This left Father puzzled, to say the least, but I read her meaning loud and clear. "Mother!" I cried. "This morning you said she was a fine girl. What changed?"

Mother gave Bobby a side glance. "I see now what she's after."

I shot up out of my chair. "He should be so lucky! *You* should be so lucky!"

But then Nonnie—quiet, none-of-my-business Nonnie—

gave Mother a sharp look and said, "I used to think the same thing about you, June."

My jaw dropped.

Mother gasped. "About *me*?"

Nonnie dabbed her lips. "Yes, dear. And see how wrong I was."

I gave Nonnie a grateful look, which she ignored, and then Mother hissed, "I'm nothing like her! It was a completely different situation! She's an—"

Nonnie's hand shot up. "Don't say things you'll live to regret." She gave Mother a sage smile. "Take it from one with experience in such matters."

Mother's eyes were huge, her cheeks steaming red.

"What is going on?" Father asked. He turned to me. "Peggy, why are you standing? What is this? Why can't we just eat in peace?"

"What this is," I said pointedly, "is Mother having awful thoughts about good people."

"What thoughts? What people?" Father asked, and Bobby looked equally baffled.

"Ask *her*," I said, throwing down my napkin and leaving the room.

"Peggy Simmons!" my mother shouted after me. "You get back here this instant!"

But I did *not* get back there that instant, or the next, or the one after that. I went outside to the orchard and loaded lug boxes onto the trailer. I was angry enough to do the whole thing myself, but before long Bobby appeared. "I got to ask you something," he said as he helped load the boxes.

"About what Mother said?"

He looked confused. "What *was* that about? And why'd you storm off? She said you're going through a phase."

I laughed. "Oh, is *that* what she said?"

"Never mind her," he said. "I want to ask you about something Ginny Rose said."

My mood immediately switched from annoyed to hopeful. He wanted to talk about Ginny Rose! And why should I be surprised? He'd helped her with the shade; he'd been grinning ear to ear when they'd delivered it. Of course he was starting to see how wonderful she was!

But then I panicked. Had she told him about her brothers? About our plans? Bobby wouldn't keep something like that to himself! He would tell Father, and then . . . the whole scheme would come out. It would never happen.

A voice in my head said, *Maybe that's for the best.*

It was a cowardly voice, I knew.

No, I countered, it was a *sensible* voice.

But then Bobby broadsided me. "She said Lisette went out with Jimmy Dickens to make Rod St. Clair jealous. Is that so?"

I stayed planted in place, staring at him. Then I hopped onto the tractor and fired up the motor. "That is one hundred percent true and accurate," I shouted at him as I ground the gearshift. "Did Ginny Rose volunteer that information, or did you ask her?"

He pulled himself onto the trailer. "I asked," he admitted.

"Then you deserve all the pain you're in," I shouted back, and revved the rig forward.

Neither of us spoke as we set the boxes, and afterward I went straight for my bicycle.

"Where are you going?" he asked as I rode past him. The

surprise on his face was understandable—it was time to wrap up the day, not ride off into the dark.

"I'll be back," I answered.

"What if they ask where you went?"

"Tell them I'd be home if they'd let me talk on the phone for more than thirty seconds."

"I'm not telling them that!"

"Then don't!" I called, and made a beeline for the road.

Inside the orchard, the day's heat had been palpable—humid and sticky—and it had created a stewpot of uncomfortable feelings inside me as my mind had churned about Lisette.

How dare she call me a liar!

How dare she toy with Jimmy's heart!

How dare she stare at Ginny Rose's shoes that way!

But the night air felt cool and calming as I pedaled my way to Lisette's house, and by the time I arrived and saw light shining through her open window, I felt more relieved than angry. We could work this out. We had to! We'd been friends far too long to let a boy come between us.

Even if that boy was Rodney St. Clair.

It was too late to ring the bell, so I stood under her open window and whispered, "Pssst! Lisette!"

Her face appeared almost immediately. "Peggy?"

"May I come in?"

Her voice was full of emotion as she cried, "Yes!" She disappeared from the window, and in a flash the front door flew open and she was throwing her arms around me. "Oh, Peggy! I'm so sorry!"

Her eyes were swollen and rimmed red, and her hair was a mess, sticking out every which way. She took my hand and pulled me upstairs. Into her room we went, past her sewing machine and a dress form draped in fabric, across her beautiful new rug, and onto her four-poster bed, where she swept aside a spread of *McCall's* and *Seventeen* magazines, then tugged my arm so I'd climb on, too.

"What on earth happened?" I asked, because clearly something had.

"I went to confront him," she said, leaning against the headboard, hugging her knees tight to her chest.

"Rodney?" I asked, which was silly, but it just came out.

She nodded. "Because of course you didn't lie. You never lie!" She looked right at me, her eyes glassy. "How could he go after my best friend? I couldn't believe it, couldn't even *imagine* it." She gave me a pleading look. "Why didn't you tell me you liked him? When did that start? And how did I not notice?"

I swallowed the answers. They went down hard and rough, but I could see that—maybe for the first time ever—Lisette was really hurting.

Instead, I forced a laugh. "I could ask you the same questions. I really thought you hated him!"

She frowned. "I didn't want to admit it, either. Or let on that I've been playing hard-to-get with him for months. And then, the afternoon we were both at the fruit stand? When Bobby came out on his horse and it was all so . . . uncomfortable? Rodney invited me to meet him at the park. He said he wanted to talk. So I met him and he was so . . ."

Her voice trailed off helplessly, so I prompted, "Charming?"

"Yes! And we took a walk down to the river and, well, one thing led to another and I . . . I let my guard down." She hastened to add, "Not completely! But enough so that I'm . . . I'm really embarrassed!" Her eyes spilled over. "I believed him! I believed all his smooth lines . . . which, come to find out, were the same things he said to you, and probably the same ones he's telling Vivian Yelsen this very minute!"

"Vivian Yelsen?" I asked. She was a classmate, quiet and reserved—one I didn't know well.

"Yes! When I called his house, his father said Rodney had gone to Dolly's. So I was on my way there to confront him when I spotted him driving the other way with Vivian nuzzled beside him." Her hands flew up to cover her face. "How could I have been so stupid?"

I moved closer. "He's criminally handsome and utterly charming, that's how."

"How can you not hate me?" she wailed. "*I* hate me, so how can you not?"

Seeing her in such pain, I found it easy not to hate her. But why *wasn't* this—any of this—bothering me more? I'd been head over heels for Rodney, and now . . . ?

I took a deeper dive into the truth and realized that the feelings I'd had for Rodney seemed suspiciously like the ones Bobby had for Lisette.

And what a sobering thought *that* was!

But I also saw that having Lisette to share my feelings with—knowing she understood completely now—was giving me conviction.

He was a cad. A smooth-talking, belt-notching cad.

And then, looking past the place inside my heart where Rodney had landed, I could see that learning more about Ginny Rose's life had distracted me and put a spotlight on something far more worthy than winning the affections of a handsome boy.

And the truth was, I liked the way being around Ginny Rose made me feel like I could stand taller, be stronger, act *braver*.

Not that my parents were appreciating the change in me, but for some reason that didn't bother me the way it might have. Maybe because the change felt . . . justified.

I was also relieved to have escaped Rodney's advances with my dignity mostly intact and felt awful for Lisette that she couldn't say the same. All told, it made me pity Lisette, not hate her. So I clutched her hands in mine and said, "He tricked you into thinking he cared. *He's* the one who did something wrong, not you. And now that this is all out in the open . . . how can I be mad at you? He broke my heart, too, you know."

She gave me a puzzled look. "After the way you talked about him this afternoon . . . how can you just push your feelings aside? And after the way I treated you?" Her eyes filled with tears. "I didn't think you'd call me back, let alone come over."

I broke away. "Call you back?"

She flicked off her tears. "Your mom didn't tell you? She said you were out working in the orchard. Was she lying? Did you tell her what I said? What I *did*? Does she hate me even more now?"

I tried not to cringe at the truth in her last question. Mother had remarked more than once that Lisette had too much drive and not enough direction, and that someone should place a firmer hand on the wheel of her life. I'd tried to shield Lisette from the disapproval, but I could see now that I'd failed.

Still, I rushed to assure her. "No! I *was* in the orchard. I didn't go back inside the house before coming over, so she didn't have the chance to give me the message. And no, I didn't tell her a thing." My voice pulled up short as I remembered my conversation with Bobby.

"What is it?" she asked, seeing my mind whirring.

"Bobby . . . well, Bobby knows about you trying to make Rodney jealous."

She waved it off. "I don't care what Bobby knows. What I really care about is that you don't hate me. Everything is such a mess! We're moving into that awful house—"

"Awful?"

"Not the house, the situation! Daddy insists it's just business, and Mom's going along with him because the house is in Oakvale, but people are gossiping and I'm embarrassed, and I . . . I . . . without you, I have *nobody* to talk to."

It was a strange thing to realize this was true. I always saw myself as being lucky because she'd chosen *me* to be her friend, thinking she could have chosen any number of other girls. But maybe the reason she didn't have other friends was because it *wasn't* easy for her to make them. I knew she was a nice person, but her sheen *was* intimidating. And since her solution to a problem was always to polish, her presence could be like sunlight bouncing back from a mirror.

And maybe the reason *I* hadn't developed a larger group of friends was because if someone else got too friendly, she began polishing. Analyzing things now, I was beginning to see that maybe she didn't *want* anyone else in our group.

As if underscoring my thoughts, she said, "And now that you've got Ginny Rose . . ." Her voice tapered off helplessly, and she began to cry again.

I moved forward a little on the bed. This conversation had not gone at all as I'd expected. I'd left the orchard upset with Lisette— angry, even—yet here I was, feeling like *I* was the one who had injured *her*. Normally, I would have rushed in with assurances.

Even an apology. But this time I couldn't—no, *wouldn't*—let her lead me down that well-worn path.

"I've known Ginny Rose since I was a little girl," I said softly. "Maybe if you think of her as being my sister? You wouldn't mind her if she was my sister, would you?"

Her head didn't shake. It didn't bob. It just hung over her lap, dripping tears.

"Lisette?" I prompted.

"That would be worse!" she cried, looking up suddenly. "A sister is like a built-in friend forever! And who do I have? Nobody!"

"That's not how I—"

"And Ginny Rose hates me!"

"She doesn't hate you."

"Sure she does! And all because my father's a banker. Like I have any control over what Daddy does?"

"Look, she's had a really hard life. And a lot of that had to do with what the banks did to—"

"I know! But I asked Daddy about it, and he told me that it wasn't the banks' fault! He said farmers overborrowed and expanded too fast, and that too much plowing and too many years of drought caused them to go bankrupt! And then they all came *here,* swarming the state looking for work when there wasn't enough of it to go around. So maybe she's had a really hard life, but bankers have nothing to do with the weather or droughts, so she shouldn't blame *me* for any of it!"

That sounded suspiciously like what a banker would say, but I didn't know enough about the Dust Bowl to argue one way or the other. What *was* clear to me now was that my hope of Lisette and Ginny Rose becoming friends was fading fast, and it made me feel stuck and *sad.*

No matter *why* Ginny Rose's family had become destitute, I couldn't just reason the effects of it away. No one should have to live the way the Gilleys had. No six-year-old should have to bury her brothers in a ditch.

So . . .

Maybe if Lisette knew about that?

Maybe if I let her in on . . . the situation?

Maybe even let her in on our plans?

No! I slammed that door shut in my mind. What was I *thinking*?

And then very quietly Lisette said, "Please tell me you're going to give her the shoes in that box of clothes."

I blinked at her, not quite sure I'd heard right. "You *want* me to?"

"Yes! Please! Her shoes are . . . well, they're in shambles. Haven't you noticed?"

"Of course I've noticed. But I didn't think you'd want her wearing your shoes."

She rolled her eyes. "Just don't tell her they're from me." Then she sighed and said, "Now can we get back to Rodney?"

"Get back to him? What we need to do is forget about him!"

"But how?" she whimpered. "He's broken my heart! And I'm so embarrassed."

"Stop that. It was *his* wrongdoing, not yours."

"So why doesn't it feel that way?"

I studied her a long time. Finally I said, "You need something bigger than Rodney in your life."

"Something bigger than *love*?"

"Something more important."

"More important than *love*?"

"It's not love!"

"Maybe not for you . . . !"

"Stop that, Lisette! Of course it felt like love! But it was just a mirage! What you need is something that *gives* you strength instead of stealing it. All Rodney did was break us down. Our knees turned to jelly, our hearts fluttered, our convictions crumbled. . . ."

She laughed bitterly. "Isn't that the truth."

But now it was her turn to study me. And I could see her actually take me in. Carefully. Deeply. And as my cheeks warmed under her scrutiny, she asked, "So what 'bigger thing' got you over Rodney?"

I turned away.

"Peggy Simmons. What are you holding back from me?" Her eyes narrowed. "What is it? *Who* is it?"

I shook my head.

"Tell me!"

"I . . . I just . . ." I threw my hands in the air. "There are *lots* of things. Things bigger than a boy."

"Name one."

"War! Famine! Death! Figuring out what we're doing after high school!"

"After high school is a whole year away, so don't try dodging with that!" She frowned. "Also, the war is over, nobody around here's starving, and there's been no death in either of our families."

Again, I looked away.

She wove her arms across her chest. "Peggy Simmons, you are not leaving until you tell me."

But how could I? I was sworn to secrecy by Ginny Rose!

But . . . thinking back . . . Ginny Rose had never asked for that. She'd only said her *parents* couldn't find out. Which, of course they wouldn't. The Bovees and Gilleys lived in completely different worlds.

I tried to stop that train of thought, but once it was rolling, it began picking up steam. Letting Lisette in would *have* to create a new understanding. After all, how could she admire Ginny Rose the way I did if she saw her as just another soul in a swarm of poor migrants? Maybe Ginny Rose couldn't hide being poor, but that didn't make her a leper. Her condition wasn't contagious! Although . . . as the train rumbled faster, I glimpsed the notion that her bravery might be.

I took a deep breath. "May I use your phone to call home?"

"Won't your mom be mad if you call this late?"

"Doesn't matter. She already is."

"At you? Why?"

I shook my head. There was so much she didn't know. "It's a long story. It involves Doris."

"*Doris?* Well, start talking!"

"Let me call home so Mother doesn't worry."

"Can you spend the night?"

I slid off the bed. "Probably a good idea. I'll tell her that's what I'm doing."

"You'll *tell* her?"

I shrugged. "I'm pretty fed up with asking."

Her jaw dropped. "Well, good for you!"

But as we tiptoed downstairs to the telephone, I couldn't help wondering if my new devil-may-care attitude might end up being *bad* for me. And maybe not just for me.

But the train had already left the station.

It was too late to jump off now.

22

Ginny Rose

REFLECTIONS

I roll in from my day of buildin' Peggy's shade to the rumble of a long freight train lumberin' by and the sight of Papa's legs stickin' out past the front tire of our truck. I notice that his leather soles are nearly worn through at the balls of his feet. I guess I'm not the only one in need of new shoes.

Curses are comin' from the truck's underbelly, so I step off the bike and call, "Can I give you a hand, Papa?" over the rumble.

"Ginny Rose!" comes his voice. "Yes! I could sure use it."

I take a quick look inside the open hood as he scoots out from under the truck. The engine block's clean as a whistle, despite it bein' nearly twenty years old. When Papa's standin' beside me, I ask, "What's wrong with her?" fallin' into the way we always talk about Faithful.

"I'm tryin' to install a rebuilt alternator, but the fan belt keeps slippin' off the bottom pulley." The freight train ambles by, and the clackin' of steel wheels begins to fade as Papa says, "If you could go under and keep it looped on while I set the part, that would be mighty helpful."

I'd hurried to fetch my things before leavin' Peggy's, but I'm still wearin' her dungarees. And since they're already in need of washin', I say, "Sure," and scoot under the truck on my back until I'm lookin' up through a space by the engine block.

Papa's face gazes down at me, and the sight of him catches me off guard. Maybe it's the shadows, or the position he's in, but he suddenly looks old. He's always been a wall of strength around us, but from my view through formed metal, rubber belts, and black hoses, I see the deeply weathered face of a man whose hard years have finally caught him.

A pang of sorrow hits me, but then I see in his gaze that he's thinkin' thoughts about me, too.

Seein' me, too.

But . . . what's he seein'?

For a moment, guilt grips me and the air goes eerily still. Then the train whistle sounds in the distance and I break my eyes from his and turn to the job at hand.

I hold the belt in place while Papa hoists the alternator, then uses a crowbar to pry the part up so the fan belt's tight. "Now come up and hold this, would ya?" he says.

I work my way out from under Faithful and keep the crowbar pried as he tightens the bolt. When it's all snug and he's tested the repair, he says, "Thank you, Ginny Rose. I wasted half an hour tryin' to do that myself."

"So," I say, doin' my best to act casual, "you think maybe you've had to patch her one too many times?"

He gives me a curious look. "Are you sayin' I should give up on something that's seen us from Oklahoma to California, and then up and down the Central Valley again and again and again?"

"What I'm sayin' is she's tired and deserves a rest."

He laughs, "Don't we all."

"So . . . ?" I ask, holdin' my breath. It's not just that between the choke, the throttle, and the spark advance, gettin' Faithful fired up and runnin' smooth is a finicky business; it's that she *is* tired. Tired and creaky and apt to rattle apart any day now.

"Naw," he says, and starts for the back porch. "She's runnin' fine and can take us where we need to go. And if she should break down, anywhere around here's walkin' distance home, so . . . no need."

But Garysville's not! I want to cry. *And I sure can't walk that carryin' a coffin!*

But we're at the porch now, leavin' me no chance to say more.

When I walk through the back door, Mama says, "You're here." There's resentment in her voice and a frown to match, and it nettles me something fierce. I want to cast off any notion of makin' her happy because . . . what's the use? At her insistence, I spent the day payin' back a kindness that didn't need repayin', only to be greeted like a dog trackin' in mud?

But then Anna Mae comes at me like a shooting star. "You're here!" she cries, wrappin' her arms around me. Then the Littles are upon me, too, chatterin' like squirrels, wonderin' at the dungarees I'm wearin' and askin' about kittens-with-umbrellas. They all seem mighty happy to see me and to know that the dress is safe, and when Anna Mae whispers, "Mama was grouchy all day," I realize that I can't quit tryin' to heal Mama's heart. My sisters need her to find peace at least as much as she does.

During supper, I don't let on about how grand the sunshade

turned out. I play the whole thing down as simply bein' done and serviceable. I also keep my answers about skating to a bland minimum. It's plain to see there's been no fun had around here, and I've got better sense than to turn up the flame on a pot already simmerin'.

But after supper and cleanup, Anna Mae corners me in the latrine, closin' the door tight. "What was roller skating really like?" she asks, her voice low and urgent.

"Fun," I confess. "Mighty fun."

"Can I go with you sometime?"

"Sure," I whisper, and suddenly I'd like nothing more'n to take her. "They rent skates for a quarter. It costs thirty-five cents to get in."

"Oh," she says, her face fallin'.

"But I have a job now, and Papa says I get to keep part of my wages, so . . . I'll save up and we'll go."

"No foolin'?" she asks, and throws her arms around me again.

"My," I say. "Where'd my cagey sister go?"

"Still here," she says, breakin' away. "And I *did* do something I shouldn't have today. Promise you won't tell?"

"'Course."

Her voice goes soft as a breeze as she cups her mouth and connects to my ear. "I know what Mama's been cryin' over in her room."

"The boys, no doubt."

"That's right, but I found a picture."

"A *picture?*" As far as I knew, there were no pictures. Not even of us back in Oklahoma.

"It's from a newspaper," she whispers. "You're in it, too, is how I know it's them."

"*I'm* in it?"

"Well, you when you were little. And Faithful is, too, loaded sky-high with stuff."

I pull back, feelin' goosed. "Where'd you find it?"

She yanks me down and whispers, "Inside an envelope under their mattress."

"Are you tryin' to get yourself *killed*?" I ask. "And when on earth did you have enough time to snoop?"

"Shh!" She yanks me down again. "She locked herself in her room and had a cryin' fit while Papa was gone into town. So I peeked in through the window and saw her holdin' something. I spied long enough to see her put it away, and later when she was tendin' to the garden, I sneaked in and looked." Her face screwed into a frown as she stepped back. "I *knew* it had to do with those stupid boys."

"Anna Mae!"

"Well, how can she love them more'n us? And don't tell me it's not so!"

There's a tap at the door, followed by Bonnie Sue's little voice. "We want to come in, too."

"That's right!" Katie Bee's even littler voice huffs through the door. "Let us in!"

Anna Mae rolls her eyes as she opens up, but she stands like a roadblock in the doorway. "There's no room."

And she's right, there's not. There was barely room for just me before Anna Mae showed up!

But Bonnie Sue pushes in anyway. "What are you doin'?" she demands.

"Fixin' to brush our teeth," Anna Mae replies.

Katie Bee has wormed in now, too, and wiggles her way between legs to pull the little step stool from beneath the sink. "I want to brush, too!"

"Shoo!" Anna Mae says.

But the Littles are wedged in and goin' nowhere. And though we can't all fit around the rim of the pedestal sink, I lift Katie Bee onto the toilet seat and set Bonnie Sue in front of me on the step stool. Anna Mae quits protestin' and squeezes in by the wall, and somehow we manage to all get scrubbin' at the same time.

And then we're all spittin'.

And pullin' funny faces at each other.

And garglin' our water until it's spurtin' everywhere.

And gigglin' until we're nothing but silly.

Mid-laugh, I see Mama's reflection in the mirror. She's standin' in the open doorway with the strangest look on her face. It's soft and sad and happy all at once, and when she sees me lookin' at her, she gives a little smile and a nod, then silently moves on.

My breath catches. Then I close my eyes, take a deep breath, and hold tight to that smile in my mind.

It fairly breaks my heart.

23

Peggy

DIGGING IN

My sleepover with Lisette had us talking into the wee hours of the morning. I began by telling her about Doris—her apartment, her life, and the real reason she'd run off with Tom. Then I explained how trying to reason with Mother and Father had created an ember of anger inside me, because I could tell that no matter what I said or how I felt, things would stay the way they were.

"Well, I don't blame you for being mad, Peggy," Lisette said. "You work so hard, and none of that seems fair to me. But I still don't understand what it has to do with getting over Rodney. What am I missing?"

I frowned. Hugged a pillow. Frowned some more.

"Peggy?"

"Okay." I locked eyes with her. "But you are sworn to secrecy."

"I am?"

"Yes. You are. You cannot breathe a word of this to anyone, understand?"

"My goodness!" she said. "What on earth is going on?"

"Swear," I demanded, wishing Ginny Rose had made *me* swear, wishing honor could save me from the urge to tell.

"All right, all right," she huffed. "I swear."

"Not a word. To anyone."

"Fine!"

I began by stalling. I went on and on about Ginny Rose, recalling every detail I could about the things she'd been through, including burying her brothers. But at last Lisette interrupted me. "Peggy, please. Where are you going with all of this?"

So I spilled the rest, explaining things in logical steps, gently working my way to what Ginny Rose and I were planning to do.

And she was horrified.

"No. No. No, no, no, no, no!" she said, holding her cheeks. "You cannot mean that. You cannot be *thinking* that!"

So I tried to explain again the reasons, the urgency. "Ginny Rose said her mother has slowly been going mad."

"So change the *father's* mind! That's what she has to do! You can't just go digging them up yourselves! *That's* madness!"

Two tracks that seemed to be laid in different directions suddenly found the same depot in my mind. If Ginny Rose's father was anything like my own, his word was law, and going against it would yield nothing but unhappy outcomes.

And then another track appeared at the station. One with Lisette tied firmly to it.

In a rush of connections, I gasped, then said, "Would your father *not* buy the Oakvale house if you asked him to?"

"*What?*" she asked, clearly confused by the quick change in direction.

"If you and your mother both wanted to stay here in Ferry-bank, or move to a different house in Oakvale instead—one that wasn't under such a . . . cloud—"

"Stop it!"

"I'm not criticizing. I'm asking you something."

"What? What is it you're asking? And *why* are you asking? What does this have to do with getting over Rodney?"

"Look, your father says you're moving, so you're moving. And no matter how much you hate the circumstances that surround him buying that house, you would never be able to talk him out of it."

"He says it's a really good investment," she said miserably.

"So is robbing a bank, if you can get away with it."

"Peggy!"

"What he's done is wrong, and you know it."

"It's legal, so how can it be wrong?"

I stared at her.

"I know," she moaned. "I hate it. Mom hates it. But Daddy says everyone will forget about it in a few months; that it's just business and nothing to be ashamed of."

"People do not forget, Lisette. They may go quiet, but they do not forget."

"Why are you doing this to me?"

"Because I'm trying to get you to see something. You don't want to move into that house, your mother doesn't want to move there, but you won't in a million years be able to talk your father out of it, because he's in charge and what he says goes." I leaned in. "It's the same thing at my house. It's the same with Ginny Rose. And talking your father out of buying a house would be a small thing compared to talking my father into willing me part of the farm, which would be a hundred times easier than talking Mr. Gilley into moving his sons." I sat back and frowned, somewhat stunned by the thoughts that had rolled into the growing switching yard in my mind.

And that's when I glimpsed my future.

"I'm tired of Father holding all the cards. I'm tired of Rodney thinking he can manipulate me. I'm tired of me *letting* them!" I take a deep, calming breath. "So I'm not staying on the track I'm on, and neither should you."

"But . . . what would you suggest I do?"

"I don't know," I said, which was the simple truth. "What I do know is that thinking about all of this is a whole lot more important to me than pining away for that smooth-talking Rodney St. Clair."

I awoke the next morning before dawn. I'd had a dream, a vivid one, about Ginny Rose and me digging.

Digging, and digging, and digging.

My throat was dry, my heart pounding.

There'd been bones in my dream.

Lots of them.

I got up, dressed quickly, left Lisette a note, slipped out of the house, and pedaled hard toward home. Once there, I got straight to work preparing peaches. By the time Mother appeared in the kitchen, the day's fruit was blanched, peeled, pitted, and sliced.

And more important, a plan had become fully baked in my mind.

"Is this your way of apologizing?" Mother asked as she looked over the bowls of finished peaches.

I tore off my apron. "This is my way of making time to attend church," I said, then pushed past her and pounded upstairs.

"Church?" she called after me.

The alarm in her voice was almost funny. "Yes!" I shouted back. "Church!"

I cleaned up, dressed for church, and pocketed the money I'd skimmed at the fruit stand. I was hoping to escape without being noticed, but I should have known Mother would be waiting. "What are you not telling me?" she demanded.

Oh, so many things, I thought, but what came from my lips was "Do you have something against me going to church?"

"Don't for a moment think I'm that gullible. Church doesn't start for another hour!" Her jaw was set, her eyes hard. "Who is he?"

My cheeks warmed under her scrutiny; my heart raced. "If you must know, 'he' is my teacher's stillborn baby and he's buried in the church cemetery. I want to go early to put some flowers on his grave."

The granite forming her face cracked. "What teacher?" she asked, and this time it wasn't an inquisition.

"Mrs. Smith," I said. "So please." I moved past her. "I'll be back in plenty of time to run the stand."

I hurried out the back door and took my bicycle from the shed. But as I was pedaling out to the road, Mother called after me. "Peggy! Peggy, wait!"

I was worried there'd be more questions, but then I saw the cut roses she was carrying—one yellow and two white—and my heart went soft. There were wildflowers in a field on the way to the church, but this was much nicer.

"The poor dear," she said, placing the roses in my basket. She gave me a pitying look. "If you'd just told me . . ."

I studied her a moment. She didn't see her role in my silence, in my combativeness, in our impasse. It was all my doing.

All my fault.

I shook my head ever so slightly and pushed off. "I'll be back to work the stand," I said flatly, and rode away.

Telling my mother I was going to visit the grave site was not a lie. Between what Ginny Rose had told me about Babyland and Mrs. Smith's child being laid to rest there, I did want to see it for myself. But that was just a small part of what I planned to do.

I entered the cemetery with an unexpected pang of guilt. It had been years since I'd gone to visit Poppie's grave. Nonnie visited it weekly and had taken me with her many times when I was younger, but that habit had faded long ago. And since Poppie had died the year after I was born, I never knew him and didn't miss the visits.

But being at the cemetery now and not going to his grave felt somehow neglectful. So I took a quick detour and laid the yellow rose by his grave marker, then tried—and failed—to think of something meaningful to say before hurrying over to Babyland.

This was the first time I'd crossed the bridge that led into Babyland, and I was surprised by how much I liked the secluded area. It was a charming, peaceful spot, but it was more than that. The stuffed animals and dolls and toys laid on the graves made it feel like a nursery. I could almost imagine baby angels—or mischievous sprites—coming out after dark to play with the toys and each other.

I could almost imagine them around me now.

I laid the two white roses on Baby Smith's grave and then sat on a bench and just took it all in. No wonder Ginny Rose wanted her brothers here.

Of course she did.

Finally, I hurried over to a side door of the church and was caught off guard by how quickly I bumped into Mrs. Poole, the reverend's wife.

"Why, Peggy Simmons!" she said, bustling along. "What a pleasant surprise." She slowed, then stopped. "I assume those peaches are keeping your family busy day and night?"

"Yes, ma'am." It had been some time since I'd attended church, and standing under her appraising look now made me squirm. I had known her my entire life, and she'd always been strict, although full of affection for her "little lambs." She was someone who could corral kids or teens at socials and ensure they played nicely together; someone I would obey without pause or question.

But the past week had changed things. I was no longer a little lamb who would simply follow the shepherds in my life. Maybe braving my own path would get me lost, but it didn't feel that way. It felt like I was finding . . . *me.*

"Is something on your mind, dear?" Mrs. Poole asked with concern. "Would you like me to get the reverend?"

I looked into her expectant brown eyes and dug for courage. "I was hoping to talk to *you.*"

"Oh! Well, by all means, then," she said, and led me down two short hallways to a small office. She indicated the simple wooden chair in front of a tidy, kidney-shaped desk and sat in the green velvet chair behind it. "So, dear," she said, her clasped hands on the desk's leather top, "what's on your mind?"

"It's about my friend Ginny Rose Gilley."

Mrs. Poole's face remained placid. "Go on," she said, her voice betraying nothing.

"I understand she's shared her family's . . . *situation* with you."

"What situation are you referring to, exactly?" she asked.

"The one involving her brothers."

Mrs. Poole sat back a little. "Ah. And how did you come to hear about that?"

So I explained that Ginny Rose was a childhood friend who had recently come back into my life and that I wanted to help her put the past to rest. But Mrs. Poole gave no reaction, and I soon found myself swept up in an urgent rush of explanations, barely stopping short of confessing our plan to find the boys ourselves.

"My," she said, once I'd finished.

I hastened to add, "Ginny Rose doesn't know I'm here. And please don't tell her or anyone else what I've shared. The Gilleys are very . . . private. And Ginny Rose is buying the grave site as a gift for her family. She wants it to be a surprise."

"She did make that clear," Mrs. Poole said. "Which you must know. So I'm wondering . . . why, exactly, are you telling me this?"

I took a deep breath. "Because the longer this goes on, the worse things will get. Mrs. Gilley is not doing well. And at the rate Ginny Rose is able to save her wages it'll take her a long time to pay for the grave, and even longer if we want to buy a proper casket."

"So . . . ?"

"So I was hoping you might be willing to do a collection to help out."

Her eyebrows crept up, but I forced myself to hold her gaze. Finally, she said, "A collection for a family that's not part of the congregation, whose story cannot be shared, and whose identity cannot be named."

"A family," I said quietly, "that has suffered immeasurably and wants to put the past to rest by moving their little boys from a ditch grave to Babyland."

Her eyes broke from mine. "I don't know, Peggy. . . ."

"They may not be part of the congregation yet, Mrs. Poole, but they are our neighbors. And doesn't the Bible teach us to love thy neighbor as thyself?"

She gave me a sharp look, which immediately fell into a troubled one, then withered in defeat. At last she sighed and said, "Is there a picture of the boys? Something I can work with? We wouldn't have to say who they are, but we won't get more than a handful of beans without some personal connection."

I nearly sprang from my chair. "So you'll do it?"

"Get me a picture," she sighed. "I'll think about it."

"Well, while you're thinking," I said, producing every penny of the money I'd skimmed, "I'd like to make the first donation."

She frowned. "You *are* determined, aren't you?"

"Yes, ma'am."

"So it would probably be wise for me to simply agree now?"

"Yes, ma'am," I said with a smile.

She shook her head and sighed, then produced an empty cigar box from behind her desk and accepted the cash.

24

Ginny Rose

HIDDEN PICTURE

Sunday's not a day of rest for any of us but Papa, and he only takes half the day, which he spends readin' the Bible and old newspapers from work, or catnappin' on the porch while Mama directs chores that'll keep us from disturbin' his peaceful contemplations. It's the compromise that was reached followin' Mama's refusal to go to worship after the boys died, but Anna Mae states weekly that she'd be more'n happy to go to church if it meant bein' free of chores.

"They'll just be here waitin' when you return," Mama always replies.

Only today Mama's not around to direct or respond. Once Papa's on the porch and she sees I've got Anna Mae and the Littles busy kneadin' bread dough, she shuts herself in her room with the excuse of feelin' poorly.

"She's not sick," Anna Mae grumbles as she works her half of the dough. "She hates us is all."

"She hates us?" Katie Bee asks, her eyes big as saucers.

"No!" I slice Anna Mae with a look. "And she *is* sick." The words fly from my lips before I even know they're there, then linger like a deafening truth as all eyes turn to me.

"Is she gonna die?" Bonnie Sue asks, her tiny voice tremblin'.

I knead my ball of dough, leanin' in hard with the heel of my hands, pushin' the damp insides out. "It's not that kind of sickness."

Bonnie Sue sprinkles flour on my hands as dough sticks to my palms—her favorite role in bakin' bread. "Then what kind is it?"

Brokenhearted sounds so hopeless, and I don't want the Littles to be fearful, so I say, "The kind that lots of hugs will help."

Anna Mae snorts and rolls her eyes, so I cut her with another look and whisper, "Quit that. You're just makin' things worse!"

She scowls and steps back from the table, slappin' flour from her hands. "Easy for you to say. You get to go to work all week while we're stuck here."

"I *get* to?"

Anna Mae just keeps on. "She won't take us anywhere, she won't do anything with us. I can't *wait* for school to start, and I *hate* school." Her chin starts to quiver, and then she's gone, the front door slammin' shut behind her.

Bonnie Sue moves in to work the abandoned ball of dough and does a kissing sound, which makes Katie Bee giggle.

I stop kneadin'. "You know about that?"

Bonnie Sue snickers. "She thinks she's the boss of us, but we spy on her all the time."

I do a final roll of my loaf, then take on Bonnie Sue's, and when I've got both loaves risin' in the oven, I set about cleanin' the kitchen, sweepin' the floors and—Heaven help me—dustin'.

Bonnie Sue and Katie Bee follow me everywhere. Whether they're a help or a hinder, they're fun to have around, and I find myself growin' impatient with Mama's absence and her attitude. If she's truly in there cryin' over a picture of the boys, she's givin' power to darkness and blockin' out the sunshine that's fillin' up this very room! And how long can she expect that sunshine to last? How long before the Littles start feelin' abandoned and put upon the way Anna Mae does? How long before her darkness snuffs out all of us?

But short of askin' Papa to help move the boys—something I'm certain would end badly—I don't know how to do more'n I already am. What I do know is I have to try my best to protect the Littles. Mama *is* sick, and if Anna Mae's any indication, she's also contagious. So when the kitchen's clean and the bread's bakin', I call the Littles over, squat in front of them, and whisper, "Who wants to make pockets?"

They gasp and their eyes go wide. "Kittens with umbrellas?" Katie Bee squeaks.

When I nod, they both bob up and down, clappin' their hands, cryin', "I do, I do, I do!"

"Then go fetch Anna Mae. Tell her if she wants a new dress, she'd better get home quick."

"Why does she get a whole dress and all we get's pockets?" Bonnie Sue asks.

"That's right," Katie Bee says with a little stomp of her foot. "She's not good helpers like us!"

I scoop them into a hug and tell them they're mighty good helpers and that I'll think on what they've said. "Now shoo," I say, givin' each a quick kiss on the head. "Go fetch Anna Mae."

The three of them are back in short order, the Littles

breathless and full of excitement at the sight of the dress laid out on the table beneath scissors, a tape measure, and the sewing basket.

I cross my arms and level a look at Anna Mae. "I'm sorry," she says, without my havin' to say a word.

"You may be upset with Mama," I say in a hushed voice, "but it's not fair to use it as a way to cut out on chores. And I can't have you meetin' up with a boy alone for that long."

"She wasn't with him," Bonnie Sue offers.

"She was pitchin' pebbles," Katie Bee says.

"At weeds."

Anna Mae looks forlorn, and when I raise a questioning eyebrow, she holds back tears with a stiff frown and says, "I hate him anyway, so who cares?"

I pull her aside and whisper, "What happened?"

"His ma says I might have lice and to stay away." She frowns harder. "I told him I don't have 'em, but he didn't listen, so I hate him."

"Well, maybe don't hate him. Maybe just feel sorry for him." I put my arm around her. "'Cause if that's how he is, he's just plain dumb, and dumb sure as shootin' is the *last* thing you want clutterin' up your life."

She laughs a little at that, and then I break the bad news. "But, Anna Mae, I'm afraid there's a price to pay for all that time spent pitchin' pebbles while your sisters worked." I turn to the joyful kittens draped across the table. "Instead of a full dress for you, it'll simply be a skirt, so we can squeeze out pockets, collars, and sleeve cuffs for them." I give Katie Bee and Bonnie Sue a smile. "They've earned them."

The Littles jump up and down, overjoyed with their improved share of the kittens, and to my surprise, Anna Mae nods and says, "That's fair."

"Okay then. Anna Mae, I'll need your dress for a pattern. Bonnie Sue, Katie Bee, we'll have to make patterns for your parts, so go ask Papa for a page or two of the newspaper."

But just as the girls are set to disperse, Mama appears.

We all hold still like she's a wounded dog we're not sure will bite or accept comfort. She stops, too, takin' in the sight of us like we're a mountain in her path, one much too steep to climb.

I break the impasse by askin', "How're you feelin'?"

"In need of fresh air," she says, and escapes out the back door.

Suddenly full of life, Anna Mae whispers, "Do you want to see it?"

At first I don't know what she's referrin' to.

And then I do.

"No!" I whisper fiercely.

But it's a lie.

I very much *do* want to see it.

"All right, yes," I admit.

"I'll stand guard," Anna Mae whispers. "Be quick about it!"

The Littles are beginnin' to buzz with curiosity, so I bring them in close and say, "Go get newsprint from Papa." And to buy myself time I add, "Tell him you need a page with an advertisement for soap."

"Soap?"

"Yes," I breathe, actin' like it's a big, exciting secret. "Be very quiet, and very polite. Don't wake him if he's nappin', or rush him if he's not."

"But why?" Bonnie Sue asks.

"Just do as I say," I whisper, my voice full of mystery. Then I put a finger to my lips. "And *shhh . . .*"

"But why soap?" Katie Bee hoarse-whispers.

"Because it *cleans*," Bonnie Sue says in a superior voice, makin' no sense at all.

But Katie Bee doesn't know better and simply says, "Ohhhhhh," and then the two of them tiptoe toward the back door like they're sneakin' up on rabbits.

I waste no time hurryin' toward Mama's room and find the picture just where Anna Mae said it would be. But once I have it in hand, my knees buckle and I find myself sittin' on the edge of the bed not able to breathe.

There they are, my brothers, barefoot and filthy, tattered and sunbaked, lookin' at the camera with curious mischief in their eyes. Even in the state we're in, they've got *life* in them. A *future* to them. They're such darling imps in this picture that if it was all you had left of your sons, I could see cryin' over it.

I could see takin' nips of it until another taste was all I could think of.

I could see drownin' in it.

Tears spring from my eyes as I sit starin' at the picture, and I'm so caught up in memories of them that at first I don't hear the noises comin' from the kitchen.

And then I do.

"Anna Mae, let go! What are you doin'? Stop that!" Mama's voice commands. "I said let go!"

I put the picture away quick and fly from the bedroom, shuttin' the door behind me.

Katie Bee's voice carries down the hallway. "Ginny Rose says hugs'll make you feel better!"

"*Will* they, Mama?" Bonnie Sue asks, and her voice is muffled as if buried in the folds of Mama's skirt.

"Where *is* Ginny Rose?" Mama demands.

I duck into the latrine, close the door a moment, then open it again and step out into the hall just as Mama enters it.

"How *dare* you tell them hugs will fix me?" she seethes. "How *dare* you!"

"How *dare* you not hug them back?" I cry, the words shootin' out before I can stop them. And then a second round fires. "How *dare* you treat them like you hate them?"

She stares at me a moment, then slaps me hard across my face before escapin' to her room.

I hear Anna Mae gasp and the Littles begin to cry, so I hurry to scoop them into my arms and promise them everything'll be all right. Then I turn to Katie Bee and Bonnie Sue and push a smile into my throbbing cheek. "Did you get me that paper?" I ask. "Because it's time to make pockets!"

"And cuffs!" Bonnie Sue cries, her tears vanishin'.

"And collars!" Katie Bee adds.

"Yes," I say with a smile. "So where's the paper?"

They race to fetch it, the hallway fight all but forgotten.

Anna Mae, though, is not so easily distracted. "Do not give up," I whisper to her. And then, because I'm pretty sure she's been toyin' with the idea, I add, "And do not run away."

She shoots me a sharp look, confirmin' my suspicion.

"I'm plannin' something," I whisper. "Something I truly believe'll make things better. And I'm gonna need your help."

"What something?" she asks, suddenly brimmin' with curiosity.

"Not now," I whisper, buyin' myself time.

To my relief, she accepts this answer. Inside me, though, is the sinking feelin' that our family will fall apart before I can put all the pieces in place, and that what little light's still inside us'll be snuffed by Mama's rising storm.

Because it doesn't matter if it's in your house or in your heart.

Dust never truly settles.

25

Peggy

SETBACKS

The fruit stand was bustling after church service. Something about sitting still for a sermon seemed to give people an appetite, but today was unusually busy, and I was sold out of pies by one o'clock. Maybe it was the cheerful new shade that caused more last-minute swerves off the road. It did receive plenty of compliments, especially from Mrs. Gustoff, who was determined to take credit for it.

"I'm delighted you heeded my advice, dear," she said, proclaiming it so other customers were sure to hear. "This roof is a big improvement!" She leaned in conspiratorially. "And it seems to have helped sales, t'boot. Maybe I should get a discount?"

I laughed, but I could see she was serious, so I leaned in, too, and said, "You're not trying to get me in trouble, are you? Mother works hard, getting up before dawn to start the baking, so she's keen to track sales to the penny."

"Of course, dear, of course," she said, patting my hand. Then with a hopeful look she asked, "Perhaps just a peach?"

I slipped her one, knowing I'd now be doing so through the end of summer and not minding a bit. In just the last week, fruit in the orchard had become impatient, dropping more quickly than could be harvested and putting flies into a frenzy over the spoils earlier each day. So what was a peach worth this time of summer? We couldn't get rid of them fast enough. We didn't let on about that to customers, though, because money from summer harvest had to last until the next one, something families with year-round income didn't really understand.

So although the pies were sold out, the peaches and preserves were not, and I continued working the stand well into the afternoon. I also continued overcharging whenever the opportunity arose. If Mrs. Poole was skeptical about raising money from the congregation, I'd get donations a different way. I went after it with calculated determination instead of anger now, because the overcharges were no longer a means to pad my allowance but a way to right a much bigger wrong.

At least that's what I was telling myself when Jimmy Dickens appeared around half past three, sporting a dusty cowboy hat and boots that had seen more than their fair share of manure.

Jimmy Dickens, who had never once stopped by the stand before.

Jimmy Dickens, who was likely here hound-doggin' about Lisette.

"Why, Jimmy Dickens," I said with an edge of caution. "What brings you to our fine establishment?"

"Hi-de-ho, Miss Simmons," he said, sweeping his hat from his head and holding it against his chest. "I'm here with an apology."

This was a surprise, to say the least. "And just what, exactly, are you apologizing for?"

"It's not from me," he said, scuffing the dirt. "It's from Hot Rod."

I laughed. "Oh, Jimmy, you poor thing. He's too much of a coward to deliver it himself, so he sent you?"

"No, I'm here in the role of emissary."

I raised an eyebrow. "Emissary?" It was a much bigger word than I'd ever heard slip past the lips of Jimmy Dickens.

"That's right. I'm here to lay the groundwork for a truce, 'cause Rod's pretty sure he wouldn't get a word out before you pelted him with peaches."

"He deserves a pelting. A good hard one. But I wouldn't waste even rotten peaches on him."

It was his turn to laugh. "Oh, we both know that's not true."

I gave him a glare.

"Come on, Peg. There's not a girl in this county that doesn't want him, so quit holdin' a grudge and forgive him already. He swears he's sorry."

I went from insulted to furious in the quick blink of an eye. And before I could think it through, I'd snatched up a peach, rounded the stand, and hurled a lucky shot, splatting Jimmy Dickens at the hairline of his hatless head.

"Ow!" he cried, cowering back.

I hurled another and beaned him in the leg. "Get gone, Jimmy, and don't you dare show your face here again!"

"What about Rodney?" he called.

I hadn't thrown a peach at anyone since I was about ten years old, and then only at Bobby. But Jimmy mentioning it had put the idea in my head, and pelting him felt so good, I couldn't seem to stop. I threw a third peach, but this time he was ready and caught it neatly with his hat. "Thanks!" he called, then took a bite and grinned. "Mmm, delicious! I can see why Hot Rod developed a taste!"

"Oh! You . . . you . . ." But all I could do was sputter as he hurried away laughing.

I closed the stand and marched into the house, straight for the phone.

"What are you doing?" Mother asked from the kitchen, where she and Nonnie were working. I could smell corn bread baking and ham roasting. "You should be out there another hour at least!"

"I'm done," I said firmly. "And I'm making a call."

"But—"

"And I'd like some privacy?"

That, of course, was a hopeless request, so I just tried to talk in code when I got Lisette on the line. "JD was here," I said, straining to keep my voice low and calm despite how furious I was.

"And . . . ?" she asked.

This threw me. How did she know so immediately who JD was? We never called him that.

And then it suddenly made sense.

"You knew he was coming?" I breathed.

"I told Rodney I wouldn't forgive him unless he apologized to you."

"So . . . you're actually considering . . ." I eyed my mother. She was too close and too still to not be eavesdropping. I edged away from her and whispered, *"Forgiveness?"*

Silence greeted me from the other side.

"You can't be serious!"

"I'm not over him, Peggy."

I felt slapped. "Did you forget about Vivian?" I managed to ask.

Her voice came over cool and casual. "What's it matter now, if I'm his one and only?"

"He said that?" I blurted, my guarded wording now abandoned.

"Yes."

"And you *believe* him?"

"I do," she said, her voice glowing. "And he's agreed to my boundaries, so no need to worry about *that*."

My knees gave way and I folded onto the stool, completely gutted. It didn't matter what I said. It didn't matter if I forgave him or not—she was a goner.

"I have to go," I choked out, and hung up.

The handset was barely cradled when Mother asked, "Boy trouble?"

I wanted to scream. At her, at Lisette, at the world! But instead, I closed my eyes, took a deep breath, and said, "I'm going out for a while."

"Where? And for how long?"

"I *could* simply use the phone, but it's a private matter between friends, and you don't seem to be able to give me a private moment, even when I ask." I ran up the stairs to retrieve a few things, then back down to where, once again, Mother was waiting.

She followed me to the back door. "What makes you think you can just abandon your post and leave like this?"

I spun on her. "What makes you think you can hold me? It's Sunday, and I've been working since before dawn!"

"Everyone has!"

"No, they haven't!"

"Well, you went to church, so it all evens out!"

My jaw dropped. "So it's a crime now to go to church?"

"Not a crime, but you're needed here! I know it's hard, but we're in this together, and we all have to work until the work is done!"

I was so spitting mad, I could almost not form words, but I managed to force out, "Unless there's been a change you haven't told me about, there's more in it for some than there is for others." I charged outside toward the shed. "Don't wait dinner on me," I called over my shoulder. "I have no idea how long this will take."

It was a rash move, I knew, to ride my bicycle over to Ginny Rose's house unannounced, especially around dinnertime and on a Sunday. But I was furious with Lisette and couldn't take being home a moment longer. And I *did* have a compelling reason to go. I needed a picture of those boys, and soon. I'd been acting brave about the plan in front of Ginny Rose, but my courage was already starting to falter. My digging dream had haunted me throughout the day, and now I could see that I'd made a horrible mistake confiding in Lisette. Yes, she was sworn to secrecy, but her giving in to Rodney made me doubt her resolve about everything. How long would it be before she spilled the beans to him? And once she'd told Rodney, how long would it be before *everyone* in town was whispering about it?

Ginny Rose would hate me forever.

I would hate me forever.

So I had to get the plan moving, and moving fast!

I'd retrieved the Gilleys' address from my room, but I'd never been to Carriage Lane and had to stop twice to ask directions. I'd missed it because it was a narrow dirt road that Y'd off another road, then ran near the railroad tracks and through wild acreage. Had she given me a false address?

But then I went around a bend, and small cabin-style houses appeared on my right. They were tidy enough, with a good bit of land between houses, but I began regretting my impulse to drop in on the Gilleys. The thought of four girls and two adults living in one of these small places suddenly made our farmhouse seem luxurious, my bedroom enormous. And where I'd known Ginny Rose was embarrassed by the results of her family's misfortunes, I now found myself feeling embarrassed by the fortunes of mine.

Good sense along with a creeping cowardice were convincing me to turn around. But as I was about to do so, I rolled by a man who was leaning over the engine of an old jalopy truck parked near a house where three girls sat on a short run of steps doing hand stitching.

Even from the road, I recognized the fabric they were working, and my heart sank. If this was the Gilley house, was *that* the truck Ginny Rose was planning to drive to Garysville? It would never make it! It didn't look like it would make it to Oakvale!

I wanted to hurry away, but the girls on the porch had already seen me. And when one of them called something through the doorway behind her, a fourth girl appeared on the stoop.

Ginny Rose.

"Peggy?" she called, her voice a mixture of disbelief and apprehension.

"Do you have a minute?" I asked.

"Why, sure!" she said, attempting to weave between her sisters, only to have them jump up and reach me first.

"Are you Peggy Simmons?" the biggest of the girls asked, and one of the smaller girls gasped, "The one who gave Ginny Rose those dresses?" which caused the littlest one to say, "Uh-oh," and hide her sewing behind her back.

I laughed. "Yes, I'm Peggy. And you must be . . ."

"Anna Mae."

"Bonnie Sue!"

"Katie Bee!"

"Pleased to make your acquaintance," I said.

"I'm sorry about the dress," Ginny Rose said. "They were wild about it, so I gave in and let them each have a bit of it. The Littles are stitchin' collars, cuffs, and pockets; Anna Mae's makin' a skirt."

"I think that's wonderful," I said with a smile. "A little for everyone."

"Why're you here?" Katie Bee asked, bursting with curiosity.

Bonnie Sue slapped her arm. "That's not polite!"

"It's fine," I said. "I just need to talk to Ginny Rose a minute."

Anna Mae studied me suspiciously. "We do have a telephone, you know."

"So do we, but my mother doesn't like me to use it." I dropped my voice as if letting them in on a secret. "And when I do, she eavesdrops."

Anna Mae scowled. "A snooper, huh?"

I laughed. "You might say!"

Katie Bee tugged on my skirt. "Can you stay for supper?"

"Pleeeeeeeeeeeeease stay!" Bonnie Sue squeaked, bouncing up and down on bare feet.

"You don't want to stay," Anna Mae warned. "Which is not on account of what's bein' served."

"All right, girls, git," Ginny Rose said, flapping her hands at them. But then she called Anna Mae back and asked, "Where's Mama?"

"In the garden, last I checked," Anna Mae replied, looking over her shoulder toward the house.

"Make excuses for me, would you?"

"Like what?"

"Just do!" Ginny Rose said frantically, then shooed her off and pulled me under the eaves, where we were mostly concealed. "Why *are* you here?" she whispered. "Is everything all right?"

No, I wanted to say. *Nothing is all right. I made a terrible mistake. I might have ruined everything. And now that I might have ruined everything, I don't know if I can help you with your plan. Especially now that I know that it's an impossible plan! We'll never make it to Garysville in that jalopy! And I don't have a car! Or even a license to drive!*

But what came from my lips was "Do you have a picture of your brothers?"

She looked stunned. And instead of answering, she asked, "Why do you want a picture of my brothers?"

So I told her about my meeting with Mrs. Poole, hoping she'd be excited. But the farther along I got, the more troubled she seemed.

"The congregation doesn't know your family, and certainly not your brothers," I hurried to assure her. "Reverend Poole won't say their names, so it's safe. And it may bring in enough money to buy a plot."

"You shouldn't have done that," she said. "We don't take charity."

"Don't look at it that way! Think of it as neighbors wanting to help make things right."

But Ginny Rose looked almost hurt and said, "But *I'm* buyin' them a plot."

"But how long is that going to take you?" I asked. "And wouldn't it be nice to have a real coffin? One that's not made from old scrap?"

She looked away. I could tell she was struggling with a landslide of emotions, and that one of the rocks tumbling around in it was anger.

"Please don't be mad," I whispered. "I just . . . I don't know how long I can hold this in. I don't know if I can take this stretching on for a year, or even months." And then I confessed, "I had a dream last night that was . . . well, disturbing to say the least."

To my surprise she asked, "About the boys?"

I nodded.

Her face pinched a little. "About . . . findin' them?"

I nodded again.

"I've been havin' them, too," she said. "And I agree. I don't know how much longer I can hold things together here, either!" She sighed. "Mama seems to be gettin' worse by the day."

I held my breath and asked, "Any possibility of taking her *to* them? Of bringing a cross or a gravestone and leaving them to rest where they are?"

"They're in a *ditch*, Peggy." She sighed heavily. "Besides, they don't seem to be restin'. They haunt every wakin' moment around here, and dreams, too."

I felt gripped with anxiety. My life was falling apart all around me—my friendship with Lisette, the boy of my dreams, my family, my future . . . it was all such a mess, and I didn't know how I could take on any more.

But I'd given my word. I'd *volunteered*. Which meant there

was no backing out. And since I couldn't take standing still, there seemed to be only one choice left.

Moving forward.

"So," I said at last, "do you have a picture of them?"

"There's a newspaper clipping," she replied.

"May I see it?"

This question brought Anna Mae out from around the corner, giving us both a start.

"You sneak!" Ginny Rose cried. "And you're supposed to be buyin' me time!"

"I can help," she said defiantly. "I'm old enough, and if you're truly schemin' to move those boys, you're gonna *need* my help." She looked me straight on. "Let's start by showin' you that clipping."

This set into motion a whole series of furtive moves that involved all four sisters inside, with me waiting anxiously under a small window outside.

Suddenly the window opened a few inches and a hand shot out, dangling a square of newsprint. "Take it!" Anna Mae's voice whispered fiercely.

I did. It was yellowed, and tattered at the edges, but my first reaction to seeing it was *This is perfect*.

And then . . . it crushed me. The boys were adorable. Full of so much life and mischief, despite being barefoot and filthy and perched on a jalopy that was piled way past overflowing, with a mattress strapped on top of the cab and chairs hanging over the sides. And right there beside the boys, also barefoot and filthy but looking dark and serious, was Ginny Rose. She had the eyes of someone much older and was giving the camera a hard stare, one filled with strong will and defiance.

I slid down the wall, taking in the picture, taking in my friend—the girl I'd harvested peaches with all those years ago. Why hadn't she looked this way to me then?

I sat, wondering how many years the Gilleys had traveled from place to place with all their possessions piled onto their jalopy, wondering how long a family could survive that way.

"Give it back!" Anna Mae whispered, her hand sticking out through the slit in the window.

"Can't I borrow it?" I asked.

"No!" she cried.

"But I—"

"Give it!" Her hand wiggled frantically. "Now!"

So I did.

"You better git before Mama sees you!" she whispered. "She's in a state."

The window creaked closed, and the next thing I knew, I was pedaling for home, feeling more troubled than ever, that picture of Ginny Rose and her brothers seared into my mind.

August

26

Ginny Rose

UPROOTED

It's been a hard two weeks at the cannery since Peggy came by the house, and a hard two weeks at home for Anna Mae and the Littles. Anna Mae reports that, more'n ever, Mama shuts herself away when Papa's not around, leavin' her to run the household while Papa and I are gone to work.

I know it's all made worse by the upcomin' anniversary of the day my brothers died.

Which, of course, is the same day as my birthday.

I've learned to have no expectations at all for my birthday, other than the inevitable fight between Mama and Papa. He forgets what day it is, whereas she seems to do a silent countdown to it year-round. I've come to dread the day and have given up ever takin' center stage on it, and instead remind myself that survivin' those times is gift enough.

Still, as the day creeps toward us, Mama's mood darkens. I've spent evenings and weekends tryin' to lighten Anna Mae's burden and lift the mood around the house, but the only time there's a sense of calm is after supper when Mama tends to the garden and chickens.

The best day we've had was this past Saturday, when Papa allowed me to drive the girls into Oakvale. "Mama needs us out of her hair, and they haven't been anywhere this summer," I told him after I'd hung the wash on the line. "I'd like to take them to the library for some books, and maybe on a picnic at the park."

Once he learned Mama was tucked away in her room, he was all for it.

So I gathered some quick provisions and promised him we'd be home in time to make supper. Then, for the first time ever, it was just the four of us girls in Faithful, with Anna Mae by the passenger door, Katie Bee in her lap, and Bonnie Sue in the middle. We rolled the windows down, and I let the girls take turns honkin' the horn—*ah-ooh-gah!*—when no other cars were nearby. I did it once myself as we passed by Peggy workin' the fruit stand, which was bustlin' with customers.

"Is *that* the thing you built?" Anna Mae asked as we went by.

"Yep!" I said, and it made me swell with pride. Anna Mae's rarely impressed, and I could see that she was.

It turned out to be a wonderful day. We borrowed a stack of books from the library, and afterward we went to the park and picnicked in the shade of a big elm tree. I'd brought along an old book I was in the middle of readin' to them in case we were turned back at the library, but since we'd all heard that story many times before, I was more'n happy to switch to *Alice's Adventures in Wonderland* when they asked me to.

After, we all waded in the river. The Littles didn't want to leave the cool, clean water—"not ever!"—so I bribed them with ice cream cones at Sully's Drugstore, where I splurged two nickels so I could split a cone with Katie Bee and Anna Mae could split one with Bonnie Sue.

On the way home, I slowed when I neared Simmons Farm. It looked like Peggy was closin' the fruit stand down for the day, and I was just considerin' pullin' over when Anna Mae reached across the Littles and sounded the horn. *Ah-ooh-gah, ah-ooh-gah!*

Peggy jumped, and I scolded, "Anna Mae!" but then the Littles pounced on the horn. *Ah-ooh-gah, ah-ooh-gah!*

I pulled over, turned off the engine, and set the brake. "I'm sorry!" I called to Peggy, who was hurryin' toward us. "They were excited to see you."

Anna Mae bolted from the truck, followed by the Littles, who wasted no time wrappin' themselves around Peggy.

"Hi, girls!" Peggy laughed. "What a nice surprise."

"We're just on our way home," I explained as I got out, too.

She noticed the wide spread of books on the seat, and I laughed at her expression. "We've been to the library. The girls love a bedtime story."

"And a picnic story!" Katie Bee cried.

But Peggy was still lookin' inside the cab and still had a curious expression on her face.

"What's the matter?" I asked.

She reached inside the cab and pulled out *Alice's Adventures in Wonderland*.

But it wasn't the book she was interested in.

It was the bookmark.

"Is this the *same* two of hearts?" she asked, openin' the book to see it.

I smiled at her. "Yep."

"You've kept it all these years?"

I nodded. "It's been my one and only bookmark."

"Oh, Ginny Rose," she said, and wrapped me in a hug. Her eyes were a bit teary when she pulled away. "That's . . . I can almost not believe it." Then she laughed and said, "The rest of the deck is long gone!"

I couldn't help laughin', too. "Well, I'm pretty sure I know where the queen of hearts wound up." I pointed to the book. "She's causin' trouble in Wonderland!"

Peggy laughed, then said, "Can you stay for a quick visit? I've actually been thinking Katie Bee and Bonnie Sue should meet Willie and Wesley."

I started to say we didn't have time, but with the Littles squealin', "Yes! Yes! Yes!" and Anna Mae pleadin', "Pleeeeeease?" and Peggy coaxin', "Oh, come on. Just for a minute," I gave in, and we all wound up in the orchard, where the Littles and the twins played tag and hide 'n' seek while Anna Mae listened to Peggy and me talk.

When at last I'd gathered the girls again and we'd said our goodbyes, I found Bobby standin' beside Faithful, his face half inside the driver's-side window.

He pulled back when he saw me and asked, "Whose is this, do you know?"

"It's Pa—my father's," I said, feelin' the need to switch . . . and unsettled about havin' done so.

He looked around, confused. "So . . ."

I opened the door and let the Littles in while Anna Mae went around to the other side, then got in myself.

"*You're* driving?" he asked.

I nodded.

"You know how to run that thing? I heard they're finicky. And complicated."

I laughed, then went through the ritual of firin' up Faithful and puttin' her in gear. "Been doin' it since I was about nine," I said, then tossed him a smile and pulled away.

When we arrived home, though, all our smiles vanished. Mama was in a state.

We were late.

Inconsiderate.

Neglectful.

I wanted to scream, *Neglectful?* but bit my tongue and escaped to take the wash off the line.

Mama went to bed without supper, and Papa did nothing to stop her. Not too long ago, Anna Mae would have used this as an excuse to duck out on chores, but she did not. And it wasn't just then, but the next day, too, when Mama stayed in her room once again.

The truth is, Anna Mae's been nothing but cooperative with me since I let her in on the secret—which she now knows everything about. I've told her she can't come along when Peggy and I make the trip to Garysville because I need her to cover for me and keep watch over things at home, and she's agreed. It's nice to have an ally in the house, and such a gutsy, sly one at that.

The plan *is* comin' along, though at a snail's pace. I've been turnin' over nearly every cent of my half of my wages to Mrs. Poole at the church. Mama thinks my share's gone to the second-hand store for the new shoes I'm wearin' and the extra clothes I've come home with, and I'm not about to tell her they're hand-me-overs from Peggy.

Mrs. Poole let me know that Peggy has also been makin' donations—something I've told Peggy to stop, though she hasn't. Even so, Peggy's right—we're ages away from havin' enough for a plot, let alone a coffin.

"The reverend's willing to ask the congregation to help," Mrs. Poole said when I saw her last. "But we need that picture."

Gettin' ahold of "that picture" has had me on edge for weeks now. I'm to phone Peggy when there's a chance for her to come over and take a snapshot of the newspaper clipping—a picture of a picture. It's the only way we figure we'll get it—or at least a copy of it—out of the house without Mama noticin'. Peggy says the camera's tricky, and she seems as nervous about usin' it as I am about havin' her here to do it. And so far, between her hours at the stand, mine at the cannery, and Mama's unpredictable time in the garden and her habit for holin' up in her room whenever I'm home, there's been no chance at all.

Papa doesn't seem to know what to do about Mama's decline, so I've decided that tonight—despite how tired I am after my shift at the cannery—I'm rallyin' the nerve to ask him about movin' the boys. It sure would be nice not to have to go behind his back.

After supper and cleanup, a gentle breeze sweeps through the house like a cool sigh of relief. Mama goes out to tend the garden and chickens, and soon after, Papa—who left the house right after supper—leans in through the back door. "Ginny Rose, come help me pull a stump. I got it dug out, chained, and ready."

Outside, Faithful's backed up near a tree stump that's surrounded by mounds of dirt that Papa's dug up from around the roots. Lyin' along the ground, there's a heavy chain that links the stump to Faithful's back bumper. It's the second time I've helped Papa pull a stump, so I know my role. I squeak open the driver's-side door, take my place behind the steering wheel, and get Faithful fired up. And after I've rolled the truck forward enough to take up the slack from the chain, I watch the mirror, waitin' for Papa's signal.

He gives me a wave and calls, "Easy does it!"

As I slip the clutch and rev Faithful forward, roots pop from the earth, sendin' dirt clods skyward. But deeper roots hold fast, so I hold her steady until Papa signals me forward again. This time I rev a little more, pullin' hard as Papa swings his ax again and again at the anchoring roots.

After he's worked the ax hard for a good five minutes, I can feel the stump start to give, so I holler, "Stand clear!" He steps away, wipin' his brow with a handkerchief, and I give more gas, strainin' Faithful forward until the stump pops loose.

Papa whoops victory and hurries after me as I drive over to the woodpile with the stump thumpin' and bumpin' along behind.

We unchain the rooty mass and wrestle it out of the way, and as Papa's dustin' off his hands and grinnin' at our feat, I hear the deep rumble of a train approachin'. Soon it'll be too loud to talk without raisin' our voices, so I gather my courage quick and ask, "Can we talk about Mama?"

His face falls and he shakes his head. "It serves no purpose, Ginny Rose. You need to let her alone with her demons."

"But the demons are winnin'!" And in a desperate rush I say, "If you would just consider movin' the boys—"

"No!" he says, his answer swift and firm. "It's not something I'll allow. Ever!"

Still, I manage one final plea. "But *why*?"

"Because I say so!" he snaps. Then he thinks better of his retort and spreads his arms toward the newly cleared soil. "The reason I'm doin' all this is to help her out of it. She loves her garden and seein' things grow, and I'm clearin' this whole area so she can work it."

The ground's vibratin' now as the train draws nearer, and my heart falls heavy inside me. Sure, Mama loves her garden, but I can see from the glow on Papa that *he's* the one who needs to work the land. He might truly believe he's doin' this for her, but claimin' every inch of soil around us is makin' *him* happy, not her.

And what he's cleared is a slice of land that's not even ours.

The railroad company owns it.

He looks at me, readin' my mind, or at least part of it. "It's not much, Ginny Rose, but you've got to make the best of where you're at. Small as it is, this patch of earth is more'n we've had since we left Oklahoma, even if it's not in my name." He gives a weary sigh, gazin' out at the strip of earth. "At least it never was."

At that moment I realize with a jolt that losin' his land in Oklahoma might have been harder on him than losin' his sons. I can't believe that's really so, and yet there's a truth to it that can't be ignored. He worked those fields sunup to dark for years, stretchin' back to before I was born, and those eighty acres seemed to speak to him in a way that I never could. Sometimes Mama would send me out to fetch him for supper and I'd find him standin' alone in a barren field, doin' nothing but takin' in the sight of it.

He never spent time that way with me. Or Mama. Or the boys. We didn't seem to fill his mind or his soul the way the land did. And lookin' back, I can see that him thinkin' he could hold on to the land—borrowin' against it for seed and supplies, only to have dust storms choke out his crops again and again until everything was lost to the bank—that's where his heart broke. It wasn't California that did it. It was Oklahoma. And despite the heartache of losin' his sons *after* leavin' Oklahoma, he can picture them in Heaven. In a life beyond the pain of this one.

But the land?

He poured *his* life into that, only to have it wither and die.

Only to have to leave it behind.

This connection snaps like a sprung trap in my mind. And though I'm findin' it hard to equate land and life, maybe understandin' him is the path to him understandin' Mama. So I turn to him and try one more time. "Papa," I breathe out, my heart racin', "the way you feel about leavin' your land back home? That's how Mama feels about leavin' the boys."

His eyes flare at me, and he raises his voice against the train's rolling thunder. "You can't begin to know how I feel. Not about any of it."

I want to shout, *Then tell me,* but the corner of my eye catches a movement, and when I glance over, I see Anna Mae sendin' me frantic signals from around the back door.

And then it's too late. Papa's steppin' into Faithful, sayin', "We need to let the past rest, Ginny Rose. Never speak of it again."

Defeated, I hurry over to Anna Mae, who's actin' like her feet are on fire. "What's wrong?" I ask, hurryin' up the steps.

"She's here!" she whispers hoarsely over the train's waning rumble.

"*Who's* here?"

"Peggy! She's out front with a camera." She yanks me inside and jabs the newspaper picture of the boys at me. "Here! I'll keep watch over Mama."

I want to ask her a million questions, but the clipping feels like a hot potato in my hands, so I cut to the most pressing one. "Where are the girls?"

"In our room. They think we're playin' hide 'n' seek." She flies out the back door as the last boxcar rolls past. "Be quick about it!"

Peggy seems relieved to see me, but she's also twitchy as a scared mouse. She scrambles to pull a black-and-silver camera from where it's hidden under a sweater inside her bike basket. "When she said the coast was clear," she whispers, "I wasn't expecting everyone to be home!"

The camera's not much bigger than a rich man's wallet. But when she presses a button, a small door on the face of it pops free, revealin' a lens the size of a large eye. "*Who* said the coast was clear?" I ask.

Peggy pulls the little door fully open, revealin' hidden bellows that push the lens outward, makin' the camera almost double in size. "Anna Mae!" she whispers, lockin' down the bellows with a snap. "She called the house and told me to hurry over." She points to the second porch step. "Lay the picture there. Hold it flat."

So I do. And as I anchor it, Peggy twitches around the camera, twistin' the lens, movin' little levers and knobs, turnin' the camera sideways, then back again, all the while mutterin' little things as if recitin' what someone's told her.

"You haven't used it before?" I ask, and my hands are startin' to quiver a little as the seconds tick by.

She shakes her head as she leans over the picture with the camera to her eye. Then she moves forward and back, then forward again. At last she holds still and says, "Don't move," and pushes a tall button on the top of the camera.

Click.

She turns a knob, which makes a little rasping sound, then gets the camera in place again and takes another shot.

Click.

"Ginny Rose!" Mama's voice growls from inside the house. "Ginny Rose, where are you?"

My breath catches. I snatch up the newspaper clipping and slip it inside my pocket just as the door opens.

Mama stands loomin' above us, while I look guilty as sin and Peggy holds the camera. "What's goin' on here?" she demands as she surveys us.

Behind Mama, Anna Mae's fallin' apart, mouthin', "I'm sorry!" And then the Littles are there, whinin' about bein' tricked. I have no words, no excuse, no idea what to say. Sounds seem buried in cotton, and it drifts through my mind that I feel like I did the day I about fainted at the cannery.

And then Peggy's voice cuts through the daze. "Your daughters were trying to surprise you, Mrs. Gilley," she says, and casts an anxious smile my way.

I'm fearful she's about to spill the beans, but ridin' high on that fear is a sense of relief. It's over. No matter how much trouble I'm in, it's over.

But then Peggy says, "Ginny Rose asked me to take a picture of the four of them. For you."

Mama stares at Peggy.

Anna Mae stares at Peggy.

I stare at Peggy.

And then the Littles come flyin' past Mama, squealin', "I want to be in a picture!" "So do I!" "Me first!" "No, me!"

Peggy laughs and says, "Well, it'll be all of you together."

Then she turns her attention to Mama. "If you'd like, I can take one of the whole family . . . now that I've ruined the surprise."

I can see Mama's cloud creep in, castin' a dark shadow on her thoughts.

The whole family's not here.

And never will be.

"No," she says at last, and turns to leave us.

Peggy looks dismayed, but I'm so relieved by her quick thinking, I could cry. Anna Mae, too, has her wits about her and is already on to the next crisis. "Quick!" she says to me. "The picture!"

"Oh no!" I gasp, because she's right. If Mama goes to her room and discovers it's missin' . . . then what?

I hand over the clipping not knowin' how in the world Anna Mae will ever be able to put it back without bein' caught, and with each passing minute, I imagine the worst.

But then suddenly she reappears wearin' her kittens skirt, her face clean, her hair freshly brushed.

"I want to wear my kittens, too!" Katie Bee cries, and she and Bonnie Sue race inside to change.

When they return in their dresses newly trimmed with scraps of kittens-with-umbrellas, Katie Bee hands me our brush. And after I've redone their hair and mine, Anna Mae says, "I get to be in the middle," and plops herself in the center of the top step, pullin' the Littles down on her left.

I almost point out that with four there is no middle, but I keep that to myself and simply sit for the portrait, grateful beyond measure to have these sisters, and a friend as courageous as Peggy Simmons.

27

Peggy

BRASH MOVES

My nerves were completely frayed when I left the Gilleys' house after taking the photos. I'd been nervous enough to begin with, not wanting Ginny Rose to know I'd borrowed Mr. Bovee's camera and then not being sure if I'd done the camera settings right or taken usable pictures. But the terse exchange I'd had with Mrs. Gilley had me shaking.

As I pedaled away, I was sure that was because I'd been doing something sneaky. But once the house was a safe distance behind me, I realized it wasn't *just* that. It was also because Mrs. Gilley had made me feel as though—no matter what reason I was there—I wasn't welcome.

But . . . why?

What had I done to make her dislike me?

And then, with more distance between us and time to reflect on some things Ginny Rose had told me about her mother, I decided that it might not be me specifically.

Maybe it was just outsiders.

Any outsiders.

This thought tumbled inside me, and I wondered at the irony of it. Mrs. Gilley hadn't said so much as hello to me. She certainly hadn't invited me in, even for a glass of water. She had simply turned her back on me and walked away. Yet people being unwelcoming to the Gilleys was a big part of what made *them* feel like outsiders.

So . . . why did she do the same thing to me? But then my thoughts turned in a different direction. Maybe Mrs. Gilley had unnerved me so much because I'd never been treated like that before. Not by anybody. But the Gilleys? They'd been shunned and turned away for *years*.

My heart caught at the thought.

What must that have been like?

My contemplations came to a halt when I reached Lisette's house and Mr. Bovee answered the door. He was still in a suit and tie, his dark hair styled neatly back, looking like his day at the bank was just beginning rather than finished. "Why, Peggy, hello! Come in, come in! Can you join us for dinner? We're just about to sit down."

"Thank you, but no, sir. I'm expected at home. I just wanted to ask you—"

He saw the camera in my hands and chuckled. "I was wondering if we'd ever see that again."

"I'm sorry I had it so long. I was—"

"Oh, it's not a problem. Not a problem at all. I just didn't want to lose the pictures that were already on it. Were there enough frames left for your project?"

"Yes. And I hope I did everything the way you showed me."

"As long as your subject distance matched the marking on the dial, you should be all right."

He was holding out his hand for the camera, but I didn't want to give it to him yet. "Would you mind showing me how to take the roll of film out so I can get it developed?"

From inside the house, Mrs. Bovee's voice sang out, "George?"

"I'll be right there, Helen!" he called back, then wiggled his fingers a little, impatient for me to hand him the camera. "I'll take care of it."

"But I should—"

He reached out and took the camera from me. "Nonsense. I'm happy to."

I was feeling full of regret for not having done things differently, when Lisette appeared at the door. "Peggy! Why are you standing out there? Come in!" Then she saw the camera, and her eyes got wide as she gave me a questioning look.

I nodded.

"George? Lisette?" Mrs. Bovee's voice called down the hallway, and this time the tone was sharper.

"Can you stay for dinner?" Lisette asked.

I was sorely tempted. The wonderful smell of pot roast had made its way to the front door. We rarely had pot roast, and Mrs. Bovee always made Yorkshire pudding from the drippings, which was my favorite. But I was already in hot water at home for having raced away when Anna Mae had called, so I shook my head. "I wish I could, but I've got to get home."

Mrs. Bovee appeared in the foyer, a cocktail glass in her hand. "George! Lisette! Dinner is getting cold!" She gave me an annoyed look. "In or out, dear. Decide."

"I'm sorry, Mrs. Bovee," I hurried to say, then started down the porch steps. "Thank you for the loan, Mr. Bovee," I called, and threw Lisette a pleading look.

She caught it and mouthed, "Don't worry!" from behind her father as he closed the door.

But I *did* worry. Even after Lisette stopped by the stand on Tuesday to tell me her father had turned in the roll of film at Sully's Drugstore and that the prints would be ready in about a week, even after she assured me on Thursday that she would check Sully's herself every day to intercept them, and even after she told me on Sunday that her father was so busy attending to repairs at the Oakvale house that picking up prints was the last thing on his mind, I still worried. That was, in part, because Valley Bank, where Mr. Bovee worked, was only a short walk from the drugstore, and Lisette had *also* told me that her father was known to take glad-handing strolls through downtown, or simply cut his workday short.

And the Bovees attended Valley Church regularly, so if Mr. Bovee got to the prints first and looked through them—which of course he would—and if Reverend Poole spoke about Ginny Rose's brothers during a service and Mr. Bovee recognized them from the picture—which of course he would—then it was just a matter of time before things unraveled.

We *had* to get to the photographs before Mr. Bovee did.

So for a whole week, I'd been feeling like I was wobbling on a tightrope, trying to help Ginny Rose without betraying her trust—or revealing that I already had—and fearing that at any moment I would lose my footing *and* my friendship. Then today, Lisette's car came flying down the road and skidded to a stop at the fruit stand. "I phoned Sully's!" she called out her window.

"They're in! I left work early to grab them. Do you want to come along?"

Even on a Monday, when things were generally slower, it was too early to close up shop, but for this I'd do it. The problem was, there was an elderly woman at the stand who seemed perfectly content to spend the rest of the afternoon selecting a single peach. She'd been squeezing—and bruising—peach after peach, trying to decide which one she wanted while her daughter—who wasn't exactly a spring chicken herself—looked on.

"Can I help you decide?" I asked the elderly woman.

She looked at me but didn't respond and simply went back to squeezing peaches, this time harder, leaving a dent from her thumb in each.

"I'm sorry," I said to the daughter, "but something's come up and I have to close the stand."

The daughter looked over at Lisette sitting behind the wheel, stylish as ever. "I'm sure it's *very* important," she said dryly.

"I assure you, it is," I said, and I could feel myself flush with annoyance.

"Are you coming?" Lisette called impatiently.

"Yes!" I called back, then handed the elderly woman a peach. "Here, ma'am. Free of charge."

The elderly woman seemed satisfied—at least with the price—but her daughter frowned and stayed planted in place. And as I began quickly moving my supplies into the handcart, she asked, "What about me?"

After a week of worry, and countless minutes biting my tongue as her mother pinched peaches, I finally snapped. "Oh, I'm sorry. Were you wanting a bill for the dozen peaches your mother bruised?"

The woman gasped, and a moment later she said, "Well, I never!" Then she huffed away, calling, "You certainly won't see us back here again, I can assure you!"

"The peaches will be most obliged," I said with sizzling sweetness.

"Such insolence!" she cried over her shoulder, and I had to agree. I'd probably never been so rude in my life. But the strange thing was, I didn't feel bad about it. Not one bit. I was tired of being pushed around.

Once we were down the road toward Oakvale, I let out a deep, choppy breath and said, "Thank you."

"I just hope we get there before Daddy does."

"I can't believe you left work early. Won't you be in trouble?"

She gave a little shrug. "I know how worried you've been about this."

Suddenly I felt like an awful friend. For the last few weeks, I'd refused to listen to anything that had to do with Rodney. I *was* still miffed at him. And even more at *her* for going back to him. Rodney St. Clair had become a thickly mortared wall standing in the middle of our friendship.

And yet, anyone could see that Lisette was happy. *Really* happy. And wasn't that what true friends were supposed to want for each other?

"I'm sorry I've been so mulish about Rodney," I said.

She glanced over, surprised.

"How are things with the two of you?" I asked, trying to sound like I really wanted to know.

"Wonderful," she said, letting it escape on a full breath of dreamy longing. "Just perfect."

"Well, I'm glad," I said, the words burning as they passed my lips, the way lies are supposed to.

There was a parking slot open on the street right in front of Sully's, but Lisette went to the end of the block, turned the corner, and parked out of view.

"Smart," I said, realizing she didn't want her father to spot her car at the drugstore in case he was out and about.

We hurried back to Sully's on foot like a pair of nervous cats, then jangled through the door. There were customers at the register, more in the aisles, and a short line of them at the pharmacy counter.

"Good," Lisette said. "It's busy."

I followed her past the register, past the ice cream counter, down one aisle, then another, and over to the camera department, which was outfitted from ceiling to floor with bright yellow Kodak promotions. A man with salt-and-pepper hair was smoking a cigarette as he stocked small boxes of film behind the counter. When he saw us coming, he rested the cigarette in an ashtray and smiled. "Why, Lisette Bovee, how nice to see you!"

"Hello, Mr. Leeward. It's wonderful to see you, too. May I introduce my friend Peggy Simmons? Her family has that beautiful peach farm in Ferrybank. The one on the road to Modesto?"

"Ah, yes, of course!"

"Peggy, this is Mr. Leeward, a good friend of Daddy's."

"How kind of you to describe me that way," Mr. Leeward said.

"Well, it's certainly true!" Lisette said. Then, without even a hint of nerves, she gently turned the subject. "I'm here to pick up some snapshots for Daddy. I heard they were ready?"

"Let me check," Mr. Leeward said, and after bending to

rummage beneath the counter, he emerged with a bulging envelope. "Here we are," he said, handing the prints over. "Shall I put
the charge on your father's account?"

"If you would," Lisette said, scooping up the envelope.

"Certainly," he said with a smile.

She thanked him and gave me a look that said, *Let's hurry,*
and we cut through the store, picking up speed like we'd just
committed a robbery. But as we were nearing the register, the
front door jangled open and Mr. Bovee stepped inside.

"Oh no!" Lisette gasped, pulling me quickly into an aisle
filled with medical supplies. We knelt out of view, pretending
to inspect Band-Aids on a low shelf. "Do you think he saw us?"
Lisette whispered.

"I don't know!" I whispered back.

"Can you see?" she asked, motioning frantically for me to
peek over the shelves.

So I inched up and watched Mr. Bovee as he greeted the ca-
shier like an old friend, then stopped to talk to a couple of customers, shaking their hands with gusto.

"He acts like he's running for office," I whispered.

Lisette stayed mum.

"*Is* he?"

"He's thinking of running for mayor," she said.

Suddenly his decision to move to Oakvale made a lot more
sense.

And felt even dirtier.

"Where is he now?" Lisette asked frantically.

I peeked back out, then quickly ducked. "Coming this way!"

We held our breath, but Mr. Bovee turned down the aisle before ours to greet some other people he knew. "Why, Mrs. Taylor, Mrs. Williams! How are you this fine afternoon?"

"Waiting for a break in this heat!" one of the women replied.

"Which is why I frequent the ice cream counter here," Mr. Bovee said with a chuckle. And after some small talk about his favorite flavors, he said, "Well, I need to pick up some snapshots, but it sure was a pleasure to bump into you ladies! Please tell Leon and Chester I hope to see them sometime soon."

With Mr. Bovee moving toward the Kodak counter, we were ready to scurry away. But then we heard one of the women grumble, "What I've told my Chester is to get our money out of his bank!"

Lisette froze, then leaned in to better listen.

"Because of what he did to Carl Sunderwood?" the second woman asked. "Leon said they were in the same bowling league."

"It's true! Smile to your face, stab you in the back. It's unconscionable that the Bovees are moving into that house!"

"I agree!" The second woman's voice was louder now, and braver. "And he can afford to come in here all the time for ice cream? Must be nice."

"Whose nickels do you suppose he's spending on that?"

"The thief," the second woman grumbled.

"Yes," the first woman said. "That's what he is. A backstabbing thief."

Lisette had gone pale, so I grabbed her hand and pulled her along, resisting the urge to look over my shoulder as I led her outside.

We all but ran down the street, around the corner, and back to Lisette's car, where we sat in silence while the color slowly returned to her cheeks. I had no idea what to say to her, so I simply said, "That was awful. I'm sorry."

"Here," she said at last, turning the envelope over to me.

It felt wrong to look at the pictures while Lisette was so upset, but curiosity got the better of me. I quickly flipped through snapshots until I reached the ones I'd taken at the Gilleys'.

All four pictures were in focus.

Centered in frame.

Perfect.

Lisette eased one from my grasp and slowly took in the overloaded truck, the two boys, the young girl. It wasn't long before tears welled in her eyes. "That's Glory Rose?" she asked as she pointed to the photograph, her voice barely a whisper.

I nodded.

"And these are the brothers who died?"

"Yes," I said, taking the picture back, mortified she'd splashed it with tears. "I tried to get this to Mrs. Poole right away."

"That poor family," Lisette said, her voice quivering. Then she swiped away her tears, took a deep breath, and squared her shoulders. "I need to have a talk with Daddy," she said, starting the car. "I am not moving into that house."

28

Ginny Rose

SECRETS

It's Tuesday evening when the telephone rings. The girls and I are doin' dishes after supper, and the sound is so unexpected that we all lurch and squawk like startled chickens, sendin' water and suds flyin' and dishes clatterin'. Despite the luxury of a telephone, it mostly hangs on the wall unused.

Papa's out back hoein' the earth, and Mama's stepped away to spend time in the garden, so it's just the four of us inside, and we all stare at the telephone like it's conductin' a stickup.

Brrrrrringgggg, it sounds again.

Anna Mae's the first to react, shakin' rinse water from her hands and snatchin' the handset from the cradle. "Hello?" she says, and after a short delay, she holds the telephone out to me without a word.

I dry off, take the phone, and weigh the Littles' wide, curious eyes as I say, "This is Ginny Rose."

"It's me," Peggy says, her voice hushed and laced with worry. "They all came out."

I can tell she means the photos and that she's bein' careful about her wording. "Good news," I reply, tryin' not to let on to the Littles how relieved I am.

"I took the first one where it needed to go," she says, her words chasin' after each other. "I told her to cut you out of it, just like you said."

"And?"

"She said she would. She wants you to stop by as soon as you can." I sense her glancin' over her shoulder before she goes on. "She knows time's of the essence."

"How can I ever thank you?" I ask.

There's a short silence, and then, "Forgive me for any missteps I might have made."

"But . . . you've been an absolute angel!" I tell her.

There's a little sigh, and then, "Mother's coming. I have to go."

The click of her hangin' up sounds in my ear, but I stand there a moment, thinkin' before I turn to the Littles. "Guess what?" I ask them.

"What?" they cry.

"The picture of you in your kittens dresses turned out great."

"Yay!" they squeal.

Anna Mae gives me a questioning look and I give a curt nod in return, sharin' information in our new sister code—a language I've grown to love. Then I turn back to the Littles and whisper, "We can't talk about it, though, okay? It'll be a surprise for Mama."

Bonnie Sue's smile fades. "But I want to see!"

"Me too!" Katie Bee seconds.

"You will, soon enough," I tell them, "but only if you don't breathe a word of this to Mama until we're ready to give it to her."

It's a bribe I hope holds, though it's not a problem if it

doesn't, seein' how Mama already knows we took a picture of us girls. But I'm hopin' that havin' the Littles believe we have a small secret might let me talk more freely with Anna Mae about the *other* picture.

"She has to get it framed and all," Anna Mae says, already helpin' out.

"Which will take a little time," I add, kneelin' down in front of the Littles. "So . . . are you old enough to keep it a secret?"

They nod with wide, earnest eyes.

"Then *shhh*," I say, puttin' a finger in front of my lips.

They copycat, little fingers in front of little lips. *"Shhh."*

Soon it's their bedtime, and there's no more talk of secrets once the Littles are snuggled around me and I begin readin' more from *Alice's Adventures in Wonderland*. Afterward, they chatter about Alice and the Caterpillar, and how the story makes no particular sense.

"Dreams never do," Anna Mae mutters, from her dangling position in the bunk above us.

"What?" Bonnie Sue cries, and a little argument starts about whether the story *is* just a dream, and it ends with the Littles decidin' that, if it is, Anna Mae's gone and spoiled the whole thing and *she's* the one who doesn't know how to keep a secret.

"So there!" Bonnie Sue says, scurryin' into her own bed.

"That's right!" Katie Bee says, doin' the same.

It makes me smile to think that tellin' someone they don't know how to keep a secret is such an offense to the Littles. Maybe they won't spill what they know in front of Mama after all.

Anna Mae, on the other hand, simply shrugs off their complaint. And after the Littles fall silent, she picks up whisperin' at me from the top bunk. "What did Peggy say?"

"Shh!" I whisper back. The walls are thin and the doors drafty. The last thing I need is for Mama to overhear a single word of what's goin' on. "We'll talk later," I tell her. Then, though it's only eight o'clock, the full weight of the day settles on me, and it isn't long before sleep takes me, too.

The next morning, I fix Papa and me breakfast, because Mama never appears in the kitchen. It's a quick meal of bread and beans, but I haven't time for anything more. He said to never speak of what's causin' Mama's dark moods again, but her absence says volumes, even if he refuses to listen.

I'm quick about packin' bologna sandwiches and apples for our lunches, then go in and nudge Anna Mae. "Papa and I are off," I whisper, hopin' not to wake the Littles. "You're in charge." I press a slip of paper into her hand. "This has the number for the switching yard, and the one at the cannery. If there's an emergency—only a *real* emergency—call Papa first, and if you can't get through to him, call me."

"We'll be fine," she says, her voice thick with sleep.

I pray she's right and hurry out the door.

I pedal hard to make up for lost time, but even so I'm almost late to work, arrivin' at my post breathless, my nerves more'n a little frayed. So at first I don't realize that the woman standin' to my left is the same one who stood there four weeks ago and fainted before my very eyes. "Mrs. Smith?" I call over the noise.

"Ginny Rose," she says as though we're old friends. "The ladies tell me you were very helpful when I collapsed before."

"I'm . . . I'm so glad to see you're doin' better."

"Work will be a blessing," she says. "It'll keep my mind off of . . . things." She casts a wary glance to our left. "I hope the other ladies don't mind that Kay put me up here. I feel like I'm cutting the line."

During the month she's been gone, I've advanced down the line to where the duty is to pull damaged peaches from the belt and dump them into a slop bucket that'll be taken away for processin' into pie filling. The "slop station," as everyone calls it, pays three cents an hour more, so yes, whoever's been bumped back a slot by Mrs. Smith's return *is* likely feelin' more'n a little ruffled. But I do my best to ease her worry. "They shouldn't mind," I call to her. Then with a laugh I say, "It's much stickier up here!"

We get down to work, and by midmorning it's sweltering in the warehouse. Fans were brought in last week, but all they seem to do is make the place noisier as they spin hot air around. I find myself wishin' for the job of loadin' the conveyor belts, or haulin' off slop buckets, or hosin' down the floor—anything to move my legs and get some time in fresh air—but those jobs are all done by men, whereas women work every single station on both belts, all the way down the line.

"Are you all right?" I call over to Mrs. Smith when I see that she's fadin'.

"When do we break for lunch?" she asks.

I check the wall clock. "In half an hour."

She wipes her brow. "How are you holding up so well?"

"The first week's the hardest," I say, tryin' to be encouraging. "And the first day of the first week's the hardest of all." I smile her way. "So after today, you'll know you can do it, and then . . . you just keep doin' it until you're used to it."

But by lunch I'm not sure she'll make it through the day, let alone return tomorrow. On our way out to the break area, I fetch a cup of cool water and press it on her as we walk. "Drink this," I tell her. "Drink every drop."

She does, and once we're outside, she waves at her teacher friends and asks me, "Do you have a group?" Before I can reply, she says, "Would you like to sit with us?"

I don't have a group, just a table I share with other women whose names I don't really know, and who don't really know mine. And I would love to accept, but . . . "It's probably not appropriate," I say at last. "I'll be attendin' Oakvale High come September. It's my understanding you're all teachers there?"

"Oh," she says, takin' me in now with a keen look. "I had no idea. You seem much more . . . mature than my students."

Her eyes sharpen on my dress and shoes like she's seein' *them* for the first time, too, so I save her the trouble of speculation. "My family's been through a rough spell," I say. "But things are lookin' up. And this job's helpin'."

She says, "Well, bless your heart," then leaves to join her friends.

I sit at my usual table and eat my lunch in silence, pickin' over the lie in what I said to Mrs. Smith. It was true that we were no longer hungry, and that we had a solid roof over our heads and real beds to sleep in. But with Mama's struggles, things felt like they were gettin' worse, not better.

And then, mid-apple, a thought strikes me.

I gather what's left of my lunch and go up to the teachers'

table. "Mrs. Smith," I say, tryin' to be polite with my interruption, "may I talk with you, please? Privately?"

All the women seem a little taken aback, but Mrs. Smith rises from the bench with a smile and says, "Of course, dear."

I know there's not a lot of time before we're back on the line, where it's much too loud to have a delicate conversation. So I throw caution to the wind and get to the point. "During my family's really lean years, when we traveled around a lot lookin' for work, my two little brothers got sick and died, and Mama's never really gotten past it. I know you've been through a terrible time yourself, and I'm wonderin' what's helped you. What got you to the place where you could come back to work today?"

Mrs. Smith proves to be a keen listener, takin' in every word. "How long ago was this?" she asks.

I look down. "Almost eleven years ago. The boys were only four and three. But instead of time healin' things, it seems Mama's goin' to a darker place."

"Oh, the poor dear," Mrs. Smith says. She shakes her head, and I can see her eyes glaze with tears. "Does she have friends she talks to?"

I consider this, then say, "Our life didn't make for developin' friendships, ma'am."

She nods as she thinks, then asks, "What about your father?"

"He doesn't want to talk about it. He says it's in the past and that's where we need to leave it."

"But it's not in the past, is it?" she says with sad eyes. "He can't see that?"

"He sees it. He just doesn't have another answer."

She heaves a sigh. "Well, I'm by no means over my loss, but

what's helped me get from under the covers is my colleagues," she says with a nod at the teachers' table. "Also, attending a weekly meeting of grievers has been unexpectedly helpful."

"Grievers?"

"It's a quiet gathering of women who find comfort in talking to others who can understand what they're going through. There are war widows, and mothers who lost their boys to the war, but we're mostly women from ordinary circumstances. You'd be surprised how many of us have deep hurt buried away inside us."

The end-of-lunch whistle sounds, and I apologize for takin' up her break time, but she's kind about it. "Nonsense, dear. I'd be glad to invite her, if you'd like."

I think the grievers' group might help Mama, but the thought of Mrs. Smith callin' sends waves of terror through me. "No, but I'll be sure to tell her about it. Thank you!"

Then we're back on the line, surrounded by heat and noise and endless peaches. Mrs. Smith does make it through the full shift, but as we're clockin' out for the day, she turns to me and says, "You promise me tomorrow will be easier?"

I give her a weary smile. "Get to bed early."

She laughs. "You see? Mature beyond your years."

Outside, I rush to fetch my bicycle as Mrs. Smith finds her friends and walks with them toward the parking lot. I'm glad she has friends to help her through the death of her child. I only wish Mama had the same.

I pedal hard, away from the cannery, over the railroad tracks, and onto River Road, intent on makin' time to visit Mrs. Poole at the church. But as I'm windin' along, I become aware of a car rollin' alongside me. The road ahead is clear, and I don't understand why the car isn't movin' past me. So I take a quick look over and am dismayed to see Mrs. Smith and another teacher watchin' me from the back seat, while the passenger up front— another one of the teachers—studies me, too.

Once I look, they speed away, and although Mrs. Smith gives a friendly wave, I know at that moment that I've made a mistake.

A mighty big mistake.

29

Peggy

UNEXPECTED GIFT

I kept trying to reach Lisette by phone. Monday and Tuesday I called because I was anxious to find out how the talk with her father had gone. Wednesday and Thursday I called still wanting to know about that, but also wanting to let her know that someone in the congregation was making a large charcoal sketch of the Gilley boys, and that it would be ready for Sunday's service.

The thought of the service tied me in knots. Would the congregation open their wallets? If they did, there'd be no turning back. And would that mean Ginny Rose and I were headed for Garysville . . . soon? We hadn't built a coffin yet because we were worried that Bobby might wonder what we were up to, but . . . should we start?

Were we really going to do this?

But every time I called Lisette's house, Mrs. Bovee made some vague, overly sincere apology for why her daughter was "not available." Mrs. Bovee was always overly sincere—something that used to make me feel special but now felt phony. Anytime I saw her, she was cinched tight in a girdle and flawlessly dressed, usually mixing a drink for Mr. Bovee and, lately, one for herself as well. I'd started realizing that the way she treated me was just a different form of dress-up. Lisette had never said so, but I'd come to see that Mrs. Bovee didn't really approve of me as her daughter's best friend any more than mine did of hers. My family farmed. We labored. We were definitely not society people, even by small-town standards.

But one night last year when I was having dinner at Lisette's house, Mr. Bovee had shared that he believed someday the whole valley would be a sprawling metropolis. "And when things move in that direction," he'd said to me, "that acreage your family's sitting on will be worth a mint."

So maybe Mrs. Bovee tolerated me for that potential? But that didn't mean she bothered to pass along my messages, or that she could resist ever so politely sharing status-confirming information the way she'd done last night, when she'd said, "Oh, I'm terribly sorry, Peggy, she's not here. She's out shopping for a dress for Saturday's dance."

"What dance?" I'd asked, sounding like a peasant who hadn't been invited to the ball.

"Oh, just the teen dance at the Community Center," she'd said with a laugh.

And *that* was how thirty seconds on the phone with Mrs. Bovee could make me feel like a goat in her parlor. Community Center teen dances were held four times a year, and they were always casual. Anyone in high school could go, and *nobody* got a new dress for it. Yet I hung up feeling inferior about everything— my ignorance, my wardrobe, my lack of a date . . . everything.

And because Lisette hadn't called back or stopped by the fruit stand on her way home from Woolworth's, by Friday afternoon I was also feeling very insecure. Could Mrs. Bovee really not have passed on *any* of my messages? Or . . . was she simply keeping up appearances—covering up that things hadn't gone well between Lisette and her father? Or . . . was Lisette so tied up with Rodney that she couldn't make time to call her best friend?

Or . . . maybe Lisette had been fired from her job for leaving work to intercept the snapshots and didn't want to let on?

I was driving myself a little mad with speculation, so as Friday afternoon wore on, I decided I would go over to the Bovees' and see if I could find Lisette. And since there were no customers at the stand and it was getting late, I started closing up shop.

And then Bobby loped up on Blossom.

"*Please* lay off," I said to him, because this was the third day in a row he'd shown up at about the time Lisette might come by if she had worked a shift at Woolworth's. "She will never in a million years like you, so just lay off."

He gave me a frown. "You think you know so much."

I gave a little snort. "*You're* the one with that reputation."

He reined Blossom to a halt and casually tossed out, "What if I'm here for other reasons?"

I nearly blurted, *Did Mother send you?* but just then, like the leading lady cued from stage right, Lisette rolled up. "Go!" I commanded Bobby, pointing him away from Lisette as I made a beeline over to her car.

Lisette gave Bobby a curt nod through the open window as he trotted away, but she stayed put in her car.

"Did your mother tell you I called?" I asked when I reached her. "You did? When?"

"Every night this week!" I exclaimed, regretting it the moment it was out of my mouth.

She sighed. "Sorry. No. But I'm here now, so what's the news?"

I told her about the charcoal sketch and got her to agree to meet me at church on Sunday, then asked, "I've been dying to know . . . did you have a talk with your father?"

She shook her head. "He left for a bankers' meeting in San Francisco before I could. He's supposed to be home tonight."

I looked at her blankly. "So I've been worried all week about nothing?"

She cringed at my expression. "I'm sorry my mom is so . . . unreliable. And I'm afraid I've been really swept up in seeing Rodney." She heaved a blissful sigh. "I'm sorry I've been out of touch." Then she quickly added, "But I was thinking . . . there's a dance at the Community Center tomorrow night. I'll be going with Rodney, but . . . why don't you invite Ginny Rose along? There'll be lots of kids from school there. We could introduce her to people?" She handed a lovely sky-blue dress through the window. "This is for her."

The dress had a silky feel, and when I held it out, I saw that it had a swing skirt that flared out mid-hip and cute little bows that ran along the neckline. "This is gorgeous," I gasped.

"It'll fit her just right, don't you think? And the color will go great with her eyes."

"But . . . she'll never accept it from you!"

She shrugged. "So don't tell her it's from me."

"She wouldn't even accept it from me!"

"Then tell her it's a loan. She'll have something nice to

wear and we'll introduce her around." She leveled a look at me. "School's starting in a few weeks. You need to ease her into it." Then she said, "Also, we need to make plans for your birthday. I told Rodney that this Sunday I was all yours, so whatever you want, I'm available. I could even help you work the stand if you can't get out of it."

I stared at her, feeling foolish and childish and so, *so* grateful.

And since I wasn't actually *saying* anything, she laughed and said, "Look, we can decide about your birthday later. For now, promise you'll give Ginny Rose the dress." She sighed and said, "I do want to help. In ways I know how."

"Ways that don't involve a shovel?" I half kidded.

She shivered, then got very serious. "I want you to know I haven't told Rodney a thing. It's been hard, but I haven't told him or *anybody*."

"Well, you *are* sworn to secrecy," I reminded her. But then I confessed, "I *have* worried, though, so thank you for telling me."

She started her car. "I'm sorry, but I've got to dash." And as she was rolling away, she called out the window, "The dance starts at seven. It's free, so no excuses!"

After she drove off, I went back to the stand and placed the blue dress neatly in an extra sack, thinking about the dance.

I finished loading the handcart and pulled it toward the house, still thinking about the dance. It was nice that Lisette wanted to include Ginny Rose, and the dress *was* a sweet gesture . . . but did *I* really want to go to the dance and see Lisette and Rodney all lovey-dovey? I hadn't seen Rodney since we'd gone roller skating and wasn't sure I could even be civil to him.

As I looked both ways to cross the road, my thoughts were interrupted by the sight of Ginny Rose. She was in the shade of an oak tree barely ten paces from me, straddling her bike as she stroked Blossom's face while Bobby sat perched in the saddle.

"She's such a sweet girl, isn't she?" Ginny Rose asked when I joined them.

I nodded my agreement, watching Bobby carefully. How long had he lingered there? Had he overheard any of my conversation with Lisette? Also, he hadn't bothered to dismount to talk with Ginny Rose . . . how long had *she* been there? She seemed really taken with the horse, so she might have missed seeing Lisette. And she was smiling, so Bobby must not have been *entirely* rude to her.

Bobby caught me studying him and nudged Blossom along with a mumble in Ginny Rose's direction. I couldn't make out his words, and apparently neither could she, because once he was gone, she gave a little shrug and switched the subject. "I stopped by the church," she said. "Mrs. Poole showed me the sketch. It's *big,* and it's . . ." Her voice caught and her eyes turned glassy. "It's beautiful," she managed.

My eyes were suddenly stinging, too, and I found myself hugging her with all my might. "We'll get them home," I whispered.

She pulled back and the tears spilled over. "Home," she sniffed.

At first I thought I'd said something wrong. After all, how could a grave site be considered home? But Ginny Rose was looking wistful, not upset, and in that moment I realized that *home* was much more than a place.

It was a condition.

"I wish I could go on Sunday," she was saying, "but I don't want to risk it."

"I'll go," I assured her. "And I'll tell you all about it."

"I almost can't believe this is happenin'," she whispered. "And if I'm bein' honest? I'm a nervous wreck. Takin' money from other folks? Mama'll be fit to be tied! And what if the church *does* raise money but I can't find the place they're buried?" Worry creased her brow. "And when I picture doin' it, I feel like divin' in a fraidy hole. What if I *do* find them?"

"We'll just take it one step at a time," I said, trying to cover up that I was afraid, too.

She took a deep breath. "I should never have pulled you into this, but I don't know how on earth I'd be doin' it without you!"

"Well, you don't have to," I said with a smile.

And I was thinking it might be the right time to confess that it wasn't just me helping her, when she said, "I've been gettin' Papa to let me drive Faithful for errands. She's runnin' fine. I'm sure she can make the trip."

I tried to look confident, but inside, I wasn't. Especially since it seemed that Ginny Rose was saying this to convince not just me, but also herself. Because besides the actual job of unearthing the boys, how we got to Garysville *was* the big worry to me. I could just see us breaking down halfway, and then what? The whole mission would be lost *and* we'd both be in huge trouble, all for nothing.

Still . . . how could I bring up my concern without insulting her?

"Say," I began, spinning a thought out without knowing where it might land, "do you think you could borrow your father's truck tomorrow night? You could pick me up and we could—"

She laughed. "You're not sure it'll make it to Garysville, are you?" she said, reading me with frightening clarity.

I hurried to sweep over my concerns. "Well, I *would* like to know what I'm getting into, but also there's a teen dance at the Community Center in Oakvale, and it could be fun to go. They'll have a band and refreshments, it's free, and"—I produced the blue dress and gave her a cajoling look—"it'd be a chance for you to wear this."

"Oh my *Lord*," she said, taking it gingerly.

From her expression, I knew she hadn't seen Lisette give it to me, which was a huge relief. "I was really hoping you'd stop by today," I said, continuing to spin, wondering just how tangled this would all become before the truth came out.

"But," she said, looking the dress over, "why don't *you* wear this?"

"It's too small," I said. "But I'm sure it'll fit you beautifully." I took the dress and placed it carefully back in the sack. "Just tell your father you really don't want to ride a *bicycle* in it."

She swept away a sudden tear. Then another. And I could see her thinking *something,* but I had no idea what. Then she gave me a wavering smile and said, "So you're okay with arrivin' at the dance in a jalopy?"

I laughed, because suddenly it felt silly to care about that when we had such bigger things to worry about. "It'll be fun," I said.

"If Papa says it's okay," she said, "what time should I pick you up?"

"Seven," I replied. "We'll arrive fashionably late."

"In a jalopy," Ginny Rose said, and we both laughed.

30

Ginny Rose

THE DANCE

Over supper, there's no mention of my birthday bein' the next day. The hard truth is, for as keen as Mama is on rememberin' the date, she holds it like a trump card for reasons that have nothing to do with celebratin' me. And since I'm not one to ask for things, let alone attention, I never point it out and am pretty sure the Littles and even Anna Mae couldn't say when my birthday is. The date just lands like a bomb each year, with Papa tryin' to patch together some sort of apology to me after Mama's played her hand. And though birthday gifts are not part of Gilley family life, I see to it that cake is—at least for everyone else.

But as supper comes to an end, I feel resentment buildin' inside me, and suddenly I get a wild hair to drop a bomb myself.

"Tomorrow's my birthday," I say out of the blue. "Peggy Simmons has invited me to go to the teen dance at the Community Center in Oakvale, and, Papa," I say, lookin' directly at him, "I'd like to borrow Faithful, if that's all right."

"It's your *birthday*?" Katie Bee squeals.

"Will there be cake?" Bonnie Sue asks, bouncin' up and down.

Anna Mae's eyes narrow, and I can see her calculatin' while Mama looks like I've served up cow pie, and Papa looks like he's just been grazed by lightning. I strain to hold a polite smile, but my heart's clappin' like thunder inside me.

At last Papa breaks the spell. "That would be fine," he says. "It's good you have something fun to do."

"You'll be goin' with Peggy, then?" Mama asks.

"Yes, Mama."

"You'll be home by ten?"

"Yes, Mama."

"Then I guess that's settled," Mama says, lookin' not at all settled.

"What about cake?" Katie Bee asks.

Mama's silent, her chin quiverin'.

Anna Mae watches her with a keen eye, then looks at me and says, "It's not right for you to make your own cake, but . . . would you teach me?"

"Me too, me too!" Katie Bee and Bonnie Sue chirp.

I laugh, but my eyes are stingin' as I say, "I would love to teach you girls how to make a cake."

The full reserve of bravery I spent at supper leaves me with none for broachin' the subject of the blue dress. So I hide it from Mama for fear that she'll have a fit about me squanderin' my earnings on frivolous things if I don't tell her it's from Peggy, and havin' to repay the kindness if I do. It bein' my birthday, I know, won't excuse me havin' this dress.

But when Mama goes out to the garden and I hurry to fetch the bag from near the woodpile where I've hidden it, Anna Mae's keen eye spots me slippin' back inside and demands to know what's in it.

So I take her into our room and show her. "It's from Peggy," I whisper.

"It looks brand-new! And mighty expensive!"

"I know, and I don't want to try'n explain it to Mama."

"How do you expect to get away with *not?*"

"I'm prayin' she'll be in her room when I leave for the dance tomorrow."

Anna Mae gives me a sly look. "Or you could switch into it at Peggy's house when you pick her up."

I blink at her.

"See?" she says, grinnin' like a fox. "You need me."

The next morning, Mama's workin' the garden early, so I set about fixin' breakfast. Flapjacks, eggs, beans, and—since Mama's not there to stop me—a generous side of bacon.

"Isn't this nice!" Papa says when it's time to eat.

Then he says, "Happy birthday, Ginny Rose." They're words I haven't heard from him in eleven years, and he says them softly now like they're secret. Maybe he's able to say them at all because Mama's still outside, claimin' no appetite. Or maybe because the bacon's crisp and salty, with enough to go around to make anyone happy. All I know is it's nice to hear those soft words and get birthday hugs from the Littles and Anna Mae.

"How's it we didn't know when your birthday was?" Anna Mae asks while we're lined up doin' dishes.

I'm done with things stayin' the way they've been, so I just come out and say it. "Because it's also the boys' death day."

The three of them stop rinsin' and dryin' and stare at me.

I shrug. "Which sorta puts a damper on things."

"Those *stupid* boys," Anna Mae fumes.

"It's not their fault, Anna Mae. None of it's anyone's fault." I give them all a little smile. "But I *would* like cake for once, so thank you for askin' and for wantin' to learn how."

"Can we start now?" Katie Bee asks.

"As soon as chores are done," I tell them, which turns out to be the quickest way ever to get them to buckle down and work.

Makin' the cake batter's a fun lesson for all of us. For me it's lettin' go of the reins, for the Littles it's gettin' to crack the eggs, and for Anna Mae it's learnin' to be a gentle teacher—showin' the Littles how to measure and stir without sloppin' batter around.

It isn't until the cake's ready to slip into the oven that Mama comes in from outside. The Littles see her and cry, "We're makin' a cake, Mama!"

She gives a tight smile and says, "How nice," then walks by sayin', "I'm sorry, but I'm feelin' poorly," before disappearin' down the hallway.

Papa's outside workin' the land, so after the cake's in the oven, I gather the girls and read a little more from *Alice's Adventures in Wonderland,* and when the cake's coolin', I work with them on their letters. The Littles love lettering lessons, but Anna Mae never has and still doesn't. I used to think she was behind because of the way we were always movin' around, never stayin' in one school for very long, but now I worry—not just because she's behind, but because there's letters that she just can't seem to get faced in the right direction no matter how hard she works at it. Letters like *b* and *d*, *p* and *q*, which *are* easy to mix up. But letters like *e* and *s* also seem to befuddle her, and I don't know why.

When she was younger, she used to sit close beside me and work at readin' aloud, but now she refuses. Despite the way she acts, I've come to believe that it's not so much stubbornness as it is not wantin' to let on that she has trouble with it. I see her mouthin' words over something like a *Little Orphan Annie* comic book that she *wants* to read, and it's slow going. It makes me sad, because havin' a book—even one I've read a dozen times—has helped me get through the rough times, helped me escape how we were livin'—at least for a while. Anna Mae doesn't have that, which may be part of why she's lookin' for other ways to escape.

When the cake has cooled, I teach the girls how to make buttercream frosting, which Anna Mae insists on etchin' *GR 17* into . . . and I don't say a thing about the *R* bein' backward.

At lunchtime, Mama still hasn't appeared and doesn't answer my gentle knock at her door. So when the girls say we should have cake for lunch, I laugh and say, "Why not?"

Papa comes in for a piece, then takes two hard-boiled eggs outside with him and gets back to work. And as we're cleanin' the kitchen once again, I find myself gettin' tearful.

"What's wrong?" Katie Bee asks, noticin' my watery eyes.

I push the tears aside. "Not a thing," I assure her. "It's just . . . well, this has been the best birthday of my life."

Midafternoon I help Papa pull another tree stump from the earth, and afterward I notice how dirty Faithful is. So I wash her down outside and whisk and wipe her clean inside, and after I fix a quick supper—one that Mama skips—Papa turns to me and says, "The girls can clean up, Ginny Rose. You've got a dance to get ready for."

So I lock myself in the latrine and clean up. It's a big job that involves washin' my hair and tryin' to use Papa's razor to shave the hair that's grown back under my arms and on my legs.

After a while, there's a rap at the door and Anna Mae whispers, "What're you doin' in there? You're takin' forever!"

I'm already skittish, and her knockin' makes me jump. "Go away!" I whisper back.

But she rattles the doorknob and whispers, "Let me in!"

I've already nicked my legs in two places, and now I'm havin' trouble with my underarms and feelin' twisted up tight over the whole business. So in a moment of complete frustration, I open the door, yank Anna Mae inside, and lock it again.

She takes in the situation: the bits of toilet tissue on my legs, the razor in my hand, my wet hair still wrapped in a dish towel. "Does Papa know?" she asks, eyein' the razor.

I shake my head.

She pulls up my arm, inspects underneath it. Pulls up the other, does the same. Then she takes the razor and tells me to hush and hold still and stop my fussin' while she works it ever so gently under each arm.

"There," she says at last, checkin' her handiwork with pride. "All done." Then she pulls the towel from my head, sits me on the toilet lid, and begins rakin' through my hair with the comb. I go to take it from her, but she slaps me away and says, "Sit still." Before long, my hair's free of tangles and she's reachin' for scissors.

"What are you *doin'*?" I whisper.

"Hush," she says. "It's all ragged. Don't worry—I'm good at this."

"How are you good at this?" I demand.

She pushes me into position. "I do the Littles."

"You do?"

She combs a section straight and snips the ragged ends. "Why do you think they're so cute and we're not?"

I laugh at this, and soon a kitten's worth of hair clippings is lyin' on the floor. "You cut a lot," I gasp, but when I stand and look in the mirror, I have no complaints. It's even and already comin' to life as it begins to dry in the warm evening air.

"Don't braid it," she says as I admire what she's done. "Braids don't go with that dress." Then she says, "I'll clean up. You go or you'll be late."

I hug her and whisper, "Thank you!" And then I remember. "Oh! One more thing." I reach into my pocket and produce the little jar of Mum that Peggy gave me.

"What's that?" she asks.

I twist off the lid and hand it to her to read, and I see her mouth "Mum" while I smear some on with my fingers.

"It stops odor," I explain, takin' the lid back. "Peggy gave it to me."

"I need a friend like Peggy!" she says in complete awe.

I laugh and hug her again. "Well, for now, you've got me."

And then I'm escapin' in Faithful wearin' an older dress and the shoes Peggy gave me, with the blue dress in the sack at my side. And though I'm late, Peggy whooshes me inside when I explain needin' to change. Before long, I've switched dresses and she's offerin' me lotion for my legs and hands, then pinnin' back a strand of my hair with a rhinestone clip that has a little heart on the end of it.

"Well, now," she says with a giggle. "Look at you."

I compliment the pretty belted dress she's wearin', and soon we're off, scurryin' out to the truck.

Inside Faithful, I go through the ritual of firin' her up. At first the motor sputters, and I catch Peggy's alarm. "That's just the way the old girl wakes up," I say with a laugh, quotin' what Papa always says. And then I keep on usin' Papa's words to put her at ease. "She's made it from Oklahoma clear to California, then up and down the Central Valley more times'n I can count." I grin at her as we putter away. "There's no doubt she'll make it to the dance."

And make it to the dance she does, but not without Peggy askin' to honk the horn.

"You're teasin', right?" I ask.

But she laughs and says, "No!"

So I let her, and *ah-ooh-gah, ah-ooh-gah,* she announces our arrival as we bounce into the parking lot.

"My!" I laugh. "I guess you *don't* care!" because people *do* look at us, and we *are* the only ones arrivin' in an old jalopy.

"Lisette says it's all about attitude," she says, sittin' taller, "so let's have some."

I feel my hackles rise at the mention of Lisette, but I do like the way Peggy's actin' and feel myself sittin' taller, too. After all, Faithful's seen plenty of hostility and even armed blockades; what's a few snickers from teenagers at a dance?

I park, and as we walk toward the entrance, Peggy takes me over to two other girls huddled outside and introduces us. "Ginny Rose will be attending school with us," she explains. "I hope you'll help her feel welcome."

"Of course!" they say with bright smiles, and then one of them asks, "So where's Lisette?"

"She'll be here," Peggy says, then conjures a smile. "She's dating Rodney St. Clair."

"Lisette is?" the other girl asks. "Vivian said *she* was."

The first girl laughs. "Next week it'll be someone else." She turns a wry smile on me and says, "Welcome to Oakvale, where you should definitely steer clear of Rodney St. Clair."

They walk off, and Peggy's smile collapses. "I was such a fool," she whispers.

"About . . . Rodney?" I ask, the words tiptoein' out.

She nods. "What was I thinking?" She shakes her head. "I do worry about Lisette. She's so head over heels for him." She heaves a sigh. "But I suppose if anyone can land him for good, it's her." After a moment, she shakes off the thought and pulls me along toward the Community Center with a smile. "Come on. Let's go have some fun."

Inside, the hall is bustlin'. There's a small swing band playin' and lots of couples dancin'. The excitement's contagious, but the little butterflies I had walkin' in have become a big swarm inside me. I've never been to a dance like this, and I sure can't twirl and flip around like the couple that's doin' a wild jitterbug in the middle of the floor.

Peggy takes my hand and pulls me into the ring of people watchin', and soon we're clappin' along to the music with everyone else. "Fantastic, aren't they?" Peggy calls over to me. When I nod, she laughs and says, "Don't worry. You don't have to do *that* to have fun!"

It turns out to be true, because after she's introduced me to a group of people she knows from school, a boy named Timothy Evans asks me to dance.

"I'm just a beginner!" I warn him.

"That makes two of us!" he says with a laugh. "Watch your toes!"

So we follow Peggy and a boy named Paul Broski to the outskirts of the dance area, and after a few minutes, I'm twistin' and turnin' and havin' a laugh just tryin' to keep up. I love the way the skirt of the blue dress swishes around my knees. It feels so *free,* and so unlike the stiff and scratchy things I'm used to wearin'. Before long, I find myself turnin' farther and faster, kickin' out higher and wider, just to feel the fabric swish around me.

When the song's over, Timothy asks, "You want to go again?"

I most definitely do, and the four of us stay on the floor for three more songs, with Peggy and me even spinnin' out and back between Timothy and Paul on the last one.

And then Peggy pulls me away, thankin' the boys and sayin', "I need to introduce her around."

"Thanks for the dances," Paul says to her, then blurts out, "You're way more fun with her than you've ever been with Lisette."

We're both so surprised by the comment that we leave without another word. And after we've had a drink of punch and Peggy's introduced me to a few other people, I notice her slyly searchin' the room.

"You're wonderin' where Lisette is?" I ask.

She nods. "It's not like her to be so late."

"And to not be in the middle of the dance floor?" I say, wishin' my voice would quit lettin' slip how I feel about her. "I'm just rememberin' the skating rink," I add quickly.

"She *is* a good person," Peggy says, turnin' her attention to me. Her look is direct but not angry. More just . . . concerned.

Then her gaze sweeps down my dress and over the shoes

she gave me. It's a casual thing, gone in the blink of an eye, but I catch a gentle breeze of unspoken thoughts, which soon twists itself into a dust devil in my mind.

The dress Peggy's wearin' is pretty, but it doesn't compare to my own. And it's true that I'm a bit smaller, but I'm sure the one I'm wearin' would fit her just fine.

So . . . why am I in this beautiful dress and not her?

Where *did* these clothes come from?

A commotion across the room scatters my thoughts. And then a raised voice makes Peggy look at me with wide eyes and say, "That sounds like Bobby! But . . . what's *he* doing here?"

Another voice shouts, "Get your hands off me!" But the words are sloppy. Slurred.

Peggy gasps, "That's *Rodney*."

Like a bolt of jagged lightning, we cut through the crowd toward the commotion, and when we get to the front of the crowd, Peggy's hand flies up to cover her mouth. "Oh no!"

In a small clearing to the side of the dance floor, Rodney's bearin' down on Bobby, swingin' wild punches at him. Bobby doesn't seem to be fightin' back, though; he's just duckin' or swattin' away Rodney's fists. I spot Lisette across the clearing from us lookin' both picture-perfect and thunderstruck, her hand also up to her mouth.

"She's *mine*, you moron!" Rodney shouts as he swings for Bobby. "I can do what I want!"

Bobby leans aside to miss the punch, then shoves Rodney hard against both shoulders, sendin' him staggerin' backward. "Not when she's telling you to lay off," he says, and shoves him again.

Rodney stumbles back but manages not to fall. "It's none

of your damn business!" he yells. Then he launches himself at Bobby, but Bobby easily sidesteps him, grabs him by the scruff, and tosses him to the floor.

"Stop!" Peggy cries, steppin' forward and spreadin' her arms wide between the two. She turns to Rodney. "What did you do to Lisette?"

Rodney staggers to his feet. "Nothin', Peaches," he says with a sloppy grin. "I swear." Then he stumbles to the floor again, all on his own.

Peggy glares at him, then turns to face her brother. "Lisette doesn't want a knight on a white horse," she says through clenched teeth. "She wants *him*."

Bobby looks at Peggy coolly. "I'm not here for her," he says. Then he scans the room until his eyes land on . . . me. At first his face shows surprise as he takes in the way I look. But then a boyish grin breaks out, and he steps toward me, leavin' Rodney and Peggy and Lisette behind.

My cheeks go hot.

Mighty hot.

"What I was hoping, Miss Gilley," he says as his golden lashes do a bashful droop, "was that I might have the pleasure of a dance with *you*."

And while the rest of the hall seems to have gone completely still, he gives me a look full of hope and courage and puts out his hand.

"Why, Bobby Simmons," I say with a curious smile.

Then I square my shoulders, place my hand in his, and let him lead me onto the dance floor.

31

Peggy

FLABBERGASTED

I was flabbergasted when Bobby asked Ginny Rose to dance. And the way Ginny Rose smiled and blushed before taking Bobby's hand? My heart leaped for joy.

But when they disappeared onto the dance floor, I immediately remembered.

Rodney.

What *had* he done to Lisette? And the scoundrel hadn't said a word to me since the roller rink, and now, staggering drunk, he'd had the *nerve* to give me a lewd grin and call me Peaches?

I was going to give him a piece of my mind!

Maybe even the slap side of my hand!

But I never got the chance, because suddenly Vivian Yelsen appeared.

And so did her father.

Vivian's eyes were red and puffy, and she was pleading hysterically with her father. *"Please* don't!" she cried, pulling hard on his sleeve.

But Mr. Yelsen shook her off and grabbed Rodney by the front of his shirt and wagged him like a rag doll. "I saw you slinking off like a tomcat last night!" he shouted. "She's told me what you've done, and now you're two-timing her?"

Mr. Yelsen is a large, barrel-chested man with meaty hands, and at the moment he had the fiery face of an angry bull. So Rodney *should* have been shaking in his shoes, but instead he grinned at Mr. Yelsen, flipped his hands in a helpless shrug, and said, "What can I say? They all want me."

"You *punk*," Mr. Yelsen yelled, then muscled him along toward the back door, giving Vivian a disgusted look as he said, "Get moving! We're going to the police."

"No, Daddy, please, no!" she cried, but followed him in a flood of tears.

My mind raced. An angry father might barge in on a dance and haul off a boy for slinking around, but there was only one reason he'd haul that boy off to the police.

Vivian was in trouble.

The same kind of trouble Doris had been in.

Which might also explain why Rodney had become staggering drunk.

I hurried over to Lisette, who was frozen in place and wide-eyed, one hand still covering her mouth. I noticed her new dress was ripped along a seam beneath her collarbone. "Come on," I said gently. "Let's go get some fresh air."

Her hand stayed in place and her feet remained planted. *"Last night?"* she said weakly. "He told me he had to help his father last night. And last week Friday, too. And"—I watched the wheels turn in her mind as she realized she wasn't Rodney's one and only—"and the week before that."

"He's a louse," I said, putting an arm around her waist and pulling her along. "He never in a million years deserved you."

"But—" She dropped her hand and looked at me, desperation in her eyes. "Maybe I'm jumping to conclusions? Maybe he was at Vivian's to . . . to tell her to stop bothering him. He did say she was bothering him."

I couldn't believe my ears. Didn't she see what was going on? How could she possibly still want to be with him?

But there it was, in her eyes, clear as the tears falling from them.

She did.

"Lisette," I said as I worked her away from the people whispering around us and into a quiet corner at the back of the hall. "I know you're in shock, but you understand how serious this is for Vivian, don't you?"

Lisette looked hurt. And confused. "Why are you taking *her* side?"

I took a calming breath. "Lisette, think about it. They're on their way to the *police station*?"

She just stared at me.

"The next stop will probably be the *courthouse*?"

She still looked confused.

"With a *shotgun*?"

Her eyes sprang open and she gasped. "No!"

I felt myself getting angry. "Lisette, wake up! He's a scoundrel! A rogue! He's been lying to you and taking advantage of your feelings for him!"

"But . . . he told me he *loved* me," she said weakly.

"You don't think he's told Vivian the same thing? You heard what he said to Mr. Yelsen!"

"He's drunk," she whimpered.

"And why do you suppose he got drunk?" I pressed. "And why did my brother have to stop him from . . . whatever he was doing to you?" I pointed to the torn seam of her dress. "That's not love, Lisette."

She covered her weeping eyes with her hands, then slid down the wall and sat on the floor. Which was not a good idea. Not a good idea at all. "Everyone's watching," I whispered. It was an exaggeration—most people had gone back to dancing, but some gossips *were* watching, and I thought Lisette's pride would motivate her to get up.

I was wrong.

She just sat there, sobbing.

Sobbing and sobbing and *sobbing*.

I couldn't seem to get her to stop, or even to look at me.

I was kneeling in front of her, doing my best to block her from prying eyes, and finally, I grabbed her by the shoulders and shook her a little. "Lisette!"

"My life is ruined," she said, looking at me at last. "Everything . . . all of it . . . It's a disaster!"

"No, it's not. It may be a mess right now, but it won't stay that way." I reached for her hands. "Get up. Get up and fight back. Do not waste your tears or your time on that scoundrel. Show him— show everyone—that he isn't worth the air you breathe out. Or the dirt you walk on! Or the—"

She gave me a little squint. "The air I breathe *out*? The *dirt* I walk on?"

"That's right!"

She stared at me for a long moment, and then very slowly a giggle bubbled through all her pain. "The dirt I walk on!"

"You know what I mean!" I pulled her so she'd stand. "Get up and fight."

"But *how?*"

"By cutting him out of your life, your mind, your *heart*. By looking through him, *seeing* through him. Why on earth would someone as smart and beautiful as you settle for a smooth-talking cheat?" I felt my temperature rising with each word, and then out of my mouth shot "You need to end up doing something better than playing cat and mouse with boys!"

"Like what?"

Her even asking that felt . . . sad. "Like . . . I don't know. . . ." I thought about the things Lisette was good at, the things she loved to do. Besides boys, the one interest in her life was fashion. She lived for fashion. "How about going to design school?"

"*Design* school?"

"Yes! They must have one in San Francisco! *That's* what you should be thinking about! How do I become a fashion designer? How can I do something *I'm* good at?"

This outburst surprised her, and it surprised me, too. In all our years together, Lisette had never even *mentioned* wanting to be a fashion designer, but in that moment it became crystal clear—*that's* what she should do. Lisette *didn't* belong in Ferry-bank *or* Oakvale, or even Modesto. And since the war, women *did* have more options.

"Don't become your mother," I breathed. "If you stay here, you'll end up moving in small-town social circles and mixing drinks for a man. Is *that* what you want?" And then the other half of all of this escaped my lips. "If *you* don't become your mother, *I* won't become mine. I'll figure out what *I* want to do, and I'll make myself be brave enough to go after it." A little sigh escaped me, because I had no idea in the whole wide world what that something might be. I just knew now with absolute certainty that it wasn't farming.

It felt like I'd flung our lives into the middle of the deep blue sea, and maybe for me there was no visible horizon, but what I'd said to Lisette seemed to be filling her sails.

"Design school," she murmured, her eyes suddenly dry.

"Why not? Why can't you become the next Christian Dior?"

She actually laughed. "Well, he *is* a man!"

"And why should a *man* be the most famous designer of *women's* fashion?" I gave a little shrug. "Seems to me it should be someone who understands being a female. Someone smart, with a flair for style. Someone like *you*."

"Hmm," she said, and I could see her sighting land. "You know, I just read that Vera Maxwell has her own line now. She started as a model and worked for other designers, and now there's a Vera Maxwell Originals label."

"See? That could be you. No, that *should* be you!"

"Do you really think so?"

"Of course I really think so! But it will never happen if you stay stuck on Rodney St. Clair. He's going to live in Oakvale, selling cars and flashing that smile at every pretty girl who happens by, for the rest of his life."

She frowned a moment, then said, "Okay then."

"Okay then?"

"I'm done with him," she said firmly. "The lying, two-timing, go-nowhere cad."

"Okay, wait. It's not *that* easy," I said. "Tomorrow you may—"

"No. Tomorrow and every day after I'm going to put my sights on becoming a fashion designer. I am done with Rodney . . . and every other smooth-talking Valley boy." She dusted off the back of her dress as if just realizing she'd been sitting on the floor earlier. "Good riddance to him and his pretty face. I don't care if I *never* see him again."

I was sure it was mostly the excitement of a new idea talking, but I wasn't going to discourage it. "Well, good for you. And I agree. I hadn't seen him since the skating rink, you know. I wasn't sure how I'd feel tonight."

She turned her eyes on me. And for a long moment she just stared, but at last she said, "I'd like to be a better friend to you. I really would." And before I could protest, she said, "Let's go, shall we?"

"Go?" I asked.

"Rodney had me meet him here. My car's outside."

"Well, I'm glad you didn't drive with him in *that* condition, but . . . I came with Ginny Rose. I can't just leave."

She looked a little confused. "So . . . where *is* she?"

"I'm hoping she's still dancing with my brother."

"What?"

"You saw him, didn't you?"

"How could I miss him? He stopped Rodney from . . . from being fresh. And then there was that horrible fight!"

"I mean, you saw him ask Ginny Rose to dance, right?"

Her hand was back in front of her mouth. "No! Really? I guess I was too embarrassed by Rodney to notice. And then all I could see was Vivian and her dad."

I grabbed her hand. "Well, come on. Let's go find her."

It had been at least half an hour since the scene with Rodney, but Bobby and Ginny Rose were still together on the dance floor, both of them rosy-cheeked and smiling.

"Gosh!" Lisette breathed. "Look at them! They're so . . ."

Her voice just trailed off, so I filled in: "Perfect together?" She was silent, and when I turned to face her, I saw that her eyes were tearing up. "What's wrong?" I asked.

She sighed. "Nothing. It's just so sweet." She sighed again. "So romantic."

Two boys came up just then and asked us to dance, but after Lisette and I shared a look, she replied, "Thank you, but no. We just want to watch."

We picked up clapping along to the music with the rest of the crowd and watched Bobby and Ginny Rose move around the floor. They weren't great dancers by any means, but they seemed to be having a great time. "Admit it," Lisette said. "I was right about the dress. It looks like it was *made* for her."

"What's there to admit?" I laughed. "You're always right about the dress!"

Then, without taking her eyes off Ginny Rose and Bobby, she asked, "Does he know?"

"Know what?"

"What you're planning."

"No!" I said. "Nobody knows!"

She watched a little longer, then abruptly turned to me and said, "I'm going home."

"Wait!" I held her by the arm, worried that seeing Ginny Rose and Bobby together had turned her sentimental over Rodney. "Are you sure that's a good idea? Maybe you should come over? Stay with me tonight?"

She shook her head. "I need to get my life in order." She frowned. "Daddy's back from his trip. It's time I faced him, too."

This seemed like a very bad idea. "Isn't that a lot for one night?"

"I've got to quit avoiding truths," she said, then clasped my hands in hers and squeezed. "Don't worry. I'll be fine." She hurried off, saying, "I'll meet you at church tomorrow morning, and then we'll do something fun for your birthday, I promise!"

"Anything with you will be fun," I called after her with a wave.

Suddenly Ginny Rose was right beside me, flushed and breathless. "Is it really ten o'clock? I have to go! I have to go now!"

Bobby rushed up after her. "What's going on?"

"Peggy and I have to go!" Ginny Rose threw over her shoulder. Then a thought seemed to strike her and she asked me, "Can you go home with your brother? Please? I'm late, and Mama will be—"

"Yes!" I said. "Go!" And in a whirl of blue she was racing out the door.

"What happened?" Bobby asked, looking terribly confused.

I laughed. "It wasn't anything you did." Then I linked my arm in his and said, "Please tell me you didn't ride Blossom here."

"Of course I didn't ride Blossom here!"

"Then please tell me you can give me a ride home."

He still seemed dazed, but he nodded.

And then he just stood there, staring dumbly at the place where Ginny Rose had been.

Well, I thought, pulling him along, *it's about time.*

32

Ginny Rose

A WARNIN'

I'm in such a frenzied state as I leave the dance that I nearly flood Faithful tryin' to start her. Ten o'clock! Where *did* the time go?

And what on earth, Bobby Simmons?

Not only did he turn his back on Lisette to ask me to dance, he only had eyes for me. He never looked over his shoulder—or mine—for her. Not once! And he wouldn't let Timothy Evans cut in. And Timothy tried. Twice!

My cheeks are still hot and my mind's in a twister as Faithful turns over and I race for home. It's not until I pass by Simmons Farm that it dawns on me that I'm still in the blue dress.

I can't go home like this!

I press the brake pedal but . . . what am I thinkin'? I don't have time to stop! I'm already late, and Peggy isn't home and might not be for some time. And it's my birthday—my *birthday*. Surely that's excuse enough to be wearin' a pretty dress. One that's a gift from a friend.

I hurry on, lettin' sweet memories from the day bubble their way through my worry—bakin' the cake with my sisters, Anna Mae's gentle help in the latrine, wearin' this magical dress, bein' introduced around by Peggy, dancin' with boys and . . .

What on earth, Bobby Simmons!

When I near our house, I cut the lights and motor and coast the last hundred feet, hopin' to slip in without notice.

For a moment, it seems I've done just that. The house is dark and still, and I feel a wash of relief as I tiptoe inside. But then through the darkness Mama's voice growls, "You're late."

I move forward and find her sittin' at the table in the dark, her hands wrapped around an empty coffee cup.

"I'm sorry," I say. Then I blurt out, "A boy I like asked me to dance and I . . . I lost track of time." I'm hopin' the truth will reach her heart; that she'll remember what it was like when Papa first asked her to dance all those years ago.

Instead, she demands to know: "Did he kiss you?"

"Mama! No!"

She clicks on the light. "That's not the dress you left here in."

"It's Peggy's," I say, my mind whirlin'.

It's not a lie, I tell myself. I will give it back. I will most certainly give it back.

"Who's the boy?"

"Bobby Simmons," I choke out, sure of what's comin' next.

"Figures," she says with a scowl, and that single word seems to hold a lifetime of resentment. Then she says, "I wouldn't go pinnin' my hopes on him. His folks are not likely to approve."

"Mama! Bobby and I danced! That's all!"

"Oh, I see the glow on you, Ginny Rose. Don't think you can pull one over on me."

"I'm not tryin' to—" I hear my voice risin' and stop myself. "Mama, why can't you just be happy for me?"

"Because no good'll come of it, and in your desperation, he's already got you breakin' rules."

"My *desperation*?"

"Your pa sees things one way, I see 'em another." She puts her cup in the sink, and just before she turns out the light, she looks me straight in the eye and says, "You need a coolin'-off period. Except for work, you're restricted to home for two weeks."

"Mama!" I cry through the sudden darkness. "It's my *birthday*."

"No need to remind me what day it is, child."

"I'm thinkin' there is!" I cry. "And I'm not a child! I've been takin' on the weight of your responsibilities for—"

"*Enough,*" she snaps. "You're now restricted for *three* weeks. And after, you're no longer drivin' yourself to socials." She puts out a hand. "Give me the key."

So I hand over Faithful's spare key.

It feels like turnin' over the key to my jail cell.

After she pockets it, she says, "That's over for good," and shuffles toward the hallway.

There's so much I want to say. To shout! But I know it'll just dig me in deeper, so I hold my tongue as she leaves the room and stand in the dark feelin' the bruise of her words on my happiness.

"She's awful," hisses through the darkness. It's soft and angry, a quiet curse on a puff of air.

"Anna Mae?" I whisper, strainin' to see.

She emerges from behind Mama's chair, where she's been hidin' wrapped in a brown blanket. It seems impossible that

Mama didn't see her, but then neither did I. She pulls me along to a kitchen window and looks me over in the soft moonlight. "You look so pretty," she says.

Tears spring to my eyes. Why couldn't Mama say *that*?

"She's been sittin' there broodin' since Papa went to bed," Anna Mae says. "She was *hopin'* you'd be late so she could restrict you."

"But *why*?"

"'Cause Papa scolded her tonight about ignorin' your birthday and neglectin' us. 'Cause when he's around and you're not, Mama can't shut herself in her room and expect you to do everything!" She frowns. "Promise me when you decide to run off, you'll take me with you."

"I'm not runnin' off!" I say. "I'm workin' to make things better."

She snorts. "It's too late for that, Ginny Rose. She's broken and set on breakin' the rest of us."

I look at her, stupefied. She may be ten, but she doesn't sound it, or act it, or even *think* like it. "Anna Mae," I say gently, "Mama is not broken. Well, maybe her heart is, but even that can be healed. I'm not ready to give up, and you shouldn't be either. If what I'm doin' doesn't help, we'll try something different." But the words do feel empty inside me. Like hope's decided it's finally time to start slippin' away.

"So when?" she demands. "When's that gonna be?"

I pull hope back with what little strength I have. "Well, Peggy says Mrs. Poole is optimistic they'll get donations at the church service tomorrow, and between that and my wages and what Peggy's been puttin' in, we should be makin' good progress."

"But *when*?" she demands.

"We'll have to wait and see!" My words sound testy, and right off I regret them. So I try to soften things by addin', "You may not remember it well, but Mama never used to be this way. Even when times were desperate, she always tried to put a good face on things." I frown as something occurs to me. "It seems the better off we get, the worse off *she* gets."

Anna Mae frowns, too. "Curiouser and curiouser," she says, quotin' *Alice's Adventures in Wonderland*. Then she looks me over again and says, "You look like her right now."

"Like Mama?" I gasp, horrified.

"No," she laughs. "Like Alice. Like a grown-up Alice." Her face turns impish. "So?" she whispers, pullin' me along. "Tell me about the dance!"

We hole up in a dark corner in case Mama returns, wrapped together in the blanket, and I start talkin'. Anna Mae does much more'n listen, too. She asks me for all the little details, especially about Bobby.

"Did you like him when you worked their orchard?" she asks.

"No." I shrug. "But it hit me pretty hard when I first saw him this summer."

Then I explain about him bein' struck dumb by Lisette and the way he asked about her while I was buildin' the shade, and I find myself tellin' her who Rodney St. Clair is and how he relates to Peggy and Lisette, and why Bobby askin' *me* to dance was such a shock.

In the end, I share things I probably shouldn't, but Anna Mae's bein' such a good listener and it feels so nice to talk about it that it all just tumbles out.

But then I remember.

She used to blackmail me.

"Anna Mae," I say, turnin' to look right at her. "I'm *trustin'* you with all of this."

"I know that," she says. "Don't be stupid."

Which is all the assurance I need.

"We'd better get to bed," I whisper, and once we're tucked in and I hear her breathing fall into the easy rhythm of sleep, I let go of my worry and drift off to the memory of the blue dress swishin' as Bobby Simmons guides me around the dance floor, his strong hand gentle on my waist.

Sunday morning breaks bright and hot, and much too soon. Chores are in full swing before I can shake off the intoxication of my dreams, and Mama and Papa act like it's any other Sunday, with no mention of my restriction or tardiness.

I wonder if Papa even knows.

The Littles are cranky with each other, and Anna Mae's short-tempered, snappin' at them to quit piddlin' around, when what it seems they need is to go back to bed. Maybe we all do!

It's late morning when a timid knock comes at the door. Mama's out in the garden, Papa's on the back porch, and the four of us girls are tendin' to wash that's been pulled down off the line—the Littles matchin' socks, Anna Mae workin' the iron, while I apply a needle and thread to repairs and loose buttons.

The four of us trade looks, not sure we've heard right, but when the knock comes again, the Littles charge for the door. In their race to reach it, they tangle up and land in a heap, and Anna Mae passes them by. Miffed, the Littles are windin' up for a fuss, but when Anna Mae opens the door and we see it's Peggy standin' on the stoop, they forget their tumble and wrap her in hugs.

"Hello, girls!" Peggy says with a nervous laugh. Her cheeks are rosy from ridin' her bike, and from the looks of her half-tucked blouse, her twisted skirt, and the hat in her basket, she went to church tidy and ended up here windblown and rumpled.

I know something's wrong, and Anna Mae sees it, too, because she gathers the Littles, sayin', "Peggy wants you to . . . to write your names for her! Can you do your names?"

"She does?" the Littles ask together.

I look at Anna Mae in wonder, then play along. "That's right," I say, kneelin' in front of them. "Do the neatest job you can. All the letters should be perfect! Can you do that? Bring 'em out when you're ready. The *last* one done will be the winner, 'cause their letters are sure to be the neatest." I guide them back inside, sayin', "Anna Mae will help you, but not too much, okay, Anna Mae?"

It's plain to see Anna Mae would rather stay outside with Peggy, but she takes the girls, tossin' me a look that says I'd better spill every detail later.

I give her a quick nod, close the door, and ask Peggy, "What's wrong?"

"Reverend Poole did a *wonderful* job introducing the sketch of your brothers and calling on the congregation to be neighborly and generous. I haven't seen him so fired up about a sermon in ages."

"A sermon?" I ask, certain she's misspoken.

"Yes! The whole talk was built on what it means to be neighbors on this earth and how it's our duty to welcome each other, especially people who've faced hardships or feel unsure of their place in our community." She takes a quick look around and lowers her voice. "And then he unveiled the sketch and explained the situation and said the church was raising money for a plot and a coffin. 'Bring these boys home,' he said over and over. 'Bring them home!' "

My eyes are suddenly stingin'. This is more'n I could have hoped for, much more! But it doesn't explain the worry still strainin' Peggy's face. "So . . . what happened?" I ask.

"People gave money! A lot of money! And Reverend Poole did say that the family wanted to stay anonymous, but . . ."

"But . . . ?"

Her face pinches. "Mrs. Smith was there."

Blood stands still for a moment in my veins.

"And after the service, I overheard her talking with Mrs. Wilson and her husband."

I give her a blank look. "Who?"

"She's a history teacher at school. It sounded like she also works at the cannery. They were discussing who the boys might be."

I try to take quick stock of the damage. Could they piece it together from what I've said?

And then Peggy comes out with it. "I heard Mrs. Smith say your name."

"Oh no!"

"So I lingered nearby and overheard *Mr.* Wilson say, 'I work with a fella named Gilley.' And then Mrs. Smith said, 'At the switching yard?' and Mr. Wilson said, 'Yes.' And *then* he said, 'I'll find out at work tomorrow.' After that, I came straight over here to warn you."

My legs go wobbly, landin' me on the step.

"I'm so sorry!" she whispers, sittin' beside me. "I thought it was such a good idea to have Reverend Poole ask for donations. I can't believe this happened!" And then she says, "But what it means is we have to go tomorrow."

"*Tomorrow?*"

"Yes," she whispers. "If we don't go tomorrow, everything will fall apart."

"But . . . tomorrow's Monday, and Papa drives the truck to work!"

"If your father gets to work, he'll find out what you're planning!"

I know she's right. But . . . *tomorrow?* It's all so sudden! I need time to think!

Peggy stands. "Unless you want to call the whole thing off?"

I stand, too. "It's too late for that!"

"No, it's not!"

I turn things over in my mind. In another year I'll be old enough to make my own way in the world. But how can I leave Anna Mae or the Littles with Mama the way she is? And maybe there's other ways to change things, but Papa's a closed book, and in her own way Mama is too. So it feels like all I've got is this desperate plan.

I turn to Peggy and blurt out what's on my mind: "I know today's your birthday, Peggy. I'm so sorry for all of this."

Her head tilts a bit, and she studies me like I'm a curious little bug. "How in the world did you remember that?"

I look down. "'Cause . . . well . . . it's the day after mine."

"It's the . . . Wait. . . . So yesterday . . . ?"

"Was the best birthday of my life, thanks to you."

"But I—"

"And I feel awful that yours is off to such a bad start on account of . . . my situation."

"But—"

"And if you want out, I do understand. But I'm goin'. I've got to."

She stares at me dumbly for a bit, then shakes her head quick, like she's dismissin' every stray thought from her mind. "We'll have to leave early," she says. "Pack whatever supplies you think we'll need and pick me up at four-thirty tomorrow morning."

"Four-thirty!"

"Any later and Father and Bobby'll be up, so don't be late!" She starts for her bike, then stops short and says, "There's no . . . *box* for them."

"We'll make do with a blanket," I tell her, tryin' to sound confident.

She gives me a doubtful look but says, "I'll be waiting by the stand with a shovel."

And the next thing I know, she's ridin' away.

33

Peggy

TRAPPED

I was plenty anxious as I rode over to the Gilleys' to break the news about what had happened at church, but my mind was positively reeling as I rode away. All the yesterdays of planning hadn't prepared me for what would be tomorrow's action.

Were we really doing this?

There had to be a better way!

But I couldn't avoid the fact that my meddling was what had thrown the plan into motion. Why had I thought no one in the congregation would piece together who the boys were? Why had I become involved at all?

But I had, and I was responsible for the situation we were in, and I could not in good conscience back out now.

Adding to my anxiety was a nagging worry about Lisette. She hadn't shown up at church like she'd promised, and I was afraid that was because last night's convictions had gone soft. So rather than going straight home to set up the fruit stand, I took back roads and pedaled as fast as I could to the Bovees'.

It was Mr. Bovee who answered the door as I stood panting on his porch. He was dressed but completely disheveled, and was holding a glass with an inch of golden liquid in it.

I blinked.

Was that liquor?

At eleven in the morning?

And then I remembered—Lisette had said she was going to have a talk with him about moving. Or, rather, about *not* moving.

"Well, look who's here," Mr. Bovee slurred at me across the threshold. "The agitator herself."

"Excuse me?" I asked.

"You think I don't know you're the one who put these confulating . . ." His brow furrowed. "Confu . . . confaluting . . ." He frowned and consulted his liquor, muttering, "Confuddled . . . con . . ."

". . . founded?" I asked.

He snapped to. "Yes!" He waved the glass through the air and cried, "Confounded!" then immediately looked puzzled again. "What was I saying?"

It seemed like a good time to switch subjects. "Is Lisette home?" I asked, like everything was perfectly normal.

"Oh, she's home!" he snorted. "And she's staying that way!" Then he called over his shoulder, "Aren't you, Lisette?"

"Lisette!" I shouted past him. "Are you okay?"

"Of course she's okay," Mr. Bovee said, sputtering saliva. "I give her everything, don't I?"

"Lisette!" I called past him again.

"But not anymore!" he boomed. "She doesn't like the way I earn a living? Let her see what it's like to live without!"

"LISETTE!"

"And she can thank *you*," Mr. Bovee snarled, his eyes squinting down on me. "You're the one who's turned my daughter against me!"

Lisette appeared, wearing pajamas and looking like she'd just woken up. But her eyes weren't puffy or red, and she *didn't* look like she'd had a relapse over Rodney. She looked perfectly fine.

"Daddy?" she said, gently taking the glass out of his hand. "Have you been up all night?"

"Don't you 'Daddy' me!" he snarled. "Go back to your room!" He turned to me. "And you get off my porch. And don't come back!"

Lisette caught my eye and pointed frantically to the ceiling as the door slammed in my face. I understood exactly what she meant and made my way around the house, where I waited beneath her window.

After a few minutes, her window opened. "I'm so sorry!" she said, half whispering.

"Are you all right?" I asked.

"Yes! He's taken away my car and my allowance and says I can find my own place to live if I don't like the one he provides. But that's okay."

"That's *not* okay!"

"It is! You are so right about design school. I am setting my sights on that."

"But . . . you have a full year before you can do that!"

"What's he going to do? Have me thrown out of this house? Not if he wants to run for mayor!" She looked behind her and then quickly turned back. "Mom's screaming for me." She frowned. "Before I talked to Daddy last night, I got her to agree to tell him she didn't want to move either, but she had a few drinks and buckled. It was pathetic." She reached her arms up to close the window, saying, "Sorry I didn't make it to church. I guess you can see why! And I'm so sorry about your birthday! I promise I'll make it up to you."

The window was starting down. "Wait!" I called. "Church was a disaster."

"What?" And then, "Oh. I did it again, talking all about me. I'm so sorry." She shot a look over her shoulder and called, "Coming!" then turned her attention back to me. "Tell me quick."

So I did, and ended with "We're going tomorrow morning. She's picking me up at four-thirty."

"Four-thirty?" Lisette stared at me for a moment. "And why tomorrow?"

"Because it's tomorrow or never."

"'Never' sounds good to me!" she said.

I could hear Mrs. Bovee screaming out Lisette's name. "Go!" I said. "And if you need a place to escape to, you can always stay with me!"

She laughed. "Oh, that would go over like a lead balloon with your mother! I think I'll take my chances here!" Then she closed the window.

Back home, Bobby clip-clopped up on Blossom as I was putting the bicycle in the shed. "Where have you been?" he asked.

This made me bristle. "Church," I answered curtly.

He frowned. "Good luck trying that answer on Mother." He shifted in the saddle as I rolled the shed door closed, and with it seemed to come a shift in his attitude. "Look," he said. "I don't know what's going on with you, but it seems to me the wheels are wobbling off the cart."

"What's *that* supposed to mean?"

"Just what it sounds like." He shrugged. "Look at you."

I did. And it was true. I was a flustered mess.

He kept his gaze firmly on me. "I'm wondering if I can help." My jaw dropped.

"You've been right about a lot," he said. Then he went on in a strangely thoughtful way. "It's helped more than you know. And it's made me think that I should try harder to stand by you the way you've stood by me."

After all the private thoughts I'd had about Bobby, I didn't feel I deserved his compliment. "I haven't been—"

"I know I can be annoying," he interrupted. "People don't always make sense to me. You usually have a way of seeing things I don't, but right now I think *I'm* seeing things that maybe *you* don't." He leaned down low. "You in some kind of trouble, Peg? Is there something I can do?"

Yes! my brain screamed. *You can build me a coffin, so if we find those boys, we'll have someplace to put them! You can grab a shovel and come with us to Garysville! You can drive us to Garysville so we don't have to go in a rattletrap jalopy! You can—*

But it was all too much, and I didn't know if this new Bobby would last or was trustworthy, or if hearing what Ginny Rose was doing would change his new feelings for her.

It was *such* a grisly thing we were planning—one that didn't mesh at all with romance! And there *was* the possibility of romance, because he had done nothing but ask me questions about Ginny Rose on our ride home from the dance. I had never seen him so flushed or so *happy*. Not a word about Lisette. Barely a word about Rodney. All he'd wanted to talk about was Ginny Rose.

So once again I swallowed my fear and simply said, "I'm not

in trouble, Bobby." I wanted to add, *I sure will be tomorrow, though,* but I bit it back. "Sweet of you to be concerned, but everything's fine."

His eyes narrowed. "You don't trust me, is that it?"

I looked away. "I'm sworn to secrecy."

He frowned a moment, letting that sink in. "Is she all right?"

"Who?"

"Lisette. Hot Rod's a jerk, anyone can see that. Anyone but her, I suppose."

So we were back on Lisette now?

He caught my look and said, "I just don't want to see her get hurt is all."

"She's fine," I said curtly.

He gave me an appraising look. "Fine like *you're* fine?"

I heaved a sigh. "Look, I've got to go. Mother's probably fit to be tied over my tardiness."

"Oh, she is that," he said, turning Blossom. "I told her to lay off on account of your birthday, but when has she ever minded a word *I* said?"

He started riding away, and my heart suddenly went soft. "Bobby!" I called after him.

He looked over his shoulder.

"Thank you. It was sweet of you to notice. And to ask. And to say you want to stand by me. I promise I'll do the same. And that I'll tell you more . . . soon."

He gave me a nod. It was firm and sincere, like a handshake. Then he rode off, and I scurried into the house to receive my scolding.

There was a cake cooling on the counter, but Mother wasn't in the kitchen. "She's outside working the stand," Nonnie said, taking in my appearance with an eyebrow cocked. "Seems your birthday's off to a rocky start."

I hurried out to the stand and found Mother attending to customers while the twins ran wild, chasing each other with sticks.

"I'm sorry I'm late," I said in a rush, taking a place beside her.

Mother was handing money back to a customer I'd seen for the first time two days before. "It's only a dollar," Mother told her.

"Really?" the woman said, then looked directly at me. "But *she* charged me one and a half just the other day."

My cheeks went hot. "Did I?" I asked as innocently as I could.

"You most certainly did!" the woman insisted. "Remember I said it was higher than market prices, and you said these were fresh-baked and worth it?"

Flames were coming off my ears now, and Mother noticed. "Take the twins and go inside," she commanded, keeping her voice low.

"But—"

"*Now.*"

"I'm sorry if I made a mistake," I told the woman, but Mother was already apologizing with a free sack of peaches. "Go!" she growled at me.

I corralled the twins, tossed aside their sticks, dragged them kicking and screaming inside, and tried to get them to play Chutes and Ladders. But they were in no mood for it, and I was in no mood to humor them. Nonnie—who had no patience whatsoever with the twins—made herself scarce, so I finally just let them run wild while I cleaned the kitchen.

I knew that no matter how hard I worked, no matter how many extra chores I took on, nothing would make up for betraying Mother's trust. But as I scrubbed, a battle raged inside me.

Why had I pilfered money in the first place? Because they'd refused to budge on inheritance, or even allowance!

But I hadn't been price hiking for myself. I'd been "taking donations" for Ginny Rose's brothers. Every penny I'd overcharged had gone to Mrs. Poole.

Yet . . . I *had* taken money.

And I *couldn't* tell Mother why!

Or . . . maybe I could?

Maybe I *should.*

But . . . would it even matter to her? My guess was she wouldn't care *why* I'd taken the money, only that I had. Besides, she'd made it clear that she thought Ginny Rose was beneath us somehow—a thought that sent me back to my anger over that, which led me straight to the injustice of sons inheriting everything, which took me right back to the beginning of the cycle of thoughts.

So I still didn't know what I was going to say—or if I was going to try to explain or simply deny my actions—when Mother came inside in the late afternoon. Nonnie walked in through the back door just then with a load of wash fresh off the line, but her presence did nothing to dampen Mother's fury. "Go to your room and don't come out until I tell you to," she commanded.

"Can I explain?"

"No!" she barked.

Nonnie raised an eyebrow in Mother's direction but said nothing.

"It's not what you think!" I said, feeling desperate to fix things.

"Go!" Mother shouted, then spun on Nonnie and said, "And stop looking at me that way! You have no idea what's going on!"

I gasped. Mother had never spoken to Nonnie with anything but calm respect.

"Oh, I think I might," Nonnie said, pushing past Mother. "I'm no stranger to ripening peaches." She cast a look my way. "They can go from sweet to rotten overnight."

I felt slapped. How could she say that about me? How could Mother not at least listen to what I had to say? How had things gotten so out of control?

I ran upstairs in tears and closed myself in my room. But Mother didn't come talk to me, and after a while I opened my door a bit so I could hear. As the hours crept by, I could smell dinner cooking, could hear pans clanking and utensils clinking. I listened as the twins were put to bed, then strained to hear waves of hushed conversation that floated up the stairs. As the night wore on, it dawned on me that I might never get the chance to explain. My trial was happening without me, and my sentence would include a lifetime of mistrust.

To my surprise, Bobby slipped into my room with a plate of food. "Shh," he said. "Hide it when you're done." He was nervous but couldn't seem to help lingering long enough to ask, "Is it true? Mother claims three customers today said they'd paid more before."

I nodded. "But I didn't do it for me."

He came in farther. "Then who?"

"I can't tell you."

"Peg, what is going on?"

I just shook my head.

"If you didn't steal it for you, just tell them why you did it!"

"I will," I said. "But not today."

He snuck out, clearly exasperated with me. I ate quickly and had barely hidden the plate he'd brought when Mother opened the door. "Tomorrow we'll lay down the ground rules," she said, "but for now, you're under house arrest."

"House arrest?"

"Yes. For the rest of summer. You're not allowed to leave the house."

I felt like such a criminal. And in a rush of regret, I said, "Mother, please let me explain."

"Nothing you say can justify what you've been doing."

I broke down. "Mother, it's my birthday!"

"Well, you've certainly made it one to remember, haven't you?"

Then she produced an old bedpan and a roll of toilet paper, left the room, and locked the door.

34

Ginny Rose

THE GETAWAY

I'm jittery as a june bug after Peggy leaves. How on earth will I get away when Mama's hidden the spare key? Never mind collectin' supplies without her gettin' suspicious. If findin' my brothers seemed like a daunting task before, just leavin' home to try seems impossible now!

Still, I press on. Between chores and with Anna Mae's help, I manage to hide a shovel, some rope, a gardening trowel, and a hand rake behind the woodpile. I do it right in front of Papa, who's dozin' on the porch with the Bible on his lap. I try not to act shifty, and I tell myself, *I'm just tidyin' up,* in case he or Mama asks what I'm doin'.

I fill a jug of water in the kitchen, take a pocketknife from the tool drawer, and am quick about wrappin' cheese, biscuits, raisins, dried apricots, and almonds in an old neckerchief. But as I'm squirrelin' the bundle away between my mattress and the wall, a voice behind me says, "Looks like you're plannin' to run away from home."

I jolt up and bang my head on the top bunk, and Anna Mae laughs when I turn to face her. I'm fixin' to scold her for sneakin' up on me when she says, "I found the key."

"You did? Where?"

"It's with the picture." She shrugs. "Easy to guess."

I sit and let the irony of it settle in. Mama's taken away the one thing that'll let me do the one thing she wants done. "She'll notice if it's gone," I tell Anna Mae. "And then she'll know we've snooped!"

Anna Mae nods. "Which is why I'm gonna get you Papa's key instead."

"Papa's? How? He keeps his key ring in his pocket at all times!"

She gives me a wily smile. "Oh, I'll get it."

True to her word, that evening after Mama's vanished and I'm corrallin' the Littles to get ready for bed, I notice Anna Mae settle on the floor next to Papa's chair in the front room. Papa's busy gnawin' the gristle of a crossword puzzle and doesn't look up from the newspaper. "Papa?" Anna Mae asks, her voice stretchin' out sweet as taffy. "Why do you have so many keys?"

"'Cause I have lots of responsibilities," he replies, still not lookin' up.

"Could I see them?" she asks.

He pulls the key ring from his pocket and passes it to her, his eyes barely breakin' away from the paper.

When Anna Mae casts a sly grin my way, I shake my head. If she manages to slip off the key, he'll *know* she took it when he sees it's missing. She may as well be lightin' herself on fire!

But she shakes her head back at me, and while Papa fills in a word, she twists a key off the ring and palms it. "Can you tell me what they all go to?" she asks as she hands back the ring.

"Oh, just work and home," he says, and shoves the keys back into his pocket.

This breaks my heart a little. Sure, Papa isn't one for chitchat. But watchin' him with Anna Mae . . . why, it's as if she's more nuisance than offspring.

My mind turns over my own experience with Papa. Nowadays I seem to be mostly a helping hand to him, but I do have memories—deep, swelling memories—of bein' much more'n that. When I perched on his shoulders in picker lines waitin' for work, when I dragged in crop that weighed near as much as I did, when I washed up beside him after a long day in the fields, I was someone he looked at with pride and gratitude.

With *affection*.

Back then, he would have shown me his keys and explained every single one.

Though back then, there was only the one to Faithful.

I puzzle over the change in him. He now has a ring full of keys but shows no pride or gratitude or affection for Anna Mae . . . or the Littles, now that I think about it. Is that because they came along after his ring began gatherin' keys?

Or because they came after the boys left this earth?

And I wonder . . . is *not* attachin' himself to the girls his way of makin' sure he never goes through such heartache again?

Or is he just tired?

I give Anna Mae another look, but it's too late. She's already movin' away, key in hand. "He'll know you took it!" I whisper when she passes it to me.

"And I'll tell him to look for it under Mama's side of the bed," she snarls. "You better be long gone by then!"

Her scowl drives home how unhappy Anna Mae is.

Anna Mae *would* run away, I realize.

She would most certainly run away.

And *then* what?

We fall into our before-bed ritual of washin', and scrubbin' teeth, and tidyin' the latrine. The Littles cuddle in the crook of each arm as I read more of Alice's adventures aloud. And though the words flow from me, my mind's not in the story. I'm frettin' about Anna Mae and how everything might blow up in my face. And each time I hear a sound outside our room, I'm terrified it's Papa discoverin' his key's missing.

Long after the house is still, my heart pounds. It pulses in my ears, makin' me short of breath as I run through the steps I'll take in the morning, and the things I need to remember—food, blanket, tools, water, key, and what little money I have.

I fret over the alarm clock, which is set for four, and which I've put under my pillow so the ringing won't carry through the house. But . . . what if the sound's too muffled to wake me? Or what if restin' on the pillow accidently turns it off?

The night drags on and on. I do doze a little, but I have a nightmare about drivin' Faithful into a ditch and overturnin' her. And then, there are my brothers, perfectly healthy little boys, pointin' and laughin' at me.

I awake from the dream with a start, breathless and dazed, then panic that I've overslept.

The clock says it's only two-thirty.

After another restless hour, the familiar rumble of a train builds in the distance. Night trains used to shake us awake, but we all learned to sleep right through them early on, and now they even *help* us sleep. But tonight, the approaching sound doesn't lull me back to sleep. Tonight, I snap fully awake, realizin' this train's an unexpected blessing.

I turn off the alarm and get up. I wish for Peggy's dungarees as I hurry to put on my oldest dress and my thickest socks, then take my old shoes and the neckerchief of food and sneak out of the room and down the hallway.

In the front room, I pick up the brown blanket Anna Mae and I sat under after the dance, then tiptoe out the back door, sit on the porch, and tie my shoes quick.

The train's near now, and I'm hopin' there's still enough time to use the noise to cover my own. I hurry down the steps and along the house under a clear sky dotted with stars. The air's cool, but not cold, and I'm grateful for the half-moon, shinin' bright enough to help me see my way around to the woodpile where the tools and the jug of water are hidden.

Faithful's parked near Mama and Papa's bedroom window, so even though the train's rollin' past now, I take extra care to spread out the blanket in the bed of the truck and lay the tools on top to keep them from clangin'. Then I pull the driver's-side door open, avoidin' the squeak, place the jug and food on the seat, release the brake, and start pushin'. I have one hand on the steering wheel, the other on the doorframe, and both feet on the ground as my whole body leans in to push.

Faithful inches forward, first like a stubborn mule but then with a little giddyup, gatherin' speed until she's rollin' down the road with me runnin' alongside. The train's almost past now, so I leap onto the running board, swing inside, pull the door closed, and fire up the engine.

My heart pounds as Faithful sputters to life, but there's a little giggle inside me, too.

This feels like such a getaway!

I try to block out thoughts of the trouble Anna Mae will be in. After the help she's given, I do feel guilty for leavin' her behind to face punishment alone. When I told her so last night, *she* reminded *me* that the Littles would need her at home . . . but there was something more to her attitude. She seemed to be itchin' for a confrontation with Mama in front of Papa. That's *not* what I want—especially since I'm doin' this to try and *fix* things with Mama—but it's clear Anna Mae will have her showdown if she decides to. I did make her swear not to say where I was goin' or what I was doin' until it was too late for Papa to stop us. "If we find them," I told her, "I'll call the house, let it ring once, then hang up. That'll be our signal."

"And if you don't?"

"There'll be no call."

Who knows what pressure she'll be put under? But the die's cast, so as I approach Simmons Farm, I try to force my thoughts forward. I'm early, so I'm not surprised when Peggy's nowhere to be seen as I putt along the length of their property. Once I'm down the road past the farmhouse, I do a U-turn, push off the headlights, and coast to a stop beside the fruit stand.

Then I wait.

And wait.

And soon darkness is liftin' and I'm wonderin' . . . where *is* she?

It must be four-thirty by now!

I tell myself I'm early and to stay calm. But as time ticks by, I begin to fret.

Did she change her mind?

Is she not comin' after all?

No, that can't be! She was definite.

And it was her idea to do it today!

So maybe she had a rough night like I did and overslept?

The moment I have the thought, I'm out of the truck and scurryin' across to the farmhouse. There's no light comin' from any of the windows at the front or side, and when I round the corner, there's no light comin' from Peggy's window, either. "Oh no!" I whimper, because it looks like I'll be goin' alone.

But as I get closer, I see that her window is open and that . . . yes . . . somebody's danglin' from the ledge! "Peggy?" I whisper, not quite believin' my eyes.

"Help!" she whispers back.

I run over and see that she's hangin' from the end of a bed-sheet that's tied to something inside her room, but she's still much too high off the ground to let go.

"Hold on!" I tell her, and run to fetch an orchard ladder.

I hold the ladder under her, but it won't reach the roofline, and even though her foot might be able to touch the top rung, I'm not sure I have enough strength to hold her weight on my own. So I lay the ladder down and whisper, "Hold on!"

"I'm trying," she warbles.

I race back to the orchard, fetch two lug boxes, set them upside down beneath her, then put the feet of the ladder on top of them. The ladder can now reach the edge of the roof, and Peggy scampers down. "Oh, *thank* you," she breathes.

"But why—"

"Mother locked me in my room!" she says, producin' a small flashlight from inside her dungarees.

"On your *birthday*? Why? Does she know?"

"No! It was for something else. Now hurry! We're running late!"

I follow her around to the shed, where she clicks on her flashlight and gathers work gloves, a shovel, and a hand trowel. "Anything else you can think of?" she asks.

I point to a large red can labeled GASOLINE. "Is there anything in that?"

She picks it up. "Yes! It feels almost full."

"Oh, good," I say in a gust of relief. "Because I don't have much money."

"I brought what I had," Peggy says. "But it's not a lot, so this is smart to take."

She hands over the gas can, which pulls down my arm like a pail of rocks. Then I follow her outside, and after we've rolled the shed door closed, we steal our way across the property and over to Faithful. And we're in the middle of loadin' Peggy's tools in the back of the truck when a light comes on in the farmhouse.

"Hurry!" Peggy says. "We have to get out of here. Now!"

But then we hear a click.

And a squeak.

And we both freeze as Faithful's driver's-side door swings open.

35

Peggy

SHOWDOWN

My jaw dropped as she stepped out of the jalopy.

This was not real.

This could *not* be real.

"Lisette?" I gasped.

"I'm coming along," she said as she moved toward us.

She was gripping a small handbag and was wearing simple tan slacks, brown flats, a blue button-down shirt with the sleeves rolled up, and a folded red bandanna around her hair.

Even at four-thirty in the morning, even on a mission as gruesome as ours, Lisette Bovee looked like she belonged on the cover of a magazine.

Ginny Rose spun on me, her eyes blazing. *"She* knows?"

"She needed help," Lisette said coolly. "Getting that picture of your brothers and"—her eyes drifted to the side—"other things."

"What other things?" Ginny Rose demanded, but then seemed to think better of it. "Never mind. It doesn't matter. You're not comin'!"

"Yes, I am," Lisette said, and began walking back toward the truck. "I didn't start a war with my father over you to get left behind."

Ginny Rose hurried to stop her. "There's no room!"

I followed, keeping a wary eye out for movement at the house while Lisette simply ignored Ginny Rose and climbed back inside the jalopy.

"She's not comin'!" Ginny Rose snapped at me. "She's not!"

Another light came on inside the house. "We really have to go *now*," I said. "Any minute someone's going to see the sheet and the ladder, and when they do . . ."

"No!" Ginny Rose cried, but now her eyes were begging.

"She *has* done a lot to help," I said gently. "And—"

"Like *what*?"

I looked over my shoulder. "I'll explain on the way," I said, climbing into the truck. I moved a cloth-wrapped parcel and jug of water that were on the seat onto my lap as I slid in, cramming Lisette against the passenger door to give Ginny Rose room.

"I brought cash," Lisette said, leaning across me. "Which, if that gas can is any indication, you probably could use."

"You think you can *buy* your way into this?" Ginny Rose seethed. "Well, you can't!"

"Ginny Rose, please," I begged. "Get in. It'll be fine."

She stood outside, glaring through the open doorway at us. "Get out. Both of you. Just get out."

"Ginny Rose!" I cried. "Don't do this."

"*You're* the one doin' it! Make her get out!"

I heaved a sigh. She was right. But before I could tell Lisette she had to leave, I saw something that gripped my heart. "Bobby's coming!"

Lisette muttered, "Well, this was fun, girls," and was about to get out on her own when suddenly Ginny Rose was inside, slamming the door, fumbling with levers and switches, cranking the motor.

When the jalopy fired up, Ginny Rose wasted no time. She pushed the shifter into gear, let out the clutch, and pulled up alongside Bobby. "Do not tell," she said. "Do not breathe a word of this to *anyone*."

He looked through the rolled-down window, taking in the three of us like he couldn't quite do the math.

"*Please* don't tattle," I said across Ginny Rose.

His brow furrowed at the equipment lying in the bed of the truck. "But . . . what are you doing?"

"I'll be home tonight," I promised. "I'll explain everything then."

"Please," Ginny Rose said, holding his gaze. Then she drove forward and onto the road.

I gave Bobby a little wave through the back window and watched him watching us go, hoping that his combined feelings for the girl he'd been crazy for, the girl he'd grown up with, and the girl he now fancied would be powerful enough for him to keep our secret.

And then, except for the *putt-putt-putt*ing of the jalopy, we rode west in silence.

Like Ginny Rose, I tried to keep my focus straight ahead, but it wasn't easy with the way Lisette was nudging and signaling me and asking silent questions with her expressions.

"We're going to Garysville," Ginny Rose finally snapped, because of course she'd noticed all the twitching Lisette was doing.

"Garysville!" Lisette exclaimed. "Why, that's hours away!"

Ginny Rose careened the truck to the side of the road. "And it's not too late for you to get out."

"No!" Lisette said. "I'm coming."

Tension sizzled from one side of the cab to the other. And when Ginny Rose took an angry turn north onto Santa Fe Road, I knew I had to do *something*.

"So," I said a little too loudly, "why are you at war with your father, Lisette?"

She looked at me like *You know why I'm at war with my father!* But when I pulled a face at her, she understood. "Well," she said, drawing out the word, "it started when you explained why Ginny Rose hated bankers. And," she added with a frown, "their daughters."

Ginny Rose let out a *"Hrmph"* but kept her eyes straight ahead.

"So I asked him about that, and he explained that what happened to the farmers wasn't just the bankers' fault, it was also the farmers'."

Ginny Rose pounced. "You have *no* idea what you're talkin' about! *Bankers* kicked us out of our house and off of our land. *Bankers* put us in a predicament so awful that all we've got left of my brothers is a faded picture! *Bankers* is who put them in their grave!"

Lisette had the good sense not to argue. Instead, she said, "I'm along because I don't like the bankers' part in it any more than you do."

Ginny Rose snorted. "Oh, sure. I can see how miserable all of it's made *your* life."

"Look," Lisette said, her exasperation showing, "I've been trying to help! I lent you my camera, I intercepted the pictures, I gave you—"

She caught herself, but it was too late.

"Clothes?" Ginny Rose asked. "Is that it? You gave me clothes?" I could see her mind whirring. "Those shoes? They were yours, weren't they? And . . . and . . . that blue dress?"

When Lisette didn't say a word, Ginny Rose looked at me. And when I didn't say a thing either, her eyes glistened with tears. She turned back to the windshield and gripped the wheel tighter. "And Bobby?" she asked. "Did you send *him* my way, too?"

"No!" Lisette cried. "I had nothing to do with that."

"What about you?" she asked me.

"I had nothing to do with it, either!" I said, which I felt was true enough. Sure, I'd tried to get him to pay attention to Ginny Rose, but my words had fallen on deaf ears and Lisette-smitten eyes. *When* Bobby had finally opened them was a mystery to me.

I took a calming breath. "Can we get back to the war with your father?" I asked Lisette.

Lisette frowned a moment, then began again. "It started when I told him I wasn't going to move into the Oakvale house. He tried to convince me the repossession was all legal and fine, and when that didn't work, I told him we overheard Mrs. Taylor and Mrs. Williams say he was a backstabbing thief, and said I thought it was wrong that he was profiting from his friend's misery."

"And?" I asked.

"And he got mad and said I needed to learn to separate business and friendship and accused me of being naïve, spoiled, and selfish."

"How's standin' up against a wrong selfish?" Ginny Rose asked. And then, seemingly as surprised by her outburst as we were, she clammed up and went back to staring straight ahead.

"He says I'm not respecting his work or what he provides," Lisette said quietly. "And since I *wouldn't* change my mind—or even agree to disagree—he took away my car and my allowance and told me I couldn't leave the house." She gave a little shrug. "So I set my alarm, sneaked out, walked over, and here I am."

Again, the cab fell silent. And it stayed that way for mile after uncomfortable mile until we passed by the small town of Edselon and Lisette said, "Look, Ginny Rose. I feel bad about what you've been through. I can't even imagine it, I know. But it shouldn't be a crime for me to want to help. Maybe I can't know what you've been through, maybe you resent that my father's job has given me an easy life, but if I'm willing to help, why don't you let me?"

Ginny Rose said nothing. She just sat stony-faced as we rolled along at forty-five miles an hour past acres and acres of farmland. Forty-five, unless we were stuck behind a tractor or farm-supply truck moseying along, and then we went even slower.

When the country road finally intersected with Highway 99 near Stockton, I was sure Ginny Rose would pick up the pace, but she didn't. She kept us at a steady forty-five as we made our way north, her eyes focused intently ahead while other cars zoomed by.

I checked my watch. It was already a quarter to six. At this rate it was going to take much longer to get to Garysville than she'd said, and who knew how long it would take us to find the grave? Ginny Rose had been pretty vague about that.

"Do you have a map?" I asked.

Her left hand disappeared around the side of the seat and reappeared moments later holding a folded map. "Here," she said, handing it over. "But we don't need it. I know the way."

Still, I unfolded the map, and I did so carefully because it was more than just tattered at the edges and smudged from years of handling. It was so worn that the folds were disintegrating in spots, and it looked like it might fall apart at any moment. But the strange thing was, it didn't feel brittle—it was more like a well-worn cloth.

Lisette held up the right side and I held the left, and we were both silent as we absorbed this . . . creation. Maybe it had started as a simple map of California, but it was as much travel log as road map now. Small drawn triangles beside notes written in fine penmanship covered the central part of the state. The notes were mostly the names of crops: *Berries, Walnuts, Lettuce* was written beside a triangle near San Bernardino; *Grapes, Cotton* beside Bakersfield; *Grapes, Peaches, Apricots* beside Porterville; and on and on, clear up the Central Valley and past Sacramento, where a final triangle was labeled *Cherries, Plums, Asparagus*.

There were neat notes written in the Pacific Ocean and Nevada—names and dates and short descriptions, each boxed in and connected with a line to a triangle. There were also hurried scrawls done pell-mell all over the map. Numbers. Addresses. Notes like *Firewood* and *No fresh water* and *Cheap gas*.

Lisette pointed to a thin cross inked in near Garysville. "X marks the spot," she whispered into my ear.

That's *just* what it looked like, and I couldn't help shuddering.

Ginny Rose's voice broke through my morbid thoughts, startling both Lisette and me. "Those triangles are the camps where we stayed."

I didn't know what to say to that, and apparently neither

did Lisette, because we both stayed quiet until a few miles later when Lisette pointed through the windshield at a Giant Orange stand and said, "What's *that*?"

I knew exactly what it was because I'd always been jealous of the orange growers who could juice their crop and sell it from such a clever stand. It was closed up tight now, but by midday it would be teeming with travelers. "You've never seen one of those before?" I asked. "They sell fresh-squeezed orange juice over chipped ice."

The stand was behind us now, and Lisette settled back in. "That sounds so good, doesn't it?" she said with a little sigh. "I can't believe how warm it is already."

We rode in silence for some time as the road cut between wide, flat stretches of orchards, vineyards, low crops, and golden grasses—fields that spread for a mile or two on both sides of us, right up to the ridges of high hills that created the Central Valley. Fields with Mexican laborers already hard at work.

At last Lisette broke the silence. "I saw that picture of you and your brothers. Is that the way you traveled from camp to camp?"

"Pretty much," Ginny Rose replied.

"But . . . where did you all sit?"

"Right here."

I held my breath. A civil exchange between them? I could barely believe it.

"But . . . ," Lisette said, "it's tight with the three of us. I can't imagine doing this with a family."

I thought Ginny Rose might give a snappy retort about *why* we were crammed in like sardines at the moment, but she seemed to almost appreciate the question. "When we left Oklahoma, the boys were little. And I was small myself. So I sat between Mama and Papa, and the boys shared lap time between me and Mama, or even sometimes Papa. That's how we came out here. But as we got bigger, I took to ridin' in back."

"But where? In that picture, there was no room for anyone to ride in back!"

She shrugged. "I just found a place. I liked it a lot more'n ridin' up here with two squirmy boys!"

We passed by a road sign—ten miles to Stockton, sixty to Sacramento. On the map, it looked like Garysville was another thirty miles or so past Sacramento. We still had a ways to go.

"So . . . ," Lisette said like she was nudging another thought through a minefield, "how long would you stay in those camps?"

"It depended on if Papa could find work. Sometimes it was just a day or two. If he found it, it could be weeks or even months."

"And every place you would . . . set up a . . . a house?"

"A few places had raised cabins with showers and a community room, but they usually cost more'n we could earn 'cause Mama had to watch the boys and couldn't help pick." She shrugged. "So usually, yep. Shantytown."

And then, to my amazement, Ginny Rose just started talking . . . almost reminiscing. She told a story about stealing potato peelings for soup, another about a fire that someone from town set one night at a pickers' camp to burn them out.

"Burn you out?" Lisette asked.

"Get rid of us. And it worked. The flames spread like wildfire from one shanty to the next. A lot of people lost what little they had."

One story led to another, and Ginny Rose took her time in the telling, setting the scene and describing the other campers, their oddities and temperaments, and their wariness toward newcomers. "Every new camper was more competition for work, and work meant food," she explained. "So sometimes people were kind, and sometimes they were hostile. From time to time, Mama would say how strange it was to belong absolutely nowhere, even when you were standin' in the midst of people just like you."

Somehow this made her recall a holdup that happened at a roadside camp where they were sleeping out in the open with one other family. "A man woke us with a shotgun and made us give over our food," she said. "He got two boiled eggs from our neighbor and a withered wedge of cabbage and some lard from us." She sighed and, more to herself than to us, said, "I was mighty jealous of those eggs."

By now we'd been traveling for over two hours, and the sun was cutting across the land hot and bright, striking Lisette and me through the open window. I noticed Ginny Rose giving a worried look to the dash, and when I leaned in closer, I saw a small, stamped metal gauge that had rotated below the one-quarter mark.

"Is that the fuel gauge?" I asked.

She nodded, her eyes straight ahead now. "Faithful needs a rest."

"And some gas," I said.

"Faithful?" Lisette asked.

"That's her name," Ginny Rose said, her eyes fixed forward. And then she backed off the gas further, bringing us down to thirty-five miles an hour.

Lisette didn't say a word.

Neither did I.

And the odd thing was, the slower we went, the tighter Ginny Rose gripped the wheel and the more tied in knots she seemed to become.

She dropped our speed to thirty.

Then twenty.

Other cars on the highway were passing us like we were standing still.

"Are we going this slow to conserve gas?" Lisette asked at last. But that's when I noticed that a vertical red band had appeared in the middle of the hood ornament.

Which, I suddenly understood, wasn't *just* a hood ornament.

It was also the radiator gauge.

Faithful was about to become Old Faithful.

"There's some!" Lisette exclaimed, pointing to a gas station sign ahead.

Ginny Rose pulled off the highway and right up to the pump, but she kept the engine running. She retrieved work gloves and a hand towel from the truck bed and was at the radiator in a jiffy.

"What *is* she doing?" Lisette asked, opening her door. "That's not where the gas goes, is it?"

"We're overheating," I explained, climbing out behind her.

A man with a deeply weathered face and grease-stained hands sauntered over and sized up the situation. "She's about to blow," he said with a chuckle. "Here. Let's get her watered."

He tugged over a hose and began lightly misting the radiator as the three of us stood by. The spray sizzled and steamed, sending up white clouds, and he kept at it for some time, slowly coming in closer, increasing the spray.

Finally, the sizzling stopped and the man said, "I think she's ready." He eyed Ginny Rose's gloved hands and her towel. "I'm guessin' you've done this before?"

"Yes, sir."

"I'm happy to do it for you."

"Thank you kindly," she said, "but I can manage." Then she covered the radiator cap with the towel, turned slowly, letting the pressure ease out, and finally removed the cap.

"Thatagirl," the man said, and handed her the hose.

Ginny Rose stuck the nozzle into the neck of the radiator, and while the fresh water displaced the hot and slowly cooled the engine, we each used the restroom. When the engine temperature had finally dropped and the radiator was full and capped, Ginny Rose pieced together two dollars in change from her pocket to pay for filling the gas tank.

Meanwhile, Lisette went over to the big red chest by the station's office door and bought three icy bottles of Coca-Cola. She put each bottle neck in the opener and pried off the caps, *clink, clink, clink,* then sauntered back to us.

I took mine gratefully and clinked bottle necks when Lisette held hers up and said, "To refrigeration!"

Ginny Rose had watched us, but when Lisette handed her the third bottle, she looked away from it and shook her head. But then, changing her mind, she produced a nickel and said, "Here."

Lisette scowled at the coin. "Oh, quit acting like this old truck," she said, pressing the Coke on her. "Just take it and cool off, would you?"

Ginny Rose frowned. "I like to pay my own way," she said, trying to force her to take the nickel.

But Lisette took a step back instead, and the two of them locked eyes, gripping their bottles like it was high noon in front of a saloon.

"So where you girls off to?" the man asked, eyeing the tools in the bed.

His nosiness brought an end to the showdown. "Family reunion," Lisette said, breaking away.

Ginny Rose looked at her in shock, but then her face twitched with . . . humor?

Lisette gave her a helpless shrug, which caused Ginny Rose to shake her head and roll her eyes.

And . . . yes . . . there *was* a little grin.

Inside the truck, Ginny Rose had me hold her bottle while she got the truck moving. I held it as she shifted gears, and then kept right on holding it for a mile, two miles, three . . . And I was just thinking that I might have to hold it all the way to Garysville when she reached for it without a word. Then, after a long, slow drink, she smacked her lips, held up the bottle, and said, "To the family reunion."

Lisette and I glanced at each other with raised eyebrows, then lifted our bottles, too. "To the family reunion," we said together, and clinked our bottle necks against hers.

36

Ginny Rose

A GRAVE SITUATION

I'm still nettled over Lisette wormin' her way into our plans like a fancy-faced weevil when she hands me a frosty bottle from the gas station's Coca-Cola ice chest.

It makes me furious.

How many times had I walked by a Coca-Cola chest at a station or market and given Papa's sleeve a hopeful tug? How many times had Papa said, "Not wastin' my money on that"? And now here's Lisette, offerin' me a bottle sweatin' with condensation, a chilly cloud risin' like a genie from inside it, holdin' it out to me like it's nothing. Like she's had more icy cold Cokes than she could count.

She stands there, arm stretched out, lookin' at me with a smile, expectin' me to take it and be grateful. But I don't want to take it. I don't want to have to *thank* her.

Also, after all this time, I do *not* want my first icy bottle of Coca-Cola to be a gift from Lisette Bovee. I'm already fit to be tied over all the other things that've come from her. I will never, *ever* wear that blue dress again. And maybe I can't give back the picture of my brothers, but I'll most definitely give back the shoes. Then, after we've put my brothers to rest, I'll save up and buy my own clothes.

But I *am* parched, and the Coke looks so good, so I take it and hand Lisette a nickel. I can see the price on the cooler from where I'm standin', so I know it's enough . . . only she won't take it! Once again, she's lordin' her station in life over me.

Well, in that case, I'll just drink water!

And even though Peggy holds the bottle for me as I'm shiftin' through the gears gettin' back on the road, I'm not gonna drink that cola. No, sir. She can hold it all the way to Garysville if she likes!

Only . . . in my mind I keep hearin' Lisette tell the gas man that we're goin' to a family reunion. For some reason describin' it that way tickles me. It also makes me wonder about *her*. I'd have thought she'd be shudderin' and squealin' over what we're doin', but instead she goes and tells the man it's a family reunion?

Which, now that I ponder it, is just what bringin' the boys home is about. And seein' it that way makes me . . . happy.

So I don't know if it's the heat outside or all that's churnin' inside me, but suddenly I'm takin' that bottle of Coke out of Peggy's hand and makin' a toast to the family reunion.

The drink goes down sparkly and sweet, and it cools me from my nose to my toes. I take my time, appreciatin' every swallow, and when the bottle's empty, I hand it back to Peggy and sigh, "That may be the best thing I've ever tasted."

There's silence in the cab as the meaning beneath my words

sinks in, and it stretches over several miles. "We do come from different worlds," I say at last.

And then Lisette surprises me again by sayin', "I'm grateful to be spending time in yours, Ginny Rose."

I laugh. "Oh, really?" Then I say, "Just be glad you've got your world to go back to."

She nods in a slow, thoughtful manner. Like she's contemplatin' the meaning of life. "I honestly don't know what's going to happen in my world when I get back," she says at last. "But I do know I'll never drink a Coca-Cola the same way."

That, too, hangs in the air for a time. Then I surprise myself by askin', "Are either of you hungry? I've packed food."

"Yes!" Lisette says.

As I pull up the parcel from where it's restin' on the floorboard, my mind's quick to turn the offer into a way of repayin' Lisette for the Coke. This relaxes me a bit as we roll along, and while we eat, we start talkin'. It begins with us each sharin' how much trouble we're in, and moves on to a laugh over how we all got put on restriction at the same time. Then talk wanders over to our folks and our families, and then around to Rodney and what a tomcat he is.

I shake my head. "I knew that the minute I heard him say *Peaches* the way he does." Right away I feel bad, because both of them have been head over heels for him. "I'm sorry," I say. "That was mean."

"But true," Peggy sighs.

"We won't share our thoughts on Bobby," Lisette says with a wicked grin.

"Thank you for that," I say, keepin' my eyes on the road. "Because after he finds out what I've pulled you into, he'll likely want nothing more to do with me."

Lisette saves us all by switchin' subjects. "Tell me about your sisters," she says. "Peggy says they're darling."

So I do. And I find myself glowin' with the telling of the Littles' antics and Anna Mae's help in my escape. And after I share that my favorite time of each day is readin' aloud to them at bedtime, and how *Alice's Adventures in Wonderland* has the Littles wantin' a white rabbit and tea sets, I confess that Anna Mae said I looked like Alice in Lisette's blue dress.

Lisette sighs. "What I would give for that."

I'm quick to say, "I plan on returnin' the dress, Lisette."

"Not the dress!" she says. "The sisters." She snorts. "I don't even have brothers. It's just me. And maybe my parents buy me most things I want, but there's never been story time or bunk-bed time . . . just alone time."

I would never in a million years have thought I'd feel sorry for Lisette Bovee, but the loneliness in her voice is heavy and real, and I find myself wonderin' what a life without my sisters would be like—a life with a beautiful house, beautiful clothes, and my own car . . . but with no Anna Mae, or Bonnie Sue, or Katie Bee. The thought makes my eyes sting.

Just then we pass by a road sign—GARYSVILLE 10—and my heart goes for a trot as I breathe out, "The camp was on the south side of town, so it should be comin' up soon."

"But . . . the camp's not still there, is it?" Lisette asks, her voice tiptoein' along.

"I'm sure it's not," I agree. "So keep your eye out for a big oak tree. My brothers called it the Eagle Tree because it has two branches that stretch way out, and the top's bent over. There's other trees around, but the Eagle Tree's the biggest."

"How far off the road is it?" Peggy asks.

"The camp started close to the road and went back almost to the river. The tree was over on the river side, but you could see it from the road." I hear my own words and worry that I sound a little touched. So I tell them, "We'll find it," like there's absolutely nothing to worry about.

Before long, though, we're rollin' into town. *Everything* comin' into Garysville looked different, and there was no sign of the camp—which isn't surprising—but . . . how could I have missed the *tree?*

"Maybe it fell over?" Peggy suggests. "Let's go back and look around."

But Lisette points to a diner where three middle-aged men are gathered out front smokin' cigarettes and chewin' the fat. "Pull over here," she says.

Seein' the diner sends me back to walkin' through Garysville with Papa. With its big statue of a smiling bear holdin' a skillet of eggs by the front door, it looks just the same as it did all those years ago. The same, except now the *No Okies* sign in the window is gone, and there's a *No Mexicans* sign instead.

I would rather hurl a rock through that window than stop, but Lisette's twitchin' in her seat like she's sittin' on an anthill, so I do as she says.

The wheels have barely quit turnin' when Lisette hops out and goes right up to the men. "Pardon me," she says with a dazzling smile. "Can you tell me where the picker camp used to be?"

"Why on earth do you want to know that?" one of the men

asks. He's wearin' suspenders stretched tight over a faded plaid shirt, and like the rest of him, his porkpie hat seems to have given up on keepin' its shape.

"We're tracing our family heritage," Lisette tells him, her voice full of pride. "A tour to honor the past."

"That why you girls is drivin' that old jalopy?" the man says, takin' in Faithful with a frown. "You Okie sisters or somethin'?"

"Cousins," Lisette says with a smile. "*American* cousins."

Porkpie twitches at her correction and counters by givin' her a long, unmannerly look up and down as he drags on his cigarette. "Ain't that somethin', fellas?" he says, blowin' out smoke. "Next-generation Okies comin' back to roost."

My blood hits a boil and I'm just fixin' to bolt from the cab to give the ol' geezer a piece of my mind, but Peggy holds me firm. "She can handle him."

"Just to visit," Lisette says, then turns her attention to the other men. "Surely one of you can point me in the right direction?" she says, her voice drippin' honey. "I'd be very grateful."

One of them grinds his cigarette butt into the sidewalk with his shoe and takes pity on her. "The camp was about a mile down the road," he says, pointin' back the way we came. "On the right side. There's houses gonna be built there now. You'll see the sign. Sunrise Estates."

"Estates," Porkpie snorts. "Ain't *that* a joke. It'll be a bunch of them toothpick houses like they put up at the north end of town."

The other man ignores him and tells Lisette, "You'll see the sign, but there's nothing left of the camp."

"Thank you," Lisette says, and quick as a wink she's back in the cab whisperin', "Let's get *out* of here."

"I noticed that sign on the way in," Peggy says as I do a U-turn. "There were bulldozers parked nearby."

All at once, I'm feelin' dizzy. "There were?"

"But it didn't look like they'd . . . like they'd *done* anything yet," Peggy says.

A short while later, we do find the sign, but Peggy's wrong— they *have* done something.

They've cleared all the trees.

There's not one standin' for acres and acres and *acres*.

And then I see the tangle of roots and stumps and branches bulldozed to the side in a long row. My throat goes tight, and I feel like a child again, lookin' at a wall of dust ten stories tall, powerless to change what's already in motion.

My eyes spill over as I pull to the side of the road. "No!" I sob. "No, no, no!"

"Let's get out and walk," Peggy says. "Maybe the tree's gone, but what else do you remember? There's got to be something."

But I know it's hopeless. We will never in a million years find the grave. And what if it was overturned when the roots popped free? What if their bones . . . their bodies . . . are scattered every-where? Still, I manage to say, "There was a big boulder. A big orange-striped boulder. It was down at the river. At a bend in the river. Their grave is straight up the bank from the boulder."

"Okay!" Peggy says. She gets me out, takes my hand, and pulls me across the cleared land. "We'll find them," she tells me. "We will."

Once we're near the river—which is much smaller than I remember—Peggy looks left, then right, then takes command. "Okay," she says, "we're looking for a bend in the river and a big boulder with orange stripes."

Lisette is silent, and who can blame her?

This is a wild-goose chase.

Still, Peggy drags us along. We walk upstream, we walk downstream. And we do see boulders—plenty of them—but none with orange stripes. We walk up and down the embankment and along the shallow gully nearby. The whole while, I'm dreadin' what I might stumble upon, but dreadin' more that I'll find nothing at all.

At last Peggy points to the river and asks, "Do you think this is the right bend?"

"It must be. But . . . I don't know!" I sound forlorn, but I just can't hide it. We've been searchin' for over an hour, and though they're not complainin', we're all miserable from the heat. I sit down on the bank as all my hopes scatter out of reach. "I'm so sorry," I say, and I begin to cry all over again. "What do I do now? I'll have to explain it all when I get home, and when Mama finds out that . . . that the boys are . . . are lost forever, there'll be no comin' out of the darkness for her. Or for us!"

Peggy sits beside me. "Don't give up now! We've come this far, and it's not even noon."

Lisette sighs and squints at the sun, then turns her gaze on us sittin' in the blaze of it. "I need to cool off a little before we start up again," she says. She pulls the bandanna from her hair and walks to the river, and we watch as she dips the cloth in, wrings it out, then dabs her face and neck before dippin' it in again.

"That looks so good," Peggy says. She stands and holds out a hand to me. "Come on."

So we join Lisette and take turns with the bandanna. "Thank you," I say, handin' it back to Lisette after the second round. "And I'm sorry. About everything."

Lisette looks at me kindly. "Maybe I could help more if I understood better about the boulder," she says. "We're at the bend in the river, but I don't see any rock with orange stripes. *How* big was it?"

"Big," I say, but even to me, it sounds silly.

"But . . . big when you were little?" Lisette asks.

I stare at her.

Of course.

Lisette holds her hand at about knee level. "So maybe this high now?"

I nod, feelin' dumber'n dirt. Why had it stayed so large in my mind?

What was I *thinkin'*?

"Come here," Peggy says. She leads me up the bank, then sits and pats the ground beside her. "Close your eyes," she says. "Tell me what you see."

These are strange directions, but I dutifully sit beside her. And though earlier in the day I wouldn't have opened up with Lisette standin' by like she is, I'm past that now. She's shown herself to be helpful and surprisingly adaptable, and—as hard as it is for me to believe—I'm grateful she's with us.

So I take a deep breath, close my eyes, and let my mind drift back. "Papa carried the boys wrapped together in a blanket. I carried the shovel. Papa had me fetch river stones while he dug the grave near the Eagle Tree, and that's when I saw the boulder." I pause, tryin' to see it better in my mind. "It looked like a scoop of orange-vanilla ice cream to me. I remember thinkin' it was nice that the boys would have a boulder like that nearby. And when I looked back to where Papa was workin', I remember thinkin' the boys would be protected by the wings of the Eagle Tree."

I go quiet for a bit, picturin' that day. And I guess I'm still for longer than I know, because Peggy's voice breaks through, sayin', "What else are you remembering?"

So I pick up from where my mind has led me. "The way the dirt smelled as Papa turned the soil out. There was mulch from oak leaves, and the dirt was damp and woody and—"

"Wait," Peggy says. "It wasn't hot and dry like it is today?"

I open my eyes, and the sun stabs them for a moment. "No," I say, shakin' my head. "We'd had a spell of heavy fog. Even a little rain."

"So . . ." Peggy stands up and looks around. "What about that one?" she asks, pointin' to an ashy white boulder about ten yards away.

It does look like a scoop of ice cream, but it's not at all orange.

Still, excitement seems to be bubblin' up in Peggy, and before I have the chance to ask why, she grabs Lisette's bandanna, races to the river, dips the cloth in, then spreads it over the face of the boulder.

"What *are* you doing?" Lisette calls as we walk toward her.

But Peggy just smiles as she peels off the cloth.

The ashy white of the boulder where the bandanna was is now darker.

And runnin' straight through it, plain as day, is a beautiful orange stripe.

37

Peggy

A DIFFERENT KIND OF LOVE

Ginny Rose gasped when she saw the orange stripe. Then she hurried over to stand in front of the boulder, facing away from the river with her eyes closed. She seemed to be getting a sightline in her mind, and when her eyes opened again, she marched forward like she knew exactly where she was going.

We followed along, but once we'd walked up the gentle slope of the embankment, the field ahead was large, flat, and completely cleared. Lisette gave me a doubtful look, which I returned. There was no sign of a grave.

But then Ginny Rose came to a halt. "Here," she said.

I looked around. There was nothing but dirt and dried oak leaves that crunched underfoot.

"Where?" Lisette ventured.

Ginny Rose waved her arms around her vaguely. "Right around here."

Fifteen feet in front of us and beyond, the ground had been

scraped, but there was a place about thirty feet wide where the earth dipped. "Do you think the Eagle Tree was there?" I asked, pointing to the dip.

Ginny Rose nodded, then moved forward, dropped to her knees, and began pawing away oak leaves with her bare hands. I joined in, but the points of the dried leaves were sharp, needling into my hands. "Do you want to drive the truck over here?" I asked. "This would be easier with gloves and a shovel."

"I want to find it first," Ginny Rose said, her movements becoming more and more frantic. "There should be river rocks. A lot of them."

Lisette didn't seem to be listening to Ginny Rose. She was looking toward the truck, saying, "You think that old thing will make it across the field?"

I stood and dusted off my hands. "I'm sure Ginny Rose can manage it."

"But . . . won't that be more conspicuous? Make people curious about what we're doing? I think we should just go get what we need and walk it back."

"And when we find them?" I asked her quietly. "Then what? Walk *them* back? I don't think we want anyone asking what we're carrying!"

"Oh," Lisette said. She frowned at Ginny Rose, who was creating a little dust storm as she pawed leaves aside. "Well, if I'm going to help do that, I need gloves."

I nodded and was about to ask Ginny Rose to please stop so we could get some tools and gloves, when suddenly she flipped into a sitting position with a smooth white rock in her hands. "It's here," she breathed out. "Right here."

Lisette and I closed in and could see that she'd dug through a good nine inches of oak-leaf mulch and had cleared a small area that exposed neat rows of river rocks.

Lisette held her cheeks. "Oh Lord."

Ginny Rose sat completely still a moment, staring at the rock in her hands. She looked smaller . . . a statue of a young girl reading a rock like others might read the Bible.

Then suddenly she said, "I agree that we should drive Faithful over here. She'll get across the field just fine, and we can park her so she lends us cover."

I nodded. "Better to wonder what an old truck is doing way out here than see three girls using shovels."

Ginny Rose stood and dusted off her hands. "You stay here. I'll fetch her."

Lisette and I watched Ginny Rose hurry toward the truck. "This is crazy—you know that," Lisette said.

I nodded.

"Which makes *us* crazy, right?" she said, but she didn't sound the least bit upset.

"We're just doing what needs to be done." I turned to face her. "And honestly? I can't believe you're here."

Lisette laughed, still watching Ginny Rose. "Neither can I." She sighed. "This is sure turning out to *not* be the summer I was expecting."

I laughed, too. "Me neither."

"I was hoping for a summer of love," she said wistfully. Then she quickly added, "I'm sorry. I know you were, too."

It was nice that she seemed to be considering my feelings more. "I think it *has* turned out to be a summer of love." I shrugged. "Just a different kind."

"The kind that has you helping friends dig up bodies?"

I grinned at her. "That kind."

Ginny Rose took a smart route returning to us, sticking close to the perimeter of the acreage, puttering along at an easy pace so as not to kick up dust or call attention to herself. And when she reached us, she parked in a way that concealed us, at least partially.

"What's the plan?" Lisette asked after we'd donned work gloves and had unloaded the tools and the rope.

"First we uncover the barrow."

"The barrow?" Lisette asked.

"The rocks that cover the grave," Ginny Rose said. "That's what Papa called it."

Lisette nodded. "And then?"

"We take off the rocks and dig. But I want to dig around the edges, not straight down." She frowned. "They're not that deep."

"So . . . not six feet down?" Lisette asked.

"Oh no," Ginny Rose said, shaking her head. "More like . . ." She thought for a minute. "Maybe only . . . two?"

My breath caught. Something about a grave only two feet deep seemed so tragic. How desperate Mr. Gilley must have been at the time. How weary and . . . destroyed.

"They're wrapped in a heavy blue-and-red blanket," Ginny Rose was saying. "If it's held together at all, I'm hopin' we can dig around it at both ends, get rope under and lift, then lay . . . the bundle on the blanket I brought and wrap it up tight in that."

Lisette and I exchanged looks. Neither of us really understood what she was saying, but it didn't matter. We just needed to get started. So while Ginny Rose and I scooped off the thick mulch of oak leaves with shovels, Lisette began moving the stones of the barrow. Compared to dirt, the mulch was fluffy and light, and in about fifteen minutes, we had cleared an area wide enough to begin digging a trench around where the stones had been.

There were only two shovels, so we traded off and dug steadily for at least an hour, slicing off sections closer and closer to where we thought the boys were. The ground was packed hard in places but was surprisingly airy in others.

"I reckon rippin' out the Eagle Tree loosened the soil," Ginny Rose said at one point.

I tried not to picture how far and wide the oak roots might have wandered. Or what yanking them from the earth might have done to bodies laid to rest nearby.

I just kept digging.

"Look!" Lisette said suddenly, pointing into the part of the trench she'd been chipping away at. "Is that blanket?"

Ginny Rose was beside her in a jiffy, taking her shovel, then using the tip to scrape around what was definitely blue-and-red cloth.

I felt a jolt of joy mixed with dread.

We'd found the boys.

We'd really found them.

The three of us stood still for a minute, staring at the dirt-caked cloth. Then Ginny Rose grabbed the hand rake and I got the hand trowel, and we began clearing away dirt around the blanket while Lisette kept excavating with a shovel.

We went around and around the grave, carefully exposing the blanket. The sun was blazing overhead, and we were all dusty and dirty and parched, but even Lisette seemed determined not to complain. From time to time, we took a break and passed around the jug of water Ginny Rose had brought along. Strangely enough, the most comfortable way to rest was sitting with our feet inside the trench we'd dug around the grave. It was cool and didn't smell at all the way I'd dreaded. But the breaks didn't last long, because we all wanted to put the job behind us and get out of the sun.

Finally we'd gotten the blanket mostly uncovered, and Ginny Rose said, "That's good enough," and handed me one end of a long length of rope. "Let's try workin' this beneath them."

She and I started at one end of the grave and sawed the rope back and forth, cutting through the dirt that was under the exposed blanket, moving slowly toward the center, while Lisette carefully scraped away dirt that still covered the top of the blanket.

Once Ginny Rose and I had worked the rope about eighteen inches in, we tied it tight at the top, and Ginny Rose cut the long end off with a pocketknife. Then we took the leftover rope and did the same thing at the other end of the grave.

After we'd tied and cut the rope there, the three of us took a minute to sit, our feet resting inside the trench. "It's hard to believe the blanket's held together like it has," Ginny Rose mused.

I was exhausted and feeling very strange about this dirty blue-and-red bundle between us. "Do you want to . . . check?" I asked at last.

"You mean *look*?" Ginny Rose asked.

Lisette got up and headed for the truck without a word.

"I just meant . . . to make sure?"

"I don't need to look to know they're in there."

Lisette retrieved the blanket Ginny Rose had brought along and spread it beside the grave. "Can we please get this over with and go home?"

"Yes," Ginny Rose said with a heavy sigh. Then she turned to

Lisette and said, "I was wrong about you. I'm truly sorry for how I judged you."

"Why . . . thank you," Lisette said, clearly surprised. Then she added, "Although you weren't entirely wrong. I had some . . . well, some things to learn."

Ginny Rose sighed. "Well, so did I." Then she looked Lisette over with a hint of a grin. "And something I've learned today is that dirt is not your color."

"Well, guess what?" Lisette countered with a grin of her own. "It's not yours, either. You look *way* better in blue."

The two of them laughed, and then the mood switched back to the task at hand. "Ready?" I asked Ginny Rose.

She nodded, and while she grasped the knotted rope at the top, I did the same for the one at the bottom. She took a deep breath. "One . . . two . . . three!"

We pulled up, but as we lifted, the middle began cratering. And I was about to put my side down when Lisette pointed across the field and said, "Someone's coming!"

Ginny Rose glanced over her shoulder, then gave me a determined look. "Now!" she said, and before I knew what I was doing, I copied her movement, hoisting the bundle and giving it a desperate swing onto the blanket.

"I think it's that man from the diner!" Lisette said, spying around the truck.

I looked and, sure enough, there was a heavyset man wearing a porkpie hat waddling toward us across the open field, his arms pumping.

"Quick!" Ginny Rose cried, frantically motioning me to help her wrap the bundle in the blanket.

We flopped one end of the blanket over, the top and bottom

ends in, then turned the whole thing like a log until it was completely rolled up. Lisette rushed to put the tools into the truck bed while Ginny Rose and I wrestled the bundle into the back of the truck and rested it lengthwise beneath the cab window.

The man was nearly upon us, so we scrambled into the cab, with Lisette wedged in the middle. "Come on, come on, come on!" Ginny Rose muttered as she cranked the motor, and when the truck fired up, she ground it into gear.

"Stop!" the man shouted as we began rolling away. "What were you girls doing?"

"That *is* him," Lisette said.

"Collectin' what's ours!" Ginny Rose yelled out the window.

"This land ain't yours, y'damn Okies!" he shouted back, his ruddy face bursting with sweat. "So *nothing* here's yours! It's bad enough your kind squatted on it for so long!"

I could see anger flare to life in Ginny Rose, could feel it inside me, too. "What a *pig*," Lisette fumed.

Yet somehow Ginny Rose kept a lid on her temper. "Is that so?" she challenged, rolling slowly along as he approached.

"Yeah, that's so!" the man spit out.

"Well, mister, there's an open grave back there that's beggin' to differ," she said, cool as ice. "And you're welcome to claim it as your own."

"What?" he cried.

Lisette leaned over and shouted, "She's telling you to drop dead!"

Ginny Rose grinned at her and pressed down hard on the gas pedal. And I guess the truck was feeling its oats, because it backfired, then shot ahead, kicking up dust in the man's face as we made our getaway.

38

Ginny Rose

RUNNIN' ON EMPTY

I'm spitting mad as we rumble across the dirt and get back on the road, but I'm not the only one. Lisette's fit to be tied. It's not just over bein' called Okie again, either. There's nothing Okie about her but a sweaty brow and a dustin' of dirt, and those'll wash right off.

No, Lisette's fit to be tied because no one's ever *treated* her like an Okie before.

"What gives a man who waddles like a duck, bulges like a pig, and smells like a skunk the idea that he's better than us? Better than *anyone*?" she demands. "Who does he think he is?"

"The one used to callin' the shots," I reply. "At least he wasn't carryin' a club. Or a gun." I shake my head. "For some reason men like him aren't afraid to use 'em."

"That's happened to you?" she asks.

I shoot a look at her but am quick to pull back my scowl. "Fear works wonders on keepin' people in line, Lisette."

"But—"

"And hungry people are known to break the law."

She settles back a little. "Oh."

I know she's still curious. Or tryin' to fit it all together. And I sure don't feel like explainin' the past, because there *is* no explainin' it—not really. But what I said came with a huff of sarcasm, and at this point I owe her better'n that. So I sigh and say, "The way Papa explained it to me is, people saw us as beggars, but all we were beggin' for was work. There wasn't enough of it to go around, and lots of farmers took advantage of that, payin' field hands less and less, while chargin' them more'n was fair at the company store. This forced most pickers to run a tab to feed their families, only at week's end, their wages didn't cover what they owed."

"Which put them right back in debt," Lisette says softly.

"Papa called it debtor's quicksand—once you slipped in, there was little chance of crawlin' back out. We spent long days workin' for what amounted to nothing, but it was that or starve." I take a deep breath. "But about what you asked me before. One time I was in line with Papa waitin' for work when they announced they'd be payin' only three cents an hour instead of the five we'd been told. The field hands got angry and made a run on the company store for food."

"What happened?" Lisette asks, sittin' a little sideways so she can face me better.

"The field bosses took up clubs and guns. Papa and I were trapped in a mob, and I saw a man get shot. After that, Papa was quick to get us out of there, and we never went back." I turn to her. "So yep. I've seen the business end of a club—and a gun—more times'n I care to recall."

While Lisette and I are talkin', Peggy's also turned sideways, but she's checkin' out the back window. "You worried about that man comin' after us?" I ask.

"We wouldn't be hard to catch," Peggy says, her eyes fixed on the road behind us.

"The boys all right?" I ask.

"They're fine," she says, facin' forward.

Lisette shakes her head and sits back, too. "This is the *strangest* situation I've ever been in."

"I told you to stay home," I tell her with a grin.

"That's because you're smarter than me," she says, grinnin' back.

I eye her. "But not as dirty!"

She looks at her hands, which are filthy and bloomin' with blisters, though she *did* wear gloves. "Can we *please* stop somewhere and wash up?" she asks.

"Sure," I say, thinkin' it'll also give me a chance to call Anna Mae with our secret signal and top off the radiator so we'll make it home without overheatin' again. "Is a gas station all right?"

"Anywhere," she says.

About half an hour later we come upon a roadside station with a pay phone out front, so I pull in. But it takes loopin' around the building twice before I see the water and air hoses along the back fence, half buried by dried weeds. I pull up and get busy with the radiator while Lisette makes a beeline to a narrow door labeled TOILET at the side of the station. But she's barely gone in when she comes flyin' out, squealin', "Euuw! Euuw, euuw, euuw!"

Peggy's beside her in an instant. "What's wrong?"

"Euuw!" is all Lisette can seem to say.

So Peggy opens the door, then closes it quick. "Oh!" she says. "That's *awful*."

Well, I don't need to know more. I just finish fillin' the radiator, which has gone low, then hose myself off a bit. The cool water feels wonderful on my face and arms and hands, and soon Lisette's standin' beside me, her neckerchief in hand. "I *really* want to wash up," she says, so I give her the hose, sayin', "Here. I'm gonna go signal my sister."

"Signal your sister?" she asks.

"To let her know we found the boys."

So while Lisette and Peggy wash up, I hurry around the building to the pay phone and place the call. When the line connects, my heart starts to gallop, and after one ring, I'm quick to hang up.

The breath I've been holdin' busts free as the coins jangle down the return chute. Suddenly the thought of facin' Papa is more frightening than the prospect of findin' the boys. And, now that I *have* found them, I'm not sure what I should *do* with them. I can't just leave them in the back of the truck!

Lisette walks up, sayin', "I should call home, too," and then Peggy's there, wantin' to do the same.

So I gather my coins and stand aside as Lisette places a collect call. "Lisette," she tells the operator, and in no time she's connected. Even from a few yards away, we can hear a frantic woman's voice through the speaker. "I'm fine," Lisette says into the phone, and then, "No! I'm with"—she eyes us uncertainly— "friends. It was an emergency. I can't tell you any more than that. I just wanted to let you know that I'm all right and that I'll be home tonight." The voice on the other end buzzes for a full minute; then Lisette says, "Mom. Mom, listen to me. I'm fine and I'll see you tonight. That's all I can tell you." She cradles the handset and says to Peggy and me, "She thinks I've run off with a boy."

Then it's Peggy's turn, and after a similar conversation, she hangs up and says, "She's *sure* I've run off with a boy!"

Then a voice out of nowhere startles us all. "You girls plannin' to *buy* anything, or you just usin' up all my water and patience."

We whirl around to see a wiry man with a shock of graying red hair wearin' greasy jeans and a scowl. Where'd he come from? And how long has he been spyin' on us?

Lisette's the first to recover. "Do you have a soda machine inside?" she asks, because there's not one outside.

"It's out of order," he says.

"So's your restroom, by the way," Lisette offers. "It could really use some attention."

He nods. "I'm thinkin' you should give it that," he says, like a cat creepin' up on a field mouse. "To pay for using my water, and all."

"To pay for—"

"I'm not runnin' a bathhouse. Or in the business of waterin' jalopies." He gives a sly shrug. "Seems the least you could do. Unless you'd like me to call the cops?"

"For *what*?" Lisette demands.

I grab Lisette's arm and pull. "For bein' Okies," I say under my breath.

Her attention snaps to me. "What?"

I pull harder. "There's no winnin' this. Let's go."

"I can't believe you!" Lisette hollers at him as I drag her away.

"Freeloaders!" he hollers back.

"Unbelievable," Lisette mutters as we get back on the road.

I look at her sittin' beside me. She's fumin', and her face is twitchin' with indignation. But it strikes me that even in her be-draggled state, she's never looked prettier.

"Why are you looking at me like that?" she demands.

I turn back to the road. "You'd have done all right as an Okie." I grin at her. "Not a compliment I give out lightly."

She sighs. "I would *never* have made it." She goes quiet for a long minute before sayin', "I guess there's nothing like having the hatred thrown right at you to make you understand how it feels."

We drive along for another half an hour or so, but I'm dis-tracted from the conversation by the fuel gauge. Why didn't I get a little gas at the station before I looked for water? Maybe that whole ugly exchange wouldn't have happened. And now . . . well, I've got to stop soon, because the gauge is dippin' below a quar-ter tank, but I have hardly any money and—despite warmin' to her—I'd never ask Lisette for help and sure don't want that awful feelin' of shame from havin' her offer.

So I'm just decidin' to avoid all of that by pullin' over and usin' the gas from Peggy's shed when there's the sound of a siren windin' up behind us. I look in the mirror and gasp, "Oh no!" because there's a highway patrol car pullin' me over.

Peggy goes pale. "Do you think that man called the cops on us?"

"Which one?" I cry. And then I blurt out, "I don't have a li-cense!"

Their eyes stretch into saucers. "You *don't?*"

"No!" I feel myself fallin' apart as I pull to the side of the road. Suddenly I'm back to bein' a little girl, scared to death at the California border.

"Ginny Rose!" Lisette's hissin'.

"Huh?" I say, blinkin'. We've come to a stop, though I don't remember doin' so.

"Switch with me!"

"What?"

"Switch with me! I have a license!"

But I can't seem to move. Why are we bein' pulled over? Was it because I said that about the empty grave? And if it is, what if the policeman discovers the boys?

"Hurry!" Lisette says frantically, archin' herself to make room for me to slide underneath her.

I snap to and scoot over, and for a moment we're a tangle of arms and legs. But by the time the police officer appears at the driver's-side window, Lisette's managed to swipe on lipstick and compose herself.

"Hello, Officer," she singsongs. "What seems to be the problem?"

He's tall and trim, and the brass star on his uniform flashes in the afternoon sun as he leans down to take a look inside. "Afternoon, ladies," he says cordially, but it's plain to see he wasn't expectin' what he's found.

"Afternoon, Officer," the three of us chime, and I pray he can't see how badly I'm tremblin'.

He looks now at Lisette. "May I see your driver's license, miss?"

"Certainly, Officer," she replies, then plucks it from her pocketbook.

He looks it over, looks us over, then looks the back of the truck over, one eyebrow raised the whole time.

"I know you're wondering," Lisette says with a laugh, "what three lovely ladies are doing in an old jalopy with shovels, looking like they've been rolling in the dirt."

"I am," he says, handin' back the license. "But that's not the reason I pulled you over."

"Then what is?" Lisette asks.

"Your speed. If you can't get this thing over forty, you should probably stick to the back roads."

Lisette nods. "We've been overheating, so we've had to take it slow, but we're turning off soon, so . . . won't you let us continue?"

He nods. "Just be aware of people coming up fast behind you."

"Thank you, Officer."

He stands by a moment, hitchin' his gun belt, a keen eye on the truck bed. "And if you don't mind?"

"Sir?"

"What's in the blanket?"

"In it?" Lisette laughs like she hasn't a care in the world. "That's three city girls' attempt at a bedroll."

"And the shovels?"

She leans toward him like she's tellin' a secret. "If you have a crazy uncle who swears X marks the spot for family treasure, don't believe him!" She gives another merry laugh. "It was an adventure, but now we're sore and tired and can't wait to get home!"

"Well, then," he says reluctantly, "I'll let you get on your way."

And just like that he's back in his patrol car and pullin' onto the highway.

"You were amazing," Peggy says to Lisette, but I'm still tremblin' like a leaf.

"He's gone," Lisette says, noticin' the state I'm in. "It's okay."

I shake my head, which is all I can seem to manage.

"What's wrong?" she asks.

Her voice is gentle and sincere, and it helps my words make their way out. "It's all of it. *All* of it. And . . . police scare me. I just need a minute."

"*Police* do?" she asks. "Why?"

I give her a doubtful look. From her place in this world it'll make no sense. But then Peggy prods me gently with "Tell her."

So I take a deep, choppy breath and say, "It started on the move from Oklahoma. When we were stopped at a bum blockade at the California border."

"A bum blockade?" Lisette asks. "What's that?"

"Roadblocks with police stoppin' people like us from comin' into California. The police *hated* us. We'd been travelin' across the desert for weeks, but when we reached the border, they turned back anyone who didn't have money or a job. Papa tried to reason with them, tried to tell them what they were doin' was illegal, that we were all Americans, but they wouldn't listen. They threatened us with guns and hit Faithful with batons until we turned around. We found a way in by some back road eventually, but it didn't get any easier from there." I heave a sigh. "We were always gettin' thrown out of places or questioned by police. They still tie me up in knots."

"That's awful!" Lisette says.

I shrug and sigh again, because what's there to say?

We come from such different worlds.

It *has* helped to talk about it, though, and soon my mind's turnin' back to what was on it before. "We're nearly out of gas,"

I tell them. "I want to use whatever's in the gas can, if that's all right?"

"Sure," Peggy says. But then she points ahead and asks, "How about we do it up there?"

Lisette squints into the distance. "Is that a Giant Orange stand?"

"I think so," Peggy says.

"Then yes, yes, yes!" Lisette cries. She turns to me and says, "You drive, I'll buy."

"Deal," I say with a weary laugh. And then I'm quick to add, "Thank you," as we switch places.

I catch the looks of surprise that pass between Lisette and Peggy, and I'm more'n a little surprised myself by how quick I'd been to accept her offer. But as I'm pullin' back onto the highway, my heart's tellin' me it's okay. I'm *not* a leaner. I *don't* have to keep a tally of every little thing.

Sometimes with friends, thanks is payment enough.

39

Peggy

TRANSFORMATIONS

There's nothing like sipping from a cup of fresh-squeezed orange juice over chipped ice when you're parched and the sky is blazing. "To the reunion," Lisette said as we gathered in the shade of a large elm tree near the Giant Orange stand.

"To the reunion," Ginny Rose and I said, wearily lifting our cups to hers. While we drank in silence, savoring every sip, I couldn't help but wish our farm was acres of oranges instead of peaches.

Oranges are hardy.

They don't bruise with rough treatment.

Or rot in just days!

And unlike peaches, they're easy to juice.

Also, there'd be no shortage of customers. We'd had to wait ten minutes in line to place our order and another five to watch them fill it. But every sip and every last ice chip had been worth the wait.

"I guess we should pour the gas in and go," Ginny Rose said after we'd all finished. "Time to face the music."

We each would have music to face, but Lisette's and mine would be a jingle compared to a dirge for Ginny Rose. Maybe recovering the boys *would* help heal her family in the end, but I could also see it tearing them completely apart. There was no way for any of us to avoid the consequences, though, so we poured gas into the tank, got back in the truck, and started off again.

Still, the closer we got to home, the more I could see that Ginny Rose was having second thoughts about what we'd done. She'd dropped out of our casual conversation way back when we'd turned off the highway, and as we passed by Edselon, I noticed she was clasping and unclasping the steering wheel like she'd done when the truck was overheating. This time, though, the truck was fine. *She* was the one under too much pressure.

Finally, as we approached River Road, the pressure inside her became too much. "What have I done?" she breathed out.

I was in the middle now, so it was easy to reach out and stroke her arm. "It'll be all right," I said, trying to keep doubt out of my voice. "And I've been thinking . . ."

She turned to me, her eyes desperate. "Yes?"

"I've been thinking that we should all go straight to Valley Church and ask Mrs. Poole for help."

"Would you?" she said at last. "Come with me, I mean?"

"Of course!" Lisette and I said together.

Before too long, we were pulling into the church parking lot, which was empty except for a creamy white Dodge sedan.

"They're here," Ginny Rose said, clearly relieved.

The three of us went up the steps to the church entrance, but it was locked. So we walked to a side door, which was also locked. Finally, we went around back to the rectory.

Ginny Rose stood on the small porch and rang the bell, while

Lisette and I stayed a step back on the walkway. The smell of roasting chicken drifted through an open window, and I suddenly realized how hungry I was.

The others smelled it, too. "We're interrupting dinner," Lisette whispered.

But then the door opened, and we were face to face with Mrs. Poole. "Yes?" she asked, then immediately said, "Good heavens!"

First she took in our filthy, sunbaked appearance.

Then she scanned our faces, blinking in disbelief when she got to Lisette. "Lisette *Bovee?*" she said at last, clearly thinking that, dirty or not, we three peas did not belong in the same pod. "What on earth?"

At last, Ginny Rose found her voice. "We've brought my brothers," she said.

Mrs. Poole stared, not comprehending. Then, very slowly, words began drifting from her mouth. "You've brought your . . . Do you mean you . . . ?"

She couldn't seem to finish, and Ginny Rose looked about to collapse, so I stepped in. "After yesterday's sermon, people were talking and piecing things together. Ginny Rose's father was against the idea, and someone in the congregation was going to ask him about it, so . . . so there was no time to do anything else."

"You're telling me the three of you . . . ," she asked, her eyes full moons now, "did it yourselves?"

We nodded in unison.

Mrs. Poole inhaled sharply. "No!"

"Can you please help us?" Ginny Rose begged, tears spilling over.

"Oh, you poor, poor dear," she said, shoving her shock aside and opening the door wide. "Come in, come in!" Then over her shoulder she called, "Reverend! Pull up some chairs. We have company!"

While Mrs. Poole hurried to add plates to the dinner table, we scrubbed up at the sink with soap. Lots and lots of soap. We took longer than we should have, but we were like early-spring birds splashing in a puddle, twittering with relief. A sponge bath had never felt so good, or so needed!

"I've contacted Mr. Merrihew at the funeral home," Mrs. Poole said to Ginny Rose when we'd finished up. "He'll take care of everything."

"Honest?" Ginny Rose said, spilling tears again.

"Yes, dear. We'll go over there in a bit. Now, come. Let's get you something to eat. I imagine it's been quite a day."

To my relief, neither Reverend Poole nor his wife asked any questions during dinner. Silently and gratefully, we simply ate.

Afterward, Mrs. Poole edged us back onto the difficult path ahead. "Do your families know about this?" she asked.

We all shook our heads.

"We did call this afternoon," I explained. "To let them know we were all right. But they don't know *where* we went."

"Or *why* we went," Lisette said.

"Or *who* we went with," I added.

"Mine may know," Ginny Rose said. "My sister Anna Mae was in on the plan. She's probably told them by now." She took a choppy breath. "I'm sure Papa's rollin' with thunder."

"So what *do* your parents think you're doing?" Mrs. Poole asked, directing the question at me.

"They think I've run off with a boy."

"And yours?" she asked Lisette.

"The same."

"Well!" Mrs. Poole said. "Are they ever in for an awakening."

And then, for practically the first time all night, Reverend Poole spoke. "I think it might be wise to gather them all here."

"Our *parents*?" Lisette said, her voice squeaking. But almost immediately she warmed to the idea. "Yes," she said. "Yes, that's actually a very good idea."

"I agree," I said, exchanging looks with Lisette, knowing we were thinking the same thing: our parents were sure to be on their best behavior in front of Reverend Poole.

"But . . . mine have no way to get here," Ginny Rose said with a cringe. "I've got the truck."

"Then I'll go get them," Mrs. Poole said. She took her napkin from her lap and placed it beside her plate. "Now let's go next door, shall we? Just drive around to the back of Merrihew's. I'll meet you there."

So we thanked Reverend Poole for his hospitality, then went back to the truck. But the truck didn't seem to want to start. "She's tired, too," Ginny Rose said with a sad smile, then broke into tears again. "Sweet, dear Faithful."

"We could push," Lisette volunteered. "It's only right there," she said, pointing to the funeral home.

Ginny Rose's face crinkled and her eyes ran fast. "I will never forget your kindness," she choked out. And then, like it had a mind all its own, the jalopy fired up. "Thatagirl!" Ginny Rose said with a tearful smile, and once again, we were rolling along.

When we reached the back of Merrihew's, there was a man standing outside an open doorway in deep conversation with Mrs. Poole. He had substantial black eyebrows—ones I'd noticed many times at church but hadn't realized belonged to the mortician.

After introductions were made and Mr. Merrihew had seen the bundle, he gently asked Ginny Rose questions—some she couldn't answer because we hadn't looked at the boys, but some she could.

Yes, they should be put in the same coffin.

Their favorite color was blue.

They loved their sock monkeys, collecting acorns and feathers, and chasing butterflies.

When the questions were done, she tearfully turned over the bundle to Mr. Merrihew, and when he'd disappeared inside with it, she sobbed against my shoulder. "The whole drive home," she choked out, "I was picturin' them on the inside of the cab, back where they used to ride." She hugged me like she might never let go. "It was their last ride in Faithful."

"A ride that brought them home," I said gently, then held on tight while she let years of heartache flow free.

When Ginny Rose had dried her eyes, we returned to the rectory to await our fate. Mrs. Poole went to get Mr. and Mrs. Gilley, and Reverend Poole retreated to a back room to place calls to Lisette's and my parents while the three of us sat in a small sitting room, surrounded by lace curtains and flowered wallpaper, imagining the worst.

The strange thing was, I wasn't afraid of whatever *the worst* might turn out to be. A soothing voice inside me kept saying it *would* be all right. Maybe my parents would never understand why I'd done the things I'd done, maybe I'd never again have their approval, and maybe I'd fail to win back their trust. But if that was the case, it would be because *they* were unwilling to bend, unwilling to listen. I liked the new voice inside me. It steadied me. It made *sense* to me.

No, it made sense *beyond* me.

For the first time in my life, I wasn't just frustrated with not being listened to—I truly felt I was *worth* being heard. And if my parents didn't understand why I'd done what I'd done, that was their shortfall, not mine. They didn't have to *agree* with all of it, but the least they could do was make an effort to understand.

They also didn't have to change their thinking on inheritance— it was their property, not mine. But *I* was not property. By next summer, I'd be an adult and I'd be free to make my own way. Not like Doris had, but certainly away from farming. It was time for me to figure out what I *did* want.

Lisette had been mulling over the future, too, because she broke the silence with "What do you think about getting an apartment together? All of us. In the city."

Ginny Rose's jaw dangled, and mine dropped some, too.

"It could be so much fun," Lisette said.

I laughed. "Well! *There's* an idea that's never crossed my mind."

"Why not?" she asked me, then turned the question on Ginny Rose. "Why not?"

"Well, I'm not a city girl," Ginny Rose offered. "And besides, I'm needed here."

"It won't be for another year," Lisette said quickly. "After we graduate." This was met with an awkward silence, which she finally broke. "Don't you look at me that way, Peggy Simmons! After what we did today?"

I laughed, and Ginny Rose gave a little grin and said, "Nothing in San Francisco will ever top this."

"You definitely should go," I told Lisette. "You *belong* in San Francisco. It's the perfect place for what you want to do." I looked down. "But I'm not sure *what* I want to do yet. I'm thinking I should meet with the guidance counselor at school when it starts. Find out what's out there. There are probably lots of things I don't even know about."

Lisette nodded. "That's a really good idea." She gave me a mischievous grin. "And know I'm all for helping you decide." But then she slouched back with a sigh. "I just don't want to lose *this*," she said, tapping her heart with her fist. Then her eyes went glassy as she whispered, "I want what's grown in here to stay."

I knew what she meant.

I knew exactly what she meant.

Because if this summer had changed me, it had positively transformed her. I could never in a million years have pictured Lisette Bovee using a shovel, let alone working hours in the blazing sun to dig up a grave. But she'd found something— something bigger than herself, more important than a boy—and she liked the way it felt.

Ginny Rose, for all she'd been through, seemed to understand exactly what she meant, too. Because she reached over and took one of Lisette's hands in both of hers and said, "You won't, Lisette." She let go and tapped her own heart. "I promise you, you won't."

Then there were voices down the hall and we knew—it was time.

40

Ginny Rose

THE LION'S DEN

Through the door we can hear the buzz of voices. It's like a swarm of grasshoppers chewin' toward us, faster and louder. Mama's voice is in it, higher than the rest, but I can't make out what she's sayin'.

Suddenly the swarm turns; the sound fades, then goes quiet. My heart flutters with dread. I know Death likes to linger in the silence that follows a storm.

The three of us sit together waitin'. Wonderin'. Lost in our own thoughts.

"What's taking so long?" Lisette mutters after we've been alone for another fifteen minutes.

Then we hear hard-heeled footsteps approach, and Mrs. Poole enters the sitting room. "Good heavens!" she says on a great gust of air. "You girls have certainly stirred the pot." She drifts into a dainty wicker chair as though her legs won't hold her another minute. "A banker, a farmer, and an angry Okie in the same small room?" Her eyes dart to me. "I'm sorry, Ginny Rose. I mean no disrespect."

"I know, ma'am," I say. "It's all right."

Mrs. Poole takes in a deep, calming breath. "So. We've given them an overview of what you girls have done, and the reverend is doing his best to set the stage for a civil dialogue, insisting that they listen with open hearts to your story. This may be difficult for them, especially for the Gilleys." She turns to me again. "You're right about your father being upset, and your mother's clammed up tight, which is hard for me to read."

"I wish I could help," I say, but I'm beyond understandin' my mother's thoughts, and once again, hope's tumblin'.

Was it all in vain?

"What about mine?" Peggy asks.

"I'm not sure," Mrs. Poole says. "Being caught between the Bovees and the Gilleys has them a little shell-shocked."

"Is my mom here?" Lisette asks.

Mrs. Poole's eyes skate to one side, then the other. "She is . . . ," she says, "but I'm afraid she's rather inebriated."

Lisette slumps back. "Great."

"So," Mrs. Poole says, gatherin' the reins. "Once the reverend has finished settling your parents, we'll join them in the front room. I want the three of you to sit side by side on the couch and each say your piece in turn. The reverend and I will do our best to keep things civil while you explain yourselves." She leans forward. "Peace will only come through understanding, and this may be your best chance to accomplish that. Say what you need to say with as much kindness as you can, despite how they may act. Keep in mind that your disappearing the way you did put them through quite an ordeal." She leans back again. "May I suggest that you each begin with an apology?"

We all nod gravely.

"Well, then," she says, takin' a deep breath. "Let's enter the lion's den, shall we?"

Mrs. Poole leads us down a hallway, through a doorway, down another hall, and into the front room. It's as large as our whole house and done up in style, with fine furniture, a grand oak desk, beautiful Tiffany lamps, and sturdy shelves of books.

Mrs. Poole stands posted at the doorway while the three of us file in, and I nearly burst into tears at the sight of my folks sittin' stiff as tombstones at either edge of a settee. Mama's eyes are cast down, and Papa sends me a hard look, then turns away like he can't stand the sight of me.

Mr. and Mrs. Simmons are in armless chairs seated close together, lookin' like they've been plucked from their chores. At the sight of Peggy, Mrs. Simmons sends her a quivery smile and my heart pangs with envy. Already, I can see, Peggy will be forgiven.

Mr. Bovee, though, looks like a ruddy-faced mule. He stands near a wall, his arms crossed, his jaw set, while his wife sits with her head leanin' against one side of a wingback chair, smilin' pleasantly at nothing in particular.

Reverend Poole is standin' beside the desk, and he nods toward the couch, which is upholstered in purple-and-gold-striped satin. I worry about the dirt on our clothes. We shouldn't sit here.

Still, in a daze, we do—Lisette on my left, Peggy on my right, all of us perched on the edge, holdin' our breath.

Reverend Poole clears his throat, then says, "Ginny Rose? It seems appropriate for you to go first."

I stand, but my legs wobble beneath me, so I sit again. And then the weight of the day, the fear in my heart, the weariness in my soul, all crash down on me at once, and I dissolve into tears.

Peggy rubs my back and whispers, "Be strong, Ginny Rose. You did it out of love."

So I pull myself together, rememberin' Mrs. Poole's advice. "Papa, Mama," I manage. "I'm so sorry if I've made things worse. I'm sorry I took Faithful. And I'm sorry to have tangled Anna Mae in this." I take a deep breath. "But, Mama, I've watched you wither away from me and the girls, and I know you're dyin' inside. We've all talked about wantin' to stay here in Ferrybank, about makin' it our home. I was hopin' that bringin' the boys here—havin' them buried in a place you could visit—would stop your heartache from buryin' *you*. And then maybe you could stop starin' at that picture of them and come back to us. Mama, your girls *need* you.

"And, Papa, I tried so hard to talk to you! I tried to explain that your ways of coping weren't workin' for Mama. That the only thing that might heal her heart would be to bring the boys home; to give them a proper place to rest. But you wouldn't listen. Anna Mae has become so angry about all of it, and I couldn't bear to watch Bonnie Sue and Katie Bee grow up in fear of Mama's broken heart. We needed to change things. Or at least to try. So punish me if you have to, but I'm hopin' someday you'll forgive me. We've been through so much together, Papa. I just want the heartache to stop."

I have more to say—much more. But my throat's clamped

down tight, and my eyes are runnin' streams. So I simply hide my face in my hands and sob.

And then Peggy's talkin'. I wipe my face with the handkerchief Mrs. Poole slips over my shoulder, and I look up to see Peggy standin' tall and defiant.

My eyes dry up in wonder.

How can she be so strong?

But she's not addressin' her folks.

She's talkin' to mine.

"Your daughter," she says, "has been in agony over this. And she's put all her wages into a fund to pay for a plot and a coffin. She's the most honorable, courageous person I know, and I'm proud to be her friend. She was only a little girl when she helped bury those boys, Mr. Gilley. She watched you dig the grave. She helped you put them in the ground and cover them with the rocks she hauled up from the river. Do you think that memory doesn't haunt her? Didn't *scar* her? So, Mrs. Gilley, won't you appreciate what you *do* have, and consider what *she's* been through? And, Mr. Gilley, don't just forgive her, *thank* her. Because it turns out they're building new houses on the land where your sons were buried. The whole area has been leveled and the trees are all gone. In a few months your sons would have either had a house built on them or been bulldozed from their grave, scattered and crushed to smithereens."

At this, Mama gasps and covers her mouth with her hands. Then slowly she turns an angry look on Papa.

It's a moment when, for the first time in my life, I wonder if they'll stay together. But that moment passes when Papa's face falls, and—again for the first time in my life—I see him break down and cry.

I rush forward and kneel before him. "Papa," I say, cryin', too. "Please forgive me."

"Oh, child," he says, lettin' the tears flow. And when Mama reaches out and strokes my hair, hope gathers inside me.

Peggy's voice begins again, so I sit on the floor in front of the settee, holdin' on to Papa's hand while Mama's rests on my shoulder.

"And, Mr. Bovee," Peggy's sayin', "I know you're mad at me. I know I've caused problems in your family, and I'm sorry for that."

Mr. Bovee remains stony-faced. So Peggy turns to Mrs. Bovee and says, "I know you think I'm not good enough for your daughter—"

"*Hrmph!*" Mrs. Simmons says, givin' Mrs. Bovee a dark look.

"—but that's something I can't apologize for," Peggy says.

"Talk to your own parents, not us!" Mr. Bovee snaps.

So at last Peggy turns to Mr. and Mrs. Simmons. "I'm sorry I was deceitful. I charged extra at the stand and used the money to help pay for the plot and coffin. But the truth is, that's not the way it began. I started doing it because I was angry at you for treating your daughters different than your sons, and for treating both Bobby and me like we owe every waking hour to the farm.

"And, Mother, I wish you'd stand up for me. *Really* stand up for me. But if you can't do that, or just agree that men deserve things we don't, then please forgive me for being deceitful and know that I did what I did because a friend needed my help.

"And, Father. You need to make up with Doris. She was hurt and angry, just the way I am now. Do you understand that both your daughters feel used? That we've worked and worked, only to learn that the plan was to push us out?

"I've been thinking a lot about what it means to be a family, and I think it means that we support each other in a *fair* way. We need to be able to talk about things, not just storm off. We've got to work at it until we find ways we can *agree*." She takes a deep breath, then says, "I know you don't want to hear any of this, but if Ginny Rose had the courage to do the things she did to try to heal her family, then the least I can do is have the courage to say I want to look for ways to mend ours."

When Peggy finishes, her face is rosy and her eyes are wet, and I know her heart's poundin' hard in her chest. But when she sits, it's with a straight spine and her head held high, and I feel my eyes well with tears of gratitude.

Then Reverend Poole prompts, "Lisette?"

Lisette stands, but she's not defiant like Peggy. And it looks for all the world like she's about to buckle under Mr. Bovee's glare. "I don't have a speech," she says, findin' her way. "Or an apology." She takes a deep breath and looks around the room. "I have a request."

Mr. Bovee frowns harder.

"Could you please just let us be friends?" She turns to Mr. Bovee and says, "We're not better than them, Daddy. As a matter of fact, I feel better about myself when I'm with them." She turns to Peggy's folks. "And I'm not an empty-headed social climber," she says with a pointed look at Mrs. Simmons, whose cheeks go red. "And clearly," she says, castin' a frown at Mrs. Bovee, "we have problems of our own." Then she turns to my folks. "And, Mr. and Mrs. Gilley? We are *not* the enemy." But then she adds, "Although I do understand why you might feel that way."

"How dare you!" Mr. Bovee shouts.

I scramble over to stand beside her, and Peggy jumps to her feet, too.

"Daddy," Lisette says, "I love you, but I'm not moving into that house."

"We can discuss this later!" he snaps.

"No. What I said before I mean more than ever. You can lock me in my room or toss me out, but I'm *not* moving into that house."

Reverend Poole looks a little bewildered. And I'm wonderin', too, how we've gotten so far off track. But then I see that we're not *off* track, we've just backed up the track to where the lines divided. To where the trouble began.

Mr. Bovee tries a softer tone. "Look, honey," he says to Lisette. "We're not here to discuss that. Let's get today's problem settled, and we'll talk about the rest of it at home."

"No," Lisette says, diggin' in. "If you don't promise to give back that house, I'm not coming home."

Mr. Bovee snorts. "Oh, come now. Where would you go?"

He sounds so high-and-mighty that my anger draws and my mouth fires before good sense can take aim. "She can stay with us!"

Mama and Papa look like they've just been goosed. But to my complete surprise, Mama says, "It'd be close quarters, but you'd be welcome, Lisette."

My jaw dangles. But then, as if not wantin' to be outdone by someone with so much less, Mrs. Simmons pipes up, sayin', "We have space, too."

From the depths of the wingback chair comes a hoarse "Promise her, George," and we all turn wide eyes on Mrs. Bovee.

"Promise her, George," she says, sittin' forward, and this time her voice is loud and strong. "Promise her, or I'll divorce you!"

"Mom!" Lisette cries.

"I might divorce him anyway," Mrs. Bovee mutters, sinkin' back into the folds of the chair.

The room goes silent, and all eyes are on Mr. Bovee now.

"You know it's wrong, Daddy," Lisette says, her voice tender now. "And Carl Sunderwood was your *friend*. How could you do that to a friend?"

"It was business!" he snaps.

"Then you have no business calling yourself a friend!" Lisette snaps back. "Friends *help* each other."

A hush takes the room as we wait for Mr. Bovee to make his move.

"Fine," he grumbles at last.

"Fine what?" Lisette demands.

"I promise."

"How do I know you mean it?"

Mr. Bovee sighs and turns to Reverend Poole and raises his right hand like he's takin' an oath of office. "As God is my witness, I promise."

"Oh, Daddy!" Lisette says, and rushes forward to hug him.

Seein' that, Mrs. Simmons stretches her arms out toward Peggy, but though I look with pleading eyes at Papa and Mama, no arms stretch my way.

So I cross the room and kneel before them again, and at last Papa says, "It's all right, Ginny Rose."

Then Mama cups my face in her hands and just *looks* at me. I see her in there behind those sad eyes and ache to know what she's thinkin'. Finally she says, "I'm so sorry, Ginny Rose. For all

of it." Then she turns to Papa. "It's been a long time in comin',
Jeremiah," she says with tearful tenderness, "but I need to ask
for your forgiveness, too."

He looks puzzled. "What for?"

"For insistin' we come to California." And as the burden she's
carried all these years sinks in on Papa and me, her eyes brim
with tears. "If you can forgive me for that," she says, "maybe
someday I'll be able to forgive myself."

"Oh, Mary," he says, and as he wraps her in his arms, I
glimpse a true ray of light breakin' through the dark, dusty cloud
of our family's heartache.

41

Peggy

HOMECOMING

Tuesday afternoon, I'd just closed down the fruit stand when Bobby rolled up in the farm truck. "They're callin' it a homecoming service?" he asked out the window.

It was unusual to see him so animated. "Who is? What are you talking about?"

"Hop in!" he said, and when I pointed out I had things to deliver to the house, he said, "Just grab the cash box and come!"

So I did.

He U-turned back onto the road, and when I asked him where we were going, all he'd say was "You'll see."

A few minutes later, he pulled onto the dirt shoulder in front of Valley Church. "See?" he said, pointing to the marquee, which read:

HOMECOMING SERVICE

&

POTLUCK FOR

LUCAS & ELIJAH GILLEY

My eyes began stinging, and I'm afraid I sniffled, because Bobby turned to look at me and said, "Are you *crying?*" And since I couldn't very well hide that I was, he said, "But *why?* I think it's swell."

"I didn't know their *names,*" I choked out, and it was true. For all the talks I'd had with Ginny Rose over the summer, for all the hours we'd spent yesterday recovering them from the earth, for all the explaining I'd done to Mother and Father and Bobby 'til the wee hours last night, I'd never called them anything besides *Ginny Rose's brothers* or *the boys.*

Why had I never asked? Why had Ginny Rose never spoken their names? Maybe it hurt her too much to say them. Maybe it was easier to keep their memory at arm's length.

But here their names were, in bold black letters for anyone driving by to see.

Lucas and Elijah Gilley.

Bobby turned back to the marquee and heaved a sigh. "Well, it does make them more real, doesn't it?"

After a quiet minute, I decided to venture into meddling territory. "Ginny Rose is worried you won't be able to look at her the same," I said softly. And when he turned a questioning gaze on me, I added, "Because of what we did yesterday?"

"What sort of person would that make me?" he demanded.

I gave him a sly smile. "Not the person for her." Then I spotted someone pedaling down the road on a bicycle. "There she is!" I said, pointing through the windshield.

We both hopped out of the truck and ran across the road. "Hey!" I called, waving her to a stop. "Have you seen this?"

Ginny Rose straddled her bicycle. "A *homecoming*," she said wistfully, then turned to me. "That's wonderful, isn't it?"

"I think so!" I gushed. "And Bobby does, too. He raced home to get me so I could see."

Bobby was standing back a few yards, scuffing the ground. "Afternoon, Ginny Rose," he said.

"Afternoon, Bobby," she replied, and they both blushed.

"So?" I asked her. "How did things go after you got home?"

"It'll take time for them, I know, but Mama and Papa went for a long walk and were holdin' hands when they returned, so I take that as a good sign." She drew a deep breath. "And I was up most of the night talkin' to Anna Mae, who demanded every last detail, of course. And then she wanted *me* to know every last detail of what *she'd* been through and make sure I'm forever in her debt for bein' on the front line yesterday with my folks."

"That's one brave girl," I said.

Ginny Rose laughed. "Oh, she's feisty, all right. And I thank my lucky stars for it, too. We couldn't have done it without her."

I looked her over and said, "I can't believe you went to work today." Then I laughed. "But you're Ginny Rose Gilley, so of course you did."

"It was easy compared to yesterday," she said. "And I'm glad I did, because I had the chance to talk to Mrs. Smith about Mama joinin' her grievers' group. She said she'd personally invite her."

"Did she know about . . . about yesterday?"

Ginny Rose rolled her eyes. "Oh my Lord. Those women. I reckon the whole county knows by now. They treated me with kindness, though." She braved a peek at Bobby, but he missed it for scuffing the dirt. "I'd worried about people judgin' harshly." She shrugged. "You know."

"Only knuckleheads would do that," Bobby offered.

Ginny Rose blushed and was about to say something, but it got interrupted by Lisette skidding to a halt and bounding from her car, looking once again like she'd never touched dirt. "Guess what!" she called as she hurried over.

I laughed. "You got your car back and you're allowed to leave the house?"

She laughed, too. "That, *and*—" Then she saw the marquee. "Oh!" she said. "Oh, that is *perfect.*"

"So," Ginny Rose asked, "what are we guessin'?"

"That Macy's is having a huge back-to-school sale starting Friday!"

She could barely contain her excitement, but the rest of us just stared at her. How could she possibly be thinking about clothes at a time like this?

"I want us all to go shopping together!" she cried. She pointed to the marquee. "For the homecoming!" She looked at Ginny Rose. "And I want your sisters to come with us! All of them!"

"But—" Ginny Rose said.

"No buts," Lisette said. "Everybody take off work on Friday." She tossed Bobby a look. "Girls only."

"I'm not dense, Lisette," he said, sticking up for himself *again* and looking downright handsome doing it.

Lisette eyed him curiously, then turned back to us. "So it's settled. I'll pick you up in *my* car and take you on *my* kind of adventure."

"But—" Ginny Rose said again.

Lisette put her hands on her hips. "Some styles are fifty percent off! This happens only once a year. So tell your mother to open up the cookie jar or I'll be forced to pay for it."

Ginny Rose laughed. "Well, we can't have that!"

"So?" she asked, looking first at Ginny Rose, then at me.

"I'm in!" I said, which pushed Ginny Rose over the edge. "So am I," she said, then added, "My sisters are gonna *love* you."

True to her word, Lisette took us all on a shopping spree on Friday. Ginny Rose managed to stretch her funds far enough to buy her sisters new shoes and dresses, and milkshakes besides. But when Lisette urged her to try on a dark gray dress with maroon buttons, Ginny Rose shook her head. "If it's all right with you, I'll just wear the blue dress you gave me," she said. "I'd like it to feel like a homecoming, not a funeral."

With all of Lisette's hand-me-downs, I really didn't need a new dress, either. But I did buy new shoes, and I found a sweet picture frame for the photo of Ginny Rose and her sisters— something I was planning to wrap and give to the Gilleys next time I visited.

Then on Saturday, Lisette served as driver for me and the Gilley girls again, so Ginny Rose and her sisters wouldn't have to ride in the back of their truck to the homecoming service. How a banker's daughter convinced Mr. and Mrs. Gilley to allow any of it is a miracle, but I have a hunch the Gilley girls banded together and got their voices heard.

And then the service itself became its own sort of miracle.

We'd arrived early, but the church was already filling up with people who placed their potluck contributions on the covered tables outside in the courtyard. The organist was playing soothing tones as people filed in, and up front, sitting on a riser draped in white cloth, was a small oak coffin with a large spray of flowers on top. As we approached, we could see that the sketch of the boys had been set on an easel beside the coffin. It looked wonderful, framed in oak and draped in blue satin, and on a small table in front of the easel were two new sock monkeys, a scattering of acorns, and a glass dome containing two Monarch butterflies.

"Oh," Ginny Rose gasped as she took in the sight, and already Lisette and I were finding our hankies.

The Gilleys were seated in the first row, and Lisette and I sat directly behind Ginny Rose in the second. Then Bobby slid in alongside me, scrubbed red, shaved smooth, and starched stiff. Ginny Rose did a double take when she caught sight of him and blushed crimson. "Hello, Bobby," she said formally.

"Good morning, Ginny Rose," he replied.

"Is that him?" Anna Mae whispered a little too loudly, earning a swift backhand from Ginny Rose.

Then out of nowhere Jimmy Dickens appeared. He slid in beside Lisette without so much as a hi-de-ho and handed her a note.

She frowned at him but took it. And after she'd unfolded and read it, she passed it to me to read.

> *Lisette my Darling—*
> *I don't want to marry Vivian. I want to be with you.*
> *Run away with me! Meet me at Dolly's at eleven tonight.*
> *We belong together!*
>
> *Eternally yours,*
> *Rodney*

I looked at Lisette, wide-eyed and worried. But she calmly folded the note and handed it back to Jimmy. "Tell that scoundrel I have better things to do with my life than waste it on him." Then she added, "And, Jimmy? If you think coming here for that is okay, you've got absolutely no class. Now leave. And *never* bring me a note or message from that coward again."

He shrugged like it was no big deal, slid off the bench, and left the church.

Lisette shook her head. "I wonder if *he's* ever going to get out from under Rodney's spell."

I gave her hand a squeeze. "I'm just glad we have."

By the time the service began, the hall was filled to standing room only. I spotted my parents and the twins about ten rows back and caught Mother and Nonnie looking around in amazement at the size of the gathering. I saw a group of teachers from the high school sitting together, clearly discussing the goings-on. And I saw regulars from the fruit stand—even some I'd overcharged—and groups of kids I knew from school. Who I didn't see were the Bovees.

"Your parents aren't coming?" I asked Lisette.

"They sent a donation instead," she whispered back.

"Don't tell Ginny Rose that!"

"Believe me, I won't."

Finally, Reverend Poole greeted the congregation and began his remarks. He talked about Lucas and Elijah Gilley, painting them into our imagination with words, telling their story—and the story of the Gilleys—while all eyes fixed on the sketch of the boys beside the coffin.

"So," he said at last, "people ask, 'How could God do this to two little boys so full of life and love?' But let me ask you in return: How could we do this to one another? How could we shut out the tired, the poor, the homeless, the bereaved? How could we let fear close our hearts?"

The hall went completely silent as the questions hung like conscience in the air. Then Reverend Poole turned the mood. "But look at this church," he boomed. "Look at all the people gathered here with open hearts and open minds. Look at all of you coming together today to welcome Lucas and Elijah home and the Gilley family into our community. It's a truly glorious sight!"

After waves of murmuring in the congregation, Reverend Poole said, "I caution you, though: It's easy to find our better selves in the sunshine of prosperity. What we must remember is to not lose those selves during times of hardship."

After a few more remarks, we sang selections from the hymn book, and I couldn't help but notice Mr. Gilley's voice. It was deep and rough and rich and . . . strong. Full of pain, but also hope. And slowly, Mrs. Gilley's voice joined in, soft and sweet and tearful.

During the final hymn, Reverend Poole pulled the glass dome up and freed the butterflies right there inside the church. They fluttered and floated above us, and as if riding an invisible wave of soaring voices, they drifted toward the open doorway and disappeared outside.

Afterward, Mr. and Mrs. Gilley stood beside the coffin with Reverend Poole, who introduced them to a long line of well-wishers and people welcoming them to the community, while Ginny Rose shepherded her sisters through the side doors and down the wide steps to the courtyard and the spread laid out there.

I watched from the top step, taking in the four of them, noticing how Anna Mae and Ginny Rose tended to Katie Bee and Bonnie Sue as they moved together along one side of the serving tables. The little girls were squealing with joy at all the choices, getting their plates piled high with food, and taking peaches from a Simmons Farm lug box.

Then suddenly Willie and Wesley were across the serving table from them, and my heart caught at the sight of Bobby helping *them* with their plates. This was a first, but then so was the way he was smiling across the table at Ginny Rose.

After a while, the courtyard was busy with people greeting each other and helping themselves to food. The air was alive with the happy sound of community, and it filled my heart with joy for the Gilleys. Then, like grace notes in a symphony of fellowship, the two Monarch butterflies fluttered together above it all, dipping and dancing in the warm air before drifting off.

"*There* you are," Lisette said, joining me. "What are you doing?"

"Just taking it all in," I said with a sigh. She stood beside me, taking it all in, too. And then I let out a thought that had crept into my mind. "I think I should try to be a better sister to Doris."

She took a moment to contemplate, then said, "It seems *she* could be a better sister to *you*."

I sighed again. "It has to start somewhere, right?"

She gave a reluctant nod. "I suppose so."

Then Ginny Rose came scampering up the steps carrying three peaches. "Here!" she said, passing them around.

"Peaches? Really?" I laughed, then pointed out Anna Mae, who was talking with a group of girls her own age.

Ginny Rose chuckled, "Their mamas better watch out!" Then

she gave a little gasp and nodded across the courtyard to where her own mother was in deep conversation with Mrs. Smith.

After a moment of watching their tearful exchange, Ginny Rose turned to me with soft eyes and said, "How can I *ever* thank you?"

I just shook my head. "No need." But then I laughed and corrected myself. "Actually, you can take back this peach!"

"Take it back?" Lisette said. "No! We should all make a toast!"

"A toast?" I laughed. "With *peaches*?"

"What a wonderful idea!" Ginny Rose cried. "Lisette, you start."

So Lisette raised her peach in the air and proclaimed, "To this summer!" and took a bite.

"To this summer!" Ginny Rose chimed in, and took a bite of hers.

I laughed because there was nothing sophisticated about the bite Lisette had taken, and neither of them seemed to care that they were dripping juice.

So I raised my peach and proclaimed, "To this summer!" and took my own juice-dripping bite. And then, because there was something silly and truly joyful about us standing on the side steps of the church toasting with peaches, I raised mine again and said, "To best friends!" and took another bite.

"To best friends!" Lisette and Ginny Rose cried, doing the same.

Then Ginny Rose took a turn, but what she proclaimed was "To peaches!"

I laughed. "To *peaches*?"

"Yes!" she cried. "To the miracle of peaches!" She bit again, but this time she closed her eyes and took her time.

Lisette shrugged and grinned at me, so I laughed and took a bite, too. And following Ginny Rose's lead, I closed my eyes and let the flavor linger, which sent my mind back to that early morning in our kitchen when Ginny Rose had waxed poetic about our orchard . . . back to her reverence for a seed's transformation into a tree, and how such different elements came together to produce something so very sweet.

So maybe it was taking a moment to see what she saw—the miracle in it all. Or maybe it was standing on the edge of that step and absorbing the miracle of this day—seeing that no matter where each of us had come from, no matter how different we once were, we'd joined together to create something sweeter than any of us could ever have imagined.

Whatever the reason, as I savored the bite, I had to admit—nothing had ever tasted so good.

AUTHOR'S NOTE

This story started with the seed of an idea planted by my mother-in-law, Rosalyn, who spent summers working in a Central Valley cannery as a teen. But it soon grew away from her experience and branched out to become a project of intense research and discovery.

This is my first historical novel and I wanted to get every detail right, so I'm very grateful to the people who helped me along the way. It was a delight spending time with Judie Hardie and Paulette Roberson, docents at the Riverbank Historical Museum, whose personal knowledge of peach farming and cannery work helped tremendously as I was beginning this book. And I really appreciate how Gary Nelson, Central Valley peach farmer and educator, patiently answered my endless stream of questions (*and* let me drive his tractor!).

I'm also grateful to all the welcoming people I've met during my many school visits to Oklahoma, but a special thanks goes to Sarah, Donna, Nancy, and especially Caradith, who proudly call themselves "Okies" and who helped me with relevant cultural and historical details.

What sustained me through the three years of researching and writing this book was identifying strongly with both narrators. As the daughter of immigrants, I understand why Ginny Rose so often feels like an outsider. And having worked for my parents at their small family business, I felt Peggy as a girl straight from my heart.

But while I relate to the main characters, over time they grew and blossomed into young women with their own unique identities, and it's their *differences* I wanted to celebrate. Like peaches being the sweet result of disparate elements (earth, air, sun, and water), Ginny Rose, Peggy, and Lisette combine forces to create change not just in themselves and their families, but also in their community.

So, ultimately, the fruit I hope this story bears is for readers to consider and discuss our reasons for labeling and treating people as outsiders, the lingering effects of economic disparity, and the fortifying power of being part of something bigger than ourselves.

BOOK CLUB DISCUSSION QUESTIONS

The story begins with a prologue of Ginny Rose Gilley's sixth birthday. Why do you think the author chose to start there?

If you didn't know about the death of the Gilley boys, do you think you would have felt differently about some characters when you first met them? Does knowing someone's history make you more sympathetic?

Each of the families in this story has secrets and things they don't openly discuss. Think about the impact those silences had on both the parents and children in each family. Are there secrets like this in your own family?

The author tells the story from two points of view—Ginny Rose Gilley and Peggy Simmons. How does that change things for the reader? What understanding might be lost if we only heard this story from one or the other character's perspective?

By contrast, we don't hear directly from Lisette Bovee. How did you feel about her at the beginning of the book, and did those feelings shift by the end?

The Peach Rebellion takes place just after the Second World War. We generally think of this as an era of growth and prosperity, but each family in the story comes from a very different socioeconomic background. How do those differences shape their lives and worldviews? What opportunities are available to each?

How do the younger members of each family see the world differently from the adults?

The postwar years were also a time when women's roles in society were evolving. Why was that? Do Ginny Rose, Peggy, and Lisette have opportunities that their mothers did not? Contrast that to the opportunities available to women today.

Each of the girls experiences love or heartbreak. How do their expectations for romance differ? How do their views shift over the course of the book?

Ginny Rose reflects on how a bike tire and its inner tube are representative of life—you carry the scars inside you, even if no one can see them. Do you agree with her metaphor? Think about the scars each of the characters might be hiding. How about the people in your life?

What do you think would have happened to the Gilley family if Ginny Rose hadn't made the bold decision to find her brothers? What if the girls had been stopped from going on this journey or hadn't been successful?

Would Ginny Rose have accomplished her mission without Peggy's support? Could she have pulled it off without Lisette or Anna Mae? How many people helped make the journey possible?

This felt like a private family quest for Ginny Rose. But every character in the book will be affected by her journey. Think about how her actions will ripple out through the community. Do you imagine there will be negative impacts as well as positive ones?

Mirroring how a peach tree combines earth, air, sun, and water to produce something sweet, *The Peach Rebellion* presents the theme of very different people working together to create positive change within their families and community. Can you think of events in your own life that have been the result of unlikely allies combining forces?

Eight weeks of survivalist camping in the desert.
Eight weeks to turn your life around.
YEAH, RIGHT.

FROM THE AUTHOR OF *FLIPPED* AND *THE RUNNING DREAM*

Wendelin Van Draanen

Wild ♥ Bird

"Riveting." —*Kirkus Reviews*

BRYCE: All I've ever wanted is for Juli Baker to leave me alone.
But there was no going back. I liked her.

JULIANNA: One look at Bryce Loski, and I became a lunatic.
But all those years I liked him? I never really knew him.

Wendelin Van Draanen

FLIPPED

New bonus material inside!

★ "Van Draanen has another winner in this eighth-grade 'he-said, she-said' romance." —*School Library Journal*, starred review